Jenn Ashworth

Jenn Ashworth was born in 1982 in Preston, where she was raised a Mormon. She studied English at Cambridge and since then has gained an MA from Manchester University, trained as a librarian and run a prison library in Lancashire. She now lectures in Creative Writing at the University of Lancaster.

Her first novel, *A Kind of Intimacy,* was published in 2009 and won a Betty Trask Award. In 2011 she published her second, *Cold Light*, and was chosen on BBC TV's *The Culture Show* as one of the twelve Best New British Novelists. She still lives in Preston, with her husband, son and daughter.

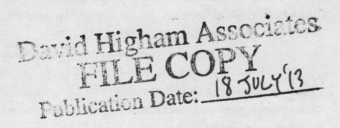

'A juicy glimpse behind the bland façade of evangelism . . . Ashworth's style is matter of fact and full of detail: the pattern of a sofa, the shape of a meal tray, the cracks on a path. She's also unafraid of ugliness . . . less interested in spreading a simple, comforting message than in uncovering the messy complexities of people, families and faith'

Jessica Holland, *Observer*

'Darkly wry . . . her familiar mix of violence and dark humour are finely wrought into a sympathetic, forgiving and absorbing portrait of family life. It is Ashworth's most confident work yet and one that strengthens her reputation as an author worth watching.'

Beth Jones, *Sunday Telegraph*

'Remarkable . . . Ashworth's characters are divided souls, with one foot in heaven, one on earth. At one point, one character, spying on another, observes the mother "pointing at the ceiling". "She could be talking about God or loft insulation," he thinks – and the poignant truthfulness of Ashworth's novel inheres in its ability to encompass and appreciate the significance of both.'

Jonathan Taylor, *Independent*

'There is high drama and tragedy – in fact there are serious crimes and personal breakdowns – but the foundation in familiar suburban family life is so sound and the tone of that life so well observed that belief is not stretched and every step of the way into the turmoil seems inevitable . . . a funny, sad and ultimately compassionate reflection on what a family can do to each of its members.'

Steve Tomkins, *Third Way*

'It is rare to find a novel that is so complex, so damn clever and yet at once readable; Ashworth effectively pares back the garments of faith and class to reveal the bare and often brittle bones of humanity . . . a truly exceptional novel.'

Helen Walsh

'Ashworth has produced a darkly comic tale of northern suburbia, one that boasts a unique cast of characters and the kind of knuckle-chewing pathos that compels you to devour it in one sitting . . . The number of Big Issues under scrutiny in *The Friday Gospels* would overwhelm a less skilful novelist. Ashworth, however, has come into her own as a writer, and themes of religious hypocrisy, sexual repression, privacy, healthcare, petty tyrannies and humiliation are dispatched with style and confidence . . . an accomplished work of satire from one of the country's most exciting young novelists.'

Beulah Maud Devaney, *For Book's Sake*

'Superb . . . It's a beautifully well-observed account of what it's like growing up in a religious family, and what it's like trying to hold one together'   *Reform*

'This may be the best mainstream Mormon novel in a very long time . . . Jenn Ashworth was named one of the twelve Best New British Novelists of 2011, and it's easy to see why. The novel unfolds brilliantly, and its handling of Mormon themes is similarly exemplary. Structurally and thematically, this is one novel not to miss. I recommend it without reservation.'

J.Nichols, Association for Mormon Letters

JENN ASHWORTH

The Friday Gospels

SCEPTRE

First published in Great Britain in 2013 by Sceptre
An imprint of Hodder & Stoughton
An Hachette UK company

First published in paperback in 2013

1

A CIP catalogue record for this title is
available from the British Library

ISBN 9781444707748

Typeset in Sabon MT by Palimpsest Book Production Limited,
Falkirk, Stirlingshire

Printed and bound by CPI Group (UK) Ltd, Croydon CR0 4YY

Hodder & Stoughton policy is to use papers that are natural, renewable
and recyclable products and made from wood grown in sustainable forests.
The logging and manufacturing processes are expected to
conform to the environmental regulations of the country of origin.

Hodder & Stoughton Ltd
338 Euston Road
London NW1 3BH

www.sceptrebooks.com

for D.

JEANNIE

5.16. There it is in square red numbers. Dawn. Fourteen minutes before getting-up time. Mouth tastes like blood and old onions. You can never pinpoint the exact second you wake up, can you? It's not one thing or the other. It's slow, like growing or your dreams wearing off. Is today really the day? At last? Eventually?

I reach out of bed and slide the switch to turn off the alarm. That's three days in a row I've woken up before it goes off. Why does that happen, anyway? Is it like your brain's been trained to it and you really don't need the alarm any more? There's black stuff, something mouldy and powdery, creeping along the seal between the window frame and the glass. It's actually really disgusting. I lean over and slide the phone out from under my pillow. This alarm is set a bit earlier, to get me ready for the second one. As I bring it out it goes off, buzzing in my hand. Freeze for a second, then turn it off.

5.19. Getting light and the first birds tuning up but if I wake Julian there'll be hell to pay and there's still a dint in the wood on my door from that time he threw his mug at me when I forgot and flushed the toilet first thing. It's maybe ten or twelve or fourteen hours until Gary gets back, depending on what the wind and the ash are doing.

Ash. It's clogging up the sky, keeping the planes on the ground, making people live in airports for days, unable to come home, late and having to eat things like Wendy's and send emails from the terminals in the airport, queuing for an hour or two every time. *I am coming home, soon, soon, soon,* all he ever says, *home soon, Jeannie, can't wait to see you, home soon.*

1

I sit up quietly and find Lewis's work number on my phone and press the button to dial. So early. There's no chance he'll be in. Apart from maybe a flood or a delivery. A backlog of work for impatient customers. Some other emergency that means he won't want to talk to me anyway. I'd ring him at home, or on his mobile, but I don't know the numbers. I listen to the ringing, and imagine the phone on the counter. An old-fashioned, rattly one with a dirty receiver. I've seen it before. Rings. I don't count. Rings rings. He does sometimes sleep at work. Rings. I don't let myself think of him sleeping under that horrible tartan blanket, but the thought, and then the smell of it, the feel of the fringe along the edge tickling my shin and now my stomach is working at itself as if it's frightened, trying to get away. So I press the red button and lie back on the pillows, staring at the ceiling until the sicky feeling goes.

There are cracks and peeling paint round the light fitting and a cobweb weighed down with dust strung across the edges of the lampshade like a hammock for a fairy. I stay still. Arrange myself so I'm exactly in the middle of the bed with my arms by my sides and my legs straight out and my feet pointed right at the door like an arrow. I put my head in the middle of the pillow and pretend I'm a cancer patient in a hospital. Shut eyes. The chair by the side of my bed with the bubbly, chlorine-smelling cup of water turns into one of those lockers and the creaky-wheeled divan gets a set of a rubber sheets and a flowered curtain falls around me and visitors creep in to admire, whispering. I lie perfectly straight like this, so good, so still.

People would be nice to you. There'd be no shouting if all you had to do was lie there and wait to be dead. I want to get that feeling I sometimes get when I open my eyes after I've already been awake for a while – that I am in the wrong room and that my body is in the wrong place – the doors aren't where you expect them to be and for a minute everything tips and spins and I could be anywhere and I want to be in a hospital. I blink and screw my eyes shut and try it again. No good. I'm not going to get it this time. I fell asleep with the curtains half open and the light is blue and grey and when I look at my hand lying on top of the duvet like a fish my skin looks dead.

Julian is going to kill someone. Me, Lewis. He won't even care who. He could have killed me straight when he chucked that mug and he never even looked around to see what it had hit. Mum was screaming up the stairs and he was off to the workshop without even getting washed and I wish it had hit me and killed me and that's a fact.

I get my journal up from down the side of the bed. Find my pen. It's a nice big red book with a hard cover and in gold writing on the front of it: JOURNAL. The large white pages are ruled neatly, all smooth and unspoiled. I flick through the pages I've filled up; the space for the family tree in the front with all our names in it. This is the place to write down all my feelings. All the things that have happened to me. And when I am dead my posterity will read it and see what sort of life I had. I close it without writing anything.

My name is Jeannie and that is half my problem. Mum says that. Half your problem is. And then the latest thing. Half my problem is I think the washing gets itself done. Half my problem is I have no idea how long it takes to plan and cook a two-course meal for five (four). Half my problem is I think carpet is free and mud disappears on its own. My problem has ten, twenty, fifty halves. And is dividing, swelling itself up into thousands.

There are no Jeannies in the scriptures – whatever version you look at. Sister Williams's first name is Ruth and Brother Fletcher's is James. His mother is Esther. There are Rebeccas and Naomis and Sarahs with me in the Mia Maids. Even Mum, nearly, because she's a Pauline. All good scriptural names. Gary was supposed to be Nephi and Julian should have been Enoch but Dad wouldn't let Mum do it to them and threatened to leave her over it both times. She brings it up every single time he forgets to take the bins out. The night he wouldn't let her have her own way over the new curtains. Curtains! *It's the first thing I've put my foot down with you about, Pauline*, he said – very quietly. *I can't magic money out of thin air.* And she erupted. *O no it's not!* she went, like a pantomime, but I didn't laugh, *O no it's not. What about the boys' names? What about that, eh?*

Curtains. I shouldn't have gone out. I could have turned the music up. I put my own frog into that pot, though, didn't I? *Curtains.* Jeannie. I wasn't supposed to be called anything other than what I am because by the time I turned up she'd given up on the idea. I am just Jeannie and it isn't short for anything and it doesn't stand for anything better and although I have checked my concordance Jeannie is not a scriptural name.

When I hear Dad start moving around I get up and kneel on the floor. Put my forehead against the saggy edge of the mattress and try to listen for something. I am the temple of the Lord. His spirit dwells inside me. I wait, feeling like an old house with the doors kicked in, and hearing nothing but the wind howling through the gaps. And the kitchen taps and the back door go as Dad gets the milk in. The radio, for the news. Bovril's claws scrabbling at the lino. Just because you can't hear something doesn't mean it's not there. Tree branches moving – the leaves rippling and showing their lighter undersides – enough to show a wind. The smell of cooking, enough to prove there's food on the way. Dad's here and part of the family forever, all the time, even when he's at work or out with the dogs just because of the dint he leaves behind on the couch cushions. I listen out some more. Nothing to say this morning. The carpet is scratchy under my knees.

I move quickly and get into my school uniform and check my phone – 5.32 – and grab my bag, which is already packed up because it's always the last thing I do before bed. Need to wee but Julian's snoring so I creep down the stairs. I'll wait and do it at Brother Fletcher's house even though the soap in his bathroom is always grey.

'You're up,' Dad says and he is standing at the cooker looking pleased and in his work uniform already and Mum who is never up at this time is there in her dressing gown, heaped and bundled into her chair with a tray across her lap, and she's smiling too.

'I'm going in early today,' Dad says, 'take you, then out with Bovril for a quick hour, then work, and,' he is talking to Mum, 'I'll be back for two so we can get the house ready?'

She is nodding but not looking at him. Scrawling on a scrap of paper with a short pencil, resting on the tray she normally eats off of.

'I'm going to have the sisters round this morning, help me get the kitchen scrubbed out and freshen up Gary's bed, and then we'll cook. You do know I'm doing a special dinner and I want you home right from school, no shallying around this time?'

She's writing so I don't say anything. I stand in front of the sink and run myself a mug of cold water and drink it looking out at the brambles in the back, the throttled greenhouse and the nettles under the hedge. The water's so cold it makes my teeth hurt and I know why that is from an advert I saw on telly: there's lots of tiny holes in the surface of your teeth and through them tiny nerves poking out and getting hurt. I think once your teeth have got these little holes in them, that's it, there's nothing you can do about it apart from buying that special toothpaste, but we only get Morrisons own because Dad says it's a rip-off and all you're paying for is the label. I look down and run the cuff of my school jumper around the shiny bottom of the sink where a few drops of water have gathered to spoil it.

'Jeannie? Are you listening to me?'

'I'll be back,' I say, and she says, 'Make sure you are,

disappearing like a cat – no sign for hours, and if there's one night Gary's going to expect us to be all here, around this table,' she leans forward and taps it with a long fingernail, 'it's going to be tonight and so that's what he's going to get. Special dinner, us all here. Yes?'

'It's Julian you want to be worrying about,' I say, and she raises her skinny eyebrows like she's about to start but my Dad empties eggs from a frying pan onto a plate, turns the gas off and puts the plate on the tray in front of her.

'Pauline, don't start it this morning, of all mornings,' he says, 'and whatever you're planning on cooking, can you leave the cracked wheat out of it, please? My guts are giving me gyp as it is.'

He's still in a good mood – they both are, and I look at Mum but she's prodding the egg yolks with the blunt side of her knife and pretending she doesn't hear him.

'Worry about me doing what?' Julian says. He's leaning in the doorway, wearing jeans, but no socks or shirt, and digging into his ear with one finger.

'What are you doing up?'

He pulls his finger out of his ear, inspects it, scratches an armpit and yawns. 'They have not shut the airspace again, have they?'

'Don't speak to me about it, Julian. I just can't stand it. Can't think about it. The best thing we can all do is pray, right now.'

'You can check the news,' Julian says. 'I will turn the telly on, shall I?'

6.12. He squeezes himself sideways past the table. A blast of his armpitty, sleepy smell as he passes. He says *forfuckssake* under his breath and no one hears it apart from me. The telly goes on, Mum fusses and mutters and hauls, forcing her chair through the gap, and we follow.

'Put that mug down, Jeannie. You're not bringing a drink into the front room,' she says, without looking at me.

6

The early morning news is on, and there are pictures of people waiting in airports – Manchester and Heathrow and Gatwick and John Lennon. All stuffed full of bedraggled passengers sleeping on floors, using their luggage as pillows. Airport staff handing out bottles of water, and nappies, and vouchers for free meals. Queues forty long for the toilets, and all the car parks full. Mum is chewing her eggs slowly and leaning forward, looking at all the people even though Gary won't be one of them, he's in the air now, right over our heads in a plane. Though we can't see it, the sky is darkening.

'He'll be all right,' Dad says. They switch to a clip of Eyjafjallajökull itself. The plume of ash and dog-grey smoke endlessly billowing out of the top, as it has been doing for days now, to cover the world. That's a funny thing, that they call the volcano a she like it's a person, a girl or a woman, like they do with boats and spaceships. Dad says they do it to boats and other things like that, sorts of vehicles, big trucks too, because they are things that carry people, like women do when they have – Dad leans over and turns the telly off to stop Mum getting worked up.

'All right! All right? Hand me that phone, I'm going to call the bishop.'

'Pauline.' Dad puts his hand on her shoulder again, takes her eggs. He moves away and his voice floats in from the kitchen. 'Bishop Jackson will still be asleep. He's got a long enough drive to do today as it is. You can ring him later. When it's a decent time.'

'Fine,' she says, and shifts round in her chair to look at me. Julian's got his feet up on the arm of the couch and is staring out the window at the sky. He looks like he's going to go back to sleep any second, except he's smiling, like he's planning something other than a day at work.

'Just make sure you're all back here early tonight. No dawdling.'

'Must we? There is a lot for me to do at work today,' Julian says, in that funny way of talking he's got – like he's planned all his lines out in advance and is just reciting them. Gary said he started doing it when he got to high school, and he puts it on deliberately. No one knows why. Dad says to leave him alone; he's not hurting anyone.

'Anyone would think you preferred spending time with Drake than being here to welcome back your own brother,' Mum says, and stares at Julian. Julian turns back to the window and ignores her.

'I've got hockey after school,' I say.

'Can't you miss it, just this once? And you,' she waves her hand at Julian, 'bring Drake, if you can't be parted from him.'

I feel my hands grabbing at each other, but Julian just huffs. He knows what Mum's getting at and he's not going to play.

'Stop moidering them, Pauline. He's not going to be back until seven, at the earliest,' Dad says, and motions over her head for me to get my bag and follow him out, 'let her go to her hockey. She'll be back long before Gary is.'

'You better had be. No disappearing.'

'I'll be back,' I say, 'it was just that one time,' and Dad catches my eye and shakes his head and I drop it like he wants me to, and before me and Dad head out the door in the usual rush she catches my sleeve and pulls me back, so close the wheels on her chair are digging into the front of my knees, and I have to stoop over her and see the egg yolk caught in the hairy corners of her mouth, and she gives me the bit of paper she's been writing on and the list, and two folded twenty-pound notes from the pocket of her stained dressing gown, and says:

'You will do this for me, won't you, Jeannie? Go to Richardson's supermarket and get them to call you a taxi and bring it all back during your dinner, then I'll have it all here in the afternoon so I can do the cooking. Will you do that for me? Can I rely on you this time?'

I look at the money and nod and take the list and Dad is holding the front door open for me with one arm and putting his other into his jacket and I duck out past him, smelling the shaving foam still clogging the little cups in the bottom of his ears as I pass.

'Come on then,' he says gently as we get into the car, 'same as usual?' and it's a game we have and I nod and we drive the rest of the way without speaking, his hands light on the wheel except when we're going round corners and then he's extra careful because winter last year he hit a cat and still isn't over it, not really.

I like the quiet. The empty roads and us driving right through the town centre in five minutes flat, with just a couple of cars on the Flat Iron and the Richardson's lorry (she) parked right up on the pavement as the early morning staff move backwards and forwards carrying in the bread. To Me. To You. The shutters are still down on all the shops, and their special yellow bags of rubbish haven't been collected yet. Smell the chlorine as we go past the leisure centre, even with the windows shut. A train goes through the station, the speed of it making the yellow and red of the carriages streak to a long blurred smear in the corner of my eye. But I don't like the way I'm trained to wake up at five or earlier even on Saturdays and get guilty if I'm ever still lying in after six. Lazy. Another half of my problem. Don't like the class every morning either – the long, confusing sentences and verses to learn off by heart and Friday quizzes and scripture chases and the certificates Sister Williams makes on her computer and gets photocopied at the Spar place around the corner. Hole-punched with a ribbon threaded through to make a bookmark. Over-critical of others' efforts. One more half. Don't like having to see them all every morning – between six and eight, every day before school, and it is seeing them all so regularly that is supposed to keep you in line. To remind you, even before you get to school, that *we are a peculiar people* and our lifelong friends will come from inside the Church and not out of it. Sullen. Antisocial. The third half, and counting.

'Things will be different after tonight,' Dad says when he pulls up and he's as glad as Mum is. I've seen him marking the days off on his Crufts' Winners calendar with the marker he uses for work.

'I know it will be,' I say.

Gary is coming home tonight. It's been two years. Since I was twelve. I have grown eighteen centimetres since then and wear a bra now and I need to suck in my belly when I walk and I am embarrassed at the thought of him seeing me. 6.58.

Gary, when you are home, finally, at last, eventually, I will tell you a story. Are you sitting comfortably? 'Gary,' I will say (I have been practising this one for three weeks and two days), 'Gary, it wasn't my fault. What it was, was just like when we went up the log flume at Camelot. You and me and Julian the year before you left. How old would I have been? Eleven? Maybe eleven or nearly twelve. Do you remember that day? We'd been on the teacups and the merry-go-round and the caterpillar, and we'd seen Merlin and Scoop doing card tricks, and when we watched the jousting one of the knights asked for a favour from a fair lady, and you pulled the ribbon out of my ponytail and stood up and waved it in the air. It made a pink S shape on the end of your hand. The knight rode over to the barrier and nodded and you pulled me up and we ran down the steps between the seats together and the knight took the ribbon, held it up and kissed it and then wrapped it around the top of his arm. Everyone whoo-whooed and my face went that red. My knight was the good one, in a blue and yellow uniform. His horse too. And signs, saying not to put your hand through the barriers because the horses weren't tame and they'd bite you. The bad one, all in black, came out and everyone booed and ssssssed, and King and Queen stood up on their platform and said some things, and rang a bell, and then they made the horses charge at each other. The knights were holding poles. My knight won, course he did, and once he'd put his pole back in the rack and collected his cup, he draped the ribbon over the barriers and Gary, I made you go and get it because he was waiting there to talk to us, I think, and I was too shy.

And then later I wanted to go on the long flume and Dad said yes. Do you remember? We were wearing those see-through plastic macs and also caps with the Camelot castle on that Mum had let us get from the gift shop. And you and Julian shouted and waved your arms in the air as the log fell down the slope and after you all said I was brave because I never made a peep she never made a peep not a sound, and you and Julian shoved me on the shoulders and Dad looked pleased with me and I still couldn't talk or smile because my cheeks were numb and my teeth stuck together with all the screaming I wanted to do. I was frozen like a stone, like I was made of cement. Something that can't move, can't run away, can't make a peep. So I didn't do anything.'

That's the end. I couldn't say any of that to you.

We have the seminary class in Brother Fletcher's front room. Mum's never been in here, but if she did she'd say this is a place that needs a woman's touch. Thin blue carpet with no underlay and magnolia walls and a grey three-piece suite with tiny red diamonds on it and some extra folding chairs he gets out for the class. There's a little wooden bookshelf and a plasma telly and no plants or photos but the picture of Jesus in the red cape on the wall over the gas fire and another little one of the First Presidency he keeps on the phone table, which is wooden too, but not the same kind of wood as the bookcase.

Sister Williams teaches the seminary with him every morning and because he's not married it wouldn't be appropriate for the two of them to be in the house together so Sister Fletcher his mother needs to come to chaperone because even though there are plenty of Beehives and Mia Maids and Laurels we don't count because we're under eighteen and anyway not married ourselves yet, although Joyce's a Laurel and she's waiting for someone to come back off of his mission next year.

Sister Fletcher usually sits in the kitchen with her knitting in a basket between her feet. She does tiny clothes for the premature babies' box and cat blankets out of old jumpers and sometimes comments on points of scripture through the open door. Angela Williams who is only five sits in there with her, eating Ready brek and waiting for us to be finished with her mother so she can get taken to her special school and she never makes a peep, but only takes some of the wool and rubs it against her lips and she's lovely.

I'm still not feeling well.

Sister Williams comes into the living room to start the class, stepping over the legs of the people who are sitting on the floor, and picks her way to the front next to Brother Fletcher, who is standing in front of the plasma telly holding the Book of Mormon with both hands in front of him like it is a tiny blue shield. Now she's here he bows his head to do the opening prayer. I fold my arms and turn my face down. Eyes closed, I hear Beth breathing next to me through a nose that needs blowing.

'Dear Heavenly Father, we thank thee for this beautiful morning. We thank thee for bringing us all safely together here to study thy scriptures and learn more about thy will. We thank thee for our health and strength, for a refreshing night's sleep and we thank thee for letting us live in a free country where we can read and worship according to thy word. This morning we ask that the teachers of the lesson be inspired and the young men and women here are able to understand, apply and remember the precepts and principles taught here today. We ask thee to bless us that we may obey thy commandments, and in particular we ask thy blessing on the health of Angela Williams, thy daughter. And we say these things in the name of Jesus Christ, our saviour, amen.'

Beth always makes sure she says 'Amen' the loudest, in this strange, sort of telephone voice. On Sundays you can hear her from the back. The rest of us just mutter. When you get up so early, closing your eyes and putting your head down for the prayer is dangerous. Blinky and fuzzy when it's over – as if wakening from another sleep. The light is too bright, the air too dry. Brother Fletcher makes a bit of a fuss of me.

'Gary's coming back! Have you heard from him yet, has he landed?' he says while Sister Williams moves slowly on her small feet, lumbering, almost, in her wide cream and blue dress.

I swallow down cold spit.

'Dinner time. His plane gets in at Heathrow and the bishop is driving him back. We're all having a meal tonight.'

Sister Williams smiles. 'So that means he'll be first up on Sunday?'

I nod and she beams at me and all of us and there's more talking and I don't notice she is carrying a tray until she turns again and shows it to us.

There's a murmur of interest. It's a tray of fairy cakes. One or two of us who have been dozing or slouching sit up a little straighter. We're not allowed to eat in the class and if you're not naturally a morning person breakfast is cold toast that is too chewy and tastes like the Tupperware you brought it in. They look funny, they're so perfect – like something out of a cookery book. All spotless paper cases, white icing and glossy glacé cherries dead centre on the top. Beth has been trying to catch my eye, so I turn myself around a bit and pretend I am paying extra-special attention to the lesson.

'Each of you young women,' Brother Fletcher is saying, 'has a very special possession. It is something you were born with, and something that, when the time is right, you will give freely to the one chosen to walk beside you for eternity.'

Sister Williams offers the plate to Beth, who takes a cake and holds it in her hand. Rebecca and Sarah take one each, and finally the plate comes to me and I don't hesitate over choosing because all the cakes are exactly the same. There are a few left, but instead of handing them around to the boys Sister Williams takes the plate back and puts it on top of the television.

No one speaks or moves. We know better than to start eating.

'Girls,' Sister Williams says, 'your job is to look after your special possession as if it was the most important thing that you own – because it is.'

Jacob sniggers loudly, swallows, and turns it into a cough.

'You know that in some circumstances it's permissible and forgivable to use violence as defence,' Brother Fletcher says.

'Nephi himself was permitted to kill Laban with a sword in order to obtain the plates,' Sister Williams says.

'And similarly you young women are permitted and encouraged to defend your virtue by whatever means are open to you,' he carries on.

They are staring at us. Our teachers and all the boys are staring at us. The cake feels sticky in my hand.

'Your Heavenly Father wants you to know that life is precious and should never be taken but just as precious is the ability to give and nurture life, something that all you young women carry within you,' Sister Williams says. 'The veil that the spirits waiting in heaven pass through in order to come to earth,' she says, properly excited, 'it's inside you. Can you think of it?'

She smiles. She might be thinking of Angela, who we can hear babbling quietly to Sister Fletcher – not real words, just noises, little cries, like a baby.

'The sacred importance of that calling, that power, is the reason for this exception,' Brother Fletcher says. He surveys us, sitting there with our cakes, and the boys lean back into their half of the room, scared to even breathe on us. 'But even better, each young person needs to choose wisely. To use their free agency and avoid getting themselves into situations where their chastity, their virtue – even their reputation – is put at risk. It's a sacred responsibility each of you has.'

He hands over to Sister Williams. I don't know if they practise the lesson, or just read the prompts out of the lesson book, but sometimes it's hard not to think of them as television presenters working on an autocue.

'Sometimes, just sometimes, a young woman can make a poor decision and that is the object of today's lesson.' Sister Williams scans our faces, staring at us in our assortment of school uniforms, grey skirts pulled down low over our knees. 'Look what happens now.'

'You, Jeannie, go and choose one of the boys to give your cake to,' Brother Fletcher says.

I stand up and wait, certain that I'm going to make a mistake. He's picked me because Gary's coming back today and the extra attention is supposed to be a treat, to make me feel special, to help me learn better and to feel like I am helping them teach the lesson, but it doesn't feel anything like that.

'Go on then, it doesn't matter who you choose,' she says, 'these bad decisions are often made hastily, without planning or discrimination.'

Michael is nearest to me and sitting on the arm of the couch looking bored and confused, so I touch his arm and shove the cake in his face. He blinks, pushes his glasses up his nose, and takes it.

'Go on then, Michael,' Brother Fletcher says, 'she's let you have it. Her own free will. It is hers to do what she likes with, after all.'

Michael starts to unpeel the paper from the side of the cake.

'The cake is to represent marriage,' Sister Williams says, 'and you're old enough now to realise that the icing on the cake represents the sacred relationship between man and wife. Now, Michael, I want you to have a go at that icing. Get your tongue out and lick it off. I was stood in my kitchen at eleven o'clock last night so don't hold back.'

Michael looks at her, at me, at the rest of us. He is baffled. Sister Williams and Brother Fletcher close in, smiling, and he opens his mouth and starts licking the top of the cake. The icing is thick and sweet and it looks wonderful.

'Have the cherry as well. Why not?' Brother Fletcher says, and laughs as if he has said something inappropriate. Michael obeys. The sugar in the icing thickens his spit, which builds up on his tongue and at the corners of his mouth. It takes him a minute or two to work all the icing off the top of the cake, which glistens moistly. The ruff of paper is damp.

'Good lad,' Brother Fletcher says, and Michael nods and holds the damp, flattened-looking cake. He wipes his mouth with the back of his hand.

'Want some more?'

Michael shakes his head.

'All that sugar so early in the morning, out of its appropriate time and place,' Sister Williams explains, 'no wonder he doesn't want it any more. You give it back to Jeannie,' she says.

Michael looks at the mess of the cake in his hand, the gunge from his tongue caught on the paper around the rim, and at me, and I shrug.

'Go on now,' she says, as if he is in trouble, 'if you don't want it, then give it back to Jeannie. What else are you going to do with it?'

Michael thrusts it back at me so I take it and sit down. Brother Fletcher nods. Now Sister Williams takes the book, and stands in front of the television, and speaks to us for a while about white-water rafting, and how dangerous it can be, and how boat crews overcome this danger by working in a team, which is to represent the family, and remind us that eternal families are built through Celestial marriage only. Brother Fletcher, who's never been married and it's probably too late now unless a widow

16

moves into the ward from somewhere else, has a large colour picture of a raft floating down a steep-looking incline, water foaming around the side and a family in matching yellow helmets and life jackets holding hands inside the boat. He stands next to her and jiggles the picture now and again.

The room is filled with her soft monotone and the click of the radiators. I sit there with the cake in my hand feeling sleepy and light-headed. We're all in a row, holding our cakes carefully. I can see the saliva shining on the top of mine and I want to throw it away but hold it off the carpet and away from the sofa just as carefully as the other girls hold theirs. Sister Williams gives us all a little clip-art picture of a raft on a river that she's printed on her computer and cut out with pinking shears and then laminated. She tells us to stick them to the inside of our lockers when we get to school so that whenever we open them to get our books we'll be reminded of the important role we play in our Celestial family and how our families rely on us to keep ourselves morally clean.

The lockers at our school don't work like that – hardly anyone has one, but the lesson book is American, printed in Salt Lake where Gary's been and where the high-school students have lockers as tall as they are that they're allowed to visit ten times a day. It isn't like that for us but because the lesson book says it, Sister Williams has got to say it and we listen and hold the little pictures carefully anyway.

When it's nearly time to leave, Brother Fletcher, as if it's an afterthought, says:

'Now, girls, the time has come and it's appropriate now for you to step forward.'

We all stand up and he nudges us into rows. I end up standing opposite James, who is six foot tall and putting in his mission papers in eighteen months, and I can't look at him. His school blazer is the blackest black I've ever seen and his shirts are white and perfect and he never comes to seminary with his tie on, but leaves his top button open with the tie dangling out of his blazer pocket. I've seen him with his collar flicked up, putting it on in the car on the way to school. I stare at a loose thread coming out of one of the buttons on his shirt. He's in the sixth form and some nights he works at the Vue outside town.

'Now is the time to give your gift to your young brothers, a little treat to remind them of the sweetness of the gospel while they make their way into school to learn the bitter things of the world.'

Us girls step forward and hand our fairy cakes to the boys standing in front of us, all in time as if we've been trained to it. Brother Fletcher looks at us as if this is inappropriate behaviour, and smiles so wide I can see the narrow gold tooth he's got in the side of his mouth. I try to hand my cake to James but he screws his face up at it and turns his head.

'And what do we have here?'

Sister Williams walks along the two rows and pulls the others into a circle by putting her hands on their shoulders and gently guiding them until James and I are standing in the centre on our own.

'And why don't you want to accept that gift?'

'It's him,' James nods with his head towards Michael, who is peering through the greasy lenses of his glasses at the new cake he's got from Beth.

'He's had his gob all over it. I don't want it. It's disgusting.'

'Disgusting. He's had his gob all over it,' Sister Williams repeats, looking around at us. '*Soiled*. Second-hand.'

'You don't want this at all then, James?' Brother Fletcher says, taking the cake off him and pushing it towards his face. 'Not even just a nibble, just to be polite and not hurt Jeannie's feelings here?'

'I'm all right, thanks,' James says, and shakes his head. Beth is smiling like a cat.

*   *   *

After the closing prayer I go into the kitchen before Beth can speak to me. The others are busy putting on their coats and hiding their scriptures in their school bags and they don't notice me. Angela is sitting on the floor, her hands knotted into a ball of wool. Sister Fletcher looks at me like I've done something wrong, heaves herself out of her chair and sucks at her lips.

'All finished?'

I nod.

'Good. I'll get in there and tidy up then. I don't know how one hour and twelve youth can totally destroy a front room but it does. Every single time. And you do know that's not what I'm here for, don't you?'

'Shall I help you?'

'Look after this one. Make sure she doesn't put the wool in her mouth.'

She closes the kitchen door behind her and I sit down on the kitchen lino next to Angela. Her chin is covered in dribble. The skin around her mouth and under her chin is red and sore. The floor isn't that clean – there are crumbs and hairs stuck to the bottom edges of the cooker and the fridge, and drips of fat that have hardened down the front of the cooker. The lino is smudged and sticky. Someone should have put a blanket down on the floor for Angela, it isn't right.

'Angela?' I speak softly but she doesn't look up, just carries on moving her fingers slowly into and out of the wool. 'Does that feel nice?'

It's hard to tell, most of the time, what she can understand and what she can't because she never talks. She's old enough for Primary now, but the bishop said she could stay in nursery for as long as she wanted. That almost never happens, but Sister Williams had a meeting with the Stake President and asked for a special dispensation. I get a bit of kitchen roll from a holder screwed into the wall near the sink, kneel in front of

19

Angela and dab at her face. Her skin looks raw in places and I am as gentle as I can be.

'This'll stop you getting sore,' I say, 'we can't have that, can we?'

I smile and try to catch her eye, but she moves her head away and goes back to the wool. It's tangled so tightly that Sister Fletcher is never going to be able to use it, so I snap a piece of it off for her and tuck it into the pocket on the front of her dungarees.

'There you go. You can play with that later,' I say, and I feel her chest move under my hand, her little heart buzzing like a tiny bird's.

'You're good with her.'

The voice startles me. I jump, and stand up and away from Angela quickly. It's Sister Williams – who just smiles, and bustles in. 'She likes you,' she says, and picks Angela up from the floor while at the same time swinging her red and yellow changing bag over her shoulder.

'Does she?'

'You think I can't tell?'

'No, I just meant . . .'

Sister Williams smiles. 'I'm her mother. I know her better than she knows herself. She likes you. Listen,' she coughs, 'the lesson we've just had. Moral cleanliness. It's important.'

'I know it is.' I have a dragging feeling in my stomach.

'I know you know. I just mean, perhaps the lesson books – maybe they could do with updating. Maybe they're a bit old-fashioned. I get the feeling you might have been a little embarrassed in there. With James.'

She pauses, her head on one side, smiling slightly. She wants to have one of those all-us-women-together talks about crushes, and Strange New Feelings, and Powerful Urges, but I can't do it.

'It was all right.'

'Well, just so you know. We've got to teach what the lesson book says. But there are better ways of going about it, in my opinion. It's a wonderful gift we women have. Bringing spirits through the veil. It's why Heavenly Father had to give men the priesthood. So they wouldn't feel left out, and like second-rate humans.'

She's watching me carefully, so I smile at her.

'I wasn't upset.'

'Good. So long as you don't feel singled out. You're a good girl, Jeannie. Angela's really taken a liking to you.'

I suppose it's true that Angela might be used to me. Sister Williams takes me to school every morning after seminary, and because she's the teacher and has to wait until the very end to make sure everyone else has got their lifts safely, I'm often in here with Angela, just chatting to her, counting on her fingers, making sure she's tidy before we leave.

'Thanks.'

'I mean it. She trusts you, I can tell. She's not quiet like this for everyone.'

'She's never any bother to Sister Fletcher.'

'Yes. Well. Perhaps that's more fear than love.' I duck my head so she can't see me smile. 'Jeannie, do you think, maybe you'd like to come over some time?'

'To babysit?'

'Well, I'll still probably need to be there. Some of the things she needs, it's complicated.'

'I can do nappies.' Angela's too old for nappies, but I bet she still wears them. Poo and wee and things like that just don't bother me any more. 'I'm used to all that sort of thing. I can do it.'

'Bless you, I know you can. But she still can't swallow very well either. It's better I'm there too, just in case anything happens.'

'Okay, sorry.'

21

'No, what I meant was – if you came to the house one Saturday afternoon then I could get on with things. I've a whole stack of ironing, and the back garden looks like a jungle. It's hard to do things when she needs watching all the time. But if you were there, to be a friend to her and keep her company . . . What do you think?'

I look up at Angela. She's rested her head against Sister Williams's shoulder and has found a lock of her mother's hair to suck. She's so used to it she doesn't even notice. Angela closes her eyes and smiles. I wonder what she's thinking about. You can tell just by looking at her that she's different. Even though she's five, she still acts like a baby. She's floppy – she can sit all right, but she can hardly walk at all. It's not her fault; she was just born like that. She opens her eyes and sees me looking at her, and puts her hand over the apple-shaped pocket with the wool, and I think I've probably given her something that Sister Williams wouldn't want her to have. Something that would hurt her.

'I don't know,' I say. 'I might not be the best person. What about Beth?'

She looks disappointed for a moment – but then she smiles. Probably no one ever wants to hang out with Angela, and she's used to it. That makes me feel guilty, but she doesn't know me well enough to want me to be a friend to her little girl, not really, so I've done the right thing.

'Never mind then,' she says, in a very high-pitched and cheerful voice. She turns away from me, swinging the bag against her hip, and speaks to me over her shoulder as she goes through the kitchen door. 'Tell me if you change your mind. It was only a thought. We'd better get going now anyway.'

I can see Angela's hand on her shoulder. I can tell I have hurt her, maybe both of them, and that makes me feel even worse than I started off this morning.

* * *

8.28. I tell Sister Williams I need to stop at the chemist's before school.

'Again?' she says. I just smile at her and nod. Dad's got this face he pulls when things go wrong: *Well, what can you do?* And I try and do it now. She knows about Mum's trouble so she doesn't ask me anything else, but pulls in at the kerb and reminds me that even though today is a special day for my family, it's important to keep up with the daily readings and she'll see me bright and early for the quiz on Monday morning, which is on the differences between the nativity narratives in the gospels of the New Testament.

She never talks to me like this. During seminary, and on Sundays, she talks like the rest of them do. *Edifying. Uplifting. Watching over the youth.* Those times she's just pretending to be someone else, and the rest of the time, like during the lifts, she goes back to normal. But she's still pretending to be the teacher now.

She must be really angry with me.

'I like Angela,' I say, before taking off my seat belt.

'I know you do. Don't feel bad. I know she's hard work.'

'It's not that,' I say. How to tell her. The words I want to say are awful – make me sound like an attention seeker.

She frowns at me.

'Are you all right, Jeannie?'

'Yes. I just think you need someone better to help you with Angela. Someone better than me. I might make a mistake. I might feed her the wrong thing or let her touch the plug sockets or she might get out of the front door while I'm in the toilet.' I pause. 'Anything could happen. Beth would be loads better at it.'

'All right, Jeannie,' she says, and her voice is tired. She doesn't try convincing me that I'm wrong, and it's obvious that I've made her see sense – made her remember that Angela is too precious to be left with someone like me.

Angela is sitting on her pink and green booster seat in the back of the car and I wave at her through the rear windscreen before turning away and crossing the road towards the chemist's.

It's calm in here and the bottles of calamine lotion and big plastic packets of nappies are soothing. I'm going to be late for school, again, but it doesn't matter. There's a carousel with blister packs of rain hoods and kirby grips and safety pins and earplugs and I twirl it gently. I see cars pass by through the stickers on the window about the smoking clinic. They're only just open and I'm first in but they don't stare at me or ask me what I want and I browse like I've not got anywhere else to be.

I didn't lie to Sister Williams. I never lie. You only have to lie if you talk more than you need to, or you're stupid. I'm in and out of chemists getting things for Mum and her trouble all the time. The big Boots in the town centre. Out on my bike at night to the late-opening one near the park if she's caught short and Dad's on a late shift. But this one is my favourite. The one I come to most often. No one from school comes here because it's run by a set of Catholics and they won't fill out prescriptions for the pill. Which means I won't see any girls from school. I've been here every day for the last week without being caught out.

One of the Elders once showed me a bit in the Bible in the book of Revelation about the whore of Babylon who is dressed in purple and told me that was to signify the papal robes and I should watch out for that, but even though they are bead-twirling papists, actually the people in here are all right. They're all old women. Sort of people you expect to be working in charity shops. The one behind the counter powers up the till and there's a dry, powdery smell in the air. As clean as a hospital but much more comforting. Like a really nice nursing home.

I take off my school tie behind the tall shelves where the baby food is and shove it in my shoulder bag. There's a round mirror in the top corner over the counter for the chemist to keep an eye on the shop while she's in the back dispensing the medicine and I use it to look at the assistants come and go behind the counter until the nice one, the one I like, is standing by the till filling up the display of Chupa Chups lollies from a cardboard box she's wheeled out on a trolley.

She's almost too old to be working but she looks soft. A wrinkled fat baby with a halo of soft curly grey hair. She always wears this same string of plastic blue beads – so cheap you can see the ridge where the mould was around the middle of each one. She wears them no matter what else she's wearing. They must be special to her because of something other than what they look like. They might be a sort of rosary or a present from her grandchild or a first love. I stare at the beads and drop the boxes on the counter quickly and she says nothing but lets her hands fall on them gently, scanning them in with the gun and the red laser and putting them in the little green and white paper bag.

It's not embarrassing. The first time it was, but in the days after, it's just like buying bread and milk. It's the way she does it, see? She doesn't rush and she takes Mum's money and puts it on top of the till while she counts out my change, then folds over the top of the bag a few times and staples it closed just like she does for everyone else. Her glasses are on a string around her neck. She hands me the bag and smiles and says they work better if you do it very first thing in the morning when urine has a higher concentration of hormones, so if you're testing early you're more likely to get a reliable result and would I like to pop into the back because there's a small consultation room with a lavatory I'm more than welcome to use?

I can't talk. She said the same thing yesterday and the day before and the day before that and I don't know if she is kind or just senile. I want to say, *How reliable are these things? Can you give me a scientific percentage of how often they are wrong? Of how often nine of them in a row are wrong?* When I don't answer she smiles again. Looks over my shoulder to the person behind me, who actually doesn't care what I am buying at all, but asks for camera film and the cheap version of Gaviscon, both of which are kept behind the counter. 8.56.

MARTIN

Most people will take one look at a choke chain and assume you're hurting your dog by using one. I walk this same path every day – two laps of the park no matter what the weather – and if I had a Polo for every time I've been stopped by some biddy who knows nothing about the rearing, keeping and training of working animals, I don't know what I'd do. A choke chain is not a corrective tool, it's an aide-mémoire to training goals already achieved. It's not a punishment any more than a knot in the corner of your hanky is. The fact is, dogs don't have hankies. Any fool can see that.

Take Bovril. Until we get past the kiddies' bit of the park, with the slide and swings and what have you, I keep her on the leash. I don't pull her along and I don't let her lead me. The chain lays against her throat loosely, almost decorative. The way the links tighten as she pulls forward, loosen as she drops back, obedient, to heel – it's a constant lesson for her. It reminds her of the gold standard: I expect self-control from my dog, and because I respect her – because I love her, even – I provide her with a gentle reminder in the form of the chain. It doesn't hurt her. She doesn't resent it. If she did, she wouldn't come out from under the kitchen table whenever I stand at the back door and rattle it, now would she?

We wait in front of the swings. I've not got a formal arrangement with Nina, not for the usual walks, but this is where we usually run into each other. A young lad getting dragged along by a boxer nods at me as he passes, and I want to ask him where his plastic bags are, offer to lend him a few, but I bite my lip.

You can't talk to anyone these days, not without getting your head half bitten off. Bovril sits nice by my leg, doesn't pull. She knows I'll let her off when I'm ready.

When I'm out in the quiet with the hems of my trousers getting wet from the cold grass, my bitch at my side, there's a feeling I get that I never get at any other time. She loves it out here. We both do. I've got my family but these days all I need is this: Bovril's wet nose against the back of my hand, or her well-proportioned haunches lolloping away from me as she fetches the decoy back in, always eager to please, always my own, always faithful and obedient – her coat shiny with first-thing sun.

Except that isn't true. The cast of the morning isn't complete until Nina's here. She is a glossy golden retriever, plump but firm about the withers and bright eyes you could fall into. I try not to compare her to Pauline, who is an overfed, incontinent Pekinese with her wet snout forever pressed up and smearing against someone else's window.

'Steady on, girl. Wait. Wait. Control yourself.'

I see Nina now, crossing the grass with her own two Labs bounding excitedly beside her. She doesn't notice me at first, and I get to watch her for a full half-minute while she strides towards me, laughing at Bracken prancing through a puddle with her tail in the air, kicking a polystyrene chip tray out of her way, tucking bits of hair behind her ears. Then she does see me and I put my hand up in the air quickly so it doesn't seem as if I've been lurking here staring at her. She smiles and waves, just slicing her hand through the air once, and I wave back and then turn away from her and look through the wire fencing around the swing park for a while to avoid that awkwardness that comes when you can see someone approaching but they're still too far away from you to strike up a conversation with them. Bovril moves closer to me. The lead hangs in a neat U from where it leaves my hand, tucked into the pocket of my waxed jacket.

'Martin,' Nina says, and her voice tinkles straight through me to the hair on the back of my knees. I turn. Nina's wearing lilac and brown Karrimor boots, jeans, a purple fleece. I stop and slip the chain over Bovril's head. My hands are cold and I make a meal out of it, keeping my head down as Nina pulls a tennis ball out of her pocket.

'Morning.'

She clucks under her breath and her bitches come to heel. She drops a hand on each of their heads. Their great brown eyes swivel to look up at her. There's only two occasions when you'll see the white of a dog's eyes. Outside of a seizure, that is. One, they're planning to bite you and two, they're starting the tie. Love and hate, hate and love. Two sides of the same thing: dogs know it, we all know it.

'Glorious, isn't it?'

Nina's not a skinny girl. Not fat, mind, just a woman who can lift her own shopping into the boot of her car. Probably doesn't need any help changing a tyre or putting up a few shelves either. Her long blonde hair is coiled up at the back of her head in a beautiful lump, still wet from the shower. The shower. I do not think about her in the shower for very long. This woman: she has ruined me. I used to be sufficient to myself. Not any more.

Bovril is nudging at my hand, her tail is swiping the air and I say, 'That'll do,' then I laugh because Nina's two are moving around too, and Nina winks at me and raises her arm in a beautiful slow arc, opening her fingers at its peak and releasing a tennis ball that flies through the air and bounces off the grass to roll down the hill. The three Labradors look at us, Bovril in so much agony she's dribbling. Bracken and Heather are whining. The crooning noises coming from their soft loose throats make my heart hurt.

'Fetch then, ladies,' Nina says, and they are away, flying like corks, racing off in streaks of gold and brown and making scuffed tracks through the dew in the long grass. I am pleased to see

Bovril out in front: Nina is a kind woman and she overfeeds those dogs. They are plump, slack and obedient but Bovril is lean and knows that if she's first on a market day I'll buy her a turkey neck on the way home.

'Bovril's always first,' she giggles, 'I think you don't feed her in the mornings, just to show me up.'

'Would I do that?' I say, and we fall into step, walking slowly along the path.

We met on a bright day like this and I fell in love with her three weeks and two days later (I am talking about Nina, not Bovril) when I observed the way she threw that tennis ball. Her fingernails are always short and neat and even though the ball is often muddy and wet with dog saliva, she holds it firmly in her palm, nothing dainty or precious about it. She hefts it into the air like a boy, and never, ever wipes her hands on her jeans. When Nina sees a dog owner holding one of those plastic contraptions used to scoop spitty balls up through the grass and fire them through the air, she laughs at them, not caring if they hear her or not.

She stops now, and tilts her head back to look at the sky.

'It's what I love about April,' she says, 'the blue is just so glorious after all those months of grey. Don't you think?'

'Nina,' I say, 'it's always a glorious morning when I bump into you.'

There's an earthworm on the path, one end wriggling, the other a mess of squashed guts and soil. Nina steps over it where Pauline would have squirmed. 'Bit of food for the birds, there,' she remarks, and we look at the sky again then change direction, leaving the path and walking slowly over the grass in the direction the dogs have taken.

'Today's your big day, what with Gary coming back,' she says.

Nina never leans into me, never takes my arm as we walk. She never pulls grass out of my hair or snaps her bobble out of her ponytail and lets the wet strands fall around her shoulders for me to touch. She never stands on tiptoe to whisper something to me, her breath hot and wet in my ear. She never lets our thighs touch each other when we sit on the wooden bench halfway round our usual route and let the dogs dither and pet. All the same, I know she knows today's a big day for more reasons than what she's just said. We don't need to say it, some things are just understood between the two of us.

'He'll be in the air now. You must be so excited.'

'In some ways, yes,' I say.

'You don't sound sure?'

We walk slowly, her stride matching mine. Her thighs are firm and bulky inside the legs of her jeans but I have never touched them. I think about what I want to say for a long time before I speak and she gives me the room to do it in and I have never touched them.

'He's bound to be different. He's been away from us in a whole other country for two years.'

'You've been able to talk to him, though? His emails and that – you've kept up to date?'

'His mother usually handles that side of things. He sent letters too. Lots of blue airmail envelopes.'

'Did you never speak on the phone? It's not that expensive.'

'No. He's not allowed. I think they make exceptions for Mother's Day, but they celebrate it on a different day in America and Gary was never sure which day the exception applied to, and he didn't want to chance it.'

'Not allowed? To speak to his own father on the phone?'

'They don't want them getting distracted from the work. They don't have any television, newspapers, no music. Nothing like that.'

'No music? What's wrong with music?'

'They sing at church, of course, but nothing else. He has a day off. P-Day once a week. But that's not really a day off the way you'd think of it. It's P for preparation. They do all their housework that day. But he knew what the rules were when he agreed to go. It's only fair he keeps to them. Sticks it out to the end. And he has.'

'That's a point,' she says, and I can see the look on her – striving for understanding, struggling not to judge. 'All sorts of cultures send their young men out on spiritual journeys. A quest before he comes of age. All that silence and solitude will help him to develop his spiritual side. That's rare in a boy his age.'

'Solitude?' I think of Gary twinned to his companion and both pinned into their matching navy suits by their little black badges. I even laugh a bit but she doesn't respond. Bracken is back with the ball and Nina kneels to catch it as it falls from her mouth. She throws it again, so hard the fleece rides up and she grunts as she lets it fly. So. Bovril was second. I look over the curve of the hill and see her panting and shamefaced. *No stop at the butcher's for you, my girl.* I think the words at her, and her ears fall flat to her head. She knows. I don't have time for the detour anyway.

'They're not allowed to be on their own. They send them out in pairs.'

She laughs. 'Like Noah's ark?'

'A bit like that, I suppose. Two of them – always together. Sleeping in the same room, eating together, working from six in the morning to ten at night, side by side. He was away to that a few months after he finished his A levels. He won't be who I remember. He won't be Gary.'

'Two years of that is bound to change a person. He'll still be yours, though. Still be your boy.'

'Nineteen when he went and taller than I am now,' I put the flat of my hand a few inches over my own head, 'he'll be the man of the house when he comes back.' My voice drops away.

There's something else to commend about Gary. If he hadn't turned in his papers we would never have had the farewell party.

And if we hadn't had the party, we wouldn't have had to do a special order from the supermarket – trays of ready-made pastry cases, plastic bowls and plates for the chicken legs, condiments, salad ingredients, eggs by the three dozen. A mixed buffet plus gateaux and trifle for seventy-five. It took us four months to pay that off the MasterCard.

Pauline's never above using her chair to get special treatment – she rang them up, said she was sending in her girl with a list, implied we'd be spending lots more than we did, and seeing as she wasn't mobile and we were a low-income local family and loyal customers, could they do something for us? *Lots of other supermarkets do*, she said.

They sent it all in a van, and it was Nina who drove it. She reverse-parked (flawlessly) in the chapel car park and unloaded all the crates herself onto the pasting tables set up in the cultural hall. There were men about, but she wouldn't take a hand from anyone. Pauline was there with her board and her list and her pencil, ticking things off and organising the sisters to unwrap the chicken and get it in the oven, put the eggs into the pans of water that were already boiling and waiting to receive them. It was chaos. She'd insisted on the wooden floors being polished, threatened to pay for it to be done herself if the ward wasn't willing to support her boy in this way, so it had been done. The sun shone in through the high narrow windows and dust floated about in the polish-scented air. Someone had brought a stepladder to put balloons up on the basketball hoops and it had slipped. Brother Fletcher had not been injured, but he was making a song and dance of it all the same, insisting on lying down on the couch in the cry room and having his wife look at his ankle for him before he'd move the ladder. Brother Lawson, his wife's uncle, came forward in the end with the oil and put his hands on his head to give him a blessing, he went on about it that much.

After four or five trips the van was empty, the kitchen was full and the steam was coming out through the hatch into the hall, making the crêpe-paper streamers flaccid. The woman sang 'Count Your Blessings' as they peeled and sliced, and Pauline cried noisily while Nina hung about in the foyer. She had on jeans and a green bodywarmer. Of course I am out in the world as much as any man and I have seen women in jeans every day of my life. But hardly ever inside the chapel, and it was that, I think, that made me stare at her. A purple bum-bag with the van keys hanging half in, half out. I wondered if she wanted a tip for making the journey through Saturday afternoon traffic, and looked about for Julian, who'd know what was the done thing. He was nowhere, Gary was at the barber's and Pauline – she were royalty that day. There was no getting near her. It fell to me. I approached, across the stone-coloured carpet, and rooted about in my pockets.

'I like your badge,' she said to me, and I've never taken it off my jacket since. It's a silver and pewter pin of Bovril – well, not really her – just a good-looking Lab of indeterminate colour, head and shoulders. A bust of a dog, if you like.

'It's a Lab,' I said, 'and it's not a badge, it's a pin.'

'I know that,' she said, and tinkled her little laugh at me, 'I know that. I've got two of my own.'

'Trained?'

She nodded. 'And registered.'

'Bitches? Or dogs? Only I've been thinking of—' She interrupted me by shaking her head.

'Bitches, both of them. I've been looking for a stud myself. You can't find a decent stud dog for love nor money round here, can you? I heard of one in Liverpool – King Wenceslas, he was called, but he was booked till January next year so I never bothered.'

I nodded. 'There was a man in Skelmersdale,' I said, 'Lancelot's Victory. A nice Lab. Not cheap, but worth it. I think he let his registration lapse.'

'Why would he do that?'

'Something dodgy about it, I reckon. Glad I never let Bovril near him.'

'Bovril! That's yours, is it?'

'Chocolate Lab. You?'

She produced her wallet – a worn black leather one, like a man's. Flipped it open and showed me a picture of the two of them running after each other on a beach somewhere.

'That's at Formby. They love it there. Both good swimmers, nice, dense coats.'

'They're a good-looking pair.'

'They're from working stock, winners on both sides.'

A pause. Not awkward. The silence settled comfortably, and the noise of singing floated through from the kitchen. They'd finished 'Count Your Blessings' and started on 'Families are Forever'. Jeannie was in there with them too, being trained on what to do for a church social. I heard her voice, special to me but as tuneless and quavering as the rest.

'Have you done the Good Citizen award with them yet?'

Nina snorted. 'That thing? They've both got Gold, but it wasn't much of a challenge. I want to do some advanced retrieving with them, try them on a few scurries, that sort of thing.'

I couldn't help it, I was impressed.

'I'm working on a controlled retrieve with Bovril now. I take her, some Sundays. If I can get a bit of the park to myself, we try a bit of clockface. She doesn't get it yet, though.'

Nina laughs. 'Labs can be daft, can't they? It'll come to her eventually, though, so long as you make it fun for her.'

I realised then that I'd not thought about all those red letters in the bills drawer, the store cards, the HP agreements from BrightHouse for Pauline's bloody leather sofa – none of that stuff – since I started talking to her. Is that all it takes? Just a few words with a new friend?

'Where do you—'

'I work them on Astley Park most early mornings. Surprised I've not seen you there before,' Nina said.

'I work shifts,' I said, 'at the sorting office.'

'Well, we're there more often than not. Do you show her? We're preparing for the next lot of trials. A long shot but,' she sucked her teeth, 'if you want to win the lottery, you've got to shell out on a ticket, haven't you?' She folded up the wallet and put it away.

'I'm working up to Crufts. That's our ambition. She's got a delicate temperament, though. Don't want to push her too hard in case it sets her back.'

'I know what you mean.' Nina nodded seriously, as if there was nothing more natural in the world than dogs with delicate temperaments, and early morning walks, and standing close to someone who wasn't your wife. 'Well, you should come, we could work them together. Maybe you've got a few tips for me. There's nothing like being first out in the morning. Nothing like it in the world.'

I wanted to invite her to stay for the farewell – to meet Gary and Julian and Jeannie – as if she'd have cared who they were. And something in me held back, thinking that it wouldn't have been appropriate, given she wasn't a member, not dressed properly and wasn't used to our ways, and Gary's last real event to spend time with his friends and family shouldn't be taken up by his father acting as tour guide to the delivery girl from Richardson's. So I didn't. But shortly after Gary left I started to have trouble sleeping, and in the end I asked them to change my hours, which they did, and now I see Nina every single day.

See how it works? Like Bovril's Kennel Club registration cards – one link to the next, going back and back, each layer pure and tied onto the next. Actions and consequences. Generations of events. You can trace them back and if you practise doing that often enough, you can trace them forward too and reject a stud that'll give you pups with lockjaw, hip splay and deafness.

'On you go now,' Nina says and I am confused until I see Bracken approach with the ball in her muzzle. Bovril is hesitating a few feet away. Second again. Maybe third. It's always the same. She gets there first, then stands by to let the others in. If I never knew any better I'd say she got it from me. Polite to a fault, to a fault. The Leekes are not go-getters, not even our dogs. Gary takes after Pauline's side – the whole Arnold clan are busy and ambitious, constantly burning to get things done. Some of us build Zion, some of us hope for it, as Pauline says.

'I'm glad he's going to see his mother again. She's missed him.'

'Has she found it hard?'

'It's been a hard couple of years all round. You know she's ill,' Nina nods solemnly, 'and she doesn't work, I'm the only one bringing in any money – and ten per cent of that has got to go to the Church. All the same, she's wanted all new things for him coming back – I've had to go to BrightHouse again.'

'Martin, I thought you were going to knock that on the head? The overtime you do. You're going to make yourself ill.'

'What else can I do? She says we need the stuff – how else am I meant to pay for it? I'm just hoping that the Housing Association will give us a bit of leeway. If they'll hold off on the arrears until Gary starts earning, well then, we'll probably be all right.'

Nina tuts and says nothing.

'And on top of that she and Jeannie have been at each other's throats the past few weeks. She isn't herself. Peaky, wound up – like Pauline. To be honest, I'll be glad when Gary gets home because it'll be less for me to deal with.'

Nina's kneeling to Bracken when Heather approaches. She fusses at them and she probably doesn't remember it's round about two years since we met, on the nose. Since I saw the rise of her ball through the air, the cling of cooling dog spit webbing between her fingers. I've counted the days since then. She nudges Heather in the flank to make it a fair start.

'He'll be a good help to you. And once he starts working, another wage coming in too. It's bound to help.'

'That's just what I was thinking. Frees me up a bit more. Jeannie's all right. She's a little princess, really. Good as gold. All teenage girls row with their mothers.'

'That's true. I was a right wildcat.'

'I can't imagine that, Nina.'

I can, though. I can.

She laughs. 'The things I got up to aren't worth imagining, I can promise you that.'

'I hope she'll settle down, once Gary's back.'

'She will do. And with Pauline being so ill, it must put a strain on her. She helps her mum a lot, doesn't she?'

I nod, thinking of the mess on the new suite just last night. A sticky, faux-leather thing indented with the shape of Pauline's buttocks. It was supposed to be wipe-clean, which is why, in the end, I let myself be persuaded on the matter of us getting it, but real life put paid to that. Pauline crying into her hands, shouting at Jeannie to bring towels, fresh clothes, sending me and Julian out of the room while Jeannie rushed in with the Flash.

'Julian's still at home, though. Shouldn't he be helping out a bit more?'

'Julian,' I say. 'Well, he's saving up for his own place. He's twenty-six years old. Pauline thinks I take board off him, but I don't. He wants to spread his wings a bit. I don't think he'll be in the house for much longer.'

'Well, that's fair enough,' she says.

'There's someone else who won't be in the house much longer either,' I say.

Might as well come out with it all now. Let her know my plans. Faint heart and all that.

'Oh Martin,' she says, and stands very close to me, 'is it that bad? You never said?'

'Sometimes I think I'm going to go mad,' I say. I don't look at her. 'It's really only you and the dog that have given me the will to carry on these past couple of years. The strain.'

'I can see that,' she says. 'You've aged. Look at your hair.' I've got my cap on, but she puts her hand up to my temple where it's started to go white. I freeze, thinking she's planning on kissing me, wondering if I should lean in, trying to remember if I brushed my teeth this morning. She moves her hand away before she touches me and flaps at a cloud of midges in front of her face.

'You can't take this all on your own shoulders. No one could. You're not superhuman, Martin.'

She takes my arm, and for a second I stiffen, glancing around us to make sure no one else can see. It won't matter much, after today. It won't matter at all. So I lean into her, and just enjoy it.

'Have you talked to anyone about this?'

'I wouldn't tell anyone before I told you, Nina. I wanted to say something to Jeannie this morning, when I was taking her to seminary. Give her a bit of a warning. But I couldn't.'

'She doesn't know? Oh, love.'

'Not yet. I've been putting it off, for weeks. In the car I nearly came out with it, but didn't have the heart. She's desperate to see Gary again. She's not eaten properly, not for days. She was sick a couple of days ago. The excitement. She's so worked up, I didn't think she could cope with anything else.'

'Maybe she's guessed. Teenagers aren't as self-absorbed as you think, you know.'

'You could be right. But I don't feel right keeping something so important from her. I know children don't need to know the ins and outs of everything, but—'

'Well, losing a parent is one of the most devastating things that can happen to a teenager,' Nina says. 'She has got a right to know.'

'It isn't like losing. It won't be the same as that,' I say, and my voice stops working before I can tell her about the plans I have. Of coming for tea some nights. Taking Jeannie out on weekends. I'll save up some money so she can still have prom dresses, and go on trips, and that sort of thing.

'I'm sorry, Martin. I didn't think. Of course. Her beliefs are going to be a great comfort to her.'

'It's just knowing when to do it. The sooner the better, I think. If only I could get the guts up.'

'You'll know when the time is right.'

'Now's the time,' I say, and pull her arm to make her stop. 'I can't wait any longer. It's only you, and the Malvern trials coming up, that give me any hope at all.'

She smiles at me, and pulls her arm out of mine.

'Maybe you should go home,' she says. 'Get a bit of sleep. Forget about the Malvern bloody trials. Bovril's a pro; it's my two we need to be worrying about.'

Home! We're up to our eyeballs in arrears and consolidation loans and debt management programmes and the letters don't fit in the bills drawer any more and even the new flat-screen-high-definition-telly-with-built-in-DVD-player-and-Freeview-box is on the drip drip. Home! The place smells like Julian's work overalls and the fat hardening in the bottom of the grill pan and the scurf in Pauline's hair. It's only here in the park with Nina that I can stop, look down the path between the trees and feel like I own something.

'Martin? What's the matter?'

There's more shades of green than I've got words for and no way to tell anyone about the way my chest feels when the wind touches the back of my neck. There's only so many ways you can talk about the smell and feel and look of grass and soil and conker trees. The daffodils aren't here yet, but they're in the post.

'I want to come home with you,' I say.

'That's an idea. Have a coffee. I made a walnut cake yesterday afternoon. We can put the dogs in the garden and go through some of the obedience tests with them.' She's brisk and businesslike. She takes her mobile phone out of her pocket and checks the time.

'We'd better get a wiggle on, though; you've got work, haven't you?'

'I mean—'

'And while we're there, I'll ring my sister. She's a home help. She'll know how to get someone to come in and give you a hand with Pauline. Take the strain off Jeannie a bit.'

'She won't have a nurse. No home helps or social workers. She won't go to the hospital, won't take any medicine.'

'Is that because of her beliefs? Like not having blood transfusions?' she asks.

I lean towards her a little. The sun is up fully now, and her hair is drying. I could do with taking my coat off, but I don't want to interrupt our moment.

'That's the Witnesses. We don't mind doctors, but she won't discuss it.' I lower my voice, so she has to bend her head closer to me to listen. She's wearing tiny silver hoops in her ears, and she's close enough now that I can see the little diamond pattern scratched into the flat edges of the hoops, the flake of yellow wax caught in the dark hole at the centre of the whirlpool of her ear.

'Sometimes I think she likes being ill. All the attention she gets. The way there's always people gathering around to help her. She can keep Jeannie close to her, keep her at home every night.'

'Martin,' she says, not unsympathetically and with a great deal of feeling. Just my name, she says, and sighs, and leaves it at that.

'I know it's a terrible thing for me to say,' I start, and she cuts in.

'It's not, Martin. Not if it's what you really think. No one can blame you for having thoughts and feelings. You're a human being, not a saint.'

'That's right enough,' I say.

'Things will get better.'

'They will now,' I say, and smile.

She nods and because she does I know she knows what I mean and my heart makes the sweep upwards like a lift, like falling or dropping, like a balloon in water, like a fall, like a swoop. What can you say anyway? I laid awake half the night listening to Pauline snoring and trying to plan it out. The smell of the house lay heavy on me. Dark, through the bedroom blinds, then light. The effort of finding the words clogged my thinking. How do people make changes? Imagine themselves into new lives, and then wake up in the morning and do what it takes? How do people do that?

'I'm glad we met up this morning,' Nina says.

She is stroking the cuckoo spit off a fireweed stem, casually searching for the froghopper within. I've seen her do it before. The pink, deckle-edged flowers nod their heads and give off their private, meaty smell. She's standing off the path, surrounded by these springy stems, and she looks like a painting. It's obscene. I feel my blood start to move and the skin across my stomach tightens and I have to look past her.

'When shall I come?'

I hate to seem over-keen but time is creeping forwards: the dew is going off, into the air. There's no real rush. I could leave after the dinner. I could leave tomorrow. Wait till he's settled in. Wait till he's earning. I could give it a few days. But I want out. Pauline tells me I've to make a speech later and the thought of it turns my windpipe into a column of cement.

'Come now, if you've got time.'

Thank God!

'Well, I'll need to go back and pack a bag. Don't worry. I won't move in all my worldly possessions. Just a few clothes. Bits and bobs. My bank book. Bovril will have to come right away. We can't be parted. Will your two do all right with another bitch? They get on well enough, don't they?'

'What—'

'I suppose I could board her, and introduce them gradually. But I'd rather – well we can sort all that out. Soon. Details, that's all they are. The most important thing is we're— What do you think?' I grope for her hand. Hold it in mine. She's clammy, and I'm cold as a fish. 'I know it's quick, but . . .'

I don't know why Nina looks so shocked. Because, perhaps, all this time she's had me down as a Christian, as a religious, church-going man? I do go to church, when I can't swing an imaginary Sunday shift at the sorting office, that is. The hours of reading and singing, shuffling between rooms, shaking hands and nodding and smiling and nodding until my neck feels like it's going to seize up. A whisper in my ear, and no idea where the voice comes from: *Go on*, it says, *believe. Just believe. What harm does it do?* It is a small price to pay for Pauline's happiness. And you pick up things, here and there, whether you want to or not.

For instance: Pauline's God says it's all right to have more than one. He does it himself. He is a man – a man turned into a god – who loves women. Gods without number, who own wives without number, merrily populating their pet worlds without number throughout eternity. We stand on one of those worlds. If I were a better-read man, my mind would trip over the facts of that, but Pauline sees no fiction in it.

I have questions I'm afraid to ask. Are all of us on this world the children of just one of the god-wives, or are we all mixed in together? Is there someone whose job it is to keep track of everyone? Birth certificates in the pre-existence? I don't ask.

Jeannie once told Pauline that her Heavenly Father lived on a ledge in the sky made of stained-glass windows, through which He looked down on us, wearing a cape the colour of grass. Pauline wouldn't let her go to Brownies any more. All that C of E propaganda had addled her thinking.

'What are you saying, Martin?' She pulls her hand out of mine, tucks her hair behind her ears and stares at me.

I go all cold. We're by the pond now, the lather of algae clouding the water so there's no point looking for minnows and sticklebacks. A memory surfaces: catching them in jars for Jeannie, pointing out the red flash on the belly of a strutting male, keeping the jars on the kitchen windowsill and pouring the stiff, foaming bodies down the outside drain before she got up. She must have been eight then, maybe less. Not the sort of thing that would interest her now. I think of Pauline at home, checking the flight times on her new Freeview internet and speed-dialling the bishop.

'You're asking to move in with me. Your wife is dying and you're asking to come and live with me?' Nina speaks slowly.

'I thought . . .'

Her face darkens. She pulls the leads out of her pockets and rattles them without looking over her shoulder to see where Bracken and Heather are. They'll come, course they'll come. I joke about her overfeeding them, but I've never seen a pair of better-trained dogs. She makes them carry eggs in their mouths, fetch them back without breaking them. They can do it with sausages, steaks, bacon: whatever you want. They are at her heels within seconds. *Dying?*

'I'm going,' she says, and clips the leads onto the girls, then walks again, briskly. 'That's your Julian over there,' she says, over her shoulder. 'He's been watching us for the past ten minutes.'

'Nina!' My voice sounds thin and weedy, like a teenage boy's. She doesn't turn, but shakes her head and holds up a stop-hand at me.

'Leave it, Martin,' she says, 'go to your son. Go to your wife.'

Julian's walking furtively across the grass at the far end of the park, heading for the gate that leads into town. He's pretending not to see me. He's not much to look at himself. Black hair in a ponytail that curls against his neck, blue overalls smeared with grease and slightly too short in the leg. He plucks them from his groin as he moves, swift and furtive in wide, long-legged strides. Julian. Behind him by a good few feet is Drake – squat, ginger-haired and damp-looking. Matching set of overalls.

I tug at Bovril's lead without meaning to, and she coughs, and I feel a great hot stab of guilt.

'I'll see you later, Nina, yes? Or tomorrow?'

She's picking up speed now, almost jogging, and the dogs are wagging their tails as they trot along beside her. Has he really been standing there watching? No wonder it put her off. I slip the collar over Bovril's head and click at her under my breath.

'Sorry, my darling, Sorry, love. Sorry.'

I don't call out to Julian. It's all right. He's with Drake. He must be out on a job. It's all right. Sorry. Sorry, love. Sorry.

JULIAN

'Is that your old man over there?'

Drake's mobile telephone is ringing. He pats the front of his overalls, top and bottom, and eventually he thumbs out the mobile with his sausagey, freckled fingers.

'I don't know, is it?'

He squints at the display, points vaguely towards the other side of the park, then turns his back to me as he answers, *Yo yo yo, baby!* Like the Fresh Prince.

Is it Dad? I turn and look and see that yes he is right and it is. Over on the other side of the green holding hands with a blonde person I have never seen before. He looks like he has just had a heart attack. His skin has gone the colour of raw chicken and he looks at her while she pulls her hand out of his and walks away. He is just stood there with the dog, looking after her. From this distance, and in his old waxed jacket and flat cap, he looks like a homeless person. His mouth opens and closes. Bovril squats, her flanks shaking. What is he doing? Is he shouting after her? I do not think he has seen me. The blonde person turns and shakes her head, annoyed with him. They have had an argument. Well, well, well. He stands for a while, and then pulls a plastic bag out of his pocket and kneels to collect Bovril's droppings. He walks away with the dog beside him, wagging her tail and nudging with her nose the knotted bag that is swinging from his fist.

'Yeh, baby? What you after?'

Who is Drake talking to? A woman? Some one-night stand? Or someone else complaining about a shoddy job we have allegedly done on their vehicle? I fill in the other half of the conversation as we walk slowly back towards the van.

'I can't, not now. It isn't convenient.'

Convenient! If I were like Drake, I would whistle and whoo-whoo and twirl at a word like '*convenient*'. He cannot be talking to someone he knows. It is a customer then, wanting a call-out. Some clumsy thoughtless person who has left their headlights on overnight and now wants us to come out and put a new battery in.

Drake charges double for that. He calls it the 'dickhead tax' and there are complex rules surrounding it: a ledger of numbers pencilled in a notebook with an elastic band around it. He licks his thumb, flicks through it, decides on a price. I think he plucks the numbers out of thin air. People who have large breasts and clothes that help you get a look at them get a discount.

We have just been out to drain a diesel vehicle that an idiot brimmed with petrol – fumes to full – and Drake charged him three hundred pounds plus call-out plus thirty pounds for a can of diesel plus he kept the petrol. Drake said the man should have known better, and as it was the park warden's Suzuki Carry, the council would be paying the invoice anyway so why not pad it out a bit? We pay tax, don't we?

'No, not this afternoon either, sweetheart.'

Sweetheart! Could it be that Drake's actually got a girlfriend? Or is this one of our large-breasted customers he is patronising? Patronise. See, they are supposed to patronise us, but almost always it is the other way round.

Dad is still waiting over there, as if for a bus. What has he been up to?

'If you're going to get worked up, we'll do it tonight. After hours. Six? Come to the shop. I can't promise anything else.' Drake laughs softly into the phone. Chucks me the keys and motions for me to open up the van. I bet I will have to drive back, too.

I know that laugh. That laugh is why I spray the counter tops with Dettol Anti-bacterial Spray every morning before I start work. It is not the grease, which has its own clean, consistent smell I hardly notice any more. It is the thought of how many sets of bare buttocks Drake has hoisted onto the counter tops. The workshop is nearer to town than his mother's house, so he often brings his girls here. The horror of my imaginings torments me. The invisible drops of saliva and ejaculate. The unnoticed smear of vaginal discharge drying to white flakes. Dettol.

I get into the van, start the engine. Pop the clutch in and let it roll forwards a few inches while Drake is getting in. It does not matter any more because after today I am taking Angela and I am getting away. I promised myself for the sake of Jeannie I would wait until Gary came back home but he is late and we have been waiting for days and days. There is no guarantee that the airspace will not close again and leave him stranded somewhere. Because of this I have decided that a person cannot be expected to live his life around the edges of an ash cloud. So today is my last day and I am finishing the most important jobs, then I am going to break a window and get Angela from her house. Then we are going.

Drake is still on the phone, listening to whoever is on the other end, nodding and starting words, only to be interrupted by whichever one of his girls he is talking to. He leaps up into the passenger seat, shows me his middle finger for no reason and then motions for me to start driving. We are not towing, so I let the clutch up gently and join the mid-morning traffic, which is light to moderate for this time of the day.

'I can't come, I've already told you. What else can I say? I work for a living, sweetheart.'

He turns away, leans his head against the window, as if I can do anything other but overhear this conversation.

'Well, if you can't come tonight, it'll have to wait until tomorrow. Up to you,' Drake says.

He is easy and unworried, which means she will come – whoever it is. Some silly girl who is dumb or desperate enough to let Drake have his own way and put his hands on her. I can see it. All heels and short skirts and broad accent. She will bring eight cans of Stella and two bags of chips and the place will stink in the morning. At least, as part of my mission to get all my work finished today, I shifted out the Volvo this morning or they would almost certainly be at it in the back of that. He rubs his hands when we get an estate in.

'Whatever you like,' Drake says, then hangs up. I turn back to him, but he avoids my eye and I pretend I have heard nothing. It is always the same.

'Right,' he says, 'back to the coalface, eh?'

'Right you are,' I say. 'All sorted?'

Drake taps his finger to the side of his nose. When I look at his face I hear crashing inside my head and I am sickened. 'Ask me no questions and I'll tell you no lies,' he says, which is one of his special sayings, and which I have come to learn means that he wants me to ask him lots of questions.

'Who is it this time?'

'Your mother,' he answers, automatically, then shakes his head and starts giggling. 'Any hole's a goal.'

'Ha. Ha. Ha.'

We cross the roundabout and Drake plays with his phone a bit, sending a text, I presume, before putting it back inside his overalls.

'Just clean up after yourself. You leave the workshop a state every single time. I've got to work in there.'

Drake winks. 'You're just jealous.'

'Of you and your seventeen-year-olds?'

'Hey, if there's grass on the pitch, the game is on,' he says, and, 'I don't make the rules,' and these are two more of his favourite sayings so as we take the corner I floor the pedal. The mess of polystyrene cups and trays, newspapers, empty cigarette packets and half-empty Coke cans slides along the dashboard and off, onto Drake, the cans decanting their sticky contents onto his lap. I am always asking him to clean up this van but some people do not learn until they suffer the natural consequences of their own actions.

'Fuck it, Julian. Steady, will you?'

I am never going to have to deal with him again after this afternoon is over. I can prevent myself from smiling only when I catch sight of myself in the rear-view mirror and realise how crooked my teeth are and how little a grin suits me. The missing tooth makes a little black hole in the side of my mouth. When I put my tongue in the hole I look wolfish, hungry and mad.

'Home sweet home,' Drake says, as we pull into the forecourt outside the workshop. He leaves me to park the van around the back while he opens up. I hurry without making a mistake. There is a Citroën that has been bothering me. Its owner brought it in last night and said it had had its head gasket and crankshaft pulley replaced at the dealership towards the end of last month and since then it had been losing coolant at a rate of knots. I did not need Drake to point out the facts but he did. A new customer, older man, probably has a second car for his wife, maybe two or three kids with their own cars. We trade on our reputation, our good name spread by word of mouth. The little things all add up. So Drake wants me to do a good job.

I tried the obvious things first, last night. Replaced the expansion tank, gave it a new radiator cap and thermostat. Took it out around the block, helping myself to a single Midget Gem from a bag inside the glove compartment, but no dice. Back to the shop, up on the ramp and me underneath, checking every inch of pipework. It is a long, slow job and today I need to finish it. It is not a good job to go out on. Thankless. Routine work. It annoys me to have to play detective for someone else's mistake.

It used to be that as soon as I had the bonnet up on a car, bits and pieces of the manual, which I had learned more or less off by heart, would appear, not in my mind, but in my mouth, and I would mutter them while my hands worked. I have noticed under-confident drivers doing it too. They chant the borrowed words of their long-departed driving instructor as they change down to take a corner: *mirror, signal, manoeuvre*. When I was much younger I nicked a copy of Hillier's from the library and read it into tatters. Then at thirteen, with my head inside the guts of a mangled car at the banger races, trying to impress, I found its phrases on my tongue. And after a while, I stopped doing it. My hands remembered what to do on their own. I can move them over the spark plugs, here, or like this down towards the fuel line – or even under the ramp on a fairly complicated welding job, and I am silent because someone else's words have rinsed right into my body and become part of me.

That is why I'm very careful about what I read these days. What I allow myself to learn off by heart. It becomes a part of your self, whether you want it to be or not. The words get in and contaminate you. I count when I am walking or talk to myself like this, nice and calm, because if I do not, my guts spew Primary songs up at me, 'Give, Said the Little Stream!' You cannot flush that kind of thing out of your head.

I inch forward, moving the light along with me. For its age, this is a car in not bad condition. Less rust than you would expect to see, and though the exhaust has been patched a few times, the bracket is sound. It is a shame, really, that some other mechanic has done a substandard job on it and ruined it for him. There are no leaks, not in any of the pipework. I am at a bit of a loss now.

'I'm going out for a fag,' Drake says, shouting above the din of the radio. 'Do you want one?'

I ignore him, pretend I can't hear. He always offers, I always refuse. I have been here nearly ten years now. Could he not remember, just once? I have never smoked, but Mum found a half-empty packet of B&H in my school bag once and then I did, had to, to make a point. I could have told her they belonged to someone else and that would have been the truth. I could have said that my laboratory partner Steven Ward had shoved the packet into my hand when Mrs Greene snuck up on us during morning break. I had stashed it then forgotten it. But even though it was the truth Mum would never have believed that. She got Dad onto me, and stood over him while he stood over me and made me smoke the lot of them.

I laid back in the garden, letting them watch me enjoying every single one of the seven fags that were left in the packet. I thought bad words at them, making the swears big and black inside my head and using my eyes to spit them over the garden. Because I knew how to smoke she would not believe that I had never done it before. But I am good at learning things. I am better at learning things than anyone else in my family and I am better at keeping that facility to myself than anyone else I have ever met. I had seen other people smoke and it did not take me more than a few sucks at the little tube before I had worked out how to take it into my lungs without coughing. I lit the new one from the last bit of the old one because I knew it would make her angrier with me.

'Don't you know how bad it is for you?' she whined from the window. I bet she was wrestling with herself as she watched me, getting tangled up inside. I think she was doing sums in her head about how bad I was. Smoking in the garden equals me driving the Spirit away from the house but smoking in the street equals retaining the Spirit plus shaming her in front of our next-door neighbour and potential investigator, Viv Potter.

'Benzene,' I said, forcing myself to smile past the burned leaves and cancer taste in my mouth. 'Acetone. Formaldehyde.'

'What's he talking about, Gary? What's wrong with him?'

I inhaled deeply and blew out a thin stream of the noxious stuff into the air.

'Tar, arsenic, hydrogen cyanide.'

I pretended to smile at her but when I thought about this so-called power I had – just one cigarette enough to drive away one third of the Godhead – I did a real smile.

We'd had the lesson in PSE. The details had stuck because I am like a sponge for remembering things, though I never liked exams and would not do them. I wondered about trying for a smoke ring, but did not have a clue where to start. I should have told her: petrolheads do not smoke. Ever. The clue is in the name.

'Martin. Make him stop. Get him to come inside.'

'I can't do anything with him, love. Just leave him.'

That is the thing that I discovered that day. Not about smoking or about my mum or dad but about myself and what is inside my head. They can control what you do. Make you stand up straight, put a tie round your neck, stop your pocket money because you will not stash half of it in the mission fund jar. They can get you when you are quite a small boy and put lots of information and ideas into your head before you know what they are up to. Before you can stop it. But once you have worked out what they are up to, you can gain total control of what gets in. (Not everyone can do this. I worry, for example, that Angela, because of her particular problems, will never be able to do this. Will be a blank canvas for them.)

I carried on smoking. My head felt like it had been barbecued but I waited till they went in, shaking their heads and threatening to get the Young Men's President to come and speak to me, then walked, very slowly, around the side of the house, lifted the lid of the wheelie bin and vomited three times.

I wonder if telling Drake this story will get him to stop offering me fags or encourage him to do it more. There is no way of telling.

I count up a few hundred in sevens, backwards in nines, then up again while I check the joint between the head and the block.

Not a bit of damp, even though the owner reported an engine weep a few weeks ago. As I suspected. I cannot see a thing, though, even with the lamp on. There is not enough proper light in this room. Well, it would not be right to say we are working in the dark because that would be impossible; some of our tasks are intricate and require the precision use of tools that could cost you a finger if wielded inexpertly. But the strip lights hanging from their thin metal scaffold in the roof do not shed real light on us as we work.

My fingers move in and around the secret part of the engine, touching gently, my head turned sideways so I can get in near. The special smells go into my nostrils but that is all right. You do not get contaminated by things just by smelling them. The light tubes flicker. I cannot allow myself to think about what I will do if I cannot get this job complete to my satisfaction by going-home time. The lights flicker again. I have suggested Drake replace the tubes and he laughed in my face. They flicker and buzz at a frequency too high for my conscious mind to be fully aware of. But my muscles are aware of it. After a few hours of this, my irises will throb and flutter as if in sympathy and my skin will crackle with static. They flicker. They flicker and I can hear them.

Sometimes the auras that occur around objects plugged into the mains become apparent to me. I can misplace words, become clumsy, drop things, lose things, lose my temper, after too long under artificial light and without fresh air.

Drake strides in, stinking of fags, and heads towards the back of the shop. 'Turn that fucking radio off, will you? I need to hear how she's turning over.'

I move away from the car, needed a stretch anyway, and turn the knob and get rid of Chris Moyles. Although now Drake thinks I am obedient to him and I do not like that at all. In order to right the balance I nudge the milk bottle off the side of the counter with my thumb. He is tucking himself behind the wheel but he hears the bottle smash and swears again.

'You're a dick, Julian, you know that?'

'You do tell me often enough.'

'Sort it out, will you, before you slip on it and go arse up!'

He gets out of the car and empties his pockets, throwing spare spark plugs and a pair of vice grips onto the counter where they skid and clatter. Drake is the sort of person who does not pass his tools up out of the pit; he throws them out. I swear I have seen his wrenches spark against the concrete. I do not like the noise he makes and I do not like the way he talks. And he knows. I think he throws his wrenches around and he shouts at me and he swears in order to spite me, because he is a bastard.

I go and stand near the open door of the garage. Wipe my hands and take in a few good gulps of clean air. Because of the day it is, I keep thinking about Gary. I have got bigger fish to fry, but I keep thinking of his case going into the back of Bishop Jackson's car early one morning; Mum and Dad crying on the step. Jeannie in her dressing gown, waving and cheering from the upstairs window. The way they talked about it, like he was going off to war. The way the ward has been praying for his safety and success. When you think about it properly it makes no sense at all. He is not dismantling bombs. He is not handing out vaccines and bottled water in the Congo. He is not even fixing cars. He is just door knocking and eyeing up spinster sister missionaries in Temple Square with a prayer in his heart.

It is hard not to think of him as lucky, though. He got away, didn't he? When I go, they will not mention my name again. Mum and Dad will take my photograph down from the wall and throw my clothes away and after a while it will be like they only have two children. It will be better for them that way because I am the one that is not right and Gary and Jeannie are the proper children. The ones who worked out according to the plan. When I go they will not mention me again. And Gary got to go, but he had to come back too.

He did get to the other side of the world. On balance I think he is lucky even if the cloud has cleared, his luck has run out and he has to come home now. Five and a half thousand miles. Sometimes they only send missionaries to the next stake – Leeds, or perhaps as far as Scotland. It is meant to be inspired; the Profit himself decides who goes where. But it always happens that the poorer families, the families that are relying on the Church to pay for the mission, have sons who are kept in the country. Some coincidence. Gary saved for years, so he got sent on an abroad mission and actually got away from the house, from this place, for a whole two years. Mum is sucking him back, though. Of course she is.

I should not think about these things and get myself aggravated. There is no point to them now. If I end up not being able to locate the problem and fix the Citroën, it is okay. It will be okay. Drake will get someone else. Angela and I will be away, somewhere else, somewhere where no one will ever think to look for us and I will not be anyone's son or brother any more.

It was my mother's fault I ended up with Angela at the party anyway. You could not have dragged me there, if I had had any choice at all. Mum found a shirt – one of Gary's – and the fair-to-decent quality pair of trousers I keep for funerals and job interviews. She woke me up and threw them through the bedroom door at me. Gary's party was the first time I had been in the Stake Centre for four years. Mum tutted at me because the shirt was not ironed properly and she made me wear a jumper of Dad's over it. I spent as much time as possible in the foyer, looking out of the windows and watching people come in and out of the big glass doors at the front of the building. The ones who recognised me nodded hello. Newer members, or old ones who had forgotten my face or who did not recognise me with a ponytail, passed by me without speaking. No one came up to talk.

From where I was, I could hear the commotion in the cultural hall and could feel the fizzing of the fluorescent lights against my teeth and in the tiny bones inside my ears. Hammer, anvil, stirrup. Brother Lawson came out of the bishop's office, striding towards me. It was not a Sunday but he was in a navy suit all the same. He was a counsellor now, on the bishopric, and I assumed they had all been in there on some church business. I let myself picture them counting tithing. Writing cheques to the Corporation of the President. All those golden Moronis do not cost nothing, you know. I remember smirking and felt the smile fall off my face when he stopped in front of me and shot out his hand. I did not like looking up at him from a seated position so I stood up and shook it.

'Brother Leeke,' he said, 'I'm so glad to see you here. We all are. It's really great to have you back in the ward.'

'I am only here for the party.'

I said that just so he would not get any ideas but I could see already it was far too late for that.

Brother Lawson did something interesting then. I have only been able to explain it to myself in retrospect but at the time it felt like the most natural thing in the world to find myself walking back along the corridor with him, towards the bishop's office, and to go inside where there was a chair in front of the desk waiting for me. He kept hold of my hand, shaking it gently, and put his other arm around my shoulders, all the while chatting to me about the food at the party, and asking after my dad, and wondering how my work on the cars was going, asking me if I still went to the banger racing on Saturdays like I used to, back when I was active, and gently, so that I hardly felt it at all, pushing me along the carpet towards the open door.

We sat down. Bishop Jackson was behind his desk. I looked for the piles of cheques and money I was certain the pair of them had been pawing over, but there was nothing. The office was bare, with a blackboard on one wall with some names and phone numbers written on it, and the painting of Jesus in the red cape on the wall behind him. First Presidency present and correct in framed, postcard-sized portraits on the sill of the small, frosted window. I started to feel self-conscious about my ponytail.

'Brother Leeke,' Bishop Jackson said, 'we're so pleased to have you in the ward today. It means such a lot to your mother – and to Gary too, of course, to have his family support him like this. His whole family.' He shook my hand over the table.

Brother Lawson was sitting to my left, rubbing his ankle and breathing noisily, as if the walk had tired him out.

'You won't know this, but your presence here, and the fact that Gary decided to invite a few of his non-member friends and acquaintances, really helped change our minds on having the party here after all. It was your mother who suggested it. A nice big send-off.'

'Suggested? I expect it was a little stronger than that.'

Bishop Jackson nodded, and smiled, and nodded. 'A mother's love for her sons is a fearsome thing,' he said, 'Heavenly Father designed it that way. It's policy not to have farewell parties any more. The brethren felt it detracted from the real work of the ward when farewells and homecomings became too much the focus of ward activities.'

Why is he telling me all this? I thought. As if I care what a set of avaricious and senile old men in Happy Valley think about anything.

'But that was always just a policy. A recommendation, not doctrine. A suggestion to solve a problem in the Salt Lake Wards where there are a lot more missionaries coming and going.'

'Okay.'

Whatever, as Jeannie's friends would say. I wanted to put my fingers up and make a W for them like I had seen them do. Not because I found it funny but because it was a joke and I wanted to see if it would make them laugh.

'In Gary's case, we decided to make a special exception. For your mother, yes – and for Gary and the example he's setting to his non-member friends who we hope, after today, will become investigators themselves. How joyful would he be to have them, baptised and active in the Church, welcoming him home in two years' time?'

'Very,' I said. '*Extremely* joyful. Should such a thing happen Gary would almost certainly achieve top levels of joy.'

He looked at me oddly but did not smile. 'The other reason we decided to relax policy – not doctrine – on this one occasion, was to give you the opportunity to come back to us, Brother Leeke. To provide an opportunity for you to get back to the chapel, see the beauty of the temple near by, and have a chance to reflect on your own eternal progression.'

'Right,' I said.

Here it comes.

'You're probably still wondering why we've invited you in here,' he said, and waved the palms of his hands at me. 'No worries if you want to go. You're not in trouble. We're not calling you in here to tell you off or anything!'

The pair of them laughed, easy, genuine laughs. As if the very idea that they would want to make me feel uncomfortable in any way, shape or form was so unbelievably hilarious, it was hardly worth mentioning.

'Okay,' I said, and stood up.

'Julian, can I call you Julian? Do you prefer it? Sit back down, will you? Just a minute.'

I did.

'Brother Lawson and I meet here every Saturday afternoon. There are some ward jobs we need to attend to, and we take our responsibilities in this area very seriously. Before we start, we kneel in prayer together and ask Heavenly Father to show us his will for the members of this ward. Their families. The individuals who used to be loved and cherished members of our family, but who have since fallen away or drifted into sin, and are no longer with us. That's what we did today. After we'd finished praying, we waited a while for the Spirit to prompt us on what portion of the Lord's work we should set our minds to next. We waited in the silence, with hearts eager to know the will of the Lord, and both of us were prompted to ask you to come in here and speak to us, to get to know you a little better.'

'Right,' I said.

'Julian, we notice you haven't attended church with your family for some years now. And before that, your activity was sporadic.'

'That's right.'

'Could you talk to us a bit more about that? Why did you decide to stop coming?'

I looked at my hands and felt my throat tighten as surely as if they had reached over and started pulling at the tie I was wearing.

'We often find that a period of activity followed by a falling away is caused by the member taking offence over some small matter. A difference of opinion about a matter unrelated to doctrine. One lady resigned her membership after she was asked not to use the ward kitchen to heat up breast milk for her baby! Revoked her temple marriage, her endowment. Put herself out into the darkness. She asked to be rebaptised a year later, and is still horrified about the danger she put herself and her family into over something so trivial. "What if I'd died, during that year?" she says, when she bears her testimony. Doesn't bear thinking about, does it? Breast milk!'

They laughed again. I wondered how many times they had told that story. If it was even true, or just something that happened to a friend of a friend of a friend, in some other ward, somewhere else. True in spirit, if not in fact.

'Julian,' he leaned over the desk, 'did someone offend you? Have you been hurt? If so, can I, as the bishop of the ward, sincerely apologise for that, and ask you, with love in my heart, to forgive, and accept that while the members aren't perfect, the gospel is. Could you do that? Would you like to pray with us and ask Heavenly Father to put the peace of forgiveness in your heart?'

There was a pause. I counted up to twelve.

'We really miss you, Julian,' Brother Lawson said. I could still feel the sweat of his hand clinging to my palm. Offend? What does offend even mean anyway? A tiny, euphemistic word for something and nothing.

But whoso shall offend one of these little ones which believe in me, it were better for him that a millstone were hanged about his neck, and he were drowned in the depth of the sea.

Offend. Offensive. A bad smell. Something to be tolerated for the sake of politeness, for everyone getting along nicely together.

'No, no one offended me.'

Bishop Jackson leaned back in his chair. It was, probably still is, a plush, padded leather one and the air hissed out of it like a fart. No one smiled.

'The other reason we find people fall away from the Church,' he said slowly, 'is sin. I can only speak to you frankly about this, out of love for you. The Lord is prompting me to open my heart to you, warning that if I don't speak plainly about the shaky foundations your eternal salvation is resting on, on the Last Day your sins will weigh on my shoulders as well as yours.'

'That hardly seems fair,' I said.

He thought I meant it. He smiled and shook his head gently. 'The mantle of a bishop is a heavy one, one with eternal consequences,' he said, 'but know this. If I could take this weight off you and bear it myself, I would. I can't do that, Julian, and the wonderful thing is, I don't need to. Christ has already done your suffering for you. Have you considered the atonement?'

'Not recently.'

'Christ made forgiveness possible. For everyone. There's a process, though. Steps we have to go through in order to become truly clean. Would you like to restore yourself to active membership? To access the full blessings available to you as a son of God? To follow Gary's example and serve an honourable mission? To marry in the temple?'

He paraded the options like they were prizes on a conveyor belt and this was *The Generation Game*. And he did not wait for me to answer. The answer was so obvious that the question could only be rhetorical.

'Do you want to be happy again?' he said. Brother Lawson had not said anything so far. His role, as far as I could tell, was to block my way to the door and nod furiously. 'It is still possible.'

'I am all right,' I said. But my conviction was failing.

It was Mum. She'd ruined me. My hands started to tremble and I sat on them, suddenly twelve years old again and convinced these people could tell when I was lying. Even if I do not know I am lying myself, they will – it is a power God gives to bishops, Young Men's Presidents and Home Teachers. And even if that does not work, after you die the events of your life will be played out on a film screen to the entirety of creation. Billions upon billions of souls witnessing every secret sticky wank, every time you put your finger to your arse and sniffed it, every peep at the undressed people in the Littlewoods catalogue, every tiny, furtive, shameful human thing.

'I want to go.' I sounded like a little boy and I was thinking of Mum then, the bulk of her loaded into her chair, her skin starting to crinkle around the eyes. She said to me once, when I was younger, that I was the special one because I was the child that had turned her from a woman into a mother, which she had always wanted to be. But she does not say anything like that any more.

'I need to go now,' I said again, and they ignored me, smiling peacefully like corpses, and I did not get up.

'You can speak in confidence here, Brother. In this room, I'm a Judge in Israel and I represent your Heavenly Father. He loves you infinitely and unconditionally. There is no judgement here. Now, the process of repentance is long, and it starts with just one step. Let's talk about your sin. Can I ask you, are you having problems with the Word of Wisdom?'

I nodded.

'Smoking?'

I shook my head. 'I drink, sometimes. Never around Jeannie.'

'There are no degrees of sin, Julian. One cup of tea a week will keep you out of the Celestial Kingdom. It's not about tea, it's about obedience. You're not a tithe payer.'

'No.'

'No fast offerings? Donations to the missionary fund?'

'You know that already.'

'It's not important what I know. It's important what you know. These are your responsibilities. We need to map out clearly how far you've strayed from the path of truth. What about scripture study? Prayer?'

'No.'

Bishop Jackson smiled, and put his head on one side. 'Julian, how can Heavenly Father reach you and comfort you, guide your path and heal your hurts, if you lock and bolt the door against him? How can your testimony grow if you keep it in the dark and starve it?'

'I don't know.'

'He can't. It won't. But we'll help you open that door again, don't worry about that. We're here for you.' He coughed. 'And Julian, I must ask you, are you involved in any other kinds of sin? How do you stand on the Law of Chastity?'

I did not answer. I wanted to say 'No comment' like they do on the police programmes Mum likes watching but I did not even look at him. He probably asks Jeannie this once or twice a year too, alone in this office, and the thought of it sickened me. I wanted to smash his face in, but my hands were still trembling, wedged between my thighs and the chair.

Mum would have put him up to this. That was why, I realised, she was so keen on the tie, though it is only a party and hardly anyone else is in Sunday best.

'Do you know what Heavenly Father wants for you in this area?'

I nodded.

'Masturbation, sexual contact outside marriage, impure thoughts, pornography. These are all sins the Lord wants you to avoid. Do you know this?'

'I don't have a girlfriend.'

Bishop Jackson laughed. I mean really laughed. He leaned back in his chair and slapped his thighs with the palms of his hands. A fraction later, Brother Lawson joined in. Obedience, you see. It is the first law of heaven, which means it is very important.

'You probably *should* have a girlfriend,' he said, grinning widely. 'I know at your age I was back from my mission and searching for my eternal companion. I dated two or three different girls a week for four months, from all around the stake. Best time of my life! Gary – Elder Leeke – will be starting that search himself, two years from now. There's a time and a season for everything. If you're finding certain aspects of the Law of Chastity . . . a challenge – do you have a computer of your own, Julian? In your bedroom? – it's only Heavenly Father's way of prompting you towards marriage. Is it something you've considered?'

I shook my head. Was about to tell him about the computer downstairs and my own personal laptop that I bought with my own money before I realised that was not what he wanted to know about. Marriage. To live with a woman. Have her stinking out the bathroom, and sweating next to you in bed when you were trying to read. Have her pulling at your arms to look in shop windows, and squeaking, and laughing, and making demands about carpets and curtains and three-piece leather suites. Consider marriage?

'Well, think about it. There are plenty of sweet young girls here, with tender hearts, who are waiting for a man to take them to the temple. Right now, you're not ready for that – but in a year, you could be. Wouldn't that be amazing? Can you imagine the joy in heaven, in your mother's heart, when you clasp a clean young woman's hands over the altar and make your covenant to her?'

'Maybe.'

'You don't sound sure, Julian. Is there something else on your mind? Some other sin you are struggling with? Do you doubt your worthiness to receive these blessings?'

I looked at him.

Read my mind then, I thought, *use your magical powers and tell me what is wrong with me.*

'Is it a delicate matter, Julian? Don't be embarrassed, son. I've boys of my own. I've been a boy. I know how it can be.'

'I'm twenty-four years old,' I said.

'It's a difficult time. A difficult time to be lost, without the gospel to cling to,' Brother Lawson chips in. 'The gospel can be your Iron Rod, through the darkness,' he says, and I want to laugh.

'Is it a problem with Same-Sex Attraction? We can help you overcome a problem in this area if that's a concern for you.'

Bishop Jackson nearly whispers it. *Same-Sex Attraction.* One of the many sins that stand next to murder, right along with pulling on your Iron Rod, tea-drinking and speaking ill of the brethren. I stood up.

'And if not, perhaps a week of careful prayer and scripture study, along with working towards becoming a full tithe payer, will remove any blocks between you and your Heavenly Father.'

That's right, I thought. *Pay and obey.*

Now I knew for a fact that Mum had put him up to this. *Same-Sex Attraction.* She could not understand that I would rather be under a car, or wandering the streets, than be at home with her. She had been making digs about Drake for weeks. *'Bring him to tea, if you can't be parted,'* she would say, looking at me carefully to see what I would do. Bag of chips and four cans of beer in the park is what I would do, rather than be subject to her staring, and another one of her store-cupboard casseroles.

'Julian, don't take offence at this, please.'

I edged past Lawson, who did not pull in his chair to make it easier for me, and Bishop Jackson talked faster, his voice following me out as I tried to leave: 'Once you become worthy to feel the Spirit again, the Lord will witness to you that what I am saying is true, and for your own good. Julian?'

Neither of them followed me out of the office, and I let the door swing closed. My shirt felt wet against my back, under my armpits. I bet I stank.

The foyer was empty, everyone gathered in the cultural hall to take the cling film off the food, file past Gary and shake his hand. Like he was charmed and by touching him something good about him would rub off on them. *Same-Sex Attraction.* If you are not breeding, shitting out four or six or even nine kids, then there is something wrong with you. You are sick, or deformed, or gay.

Gay!

I walked quickly away from the office, towards the doors. I could take Dad's car. I would not need a key to get it started, of course – strictly speaking that is not good for the engine, but it did feel like a bit of an emergency and so I was sure he would not mind. He might moan a bit about it, but it would be half-hearted. He would understand I needed to get out and he would have to chunner a bit and pretend not to, for Mum's sake.

But as I looked out through the glass doors at the front of the Stake Centre, my arms and legs shaking so much it was like the worst hangover I've ever had, I saw the car park was overflowing and that people's cars were wedged in at all sorts of weird angles. Blocked in.

I sat down on one of the benches and started my counting before I smashed the windows. I was into the eight hundreds and pouring with sweat when little Angela appeared. And after that, things were suddenly much, much better.

'Julian? Get back in here and pick up that glass before someone cuts an artery. And take your thumb out of your jacksie and fill out the tyre order. What's your problem? Are you on your period or something?'

'Sorry,' I say, once a span of time long enough to irritate him further has passed. I go back in and use my left foot to kick an oil rag over the spill.

'If you're that sorry, you can make us a pair of brews.'

His voice is hollow and not as deep as he would like it to be. I often think Drake would be more of a gentleman if he did not have ginger hair and a voice that, at times, verges on the shrill. He was probably bullied worse than I was, and I was the goody-goody boy who was not allowed to go out on his bike on Sundays.

'I would, but that was the last of the milk,' I say. 'And it is your turn to go to the shop.'

I will admit it is petty but I cannot make myself pretend I am not enjoying this. Why wouldn't I? Get him all worked up and then disappear. I am imagining his face in the morning, turning up an hour late, like he usually does, expecting to find me here working on the cars he could not be bothered to finish and get shifted out last night. He will have to ring the apprentice and see if he is available to do a bit of overtime. Put an advert in somewhere. He will be absolutely fucked. I think of the Citroën and feel a little thrum of guilt but I can only do what I can do.

'You fucking cock-sucker,' Drake squeaks, 'you absolute *tit*.'

The light and the noise and the filthy smell floating from Drake's body combine. I am overcome with an urge to get out of this place, to get out into the air and into some real light. There is no real point, I decide, in suffering through the rest of the day. Not when I do not have to.

'I will go. I will go out to the shop now and get some. Keep your knickers on,' I say, and pick up the glass, resting the little pieces inside the largest piece – the jagged neck of the bottle. I put the whole lot on the counter near the telephone and pray silently (*inthenameofourlordandsaviourjesuschristamen*) that he will slice open his hand the next time he calls his brother. My vision flickers and the noise of Drake clattering his tools around takes on a bitter, citrus taste like underripe limes. I need to get out. I need to get clean. I need to be around people who do not know words like 'twat' and 'Same-Sex Attraction'.

'I might as well take my dinner now as well,' I say, lifting my jacket from its hook near the tool cabinet. The door is half open, and inside – my tools. Priceless. I have been saving and collecting those since I was thirteen. Can I leave them behind?

'You're bloody not! Not if you plan on leaving early tonight, you're not.'

Drake has his head under the car, so I get my tool bag and start chucking things in. The mountain nose pliers set I saved up for. My socket wrenches. Drake's vice grips, which I have always admired. Dad was pleased about me taking the apprenticeship. 'You've got your tools with you,' he'd say, 'you're never going to go hungry.' I zip up the bag. Perhaps I can learn to fix up some farm machinery. It is true that I have never worked on a tractor before, but I learn new things fast.

'All right,' I say, and leave my sandwich tin under the workbench so he will not pester me.

'Get some milk and come right back,' he says, his voice rattling out from under the Peugeot. I glance at the ramp hopefully, picturing an abrupt collapse, a heaving groan of twisted metal, dropping car and screaming boss, but Drake checks the mechanism before he drives a car onto it every single time. Because it concerns his own skin – his own nasty sack of flesh and semen, it is the only thing in his work he is fastidious about.

'I mean it,' he warns, 'we're snowed under. You're going to have to finish fettling the—'

I do not bother to answer. The Citroën will have to sit there until someone else figures out what is wrong with it, or Daddy-Four-Cars can take it somewhere else. It will not be me who solves the mysterious case of the vanishing coolant, and it certainly will not be Drake. He might be gifted with women, but as a mechanic he is merely adequate.

I whistle and rattle the change in the pockets of my overall as I leave the workshop and head towards home to get the rest of my stuff.

PAULINE

Ruth Williams has her hand cupped under Angela's chin and is encouraging her to spit out whatever she's choking on, like a good little girl, and I've got one beady eye on the carpet. 'Come on, spit it out for Mummy, don't be silly.' Ruth's not paying enough attention to her daughter – she's too busy wrapped up in what Maggie's saying. Someone needs to give her a tissue but you don't want to make her feel uncomfortable, not with Angela the way she is, it's not her fault. But all the same. 'Her mother asked to be released from Relief Society, she was so humiliated. How, she said, could she stand up there next to the President with her own daughter in the front row – round as a barrel and everyone looking the other way and just pretending they thought she'd put on a bit of weight?' Maggie says. She's pairing up socks, laying the odd ones over the arm of the couch to wait while she finds their husbands. 'I never heard that,' Ruth says, still sweeping her finger around little Angela's mouth. The girl's chin is slimy with slaver but she's not giving it up. It was a stupid idea to give her a biscuit in the first place. I should have known.

'Oh yes,' Maggie goes on, getting nice and comfy up there on her rameumptom, 'she *definitely* getting released, and she's only been in her calling nine months.' 'Perhaps she just wanted to free some time up to support her, and help look after the baby when it comes?' Maggie shakes her head at Ruth, but doesn't bother answering. 'Do you know what his name was? The father?' she asks, tucking her chin into her chest while she smiles. Ruth looks up for a moment, her face flushed. She's already heard the rumours, but Maggie doesn't wait. 'Ahmed! I ask you. *Ahmed!*' 'Oh, well . . .' 'Rachael was devastated when she found out. It meant there'd be no wedding – not even a small one in the chapel. They're still trying to find some members in another Stake for an adoption. It's hard to get the right sort, though. You don't want the poor little thing to stick out. He's going to have a hard enough time as it is.' 'She's having a boy?' Ruth asks. 'How lovely.' Maggie nods. 'Fit and healthy, as far as they can tell. She's twenty weeks already. How they didn't tell from looking at her, I don't know.' The socks are all done now, and Maggie puts them into the basket. 'Here you are, Pauline. Shall I take these up now or leave them with the rest?' 'Leave them, Maggie, no point traipsing back and forth if you don't need to.' 'Poor thing, having it on her mind all that time and not being able to tell anyone. She must have been going mad,' Ruth says. She rubs Angela on the back. 'It's a hard time for anyone, never mind someone going through it on her own. She must have been so scared to feel like she had to hide it.' 'She was always small, though, wasn't she? Skinny, like? Maybe she carried it high. It's easier to hide that way,' I say. 'Maybe that's what it was like for you, but *I* was showing at nine weeks with all of mine,' Maggie chips in, sighs all nostalgic like, then plays her blinder, 'but mine were all nice big boys. Not one under nine pounds.' 'Is that right?' I say. Ruth glances at me and smiles. 'Anyway,' Maggie says, swishing sheets through the air, 'I think Carole kept it to herself because she was holding out and hoping for a miscarriage. The daft little sod. Her mother's side of the family is prone to them, apparently. Rachael had an ectopic in '97, do you remember?' We shouldn't be talking about things like this in front of Ruth. I think she lost a couple, before Angela. And then Angela came out – all knotted up in her own cord, bluest, limpest thing any of the doctors had ever seen. She's lucky to be here. She coughs and a long thread of spit dangles from her mouth, swings and then falls. Not the carpet! It's too late. I don't even think Ruth has noticed. She's got enough on her plate, though. Angela might be a Choice Spirit, but she's hard work, even I can see that. 'It's definitely fit and well, though. A boy. She's had the scan. *And* there's not going to be a wedding. *And* time running out to find a family for an adoption. *And* do you even know what Ahmed is short for? I'm not even going to say it. You'd have a fit! I don't think Rachael herself knows. Someone should say something, but I'm not going to.' 'Would Rachael not consider bringing the baby up herself? I'm sure Carole would be all right if she . . .' Ruth says. Maggie shakes her head. 'She won't think of it. He wouldn't blend in, would he? They'd be explaining him away for the rest of their lives. Wouldn't be fair on them. Or him.' 'Well . . .' Ruth's a funny one. I'm not entirely sure how to take her, sometimes. When Angela was first born the Elders went around to give her a Blessing and Ruth turned them away at the door. Her Andy had called them from the hospital as soon as it were clear Angela was going to live so him inviting them and giving permission should have been enough, but she overruled him – stood there in the doorway with her dressing gown on! Bold as brass! Brass! 'Get on home,' she said, still all pale from her operation. Limped to the door, she did. She told them to turn around and go home to their wives and mind their own children. There was no need for a Blessing for the Sick, she said, because her baby wasn't sick, but perfect as she was. A Spirit so pure she'd been sent from the pre-existence to get a body, with no need to know right from wrong because she didn't need to prove herself to anyone. Not sick, not damaged. Perfect. I know every mother thinks that. Course they do. Look at me, with my three. Even Julian, to a point. But Ruth, love, get a flannel to that carpet, will you? Perfect? One biscuit, and her dress looks like Armageddon! 'No, it's not racialist,' Maggie is saying. She's dropped the sheet and it's draped over her knee, inching towards the floor as she points at Ruth. 'They aren't racialists. I said to her mother, you're right. She is right. It's not his colour that's the problem. Ahmed! It's the culture. Not colour. Culture. Two entirely separate things. That baby isn't going to know where it belongs. They'll have a hard time finding a mixed-member family. Hard pressed indeed. I don't know if they even exist. In a Ward down south maybe, but not round here.' Maggie shakes her head and tugs the sheet into a bundle then drops it into the basket. Ruth folds a pair of pillowcases, still warm from the iron. That's no good. She might as well have ironed them into quarters; the creases will hold now. Still, her help is worth about what I paid for it, as Martin'll tell me if I mention it later. What gets me is that they're meant to be here helping me clean up and sort out for Gary coming, and all we can talk about is Rachael's less active daughter, Carole. That's old news. News it's been a near-on constant effort for me to keep from reaching Gary's ears. What he does not need, not now, nor at any point during his Mission, is bad news and distractions about problems at home. Carole was a possible for him at one point, perhaps, but there's no point thinking about all that now. And no point him hearing about it when he's so far away from the comfort of his mother's arms. End of. But it doesn't stop them talking about it non-stop in the Ward, mouths whispering nineteen to the dozen between classes and Sacrament Meeting, after Sacrament Meeting and out, into the car park, low-voiced chattering that even now, in my own home, is taking the focus away from where it should be. Which is on Gary, and the preparations for his homecoming. Maggie's starting up again, the bed valance looped over her arm, when Ruth, who is kneeling on the floor fiddling with Angela, leans back on her heels and screams. Angela chooses that minute to finally spit it up and a chewed bit of biscuit falls to the floor and drops halfway under the brand-new leather recliner. 'What? What is it?' Ruth is looking at the window. My heart leaps into my chest and I think, stupidly, that it's to do with Gary. His flight. There's been an earthquake or a terrorist and his plane has fallen out of the sky. 'Nothing.

It's just your Julian,' she says, putting her hand over her chest and shaking her head. She laughs at herself, a bit out of breath. 'Oh my goodness me, he gave me a bit of a shock, banging like that.' Julian is standing in the garden with his face pressed against the glass, grinning, and his hands against his temples like he's got a headache. I hope he's not starting a migraine. He said he'd be at work today. His forehead is flat against the window, his hair pushed back. He's making a sweaty mark. 'Hiya!' he mouths, his one eye-tooth gleaming. Maggie and Ruth wave at him, then Ruth reaches down for Angela, who, rid of her biscuit, is turning pages in the Primary songbook and tracing her finger over the illustrations. Ruth says she thinks she can even read a bit – how she can tell, I don't know, but I wouldn't put it past the little one. She's got wise eyes, that one. Not her fault she's the way she is. 'Ignore him,' I say, but we can't, because he's banging again and puffing out his cheeks, trying, I think, to catch little Angela's eye and make her laugh. I won't reach that biscuit for love nor money, and it would seem bad manners to ask Ruth to do it, so I resign myself to leaving it there. Gary won't notice a speck of biscuit on the floor when there's a brand-new chocolate-leather three-piece suite and hall carpet to look at, and that's banking on him noticing the suite, which there's no guarantee of – there'll be far too much else going on when he walks through that door! 'Give it over!' I shout, making sure he can hear me through the double glazing. 'Get inside, you're smearing the windows.' Julian disappears round the side of the house. At long last all the begging and pleading I've done has worked – he will finally come in the side door without being asked, and save the brand-new carpet in the front hall. 'Look at the state of that,' I say to Maggie, who is standing now and sorting out a basket of washing into piles – folding shirts and vests and tee-shirts. One for Jeannie, one for Martin and me (we share a wardrobe – she knows that) and one for Julian. His clothes are so marked with oil they look like they've never been washed at all. No point running the iron over them – he'd never notice. He's dirty, that lad. Maggie smiles. 'Boys, that's what they're like, Pauline,' she says airily. 'You know it yourself. He'll have forgot his pack-up. Shall I make him a sandwich?' Maggie's got five sons and every single one of them has served an Abroad Mission, has his health and a wife he's taken to the Temple. She's overrun with grandchildren – the wives are constantly pregnant. And she never fails to rub it in. 'Let him make his own sandwich,' I say, and I know I sound crabby but I can't help it. 'He's big enough and ugly enough to put two pieces of bread together.' Sometimes it's more than I can bear not to let Maggie in on the fact the whole Ward knows she made her husband go and live at his mother's for three weeks after finding filth on his computer last spring. Men are men and they've been designed to be visual creatures so we can procreate, I know that. But it wasn't normal. Tying-up filth, is what I heard. Julian comes through into the living room. Unusual for him. He takes himself away, more often than not, especially when I have the Sisters round. He doesn't like hearing us talk about the Gospel but this time he drapes himself over the end of the suite, leaning on the arm and turning the pages of Angela's book for her. 'Morning,' he says. 'Julian, have you seen your sister?' He shrugs. He needs to eat more. He's so picky. 'I'm expecting her. I can't cook what I'm planning to cook until she turns up with the shopping. Are you sure you didn't see her?' 'I didn't see her.' He puts three fingers up, a mock boy-scout salute. 'I promise. I do not know where she is.' Maggie moves the washing. 'Here, Julian. Sit properly. What is it you're after? Do you want something to eat? You've a fresh pair of overalls here. Do you need them now, or shall I put them up in your room?' 'Upstairs please, Sister Travers,' he says. He's smiling, but he's not looking at her, he's staring at Ruth. Ruth has always been funny around Julian – probably because he's in the habit of walking round with his shirts unbuttoned, and there's not a thing you or I or anyone else could say to him that would stop him. She smiles at him, and moves Angela closer to her, so she's almost sitting between her feet. 'She is all right where she is,' Julian says, 'don't mind. Suffer them to come to me, and all that.' The three of us exchange looks with each other. Julian laughs to himself. His glasses always take a while to adjust when he comes inside. He looks at us through smoky shaded lenses and it's a bit disconcerting that we can't see his eyes, can't tell who he's staring at. 'Should my ears be burning or something? What have you been chatting about?' Maggie and Ruth wait for me to answer. 'Don't be daft,' I say, briskly, and hand Maggie the ironing spray. I like to have everything smelling nice before it's put away. 'Julian, make sure you're around later to help your father move the table into the front room. I want it all nice in here, with candles, like we have at Christmas. You'll have to push the suite back and move the telly back a bit – he won't remember how we have it – so you've got to be here to sort it out. All right? Don't let your father scrape the corners of the table against the wall like he did last time. And keep Bovril off of the suite.' 'Okay,' he says, amicable enough, and still looking at Ruth. She's edged around and has her back to him now, getting between him and Angela. 'You must be very proud of your brother,' Maggie says to Julian, 'not every missionary makes it all the way to the end.' I never get sick of hearing it. It does mean a bit more, coming from her, but I'm not going to come out and say that. I look at Julian, just to make sure he's not offended. He's the older son, after all. But he's hardly interested. 'I know,' he says, as if he's had an idea. 'Spit it out, then,' I say, 'and then get back to work. You're getting in the way of the hoovering and Drake won't let you out early if you have a two-hour dinner, will he?' 'I reckon Ruth should come to our dinner tonight,' he says, pleased with himself. Ruth has her head down and is suddenly finding something interesting about my carpet. Not to the extent of lifting up that biscuit, but where there's life there's hope. Julian can't be soft on her, can he? She's heading fast towards forty and nothing much to look at – she never got herself together after Angela was born, which is why, despite her being five now, Ruth has never had another, I reckon. Someone should tell her. Even stuck in this chair and suffering with my own afflictions, I still make time for a hot flannel in my creases and a bit of lipstick every morning, so she's got no excuse. It's not right to have an only child. But babies or not, she's a married woman and I've brought Julian up to know better than that. Maggie is staring at the wall, her eyebrows almost off of her head. If invites are going out, she should be getting one too. She's the Mission-momma, after all. It's written all over her. 'I don't think I can,' Ruth says, and finally brings herself to look up at Julian. He's not looking at her, but at Angela, who is tracing her little finger round and round the pattern on the cuff of her sock, and oblivious to everything else. 'These things are usually just for family, and anyway, we have plans for tonight.' Julian doesn't just look disappointed, he looks angry and even a bit hurt. Soft on her? I can't see it, but stranger things have happened. Maggie relaxes slightly but no one says anything for far too long. 'No, Mum's going to be feeding the five thousand. We'll have more food than we can handle, honestly,' he says, and laughs. It's too loud. 'No, Julian,' Ruth says quietly, 'I don't think that would be appropriate, do you?' 'Suit yourself. I only asked,' he says, not bothering to hide that he's irritated. 'Just thought it would be nice for you and Andy to have a nice meal together. I could take Angela out in her buggy, push her round the block until she falls asleep. Give you all a bit of natter time.' What is wrong with him? 'Maybe some other night,' Ruth says, 'this one's for Gary, isn't it?' 'Get on then, leave us to it,' I say, and he heaves himself off the arm of the chair, and heads off upstairs. 'Take your washing, Julian!' Maggie says, but he lets the door shut hard behind him and pretends he doesn't hear her. Maggie coughs and folds. 'Has there been any improvement with him?' she asks, in a lowered voice. 'I don't know how I'd cope if one of my sons fell away from the Gospel.' 'His heart isn't open,' I say, 'I keep him in my prayers.' 'You should put him on the prayer roll at the Temple,' Ruth says, 'I put Angela on there every month.' 'Does he drink?' Maggie asks. 'Or smoke? That's one thing I couldn't stand. You can hate the sin and love the sinner, but there's no need to let the sin stink up your house and shame you in front of your friends and family.' 'He doesn't drink,' I say, 'nothing like that. He's just having problems with his testimony.' 'Did it start when he left school?' Ruth asks. 'It's very common among the Youth, you know.' Maggie nods. 'My Graham says he sometimes thinks it would be a good idea to limit the education they get at that age. Out in the world, you know. Too much information at too early an age confuses them. They turn to science and psychology instead of the word of the Lord, and they aren't mature enough in the Gospel to make the distinction between useful knowledge, and knowledge that could harm a testimony.' 'Julian never went to college,' I said. 'He did an apprenticeship, learning to fix cars.' 'At least there's that,' Maggie says, 'he's got a trade. He's employed. That's important.' 'Has he got interests?' Ruth says. 'Could he be depressed, do you think?' 'I couldn't tell you, that's the truth of it,' I say, 'if he's not at work, he's out roaming the streets all hours, or locked up in his bedroom watching his telly. I can hear it through the walls – Martin bought him a pair of headphones but he won't use them.' 'What's he watching up there?' Maggie asks, all suspicious. 'The other day I saw two men kissing – *each other* – and that was in the middle of the day. You just don't know what you're going to get these days. There should have been a warning in the telly paper. I wrote in and told them.' 'He's not watching anything like that,' I say, 'it's his DVDs. He collects them. Nature programmes, Carl Sagan. There's something about the coast he watches – islands in Scotland. He got obsessed with that one, started collecting camping equipment in the loft and saying he was going to take himself off up there.' 'Hiking's an interest,' Ruth says, 'the great outdoors. Maybe a little holiday would be good for him. Some peace and fresh air and time to reflect.' 'Reflect!' I say. 'The less reflecting that lad does, the better. He's on his own too much as it is.' 'Do you think he's got anyone he can talk to?' Ruth says. 'About his worries? I've noticed,' she pulls little Angela in close to her, rests her chin on her head, 'he's often walking up and down our street. I wondered if he was lonely. I sent Andy out once, told him to tell Julian we were having car problems and could he come and have a quick look.' Andy. Now I like Andy. He's one of those men you could see making Mission President one day. Maybe even Area Authority, if Ruth wound her neck in a bit and started to behave herself. 'He wouldn't come in, though. Said he had too much on.' 'That's our Julian,' I say, 'he's not generous with his time – you could never say that about him.' 'He's never had a girlfriend, though, has he?' Ruth probes. She can be as bad as Maggie sometimes, who is just sitting there listening, a little smug smile plastered all over her beak. 'Well, better that than the other way,' I say quickly, knowing full well what she's implying. 'Better a young man liking his own company than him getting some poor girl in Carole's predicament.' Ruth nods. 'Well, maybe a little camping holiday would be a good thing then. If he's interested in Scotland, send them there. Heavenly Father answered Joseph's prayers in the woods, didn't he? Jesus went into the wilderness to pray.' 'That's a thought,' I say, 'maybe I'll mention it to Gary – once he's had a bit of sleep and caught up with himself, they could go together. Maybe Gary would talk some sense into him. I got an email from him yesterday,' I say, 'do you want to hear it?' I move over to the computer. Julian adjusted the table so the bit where the keyboard sits can be lowered right down onto my knee so I can use it. Ruth smiles and sits back, waiting for me to read, but Maggie takes it as her cue to start chirping up. 'Still, it must be like a knife to your heart, knowing he should have led the way for Gary. And now it's probably too late,' she says, like a dog with a bone. 'I don't know how you sleep at night, having all these worries about him. I mean, you will want grandchildren at some point, won't you?' 'Gary was always very good about emailing,' I say, 'sent lots of pictures. And letters too. Anyway. He says he won't have time to email me again before he comes home, and he's put in all the details about his flights to send to Bishop Jackson so he can get down to Heathrow in time and pick him up. Don't want him waiting at the wrong terminus.' 'Terminal,' Maggie says. 'Still, I suppose my boys have had it slightly easier. Graham's always been a strong influence on them being active – making sure they have a living breathing example of what a man in the Church can be. Priesthood in the home makes such a difference.' 'My Martin works shifts,' I say, feeling the heat come up my neck and into my face, 'he works twelve-hour shifts to support his family. When he can get to church, he does. That's what a man should be doing.' 'Last time I looked, we didn't get post delivered on a Sunday,' Maggie says lightly. 'I'll just put my password in and get his email up for you now,' I say. 'It's very convenient, having the computer in the living room. Avoids any temptations for the boys too, you know what young men can be like. The struggles they face. Satan's grip on technology. We didn't even get the internet put on it,' I tap the monitor, 'until Gary was called. Such filth on there. Like a sewer pipe right into your living room.' Maggie is squirming and it serves her right. She shouldn't dish it out, not if she's not prepared to take it. 'I heard a story once,' Ruth says, very quietly and not looking at either me or Maggie, 'perhaps in Relief Society last year. Maybe General Conference. A woman who'd go around to her neighbours snuffing out their oil lamps. Jesus saw what she was doing and called her to him and told her, "Extinguishing the light of your neighbour's lamp doesn't make your own glow brighter, Sister." I always remember that story. It's such a moving parable, isn't it?' Maggie raises her eyebrows and then starts forcing Jeannie's school shirts onto hangers, pushing the buttons into the holes and hanging them up on the door frame so the sleeves move in the draught from the hall. Gary's email finally comes up on the computer screen, but the moment has passed now, and anyway, Jeannie will be here any minute with the grub. 'Your Jeannie looked a bit off this morning,' Ruth says after a decent interval. Maggie and I turn to her, relieved. 'She behaved herself, I hope?' 'Like an angel from Heaven, as usual,' Ruth says, 'that's not what I meant. She was pale. I asked her if she wanted to come over and play with little Angela some time, and she said no. I wondered if it was,' she looks at the door, as if she's imagining Julian out there – listening, 'her time.' 'Oh no, nothing like that,' I say, 'she'll just be excited, that's all. Not one of us has slept in a fortnight.' I look at the clock over the gas fire. Nearly one. I've missed *Doctor Quinn, Medicine Woman*. 'Although where she is, I don't know. I'm going to have to go out and get the food for tonight myself.' I say it lightly, hoping one of them will offer to do the list for me, but Julian has ruined everything. Even though I am here and his mother, they don't feel comfortable as women in the house with a less active and adult man around and unmarried at that, and Maggie has her coat on and Ruth is already putting Angela's things into her changing bag, packing the books and crayons away. 'Looks like it's going to rain, on top of everything,' I say hopefully. 'My chair's a right death-trap once the pavements are wet. Like an ice rink under those wheels. And the bus drivers. Don't get me going!' They hug and kiss me on both cheeks and they squeeze my hands and Maggie, with tears in her eyes, tells me the feeling when they come home safe is akin to the aftermath of giving birth, and she doesn't know about me, but she'd rather her boys came home in a coffin than dishonourably, and five times (the show-off) she's had that pleasure and she knows just what I'm going through, and what I'm feeling now, and what I'll be feeling later will be worth it all – and she wishes she could be here to see it. With a snaky look at Ruth. And they smile and kiss me again and Maggie takes out a bag of washing but they don't offer to do a run to Richardson's for me and where is Jeannie? I go back into the front room and try Jeannie on her mobile phone. It rings and rings until the phone connects me to her voicemail service. Martin pays for her to have a tenner a month on that phone so she can get in touch with us for emergencies, and that's after all the fuss he made about my curtains and knowing full well she never answers it if she sees it's me ringing. What about *my* emergencies? I should never have trusted her. I go to the computer and look at all Gary's emails. I've saved them inside my computer, as well as printed out and kept for posterity. It's a record of his achievements, of the leaps and bounds he's made in his own spiritual development, and for the Church, as the Lord's instrument. Gary's homecoming is going to be a real triumph for me personally and for our family generally. He sent me his picture to show he'd been keeping himself well. I click on the attachment and wait for it to appear. He's a good-looking boy and who knows where he gets that from? Light hair. If he were a girl you'd call it strawberry blond. Clear, good skin – a gift from my grandfather's side, that is. The Arnolds always had fine complexions. Eyes you could fall into – and the smile! There's not a bit of guile in him. Everyone says so. *Your Gary is a good boy – he carries the Spirit with him.* The amount of spirit clinging to that boy is *phenomenal*. Incredible. That's what they said while we were cleaning up after the party. The whole Ward got to see him really shine. *He's a credit to you*, they said. Me! I shout Julian a few times from the downstairs hall but he doesn't come. When he went I was in pieces. Of course I was. Bishop Jackson made a personal visit to the house. He knelt on that carpet right there, before we had it changed, and prayed with me and gave me his personal revelation that Gary would return home in glory. I thought for a minute he was revealing to me that Gary was going to die on his Mission, a persecution or an accident of some kind, and I screamed the house down. When he explained it was a poor choice of words but what he'd actually meant was that Gary would return here, to his temporal home with me, and that the glory would be an earthly kind of glory or a pride we all feel when our children have done well, I felt better. Home in glory! And his glory will be mine too. A mother never loses that special link she has with her children. There's a connection that goes from each of them back to me. I know what they're doing, what they're feeling, what their worries are. I can picture them out there in the world, doing the things they do. It's not that I'm saying I'm psychic or anything like that. The Bishop has revelations for the Ward, the Prophet has revelations for the whole Church. And little me, I have the revelations for my children. I have seen Gary dressed all in white, tie and socks included, and standing in the baptismal font with his arm raised to the square. Blue water to his waist, nicely heated so it's not a shock when you go under – but never reminiscent of a bath. The person he's baptising – a young girl this time. She's looking up into his eyes, knowing he'll be the last thing she sees in her old life and the first thing she sees in her new one. He shows her how to hold onto his left arm so that when the time comes he can lean her back into the water. He'll say her name, and *having been commissioned of Jesus Christ I baptise you in the name of the Father, the Son and the Holy Ghost. Amen!* There's no splashing or fumbling – Gary is an expert in it by now – she swoops backwards and up again, water streaming from her hair. Lies back as into the grave, and her saviour Gary on behalf of Jesus Christ pulls her out and she is reborn to cleanliness and her new family in the Gospel. Ah. She's probably crying. She heads up the steps on the other side of the font. It's not an easy walk – the long sleeves and skirt of the heavy white dress cling to you something terrible. I remember it well. But her new sisters in the Gospel are waiting to help her up the steps and into the dressing room. Gary waits in the water alone. Puts his hand to his hair – not vanity, but just making sure he's neat enough for such a sacred event. He knows all the pitfalls. No cheap shirts – nothing that would go transparent in the water and reveal his Temple garment to any non-members watching. He's reverent. A credit to me. The family and members waiting around the font (it's probably the same in America as it is over here – something built into the floor of one of the downstairs classrooms. You get a couple of the Youth to pull up the floor and set the taps going an hour or so before) start to sing "I am a Child of God" just to pass the time until – until what? Until the rest of the girl's family emerge! All in white. Father, mother. A few brothers and maybe one younger sister who's not old enough yet but wanted to wear the clothes and get a blessing along with her family. Which is nice, isn't it? Gary does them all. Seven. Seven! So yes, while of course there are practical worries about the day, now that Jeannie has done her vanishing trick *again* and let me down, I can still be positive and reflect on what really matters, which is Gary's success for this family. Still, if she thinks I'm letting her off with that, or with the money, she can think again. Martin's not due back for ages. I shut down the computer anyway, before he gets back and starts whining about how much leccy it sucks up when I forget and leave it running. Go to the foot of the stairs and shout Julian again. No answer, surprise, surprise. Shuffle myself back into the living room. Turn the telly on, flick through, and then off again. The Littlewoods carriage clock ticks and ticks. Quarter past. Julian says the noise drives him to the brink of insanity. The very brink. I never hear it when I've got the big telly on but it's off now and I can suddenly see what he means. Where is that girl? The thought of Gary coming home to a meal made out of what I happen to have on hand is intolerable. But Gary has had to overcome hardships to get his glory and it seems Heavenly Father is telling me that I have my own hardships to endure for this day. And if I've got to go and deal with this myself, I'd best go and take care of business upstairs first. Julian is waiting on the landing, his shadow falling down the stairs. They are narrow, our stairs. He stands and watches as I climb up them on my hands and knees. Faded and bristly carpet against my palms where it's worn down on the tread, I keep meaning to get Martin to take it up and lay it the other way. Getting up to the bathroom is always a bit of a production. 'I was shouting on you,' I say, panting. 'A bit of help wouldn't be too much to ask, would it?' 'I am busy,' he says, curtly. He's got a big rucksack in his hand – the one he takes when he goes out camping in the Lakes. 'What are you up to? What's in that?' 'Mind your own.' 'Charming! I like that!' I can't say anything else, too busy huffing and puffing myself up the stairs. Why the Housing Association won't chip in any money for some adaptions, even a little chairlift, which would make my life one hundred and ten per cent easier, is beyond me. 'Shouldn't you be thinking about getting back to work?' I say once I get to the top. He shakes his head and looks right past me. Tutting, like he's impatient for me to get out of the way. Never offers to lend a hand, and I'm puffed out so I sit on the landing for a minute to get my breath back. 'I have plans,' he says. I could shufty up a bit so he could squeeze past me if I wanted to, but I won't do it if he doesn't ask me. 'What's to do? You've got a face like fizz. Is it because Ruth isn't coming?' 'Don't be stupid.' 'Well, what did you go and ask her for then? Making a fool out of me like that? I was going to get them to stop a bit longer and ask them to take me into town to get the food shopping, but you've run them off now.' 'Run them off?' He says it like he says everything, calm as anything, with a bit of a sneer to it. 'Don't pretend like you don't know what I'm talking about. And if you've set your sights on Ruth, you can just go on and reset them. She's a married woman.' 'I am not after Ruth,' he says, and laughs, like whatever it is he is after should be more than obvious. 'Well, isn't it about time you started thinking about your future? There are so many nice girls in our Ward. And next month, there's a singles dance. Gary and you could go together!' 'You want me to take Gary out on a date to a Stake singles dance?' He laughs. 'Well, I have heard some things but that just about takes the biscuit,' he says, in a funny-sounding voice, and I realise he's trying to do an impression of me. 'There's nothing wrong with it. There are some lovely girls there.' 'You sound like Dad. Why is everyone obsessed with me getting a girlfriend?' 'You're twenty-six years old, Julian. You can't live at home with me and your dad forever. You need to get yourself back on track. Why don't you let me iron you a shirt and you can come with me to church this week? Your dad's said he'll come. It'll be the five of us again. Just think how nice we'd all look together!' Julian laughs quietly. 'I think it's going to take more than a clean shirt, Mum,' he says. I get the feeling he's going to start on one of his rants. Tear down everyone else's faith because he's not got any of his own. Or worse than that, start tearing down the house. He's never raised his hand to me, not his mother, but he's come close before. I've seen it in him. That darkness. He clenches his jaw and I flinch a bit. Not scared of my own son, course not. That'd be stupid. Just realising that, right now, I've got bigger fish to fry and one of them is Jeannie. 'I've not got time to sit here debating with you, Julian. This is your brother's day and I've got stuff to be getting on with. Come on. Give me your hand. Help me get up, I need to get into the toilet.' He stands still, his teeth clenched. He's breathing out slowly, as if he's counting to ten and trying to keep himself from exploding. He doesn't put out his hand. I can't remember the last time he let anyone touch him. 'Is Jeannie not back yet? She is supposed to help you with this. I need to get out.' I am still blocking the way, and Julian starts moving from one foot to the other, rubbing his hand up and over his forehead to slick his longish hair out of his eyes. It's a habit with him, because he lets it get so long between haircuts. Just to embarrass me and his father, I'm sure. It would take so little effort from him to bring himself into line and get this family back on track, it really would. But will he make it? Nothing his father and I have tried yet, not since he was fourteen and started refusing to go to church, has had one bit of effect on him. Sometimes I think that boy has got a bad spirit. It's not a nice thing to think about your own son, but there you go. 'I don't know where Jeannie is! That's the point!' Julian just stares, waiting for me to move. 'Look. If you're not going back to work, you can go out and get the food for me. Can't you? It's not a lot. You'll have to use your own money, though, because I gave Jeannie what was left of the housekeeping and what she's done with it I dread to think. I can't stop to think about it now. The most important thing is that Gary gets home to a proper, hot, nice meal in a clean kitchen and his bed is made fresh and ready and we are all of us sitting around that table.' He shakes his head. Drives me mental. 'I have got plans. You will have to sort this out yourself. It is not my job to deal with it for you.' 'Julian!' He loses patience then and just steps over me, nearly tripping on the top few stairs as he leaps down. He's always the same. 'Julian! No matter what sort of childhood you've had, however hard you think you've been treated – there comes a point for all of us when we've got to stop blaming our parents and stand on our own two feet. Get on with things and take responsibility for our own lives.' Julian just stares up at me from the bottom of the stairs. Very strange look on his face, like I'd told a joke but he was still waiting for the punchline. 'What made you say all that to me, I wonder?' he says, like the Smart Alec he is, but he never hangs about for me to answer. Doesn't slam the door on his way out, but he doesn't need to. And where he's going off to now with that big bag I don't know. Off out and up to no good with that Drake, no doubt about it. I know he goes into pubs: Maggie saw him once, and wasted no time in getting on the phone and letting me know. No point waiting for help. I move along. In the bathroom, there's a towel knotted to the radiator. Don't think of something stiff and mucky. Martin puts a new one out for me. It serves two purposes. When he and Jeannie are out at work, I can use it to heave myself from the floor, up into a crouch, and then onto the pan. I don't really need it, but it's reassuring to have something to hang onto. The other use is the one I put it to now. For a while, after Jeannie was born, the neighbours would bang when I was in the bathroom. It would make me ashamed and I would cry. Martin would explain it to me. Very patient, and using the same words every time so it became like a story I still remember and comfort myself with today. 'They expect to hear the baby crying at all hours. They know about that – they'd have time to get used to the idea, same as we have. It's a natural sound. Jeannie's not in pain, she's not frightened. Just hungry. They've kiddies of their own. They've been through it before. But Pauline,' he'd say, and clamp onto my shoulder so I knew he was speaking in kindness and not in criticism, 'they don't expect to hear you shrieking day and night, and if you're not going to take the codeine, we need to put other measures in place.' Measures. The hand towel on the radiator is his measures. Fourteen years. It works, more or less, in that the neighbours have never complained about me since. I lower my underclothes and garments and change the inco-pad without looking at it. It feels hot and heavy and I knot it into the little plastic bag from the box we keep up here for this purpose. The fresh ones are laid out on the side of the bath, white and soft and innocent looking. I lean forward from the hips and rest my feet on the little stool. I take the end of the towel and put it between my teeth and bite down hard on it. Sometimes I can feel my teeth move in their sockets. I grab my knees, feel the damp of my hands against the hair there, and push. The pain is unbelievable and rises in a knot against the pressure in my throat as I strive to endure without disturbing the neighbours, who did not ask to share my burden with me.

Even though I feel it every day it never becomes ordinary. My eyes are dry. The smell is warm and grassy and familiar. Pain stretches the seconds: everyone knows that. But what's a few minutes six or ten times a day compared to eternity? Flesh is grass. And it is my testimony that after the resurrection my Heavenly Father will translate my body into Celestial flesh, which is perfect and shining and will never feel pain. I need to empty myself out completely so there'll be no accidents later. Twenty minutes or so pass. I wash my hands and face and put on some make-up. My outside coat is hanging on the back of a chair in the kitchen. Purse near the bread bin, plimsolls on the back doormat and keys in a bowl on the new coffee table. I go around the house slowly and collect these items. My hands shake. It's a secret, you see. We keep it to ourselves, the fact I prefer to stay indoors. It's not like it's a phobia. The Priesthood aren't keen on emotional conditions. They speak as men, not understanding the difficulties that belong to women. I can go out, if I want to. I go to church, don't I? I do my Visiting Teaching via phone calls, but that's all right – we all serve according to our ability, take according to our need. I just prefer not to go out too much, unless I've got to. It'll be better when Gary gets back. He can wheel me places, we'll go on walks. The door handle rattles under my hand. I push the chair out first, then hold onto it while I mange the front step. The air smells like broken leaves. It's so bright out here. The whole world is drenched in light. It hurts my eyes. The more light there is, the less you can see.

GARY

SLC International to Chicago O'Hare. A six-hour layover in Chicago. Then on from O'Hare to JFK. Nine hours in JFK, for most of it waiting in a queue that snakes all the way from the boarding gate to the baggage check-in, sleeping leaning against a wall, on my feet, or with my head on my rucksack. They brought us bottles of water and vouchers for McDonald's but I was too tired to eat and too keyed up, by the constant stream of chatter, tannoy announcements and the stuck-record failure broadcast my own mind had been playing me for weeks, to relax. Finally, the announcement comes that we can board: the ash cloud has moved and, for now, the airspace is open and Heathrow will accept us. Coach all the way, of course. And all the children are screaming and even their screaming is not loud enough to silence the not-so-still and not-so-small voices that I can hear in my head: *Elder Gary Leeke: the Blooper Reel.*

The seats are blue plush with a trim of red piping. I force myself not to pick at it. (*'Keep y'eyes to y'self and put that literature away. I am not interested, get it?'*) There is a tray that folds down from the seat in front to make a small shelf that, depending on the height of the passenger and the relative position of their knees, drops to form a table at an angle somewhere between ninety and forty-five degrees. When I breathe, it rocks.

There on this tilted plastic shelf is a tray made from moulded yellow plastic. There are pockets in this tray, and inside these pockets are foods, of various kinds, encased in plastic bags that are impossible to open. Kraft Cheese, biscuits and a squat plastic tub of OJ that can be accessed by peeling off the foil lid. The apple slices have wilted; there are beads of perspiration inside their plastic bag. There's a small carton of lime-green Jell-O salad flecked with grated carrot. Here there are several wet wipes in foil packets, arranged on the plastic plate like a fanned-out deck of cards. A plastic knife with a serrated edge. A spork. *('Go on now, don't make me have to call the police . . .')*

The food is untouched. I am fasting for a last-minute miracle.

This is only the second time I have been on an airplane in my entire life. All us passengers were awarded with a complimentary Ziploc baggy with more wet wipes, Q-tips, a mini emery board and a plastic box that looks like a puncture repair kit but actually contains a folding toothbrush and a miniature tube of toothpaste. Everything carries the blue and red logo of the airline. They usually save these for business-class passengers – but these are our prizes for being delayed for so long.

A woman three rows down and to the left of me has been singing the same song, on and off, for the past three hours.

'I *will not* put a lid on it. This is a medical requirement. I am singing away my fears. I am distracting myself from thoughts of the in-ev-i-ta-ble,' she says, and launches into another wavering chorus of 'Nearer my God to Thee', which, as she's mentioned several times over the past few hours, the doomed passengers and crew sang to comfort themselves as the *Titanic* went down. *('I'm going to give you ten seconds to get off my property, and then I'm going to go back inside and get my gun.')* It is evidently not a comfort to her because now she is crying. *(Could I leave one of my . . .)* Someone tells her to 'knock it off', but her response is muffled by a conversation closer at hand – two boys playing with hand-held Nintendos and wondering aloud if their games could interfere with the plane's navigational system. Further away, a woman is complaining to the stewardess: she wasn't allowed to bring her knitting needles with her onto the plane.

'I'd understand a steel needle, miss, but these were *plastic*.

You could do more damage with this flatware you've given us and will someone *please* shut that woman up? I am not a terrorist but she's tempting me to turn into one.'

We have reached our cruising altitude of thirty-five thousand feet and the seat-belt lights have been off for some time now. The weather at our destination is 55.4 degrees with broken cloud. The onboard films available include Jennifer Aniston and Vince Vaughn in *The Break-Up*, Disney's *The Little Mermaid*, or Sean Connery and Nicholas Cage et al. in *The Rock*. Onboard meals, beverages and snacks are offered in the cashless cabin. We are to have our credit or debit cards ready. (*'Bolt the door! The Morg Are Here! Harharhar.'*) The air smells like socks and gas and sour milk. We are above the clouds and the light reflecting up at us is silvery, liquid bright. Thirty thousand feet closer to God. I send up a prayer.

'Or if on joyful wing, cleaving the sky, sun, moon and stars forgot, upward I fly . . .'

She hasn't got a bad voice. Not really. And it is a hymn I have always liked. I could have asked to switch seats so I could sit next to this frightened woman. I might have held her hand while she sang out of fear and distracted herself from thoughts of the in-ev-i-ta-ble. I could have spoken to her about the real balm for all her terrors, about the truth of what lies waiting for us beyond the sky. I could have sat silently with her, sharing her anxieties, keeping her company in her distress. I could have shown her by my words and deeds that she was my sister and she was not alone in the world. (*'Go on, get out of here.'*)

I did not. It wasn't the first opportunity I'd missed. It's my Blooper Reel. My confidence is gone: shot at. No one wants to hear what I have to say. When we first boarded the plane, the sweating man sitting next to me looked at my suit and black badge and then turned his whole body away from me. His knees and elbows jabbed me.

'Can't you shove up a bit, son?'

I offered him the aisle seat so he'd have a little more room to sprawl, if that's what he wanted, spitting and whistling over 'seat' until I needed to give it a note and sing it out – but he only shook his head and turned his face to the window.

'Long way down, huh?'

I followed his eyes through the lozenge of plastic and along the grey bar of the wing. I noticed the milkiness of the sky as we ascended. The peculiar, bathroom-bright quality of the light. The city below, all grey boxes and roads laid out in grids. A honeycomb of brothers and sisters, all buzzing through their temporal existence, unaware. The fluorescent blue of all those backyard pools. Everyone walled off from one another, trimming their own grass; cooped up in their own cars. I tried not to imagine that I was seeing the world as our Heavenly parents do, looking at these silly boundaries we put between ourselves from a more elevated perspective, but I couldn't help it.

And yet I put up my own boundaries too, didn't I? Shoved the armrest down between us and didn't bother to ask him how he felt about where he was headed in life. When I folded my arms and bowed my head to give a silent prayer for a safe flight, the man next to me huffed and shifted, jabbing me again and calling over the stewardess to demand, ostentatiously, a double bourbon over ice. His eyes moved over me, from my face to my badge and back again. Suspicious, though I'm the person on the plane least likely to rob him in his sleep. He drank three of his foul-smelling, brown drinks and then passed out. He's been unconscious and snoring ever since, his racket competing with the steady vacuum-cleaner roar of the engine.

Gently, so as not to disturb him I rest my hand against his so our pinkies are touching. Father, bless your son and keep him safe from harm and when he awakes may his sleep have refreshed him and opened his mind to truth and light. In the name of Jesus Christ, amen.

*　　*　　*

Are there any missionaries at all who come back home without having baptised a single person? Not even the children of a less active member? I got so worried about my failure at the twenty-three-month mark, when most Elders would have been getting trunky, that I visited the ward clerk and asked to look at the old *Ensigns*. I don't know what I was looking for. The scriptures are one thing, but the brethren know that many members find it difficult to apply the Book of Mormon to their everyday lives and struggles, so the ancillary church publications aim to assist with this. Year by year they cover everything.

The old man unlocked the cupboards for me and heaved out boxes and files, some of magazines yellowed and tattered at the edges. They're all digitised and online now, but Elders on normal duties aren't encouraged to use computers more than once a week – which is why, I suppose, these magazines are kept.

'You looking for anything in particular, Elder?' he said, leaning on the cupboard door and watching me as I hauled out boxes. My companion, an acne-spattered German fresh out of the Missionary Training Centre at Provo, so green he still called in his sleep for a girl called Clara, sat cross-legged on the carpet, squinting at the third discussion, which he was trying to memorise.

'Just reading,' I said, not wanting to confess. Shame, for the failure, and shame to admit to pride, which made me care about the failure.

'Godly way to spend your P-Day,' he said. 'You call me when you're done and I'll put everything away for you. There's some cookies on that table over there from my wife, and neither of us would notice if they weren't there when we came to lock up.' He winked.

Some of the magazines were so old they fell apart in my hands. Articles about preparation for Temple Marriage, Helping a Spouse who Suffers with SSA, Teaching the Youth about Tithing. How to Talk to Investigators about Difficult

Issues like Polygamy, Blacks and the Priesthood. The Three Evils of Feminism, Socialism and Intellectualism. Supporting Missionaries. Saving for Missions. The Special Challenges for Sister Missionaries. Single Sisters: Your Special Place in the Gospel.

Nothing at all to help missionaries who, sent out in fields that are white and ready for the harvest, fail to rescue a single brother or sister. Not one. Elder Keller and I went home. He stuffed his pockets with cookies and recited the third discussion, word perfect, as we went. The flat, when we got back to it, was cold, bare and empty. Keller had pictures of him and his brothers fishing tacked onto the front of the kitchen cupboards.

'Elder Keller? We need to talk about our targets.'

Every Saturday evening we would sit together and pray about this. It was never an easy experience for me. Green though he was, Elder Keller wouldn't even try to hide the fact that he was reading unapproved literature, or listening to music. One of the sister missionaries had sold him her radio before transferring out to another area and he'd lie in bed at night with it against his ear, listening to rock music and mouthing the lyrics into the darkness. I tried to intervene now and again, and even offered a compromise by tuning it to KBYU and dialling the volume down to four, but he wouldn't have it.

'All right, Leaky. Let's get this over with.'

'Over with? Come on, Elder. The S-spirit won't be with us if you have an attitude like that. This is really important. Set-set-set-setting goals for our missions is a way to sh-sh-sh-sh-show obedience.'

As I was the more experienced Elder, it was my job to teach him the way things were supposed to be. To guide him, and chasten him where necessary. The role and the expectations attached to it made some of the Senior Companions sanctimonious – picky over the colour of a tie, the shine on a shoe, whether it was permissible to wear a rucksack on one shoulder, or if two made a better impression. I was never like that. I just wanted Keller to be happy in the work, and for us to be successful in our service.

'All right. All right.' He flopped onto the chair opposite me and pulled his organiser out of his bag. 'Are we talking baptisms or discussions?'

I brought out the blue loose-leaf papers we had to fill in with our 'estimates' and 'actuals' each week, smoothed them out on the little table and took the top off my pen.

'Let's s-s-s-start with baptisms. How many baptisms do you think we'll achieve this week?'

'None.'

'Elder Keller!'

'What?'

'Have you so little faith in the Lord?'

'We can't baptise people we aren't teaching. And we haven't got past the first discussion in ages. We haven't got past a front door in ages – unless you count Herr Fundamentalist and his wives last month. Did you mark that up as a discussion in our figures?' He winked at me. 'Don't blame you, actually. I would have done the same.'

'Keller . . .'

'You should put it down as four discussions. Maybe five. How many of them do you think there were?'

'Can we please focus on what we're doing?'

'I already told you my answer. None.'

'I can't write down none.'

'It's realistic.'

'It isn't showing any faith at all in the Lord. If we are pure enough then he'll help us do his work. Have you been praying, Elder? Are you sure that radio of yours isn't the reason why we haven't had much suc-suc-suc-suc-success lately?'

'Lately? The only time my feet get wet is when I'm in the shower.'

'Elder Keller. Please.'

'All right then. Let's write down thirty.'

'Thirty baptisms? This week?'

'Why not? Put thirty-five. Put forty. With God, nothing is impossible, is it? Write down fifty. Let's go all-out. We'll take the car down to St George for the weekend and round up the Polygs. Dunk them and all their kids. We'll be heroes. They'll put our statues up in Temple Square. You, me and Brigham. Heroes. Legends.' He punched the air, said something in German and grinned at me. 'How about that?'

'Elder Keller. Right after this I am writing my letter to the Mission President. I don't want to mention your attitude to him, but if I have to, I will. There's a good reason we're not allowed to use the car any more.'

'What's wrong with what I said?'

'It's not realistic. We don't tempt the Lord like that.'

'Okay. Three. Put down three. This week Elder Leeke and Elder Keller will baptise three investigators. Can I go now?' The top buttons of his shirt were undone and he pulled the fabric back and forth against his chest, grimacing. 'I stink. I want to take a shower.'

'Three?'

'Sure. *Eins, zwei, drei.*' He held up his fingers, grinned again. 'That's realistic.'

'But we're not actually teaching anyone right now, are we?'

'That's true, Elder. But I have faith. I have a great deal of faith that you'll solve that problem. I never knew a missionary that prays as much as you do. Don't you worry about wearing out the knees of your pants?'

'I'll put down one. One for this week. And we'll review *Building Relationships of Trust* and s-s-s-s-see how we get on.'

Elder Keller had already left the room. We were supposed to do a companionship inventory, to finish with a prayer for harmony between us. But he'd gone. The tinny sounds of the radio floated in from next door along with the chug of the faucets. He started singing along to some pop song, and I knew if I asked him to turn it off he'd only tell me it was a Saturday, have some mercy, and anyway – it was his way of perfecting his English.

Eventually the man next to me wakes, startled, and looks around for the noise that disturbed him even though it existed only in his dream.

'Would you like me to ask the s-s-s-stewardess to bring you some water?'

He pulls at his tie, runs a trembling hand over his thin, greasy hair, then shakes his head.

'No, no. I'm all right. Thanks.'

He's ashamed, I can tell, to be caught muttering and chomping through his dreams like a child. I watch him, shuffling in his seat to try to find a bit of comfort. Like all of us.

'S-sure?'

'Maybe some water. I guess I got a little loud back there?'

I press the overhead button to summon the stewardess. The man is overweight, buttoned into a shirt a size too small and his shining head rises out of the top of his hair. He's ashamed of this too, and pats it again, protectively. Perhaps he didn't mean to drink as much as he did. I've heard alcohol can affect you differently at high altitude.

'It's fine,' I say, 'you weren't s-sleeping long. Do you feel better?'

He starts coughing, clutching at his collar and banging on his chest with a fist.

'Are you all right, s-sir?'

It takes me longer to find the S words, but people here notice if you don't use 'sir' when you're speaking to them so I trained myself never to miss it out – even though half of the speech therapy I've ever had taught me to avoid the words I couldn't say, think on my feet and construct sentences using 'green' words rather than 'red' ones.

I do all right, though, I do all right. I lean on the Lord, who made me a promise not to test me with more than I was able to bear.

'I'm a little sick,' he says, 'I don't feel so good.'

'Sh-should I . . .'

The coughing fit passes. The stewardess arrives with her trolley and she pours him a plastic beaker full of water from the chilled bottle she is carrying. She looks at him doubtfully, and motions towards the compartment in the trolley where the paper airsickness bags are stored.

He waves his hand.

'No, thanks, ma'am. Just the sight of one of those little paper bags is enough to make me want to puke,' he puts the back of his hand against his mouth fastidiously, like a woman, and belches wetly behind it. 'Excuse me. After years of air travel I have developed an unfortunate association with those paper bags.' He grins. 'You can imagine how sick I get at the grocery store.'

'Maybe you sh-sh-sh-should try and go back to s-sleep?'

He shakes his head and frowns – as if I'd suggested he should elbow his way through the window and leap out onto the wing.

'Can't do it. I cannot do it. It's the time difference. If I sleep one minute longer I might as well set fire to the rest of the week. I've been down too long already. Nope. My only job now is to keep myself awake for the duration. Does it ever get to you that way?'

'Haven't travelled enough to be able to tell you,' I say, 'but I had a friend who was almost crippled by jet lag. There is a medication you can get for it, isn't there?' (US chemists will sell you just about *anything* over the counter.)

I haven't slept properly in almost four days. My eyes are so tired that when I close them the aching of the muscles there and in my temples forces me to open them. I've been strapped into this seat for hours, patting and rubbing at my face and looking for that comfortable spot on the thin airline pillow.

'The best thing I can do for myself is have another drink. A little something to help me relax.'

He motions for the stewardess to come back and insists several times that I order something on him. He's pretending that he hasn't noticed my stammer and chats away about melatonin tablets and airsickness wristbands, Pavlovian associations, the mysteries of travelling through time zones and the meagre servings of the airline's in-flight meals while I sip at my warm, oily OJ.

'I never got it that badly on the way out,' I say, 'but they tell me I'll feel it som-som-som-something awful when I get back home.'

He nods. 'That's because of the way the earth spins. Something like that. At least you know to expect it.'

He's acting like he's a friend of mine and like we've known each other for years. I wonder, as I always do, if he's someone I was close with in the pre-existence. Perhaps when we heard our fates I shook his fat, trembly hand and promised him that I'd become a missionary and find him on this plane, and bring him back to the Lord. My job to find, and harvest. His job to be found, listen and accept. Maybe part of him recognises me and that's why he's been so decent and not mentioned the stammer.

Or maybe (this is something to think about later), he really doesn't notice. Maybe I am wrong, and my stammer is not getting worse the more miles the airplane eats up, the closer I get to home. Sometimes the words feel like stones in my throat, battering against my teeth and choking me to death.

'I get so bad I don't even know what time it's supposed to be,' he says, 'it could be breakfast time, for all I know.' He raises his beaker. 'Cheers.'

We're over the water now. Or maybe ice. Perhaps heading through the cloud, particles ready to clog the engines, throw us off course and darken the sky. The plane doesn't go around the world, it goes over the top. My first companion told me that. I don't know if it's true. I glance at my watch, already set to UK time.

'We've another four hours before we land,' I say, 'it's lunchtime there, or roundabout.'

'Oh really?' The fingers around the edge of his beaker tighten slightly. He's afraid of flying. *(Hello, miss. I belong to the Church of Jesus Christ of Latter-Day Saints.)* I want to touch his arm, to tell him that it will be okay. *('Turn around now, go on. Back the way you came. Don't come to my door trying to sign me up. We're Episcopalian and Episcopalian we're staying.')* It's not the flying we have to worry about: it's the falling.

The smell of the bourbon is not tempting. His cheeks are redder now, and his forehead is shining. A yeasty, unwashed smell emanates from his shirt, wafting up my nostrils when he moves. He is my brother. Everything I was taught about myself applies to him too. We arrived in this world in these Latter Days, the last dispensation, because we were especially valiant spirits. It is likely we fought side by side in the pre-existence against Satan's vast armies. Blood was shed for him, just as it was for me. The same blood, the same value.

'Well, now you're awake,' I say, 'maybe we could visit a while?'

'Anything to keep me awake. Where you from, son?'

'Lancashire, England,' I say, 'but it's where I'm going that matters. Where you're going too, if we can talk about it?'

He laughs. Ropes of spit tie the corners of his mouth together. 'Heathrow, London, England is where we're going. All of us. Arrivals, customs, baggage carousel, taxi and a bed booked in the nearest Holiday Inn my company could find for me. That's where I'm going. After that, room service, sleep and, in the morning, a meeting with the biggest client my business has in northern Europe.'

Just as I'm thinking that he's going to give me a rundown of his entire itinerary, he stops and knocks at the little window with one crooked finger.

'I hope so, anyway. Does this sound fixed-in to you? Don't want to get sucked out now, do we?'

My rucksack is in the overhead locker. Reaching for it too early would disrupt the flow of this conversation. You've got to reel them in, so very, very gently, on a thread as fine and as easily broken as silk. Bring them unto him. We are fishers of men.

'Can I ask you, s-sir, are you a religious man?'

I'm not stupid. I know he knows, or thinks he knows, who I am. I know he's drunk. But I've got to try. I glance at my watch without letting him see me do it.

'Can't say I am.' He narrows his eyes. 'But *you* are.'

I nod.

'Going home to your family? Done your time.'

I nod again. It's a bad habit – 'yes' can be an amber word sometimes, and it's so easy to avoid that I forget, sometimes, to make the effort it requires of me.

'I thought so. My wife's cousin – he's done what you do. They're from Arizona. You ever been there? No? A desert out there. He fried himself senseless.'

'Are you—'

'No, never have been. My wife neither. We don't go in for all that sort of thing.' He changes the subject abruptly. 'Say, how many did you get?'

'S-s-succ-ccess is not measured by counting the number of s-s-souls s-saved, but by the number of s-seeds s-s-sown or s-scattered and the degree of s-service given.'

It takes me a few attempts, machine-gunning through the words and ignoring the heat rising from my cheeks, but he waits patiently and without smiling, until I finish. 'Success' is the hardest word of all.

'How many wives has your father got, Elder?'

'One,' I say.

This is a question that comes up sooner or later. Every time.

'It's the fundamentalists that practise polygamy, not us. They're not LDS-s-s-s-s. It isn't san-sanctioned by our leadership. If you've met Latter-Day S-s-saints that s-s-say differently, they're lying, s-sir. We abide by the laws of the land wherever we may be.'

'I'm just yanking your chain,' he says, and laughs. Something about what he's just said amuses him, because he giggles for a long time, tapping his knee occasionally.

'Not a bad idea, though, eh? I can see why you people get so many through your doors on a Sunday. That is one Unique Selling Point.'

'There are a number of differences,' I said, 'between the true restored Church and any breakaway group you might have had contact with. We're very family orientated.'

'And you're just itching to tell me all about it for the remainder of our time together. Get me to join that big happy family of yours. Yes?'

'I wanted to bear my testimony to you, s-sir. I wanted to tell you that I know, without one shad-shad-shadow of a doubt, that what I'm about to tell you is true. With every fibre of my being, the Lord has told it to me with more cert-certainty than I know anything else. And I'd like you, if you could, to listen to me tell you a s-story about a boy called Joseph S-s-smith who not s-so long ago, in Palmyra, New York, met the Lord our Heavenly Father and his s-son Jesus Christ in the flesh and blood of their resurrected bodies. From them he received the keys to restore the one true gospel to the earth in this last dispensation. This boy was given plates of gold upon which was written the Book of Mormon, an account of Jesus's dealings with the Lamanites in these lands. And who, by the power of the Holy Ghost inspiring him, was able to translate the message on these plates. I have a personal witness that the message on those plates is true, and I want to tell you how you can have one too.'

'That's a mouthful but you've got it down pat,' he says, 'all the young Mormon boys do. Never fails to impress me.'

My jaw hurts too much to reply. I try not to touch my face or shake my head when I talk. If I had my bag, I'd be presenting him with the Book of Mormon right about now. Pressing it into his hand. We don't charge for them – not like the Krishnas.

'My wife's cousin, he knew half of that weird book of yours off by heart too. He started when he was fourteen – could recite big chunks of it off the top of his head. No problem. How do they learn it you?'

'S-s-saints, s-s-s-sir.'

I feel the cramp start around the back of my head and radiate into my jaw. (*What's the matter with you? Why are you talking like that?*)

'What?' he says, smiling lightly. He knows what he's asking me. I look at my watch. Miles and miles to go – but not enough time.

'Mormon is the name of a prophet, and of one of our books of s-s-scripture. The Book of Mormon, s-subtitled Another Testament of Jesus Christ. We are Latter-Day S-s-s-saints, and like to be known as su-su-such.'

'Saints? Saints Saints Saints. Is that a fact?'

'That's what we're called.'

'Tell me this,' he says, and I lean forward in my seat.

I know every discussion. I've known all the seminary scriptures, the Thirteen Articles of Faith, the entire *Strength of Youth* booklet and even the Young Women's Motto, off by heart since I was fourteen years old. (*'Is it because you play with yourself too much? They don't let you get at the women, do they, boy? You been jerking off? That why you talk like that?'*) I completed four years of seminary – the certificates are probably still up and framed next to the school photographs in my mother's front room. I can sing 'The Armies of Helaman' in nine languages. I'm ready for this.

'Yes, s-sir? I'm happy to answer any questions you've got about the Restored Church of Jesus Christ. And if you tell me where you're headed, I can put you in touch with the local members. Your brothers and s-s-s-s-sisters. What questions do you have?'

'Well, it's like this.' He pats at my leg. 'Have you ever considered speech therapy? That's a hell of a stammer you've got there. Man to man, I can't understand one out of three words you're saying to me. There's spit all over your shirt, son. Your eyes look like someone's got their hands round your throat. Now don't look like that. I don't mean anything by it. Like you, I'm in sales (health, beauty and home care products primarily, although we both know this wicked world is changing fast and my business is expanding into the home medicine and supplement sector – here, take a card) and I can tell you now that you're losing your customer. You need to get the message across loud and clear in the first five seconds. It's a basic rule of advertising. Didn't they teach you *anything*? If your customer can't understand you, he isn't going to buy what you are selling. Have you seen a doctor about it? Nothing to be ashamed of. One of the kings of England was a terrible stammerer, or so I believe. So, I've heard tell, was Teddy Roosevelt – although I don't think that can be true.'

If one more person takes me to one side and tells me Moses was a great man, a great prophet, a leader beloved of God, and he also had a stammer that troubled him, and had I considered praying on it, I don't know what I'm going to do. My teeth are made of glass and if I clench my jaw any more they will break. I count, and breathe, and do my anxiety exercises. He is my brother. He is my brother. Brother. My brother.

'No? You've never been to see a therapist about your condition?'

'I guess I haven't ever gotten around to it,' I say. It isn't true, of course. I've spent more years in NHS therapists' rooms than this man here has spent asleep *and* drunk, but it is the politest thing I can think of to say. His face lights up – he's suddenly more excited than I've seen him previously.

'Elder, I'm going to give you something that's going to change your life. It truly is. And maybe when I've had a nap and I'm feeling more myself, I'll tell you a little bit more about it. But for now, son, look at this, will you?'

He shows me the magazine he's been studying. It doesn't look like a real magazine – there don't seem to be articles, but lots of pictures of people cleaning things, or washing their hair, or standing in gardens or next to their cars, holding hands and smiling. I worry, just for a second, wondering if I've got myself mixed up with a Witness. Doesn't look like a *Watchtower*, but you never know – they spend about as much as we do on their PR and they might have got some new designers in.

We're not supposed to proselytise to Witnesses or Muslims. Not that they aren't Heavenly Father's children too. No, we all are. And they walk a path that contains a little bit of the truth and walk it in sincerity, meaning well. But they don't walk in the full light of the restored gospel, their truths are distorted and incomplete, their priesthood lacks real power and they really don't like being told that. For the sake of harmony, we try to avoid them.

He flicks to the back of the magazine, and tears out a page. It is blank apart from a small red circle in the middle of it. And inside the circle, a little coil of words, printed in a font that looks like handwriting.

This is a tuit. Guard it with your life as tuits are hard to come by, especially the round ones. This is an indispensable item. It will help you to become a better worker. For years Amway Associates have heard people say, 'I'll do it as soon as I get a round tuit.' Now that you have one, you can accomplish all these things you put aside until you got a ROUND TUIT . . .

'Great, isn't it? Did I give you my card?'

'You did, s-sir.'

'Put it in your pocket. My name's James. Call me James, for Christ's sake.'

'James.'

'That's right. Good to know you. And what's your name? Tell me your name?'

I point at the badge.

An Elder's name is not a secret, but we're not supposed to allow even our companions to address us as anything other than Elder. The Mission President counselled us to use our wisdom and take the matter to the Lord, but he for one could see no good reason why anyone of the Church or out of it should know our first names during this season of our lives. He invited us to come up with a reason and raise our hands if we thought of something he'd missed. And paused. Nothing in the room but suits, coughing and the creak of plastic chairs. No good reason.

'Come on,' he says, 'your real name. You cannot establish a personal relationship with a suit and a name-tag. You'd do better if you let yourself go a bit. The personal touch. Ain't you ever read any marketing literature?'

'It's Gary,' I say. I realise I have not said my own name out loud in months. They told us, in the training centre, about BRT – building relationships of trust – and about finding something you have in common to chit-chat a little while about before launching into the first discussion. That's where I was going with the chat about the jet lag. They taught us about the commitment pattern, about issuing challenges to investigators. I know all that. But they never said it would help to use our first names.

'Gary. Not short for Gareth, just as it is.'

It sounds strange, like a word I have stolen from a foreign language. Like the first time I noticed myself saying 'sidewalk' without having to do the mental translation first. Could care less. Gotten. The slow, singy way I have to speak when the stammer gets really bad. I glance at my watch.

'Take care of yourself, Gary. I mean it. Look after yourself and get home safe to your family.'

He grabs my hand and shakes it. The Americans usually reserve this degree of affection for their armed personnel. I don't know what to say to him and without knowing how he has done it, as we're both sitting here in the same places we were when we started and will be for a good while longer, I know I am dismissed and this conversation is over. He rests his head on his wadded-up jacket and falls asleep quickly and without fuss, like an innocent.

They should get people like him doing the training in the MTCs, I think, but that's a wrong thought and I put it away from me.

I watch James's chest go up and down, and think about calling over the stewardess again. (*All my family are members. My wife's family too. And her brother and sisters – all active. And their husbands and wives. Back to the covered wagons. Come on in and I'll show you my genealogy charts. We can trace ourselves back to the Navoo Temple.*) I could ask for more water, and ask her if she's feeling tired, or if anything unusual has happened on this flight. I could ask her if she ever gets scared of crashing and use that to move towards the idea that, after this life, she'll be returning to report to Heavenly Father.

If the plane crashed, I wonder if they'd tell us we were going down. If the ash really did clog the engines and they started to sputter, we'd notice ourselves falling, wouldn't we? (*And you don't know any non-members who might like to receive the discussions at all? No one?*)

I think if there was a real emergency, the sort where the oxygen masks fall down from the ceiling, Heavenly Father would take this stammer away from me and I'd be able to stand up and help the children into their life jackets and pray with the mothers and fathers and put my hands onto the plane and command it, in the name of God, to take us back home. I could do that. There's no one else on this plane who's been anointed, a select representative of Christ in the world. (*'Not round here, Elder. This is Mormon country. The only non-members you'll find round here are Antis. You know that.'*) I fold up the paper with the Round Tuit on it very small and put it in my shirt pocket. It'll give Jeannie a laugh when she sees it. As soon as I think about her, her face comes into my mind – smiling, with her dark hair tied up in those pink bobble things she has to wear for school. Julian too, his long hair and those funny glasses he wears – the both of them looking so much like Dad that it doesn't seem they're related to me and Mum at all. I shake my head and look out of the window, get my mind back where it's supposed to be.

'You're not home until the bishop puts his hands on your head and releases you,' the Mission President had said, in my last interview. 'Badge on, mission standards all the way and I don't care where you are. Take your pamphlets in your hand luggage. Plenty of missionaries have clocked up one last baptism – last year the ward bishop was waiting in the arrivals lounge and the returning missionary met him with an investigator so keen for baptism that they unlocked the chapel and filled the font on the way home. Think of arriving home late with that story to tell your mother, young man.'

I won't take my badge off, of course. But it will be strange not to reach for this every morning. Black plastic that shows every finger mark. You're supposed to give it a little polish with the edge of your tie once in a while. One of the sister missionaries used the hem of her skirt in a fast and testimony meeting once, and was pulled up before the zone leader for impropriety.

My mother writes to me and tells me that my time will not be counted a waste. That I will have planted seeds that may not bear fruit for years to come. That I have demonstrated obedience. That my real mission might take place in the world, or in my very own family. I know she is thinking about Julian. Jeannie writes that he is getting worse; that he speaks like a robot, that a family from the ward have complained to Dad about him looking into their windows. *He's going to do something*, she says, *he's going to blow a gasket. Come home soon.*

I wonder what Julian is doing. When he blows a gasket, what it will look like? Arrested drunk and kicking in shop windows, perhaps? Or something to do with a girl? Perhaps Jeannie's right, and he's heading into the darkness. And it's my job to save him. To catch the back of his collar and bring him back from the brink. Father, help me be an example to my brother. Draw close to him and comfort him and let him know thy will. Send someone to bring him peace. Show me what I need to do to help him feel loved. I close my eyes to look inwards but there's no clue there. No visions of a young woman waiting for Julian to get his act together and claim her. No visions of Julian in a suit, wearing a tag like mine. I just see him as I did before I left, skulking around the back of the house, waving goodbye with his back to me, his mind already on other things. *He's worse, Gary. He's planning something. You won't recognise him.* The Lord will show the way. Just not yet.

Out of the window, past James and the empty plastic beakers lined up on the flip table in front of him, I can see fields, yellow and green, becoming visible through the carpet of cloud below. I am coming home.

JEANNIE

13.02. Beth is twisting her hair into a ponytail and sticking it down the back of her school jumper.

'Are you all right?'

The words come out funny, because she has her slides in her mouth. Her chin skin is all spotty and I try not to stare at it in case she notices and her feelings get hurt but it's loads worse than it was last week.

'Fine.'

'Did you get through to him yet?'

13.04. I slide the phone back into my bag.

'Yes, at break-time.'

'And he's off the plane now?'

'He's landed. You heard me talking to him, didn't you?'

She's crackling with static. Fluffy baby hair flies up around her temples and she clips it back roughly. She ducks her head into her apron, and turns so I can tie it at the back for her. There's a wet smudge of gravy on her collar. We're full of chips and sausage rolls, sleepy and ready to go home already.

Mr Teasdale walks around the room, pushing his wire trolley, delivering our projects to us as he weaves between the benches. I didn't expect Lewis to message me, not really. But he could have. He could have wondered why I wanted to see him. What was wrong. He could have confirmed he'd be there. Ask me if I was feeling all right. At least act like he was bothered. *Sorry, can't talk now. Will C U 18r.* Something like that. Anything. I pull the strings on Beth's apron too tightly, feeling stupid and angry and making myself promise not to check the phone again this lesson.

'Steady on.'

'Sorry.'

'What's wrong with you?'

'Nothing.'

'You're not going to meet up with him?'

'Tonight. After hockey.'

Beth tuts, and puts her hands behind her back to loosen the knot in her apron.

'I don't think you should,' she says, 'it's not right.'

She thinks I've got a boyfriend. I told her one little thing, about meeting him in the park, and it raining, and that was it. I'm not going to argue with her about it. I don't want to tell her anything else. Dating before age sixteen is bad enough. But she stares at me out of narrowed eyes, suspecting something, and I turn around so I don't have to look at her.

'Do mine, will you?' I say, and feel her tugging gently at my apron, tucking it around my waist like she's my mother.

'I'm concerned about you,' she says. *Concerned.* I can feel her breath on my neck. There's no way to explain it, though. We're on separate sides of a moat: me in the castle, her in the garden. Before, and after. And between us, the dark water. Murk and monsters. She hasn't got a clue. 'Will you talk to me?'

'Let's just get on with it.'

We're supposed to be making bird houses. The plan was to get them finished for the Friday before Mother's Day so that on Mothering Sunday itself we could present them along with the usual bunch of wilting daffodils and corner-shop Milk Tray.

Mr Teasdale bellows at us as he pushes his trolley to the front of the room. 'Right, you lot. Let's get on with it, shall we? Those of you who are missing your usual bench partners because of the trouble we've been having getting everyone back from their half-term jollies can either work together, or join another pair to make a three. And you can thank Mount Unpronounceable for that and not me. On you go, you're already behind and if

112

they're not done in the next two weeks, you'll be taking them home in bits and finishing them yourselves.'

At the start of term Michael Rawlings was caught doing something stupid with a hacksaw and the vacuum former so Mr Teasdale made us spend most of the lessons before the Easter holidays writing and illustrating a magazine on the subject of classroom health and safety so no one's bird house was ready. I got Mum a box of Roses and a hyacinth from the market instead and I don't think she was that bothered, actually. 13.14.

Mother's Day at church is something else. During the Sunday-school classes the Primary kids put lots of crocuses sprouting in plastic cups along the wooden rise at the front of the chapel. Hundreds of them. They planted them at around Christmas and have left them on the windowsills in all the classrooms, the mothers in the ward pretending not to notice in the months between then and now. And then at the start of sacrament meeting, all the Primary kids and the youth have to go to the front and sing a song, and then take a plastic cup from the display and walk down the aisles between the pews to find their own mothers, who get presented with it. And after all the mothers have been done you've to go back and get another and hand it to the nearest grandmother or widow. And once that's been done you need to go back again, and give whatever's left to any pregnant women. It takes ages.

Last month, just as all the youth and Primary children got back to their seats and the pianist was starting the introduction to the opening hymn for the proper sacrament meeting, Sister Travers's (not Maggie, her middle son's wife Melanie) husband Samuel jumped up and took one of the last plastic cups and walked very slowly down the aisle back to her holding it. It was one of the rubbish ones – it had been in the shade and never sprouted properly and so everyone else had rejected it, but as he walked back to his seat and finally gave it to his wife, who was blushing and smiling with her eyes all wet, I cottoned on to the fact that this was their way of telling the ward that she was pregnant, and there was a little sigh, and Maggie kind of grew in her seat and sucked at her lips, and I saw Mum's hands tighten around her own crocus so some of the soil spilled out and tumbled across her skirt and onto the floor. But it was a nice thing, a happy thing. You could tell because even though talking or clapping at that point wouldn't have been appropriate, everyone smiled a lot and sang the opening hymn that afternoon especially loud.

It's good to be pregnant, to hold hands with Heavenly Father and provide a body for one of his Spirit children. Better for church members to have children than other people, because our children are born in the covenant. The Saints should have lots of children. Small families are a bad idea – means you care more about buying cars or going on holiday than providing vessels for the spirits waiting to come.

When I tell this story to Gary I will start by saying, 'It was April Fool's Day when it happened, believe it or not,' and he'll laugh. Or I'll save that line for the end, and then it will seem more, what's the word, more *ironic*. It will show him I've still got a sense of humour. Can still crack a smile about things. That I have not been murdered, wiped out and destroyed. No matter what it feels like. It was April Fool's Day when it happened, and it started with Julian, who was getting one of his heads on again. Are you sitting comfortably? Then I'll begin.

Julian had been being right weird – running up and down the stairs and making the house feel small with his shouting and moaning and moving things around in his bedroom. He thundered down the stairs, into the kitchen, and slammed the door so hard it bounced off the fridge. He acts worse than I do, and gets away with more, and I'm the actual teenager, not him.

'What's wrong with you?' I said, which goes to show how irritating he was being because I never talk to him – not if I can help it. Dad says he's just awkward and I should give him more of a chance, but he's creepy and he scares me.

'Where are my tablets? Where are they?'

I went through and he had the kitchen junk drawer out, emptying a jumbled mess of envelopes and tape measures, old sticks of glue, boxes of matches, birthday cake candles and shoe brushes onto the kitchen table. I could tell by looking at him he had one of his headaches coming on. He put his hands into his hair, laced his fingers over his head and squeezed like his head was a boil about to explode.

'Give it here. Here. Here they are.'

I found the packet and passed it to him. He took four of the tablets, grinding them up between his teeth and swallowing them without water, then put the packet in his back pocket.

'Are you supposed to have that many?' I asked. Not that I care, I thought, but if he's going to drop dead on the kitchen floor I'd rather just know in advance, you know what I mean? He basically just growled at me, like I'd insulted him or something. Fine, I thought, you be like that. I was only asking.

'I am going out,' he said, 'tell Mum and Dad not to save any tea for me. I will not be back until much later.'

'On one of your stalker-walks, again?' I said.

'What is that supposed to mean?'

I don't even know why I was winding him up, except I didn't want him to leave me in with Mum and Dad on my own, because I could see they were shaping up for a row too. It must have been something in the air. April showers – rain and thunderstorms. The atmosphere in the house was terrible – heavy and crackling. Nosebleed weather. I suppose I was a bit out of sorts too.

'I know where you're going. Off to spy on Sister Williams. See if you can spot her getting out of the shower.'

Julian moved so quickly I thought he was going to hit me, but he was just grabbing his wallet off the kitchen counter.

'You know nothing,' he said. But he didn't leave. 'Where did you hear that?'

'She saw you,' I said, 'she always sees you. She was asking Maggie about you the other day. You don't fancy her, do you?'

Julian put his hand over his mouth and then laughed around his fingers. He looked like he was about to say something, then he shook his head and laughed again.

'Forget it,' he said, and went out the back door.

I should have gone out with him, Gary. Should have followed him – asked him to take me for a McDonald's, or give me a driving lesson, or anything. Mum and Dad started having a long argument about whether the curtains needed replacing or could just be sent away for dry cleaning and if they did get sent away what would they do about people peering in the windows in the meantime. You know how it goes. Mum was wondering if she could borrow something from Maggie and Dad was saying he wasn't going to ask for nothing from that woman, not even the steam off of her crap, and if it was down to him she wouldn't even cross the threshold and anyway (he went into the top drawer and pulled out a pile of opened letters) what did she think all this was (he shook all the letters at her and threw them into her lap like he was hitting her) and she still wanted to spend another bloody ninety bloody pounds on bloody curtains, then Mum went on about his language and I could see they were settling in for a good one – an all-nighter – and all about *curtains*.

You can see how it was going to go, can't you? Why I had to get out? They'd carry on – me upstairs making a tent out of my blankets and Facebooking Beth on my phone, then (I could just see it) Mum'd shout up the stairs, polite all of a sudden: *Jeannie, Jeannie darling? Will you pop down and bring a basin of warm water with you?* and it would be business as usual with the moaning and groaning and mopping up and because

Mum would cry about the mess Dad would have to stop, and she'd take her chance and get round to the state of the garden, in particular the embarrassing state of Gary's greenhouse. She'd point out, because she always did, that in her opinion Dad consistently prioritised the health and well-being of Bovril over that of his own wife and family and would he like to explain why that was, if he wouldn't mind, thank you very much and the smell – the smell, that you don't get used to, no matter what, would be hanging around the house all night and before I could think about it any more, before I could start wishing that I actually was dead just so I didn't need to hear them for one minute longer, I did what Julian had just done and walked out the back door. I didn't plan it (never plan anything, never think, head not screwed on, etc, etc) but I ended up in the park.

It had been raining and the grass was wet but I walked along the tarmac path following other people's wet footprints. The side of the park that is nearest to town backs onto the main street and as I went I kept hearing bits of music and talking and the damp fags and pub smell floating out through open doors. Tree roots have come up under the path and ruined the finish – it's cracked right open, mossy and slippery in places and flat and brand new in others where it's been patched up so you've got to be careful how you go along it or you'd break your neck and kill yourself as easy at that. I went slowly, staring at my feet, scuffing my shoes, humming a bit. It wasn't cold. It was all my own fault really. How many times did Mum need to tell me about walking on my own in parks. About older boys. *You don't listen, Jeannie*, she says, *that's half your problem*.

Astley Park is mainly grass with ponds and trees and paths and green spaces – Dad takes the dogs out there – but there is also a petting zoo they lock up at night and a fenced-in place with swings and roundabouts and miniature motorbikes on great metal springs you can bounce backwards and forwards on. The swing park is right next to the petting zoo and there are always peacock feathers threaded in the chains of the swings and in the links of the fence. Sometimes big white goose feathers, sometimes fluff blowing about from where a cat has got hold of one of the little chickens, but always the peacock feathers in the chains of the swings. High up. It's sort of weird looking and even though it's not like I've never seen them before, I was staring at them when someone shouted at me.

'Jeannie!'

I flinched before I recognised some girls from school – sitting on the roundabout in denim skirts and fluffy boots, pushing the roundabout around slowly with their heels and leaning against each other like dolls with half the stuffing come out. I walked a bit faster, tried to pretend not to hear. I'd only come out for some fresh air. Get out of the place for a few hours, long enough for Mum to get her own way and Dad to stop chunnering about it, then I could go home. I remember thinking there was only a bit to go. Just till the end of the month, then Gary would be back. Then things would be different.

'Jeannie, don't ignore, us, you bitch. Have you got any fags?'

I walked over, looked at them through the diamond shapes in the fence.

'She won't have fags.'

'I've not got anything.'

'See.'

'Are you coming in, or what? Toffee-nosed cow, you are, aren't you?'

I went in through the little gate and walked over to them, said hello. But they didn't move up on the roundabout to make room for me. From the limp way they were lying I wondered if they were drunk, or had been taking drugs or something.

'Hello.'

This made them laugh.

'Why are you still in your school uniform? Why haven't you got changed?'

'I wasn't planning on coming out.'

They didn't look like they did when they were at school, but they were still wearing their own sort of uniform. Sister Williams told us, and I think she's right, that following fashion slavishly robs you of your free agency, and ripped stripy tights, black eyeliner and hooded tee-shirts are as much of a uniform as the ones people who work in banks have to wear. They've all got the same hair, lopsided and poker straight, with choppy layers and heavy, asymmetrical fringes. Modesty isn't just about making sure your skirts are long enough to cover you and your tee-shirts aren't so tight that they'd cause others to stumble. It's actually about not wearing things that shout out at the world, *Look at me! Look at me!* That's not modest, it's very tacky. I felt sorry for them. They must think they don't have anything else to offer the world but their skin, their hair and their eyes.

'Let her sit down.'

'There's no room on here now. I can't be arsed moving.'

'It's all right.'

There were big puddles of water on the benches and on the seats of all the swings. I took off Julian's hoodie and used it to mop down one of the swings and then sat on it, near enough to talk to them, but not so near I could hear them if they wanted to whisper about me.

The three of them called and whistled and laughed – I could tell they'd been doing it for a bit: shouting and jeering at anyone who walked past the park.

'Look at him! Who's that? Who's that?'

The swing moved backwards and forwards. I held my legs out straight not because I wanted to pick up speed (swinging's for babies) but because I wanted to keep my shoes out of the dip under the swing that was filled with brown water.

'Hot stuff, Ginger!'

Lewis was coming but I didn't know that's what he was called then. I followed him with my eyes as he made his way along the path, taking the short cut from town to the estate behind the park. When they started to whistle and jeer at him, he didn't turn his head away or pretend not to hear, but smiled, and walked over – his hands in his pockets. He stood on the other side of the fence watching me on the swings. I tucked my legs right under and the swing stopped. He had green eyes and loads of blackheads on his nose.

Paula heaved herself up from the roundabout and walked on bendy knees, one foot in front of the other to make her hips sway immodestly, and jumped up on the swing next to me. She held onto the chains.

'All right,' she said, and spat her chewing gum at him. He took a step backwards and ignored it.

'What you girls up to?'

The others, who had floated over with Paula and were leaning on the metal frame the swings were attached to, kept their mouths shut, until finally Paula, the ringleader said, 'Nothing. Nothing you need to know about. Just hanging about. You got any fags?'

He shook his head.

'You,' he said, and squinted at me, as if I was very far away, 'I know you, though, don't I?'

'Do you?'

It was my own fault. I was just trying to be clever. Paula whistled and the others laughed, which if I'm properly honest with myself was the sort of response that I wanted. Wanted her to see me being cool with him. In charge and not shy and out of my depth, which is actually what I was really feeling like, deep down inside.

'I reckon I do,' he said, and smiled. Like he knew I was only pretending. I should have just gone home.

'Have you fucked him?' she said. She jumped off the swing and pushed mine sideways, so I was rocking then. I started feeling sick. I stopped it with my feet, and stared at the man.

I did know him a bit, I thought – or I knew his voice, at least. But then maybe I was just thinking that because he said so, because he sounded so sure. I can't say that I recognised him, not for certain.

'I'm Lewis,' he said. 'I know your brother. I seen you, you came with him once, didn't you?'

'You know our Gary?'

'T'other one.'

'I don't go anywhere with Julian,' I said.

He laughed. 'Suit yourself then. Do you want a bag of chips?'

He never even looked at Paula or her friends. And the way he said it: so everyone knew he was talking to me and not to them. Singled me out, and I felt like my head would explode, my face felt so hot. Just me.

'Ooh! He's asking her out. That Ginger's asking Creepy Jeannie out for a bag of chips!' Paula and the others started to cackle, and gather around me, laughing and jostling. 'Are you going to go? Going to go out and get some chips with your new sexy boyfriend? He's delish, isn't he?' Paula stuck her fingers in her mouth and made gagging noises. 'He's gorgeous.'

Lewis didn't look at her, but kept his eyes on me.

'You can stay here with this lot if you really want to,' he said, half smiling, 'don't let me interrupt.'

I didn't say anything for a long time until he shrugged again and started to walk away, and then Paula elbowed me in the side and said, 'He wants to get off with you,' and because I didn't answer straight off she pushed me in the back and·I fell off the swing, forward and heavy onto the soles of my feet. Creepy Jeannie. That's what they were calling me. And not like they'd just made it up on the spur of the moment to try and get to me, to show me up in front of this man, but like they'd spoken about me before. Lots of times. And when they did they called me Creepy Jeannie. Lewis turned around, smiled at me and pushed open the spring-loaded gate to the play park.

'Come on then,' he said, 'I'll buy you a bag of chips and take you home.'

I might not have gone, but then he said, 'You shouldn't be hanging around with all this lot,' and because I knew he was right, I walked away from the swing and got my feet wet and all the girls behind me whistled and whoo-whooed and laughed as I walked after him.

13.54. Beth presses her frizzy hair against her head with the flat of her hand and grins at me.

'My older sisters have got a bet going,' she says, 'they reckon your Gary will be married before Christmas.'

I stare at her. Why can't she just make her bird house and shut up? It won't even be a real bet. We're not allowed to bet. But they'll have it written down somewhere, their prediction, names signed in the back of someone's journal in loopy, girly handwriting. Helen, Beth's oldest sister, has been writing to Gary since he went out. She sends care packages once a month. Socks with chocolate bars and pictures of herself tucked inside them. She's obvious – she does it every single time a missionary from our stake goes out and she's twenty-five now and what good has it done her?

'What did you bet?' I ask her. She isn't going to shut up. Never does. So you may as well join in.

'Well, I've got insider information,' she says, and pats the side of her nose. 'Poor Carole. I've said two years. Maybe even three.'

It was Gary's idea to keep his feelings for Carole quiet. Not that he'd done anything to be ashamed of – he always told me himself that he'd never be in a room alone with her, never say anything to her that he wouldn't feel comfortable saying if Jesus was standing right there with him. There's no rule against kissing, not really. But Gary said that keeping the rules was like driving a car along a cliff edge. You don't, he said, see how close you can get to the boundary, but you pride yourself, if pride is the right word, on keeping as far away from the danger at the edge as you can.

So I don't reckon he's ever even kissed her. But he didn't need to. Anyone could tell. He'd smile when he talked about her, find excuses to bring her name up and shush people who whispered while she was bearing her testimony. Anyone who had eyes could see that he had plans for the two of them. He let me in on the secret, though. Just before he went. Telling me to look out for a nice dress. See what colour Carole and her sisters liked best for bridesmaids. Blushing like his head was on fire, and grinning so much he could hardly talk. It was a nice thing for me to think about while he was away. To have something to look forward to.

We thought we'd managed to keep it from Mum – which was the main reason for Gary wanting to be discreet, really, he didn't want the drama and the hassle – but when Carole started to fall away and then turned up back at church three dress sizes bigger than she had been when she left, Mum was frantic, going round making sure no one would mention it in a letter to Gary. There hadn't to be any distractions at all. So she must have guessed anyway. Beth did. And the bishop always says you can't bank on keeping a secret in our ward. We're extended family to each other and that's how it should be.

'It might not make any difference,' I say, and Beth snorts at me, like I'm too stupid to understand about sex, and getting pregnant, and the sort of things returned missionaries are looking for when they come home.

'Course it will,' Beth says. 'She doesn't even keep church standards any more.'

Church standards are the reason, I think, I am best friends with Beth and not any of the other girls in my class. Even though she's smug and always has been and it's bad to say so but I don't even like her that much. It's just easier not to have to explain things all the time. Like the way we've got to be careful about how we dress. We don't stand out, but it's easy enough to tell when someone isn't doing it right. We have been advised, for example, to check our appearance standing, leaning, bending, reaching and sitting, before leaving the house. There's a full-length mirror on our landing at home – a crack across the bottom of it because Julian got sick of jumping at the sight of himself as he jogged up the stairs and lobbed a shoe at it one morning.

Young women should wear only one pair of earrings, if they must have their ears pierced. Hairstyles should be modest, and not draw undue attention. Short skirts, low or sleeveless tops are out – that goes without saying. We don't wear them yet, but one day we will, so we should get used to a manner of dress that takes seriously our covenant to wear a temple garment. Modest attire includes refraining from the wearing of clothing that in its fit or construction draws attention to the form of the girl. Most of us like to wear tights to school and leave our hair long, but there's no written rule about that. No trousers for church for women, or on Sundays at all, really. I don't know anyone who ever dared. Investigators, yes, but the bishopric always notice and usually get Sister Jackson or Maggie to have a quiet word about it, just to let them know what the church standards are.

They always tell me I am lucky because I've been born in the covenant so I've been able to pick these things up from when I was a baby. But that also means that there's more pressure, says Mum, on me to get things right. Which doesn't seem fair when you're pitted against converts who have every little thing spelled out to them so they won't mess up, but the whole reason I was born in the covenant and didn't have to find the gospel later in life and convert was because I was valiant in the pre-existence. Not a week goes past where someone or other does not remind me of it. So more is expected.

There are tips in the *New Era*. Like kneeling on the floor to make sure your skirt touches it. Standing in front of a bright light and spreading your arms and legs so you can make sure the silhouette of your body doesn't show. Sister missionaries have the highest dress standards. Modest, but attractive. We should all try to dress like them. It's important not to be frumpy. People mustn't think LDS women are out of touch, or unfashionable. We all want to get married, don't we? The older women like to wear cardigans and long skirts. Maxi dresses with long-sleeved tee-shirts underneath. There's some confusion about open-toed shoes and nail varnish. We await guidance from the Prophet, the bishop and our fathers. Women can fellowship each other in this area. There are *What I Wore to Church Today* Flickr groups. Facebook pages: *Modest is Hottest*.

So not many actual rules. Mainly it's about checking the way you feel. Like, would you wear this if you knew the bishop would be there to see you? What about Jesus? Would he be pleased to see one of his sweet sisters decked out in black eyeliner with red streaks in her hair? They might not give you a black and white list of what you're actually allowed to do (which is why you'll sometimes see American Mormons drinking Coke) but they do their best to help you learn to feel the right way: to feel bad at the right time. To notice when the Spirit leaves you because you're not dressed properly. By, say, taking you out of your lesson, or a dance, for a loving word if you don't look right. By showing concern, and passing a little note along the row at sacrament meeting. *I'm sure you're not aware of this but I just thought you'd like to know that split in your skirt is showing the back of your knees and beyond. In sisterly love, a friend.* We sit in rows, plucking at our blouses to make sure our bra straps don't show. Girls in short skirts don't get asked to do the opening prayer. The boys don't speak to them. Men respect those who respect themselves. Poor Carole.

I almost always check. I do. But the day I went to the park, I didn't. Just ran out of the house, grabbing Julian's big grey hoodie from where it was draped over the upstairs banister, and slammed the door against the rising noise of the argument. When I got home I went into the bathroom and put my head under the cold tap. Mum was moaning outside. I stared at myself in the cracked mirror. Pulled my wet hair out of my eyes. Rubbed the sore place on my neck. Looked hard into my own face as if I could see what was missing. Tights snagged on one knee. But nothing else.

'Helen'll have a fit if your Gary takes up with Carole again anyway,' Beth says, and shakes her head, scandalised. 'Mum had to buy her tickets for Eurodisney when the other missionary – the one from Leeds – fell through at the last minute.'

I clatter tools about, sweep shavings onto the floor, pretend I can't hear her. But she stares at me, Mum in miniature, enjoying herself and demanding an answer.

'Well, Helen better start looking around,' I say. 'Gary's not like that. He's very forgiving and understanding.'

I'll explain to him about the rain. That it had started to rain and I got soaked and hadn't planned for that. He'll understand. The paper wrapping up the chips got wet and started to stick and tear in my hands. Lewis had a pie and he'd peeled back the foil tray it came in. We stood in a bus shelter and he took a great bite of it, found it too hot and tried to suck air in around it through his half-open mouth. It didn't work, and he spat out his mouthful on the pavement.

'Fucking hell,' he said, 'free skin graft with every frigging pie.'

'Do you want some orange?' I offered him my can, he'd bought me it, hadn't he? He took it off me, drank half of what was left in three massive swallows, and then gave it me back.

'Ta.'

For a while we just stood there, watching the cars go past in the rain, the occasional bit of blue showing between the clouds.

'Thanks for the chips.'

'Your brother wouldn't want you out on your own. Not hanging out with that lot.'

I didn't say anything. Julian could keep what he did and didn't want to himself.

'He wouldn't be pleased with me if he found out I'd walked past you and not even offered you a lift home.'

'I can walk home.'

'Not in this weather, you can't,' he said.

I didn't know if we were waiting on a bus, or just sheltering. The puddles on the pavement widened and the water ran down the Perspex windows of the bus stop. Far away a rumble or two of thunder, and I wondered how Mum and Dad were getting on, but although the storm came to nothing and there was no lightning to come, the rain didn't stop either and the insides of the Perspex got steamed up.

I picked at my chips.

'You done with them?'

I nodded and he took the polystyrene tray out of my hands and started throwing the rest of the chips into his mouth, two or three at a time. I watched him while he ate, his tongue moving, his jaw working.

'I'd better go,' I said. 'Thanks for the chips and that. It was dead nice of you. Those girls aren't really my friends. But my mum doesn't know I'm out.'

He smiled.

'Doesn't she? You sneak out on your own?'

'Just wanted a bit of space.'

'Come on,' he says, 'you look like you've been swimming. I'll take you back to my work and let you get towelled off before I drive you home. You can't go home like that, can you? She'll know you snuck out as soon as she looks at you.'

There was a car in the garage he took me to. I don't know what kind it was. Blue, I think. The bonnet was up, and the back door on the driver's side was open. He said it wasn't safe to turn the engine on because of the fumes, but we'd be all right just sitting in it, in the dark. That I'd soon warm up, and he couldn't find a towel but there was a red tartan blanket that came with the car, and did I want to use that instead.

14.09. You're supposed to start with a sketch of what you want your bird house to be like, then you decide how big you want it to be and from that work out the sizes of the bits of wood you are going to need. It all needs to be done properly, and before you're allowed to start you need to hand in a list to Mr Teasdale with a list of wood and any other bits and pieces – glue, screws, hinges for the lid, everything. If he doesn't think it's right, he won't tell you, but get you to make a model of it using scaled-down bits of balsa wood, just to check. He says that's what's teaching is all about. Letting us make our own mistakes and learning from the consequences. Creating a learning environment where the failure is as fruitful as success, if we've got eyes to see it. Even if your bird house falls apart, you can still get full marks by writing a good evaluation that works out what you did wrong and says how you will do it better next time.

Balsa wood is weird. It feels like polystyrene, and if you bite it, you leave a mark from your teeth in it. I missed that week. I was feeling bad, and instead of coming to the lesson I went outside and walked along the cross-country route on my own. I didn't get caught, and because I never get in any sort of trouble I can stretch it a bit now, and no one at school even thought to ask where I'd been.

'Just ill,' I said, 'sorry, sir,' and he nodded and put a zero in his register and told me to get the wood from the racks in the room off the main classroom. I did, and we left it at that.

I have been watching out for any sort of difference in the way I feel. I've looked things up. It could be a mistake, some problem with the tests or something I've been eating that makes my pee funny. But this morning I had that bad taste in my mouth again. And there's a humming or a vibration between my hips. The crackle of something electrical happening. I am certain it can't be my imagination. I suck myself in as I walk past Mr Teasdale with my half-finished bird house in my arms.

The bird house is going to have a sloped roof and, just for kicks (*before*, there was such a thing as jokes, and kicks, and bird houses that felt important, *before* the park, *before* the Easter holidays), I cut a little bit off the end of a piece of balsa. Measured the angle, and set the mitre at forty-five degrees so that after I sawed it, I could glue it onto the sloped side of the roof. A chimney.

14.26. Mr Teasdale comes past my bench just as I'm holding the sawn edge of the wood against the roof, checking that I've measured the angles right and it fits properly. It does. He smiles.

'Are you going to put central heating in there as well, Jeannie?' he says. 'Maybe bob next door to textiles and get Mrs Underton to run you up a little pair of curtains, eh? Home sweet home.'

14.28. I blush, even though I know he's only joking. I'm not stupid – I know better than he does now that what I'm doing is silly and I know something else that he doesn't – Mum is scared of birds and if I give her this she'll keep it in the kitchen and use it to put wooden spoons in. It will end up trimmed with lace and sitting on top of a cabinet somewhere.

'How are you going to stick it on?'

'I was wondering if I could have a bit of wood glue, sir?'

Mr Teasdale doesn't like us using wood glue. He says it's an overused resource and something lazy joiners turn to who don't trust themselves with a drill bit. He taught us, in the first lesson, how to check the joints on a drawer or a chair, to tap on the inside of a kitchen cupboard, to inspect the dovetail and dowel joints on park benches. He doesn't like short cuts. He says you're only allowed to cut corners once you've learned to steer your way around them. He means if there's a hard way to do something, that's the way we need to do it.

'You'd be better screwing it in,' he says, 'I'll go and get you what you need.'

Beth pulls a face at me. 'Can you be bothered?'

I shrug. 'We're here for another hour whether I mess about with the bird house or not. I might as well do something.'

Beth is further ahead than me, because she didn't skip the week before the holidays, like I did. She has a paper cup on the bench next to her, into which Mr Teasdale has decanted some black wood stain. She's messily slopping the stain about into the joints, dripping it everywhere.

'Here you are.' Mr Teasdale puts a screwdriver and two or three screws and plugs on the bench next to me. 'It's good practice,' he says, 'but give it here and I'll drill it first with the machine, to get you started.'

I watch as he takes the box over to the pillar drill and slots it into place, clipping it steady and then pulling his goggles up from around his neck before leaning in and using the pedal to set the drill going. The noise is a high-pitched whine – designed to drive you nuts – and the sawdust flies off in little flurries, powdering his hands and falling against the plastic protective shield around the bit.

I don't know why they have this here; we're never allowed to use it. They just make the first years stand next to it and tell them gory stories about what happened to some girl years ago who disobeyed the safety rules and had her finger ripped off because she was wearing a ring that got caught in the spinning mechanism the drill bit is embedded in. Or that other girl, maybe the fingerless girl's best friend, who lost her hair and most of her scalp after she decided to disobey the rule about having your hair tied back in the workshop at all times.

Mr Teasdale takes the house out of the clasp, blows into the tiny hole he's made through the roof, and then passes it back to me. 'Let me know if you have trouble,' he says, 'it's a tricky angle, that is.'

14.37. Beth is still sloshing wood stain about when I get back to the bench. It's smeared on the back of her hand and spattered over the front of her canvas apron. She holds up the house, getting more stain on her shirt cuffs, and looking at it carefully.

'I think you missed a spot,' I say, and she looks at me, lips jammed together. 'Joke.'

'Ha. Ha.'

I pick up the screwdriver and examine it. The handle is a moulded lump of hard transparent yellow plastic, its edges slightly scuffed. There's a blob of Tipp-Ex on the end and a number written onto it. 8C. It must mean something – the place in the tool cupboard this screwdriver lives, its home in a set of ten, or the point in the curriculum they reckon we're tame enough to be allowed to handle it. The number doesn't mean anything to me. The metal end is thin and straight and very shiny.

I want to be able to say to you, Gary, that I did everything possible. I like the feel of it in my hand and put it into the pocket on the front of my apron as the bell rings.

14.40.

PAULINE

The taxi driver drops me off outside the tall red-brick building of the library. I get him to take my card out to the machine across the road. 'One two one two,' I tell him. Martin's and my anniversary – the year and the month. Testing, testing, he said, when we set the date. 'Are you sure, love?' The taxi driver talks too loud, as if the chair makes me deaf and dumb as well as big and slow. It's not ideal, but none of this is. 'Don't argue, just get over the road and get your money out. Don't be all day about it either!' He unfastens his seat belt instead of answering. We're parked on the edge of the road and the traffic moves quickly around me. Even through the glass I can hear engines thrumming and car radios leaking noise into the air. Kids no older than Jeannie pushing prams, yanking on the arms of sticky-faced toddlers, thin lips clamped round cigarettes. The things they wear. Leggings that look like they've been painted on, and shiny tops with necklines scooped out so low it makes you wonder why they bother putting them on in the first place. 'Here you are.' The driver counts the notes slowly in front of me as if he's afraid I'm going to ring up the taxi firm as soon as I get home and accuse him of swindling the infirm. 'I had to leave the meter on for the loading and unloading,' he says, 'the ramp, you see. It takes a while.' He looks away. 'So it comes to eight-fifty. Righto?' Half of next week's gas money out of the jar and gone, just like that, on a taxi ride, when most of the members in the Ward have able bodies and working cars! Maggie should have offered a lift – she's no kiddies at home now, what else has she got to do during the day? The wheels of the chair are rough against my hands. Martin usually pushes me when we go out. It's not easy and it's only when the taxi driver has pulled away and made the turn at the bottom of the road towards the leisure centre that I realise I should have booked him for the way home. That Jeannie! I saw on a telly programme that in most supermarkets they pipe the smell from the bakery through the vents and puff it out at you at the front door to make you hungry as soon as you get in, but the magic works even when you know how the trick is done, doesn't it? 'Can I help you at all?' A young woman with a familiar look about her approaches me as soon as I pass through the automatic doors. I'm not keen on the idea of someone following me around with a basket. I've got my pencil and paper and you'd be embarrassed to do your totting up in front of a stranger, wouldn't you? I'm looking about for the Inconvenience, trying to figure out the quickest way to get to it from various corners in the supermarket if it comes on me sudden, like it always does. 'I can manage,' I say, looking at the shelves and aisles and not really knowing if I will. There's the usual Ladies and Gents, a baby change, but they've tucked the disabled toilet around a corner somewhere and I can't see it. 'What about one of these?' She points, and smiles. She's got a lovely set of teeth. Peaches and cream skin. Pity she's not a member or she'd do very nicely for our Gary. She's pointing at a little three-wheeled car with a shopping basket on the front of it. 'They're dead easy to work,' she says, and laughs, 'I've had a go on one myself. It's fun!' I'll decide what's fun or not, thanks very much. 'They don't go that fast. You can put all your shopping in the front of it. Save your arms. And we'll lock up your own chair here for you.' She points again, to a little row of metal arms screwed into the wall with shiny chains and padlocks attached to them. 'Go on, give it a try,' she says, and smiles like she's telling me to help myself to a box of chocolates. It does look very swish, though. Nice and narrow, for getting through the tills, which was one thing that was on my mind. I don't know if Richardson's is just that sort of shop, or she's giving special attention to me. I am sure I don't know her. 'There's no charge for it, no deposit or anything,' she says, and holds out her arm. 'Tell me what help you need and we'll get you settled on one of these. They're brilliant.' 'Go on then,' I say. She's that nice you can't help but smile at her. 'Good!' She acts like a daughter should: helping me out of my chair and into the scooter, chatting to me about the weather and the special deals on the meat and fish counters while she makes sure my skirt is tucked in nicely. 'You put your feet here,' she taps my shoes, 'and your hands up here. And when you want to go in a certain direction, just turn the wheels. It's easy.' 'It is, isn't it?' 'And your handbag will fit in there on the front. And look at this,' she grins, and pulls up a tiny metal clipboard attached to the wheel. There's even a pen attached to it. 'You've brought a list,' she says, 'put it on here under that clip so you can cross things off as you go along.' I do, and no one stares. 'It's not bad this, is it?' I say, moving it backwards and forwards on the spot by pressing with my foot, just to get the hang. And when I say that, this girl's little face lights up from inside and she looks that pleased with herself I almost want to cuddle her. For the first time since I left the house I can feel my heartbeat go back to its usual speed. 'Just give me a shout if there's anything you can't find,' she says, and heads back to her flowers. Jeannie could learn a thing or two from this one, I think, as I give her a little wave and set off into the shop. Soup first. I zoom off and hunt out the tins aisle. Jeannie's been getting worse. Half of it's her age, but the other half of it is sheer bloody-mindedness. She never pays me the blindest bit of notice. And I have tried. She thinks I don't know what it's like to be a young woman in these Latter Days. Times more dark and more wicked, holding more temptation for the Youth than any other time in the world's history. 'But that's not any excuse for your gallivanting,' I told her. 'The rot stops here!

There's no excuse for coming home after dark in a state like this.' She just cried, ran up the stairs and shut herself in the bathroom. I shouted up after her, and the cheeky cat poked her head out of the door and shouted back! 'Just leave me alone!' she said. 'I never ask for anything except to be left alone!' 'I'll go up and speak to her,' I said to Martin, 'through her door if I've got to.' We were watching *Family Fortunes*, and he turned the sound off and frowned at me. 'Leave her, Pauline. She knows what she wants. A bit of peace and solitude. Let her cool down and she'll come to you in her own time.' 'Martin,' I said, 'you wouldn't expect me to stand by and watch her put her hand into a fire, and I'm not prepared to stand by and watch her throw herself into the very jaws of mortal danger either. Help me up them stairs.' 'She needs comforting, not criticising,' Martin said. 'She'll have fallen out with Beth. Take her some ice cream up and give her a fiver.' 'Do I tell you how best to do your round? To sort the letters? To deal with parcels? Do I encroach on your area of expertise?' I said. He didn't answer. 'Well, do I?' Eventually, he saw my point and shook his head. We'd already had a set-to that evening to do with the wretched state of the drapery in the front room and I could see that he wasn't in the mood for another. Half of marriage is persever-ance – that's what I tell the young sisters once they get engaged. Never give up. There's always something better on the other side of a disagreement, and resolved arguments are the glue that hold a family together. I got Martin to help me up the stairs. 'It's not right to sneak off and keep things to yourself,' I said. No answer. 'I'm your mother, and I've got a right to know what kind of situations you've been putting yourself into.' The bathroom door was locked, and I rattled the handle and listened to the water running. 'Your dad's turned the immersion off again,' I told her, 'so don't think you're lying in there soaking all night. You'll have to come out some time.' I knew full well she could hear me because I'd had to do the same thing with

Julian during his teenage years. Gary was never a bit of trouble, but Jeannie forgets the hassle I had with her brother, and what an old hand I am at dealing with situations like this. I waited for a few seconds, looking at the peeling stickers of pink unicorns and fairies that she had stuck to her bedroom door. 'You only need to look at your life to know how privileged you are. What a valiant spirit you were in the pre-existence. You're a lucky girl. The Lord sent you down here to a family of members, in the oldest Stake in the world. Literally minutes from the temple you're going to get married in. You're white, you can read and write and *unlike some of us* you've got your health and strength. A lot's been bestowed on you.' I heard the taps going off, and before I could get myself ready for it, she flung the door open. Her hair was wet and dripping onto her face. I used to have red hair so long I could sit on it, and a man in Southport bus station once offered to pay me forty pounds if I'd let him run his fingers through it. I was well known for my hair, actually. People used to say I was stunning. The memory comes back to me, just like that, out of nowhere, and I couldn't tell you why I cut it all off after having Jeannie except it seemed more practical. 'Take your school uniform off, will you? It needs hanging up. Sort your hair out. You're a right mess.' She just stared at me. 'Jeannie? Are you listening to me?' Silence. 'Is it your friends? Have you fallen out with someone at school?' No answer, but she moved past me quickly and went into her bedroom. Shut the door. I heard her bed creak. No point trying the handle; she puts a chair against it when she's in a mood like this. 'Not Beth, is it?' Nothing. 'Non-member friends? Jeannie, my love,' I sighed, and waited for inspiration. Girls can be cruel. It's all about belonging, being in the right crowd. 'There's always groups, things everyone thinks you've got to be part of. It's all very well and good if belonging means having the right trainers or backpack or haircut. No one wants to stand out. It's natural enough. But you can't,' I heard her move again, 'get too concerned with all that. One day it's trainers, the next it's pierced ears, late nights and inappropriate behaviour. Not wrong themselves, but a step on that slippery slope. Actions that send out the wrong message. There's a reason why we don't let you do these things.' 'Pauline?' Martin shouted up the stairs. 'Your programme is starting.' I waited for a few more seconds, my hand against the door. I could cry over it all, I really could, but being in the world and not of it is a hard lesson to learn, and she's got to learn it, and she might as well start now. 'You're too stubborn. That's your problem,' I said, losing my patience. 'There are people around you watching over you, who love you, who are just dying to be asked for a bit of help and guidance. But no. You know it all already, don't you?' Muffled sounds from inside. Is she laughing at me? Or crying, could be either. I gave up. When she's decided she's keeping something to herself, you couldn't crowbar her gob open. She'd probably stuck her head under the pillow. I smiled. Heavenly Father makes us into parents so we can understand his frustrations when he speaks in his still, small voice to us, trying to turn us away from sin. We have children so we can learn to be better children to him. Have I ever been guilty of putting my head under the pillow? 'Suit yourself then, sulky.' I banged on the floor and Martin came up to help me back down the stairs. 'I'm going to get Bishop Jackson to talk to her,' I said, once we were settled on the couch. 'Why not wait until Gary gets back?' Martin said, and that was the first bit of sense I had out of him all night. 'I don't want to leave it that long,' I said, 'I want to know what she's up to.' 'It's only three weeks now. Once he's settled in we can lend him the car and get him to take her out on a drive. He'll talk to her.' 'I'll try it,' I said, thinking, though not saying, that Gary would be a better choice than Bishop Jackson anyway, because Bishop Jackson would only consult Maggie because he'd want a woman's opinion on the matter, and then Maggie would come to me and want to know why I hadn't spoken to her myself. And I had enough of all that off her when we had our trouble with Julian and he became inactive. I'm not planning to go through it again with Jeannie. Gary will get it out of her. Three tins of soup, and now onto tuna. Jeannie says we've to get the line-caught kind or she won't eat it, but I haven't time to be stood here staring at labels and the price of it has got astronomical recently. She can have all the ethics she likes when she's putting something into the pot, and not before. John West's will do. Two tins of Campbell's Condensed. Better make that three, actually. They know me, never knowingly undercatered. All I ask from her in the way of contribution is a bit of help around the house, some assistance now and again. It should not be too much to ask. She couldn't even be bothered to turn up at home today like she said she would. I have a ticklish feeling, a bothered, can't leave it alone sort of thought, that Jeannie is dancing too close to the line and is going to get herself in trouble. There's one thing going for Richardson's, and that is that it's a supermarket that attracts the better sort of person. Even the staff march up and down the aisles in nice little green aprons with matching checked shirts and fleeces. That girl from the front has peeped around the aisle once or twice just to give me a big thumbs-up and a smile. I'm not that sure that I don't actually know her, she might be a less active member trying to find a way back, so I make sure to give her a smile and a little wave whenever I see her. But it is pricey in here. And this scooter thing is absolutely brilliant. Might as well get my money's worth. The engine on it – well, it'd be a battery but you know what I mean – is near enough silent, and as I work the pedals and turn the handlebars to negotiate the turn at the end of each aisle, I wonder what's been keeping me in the house this long, and why Julian's never thought to build me one of these things for myself. I bet Maggie's sons would just club together and buy her one – top of the range – if she was in need. The soft music and the clean floors soothe me. I'm not half as nervous as I was. The thing is, I could be, gliding up and down the aisles and price-checking tins of soup and different sorts of crusty bread, the same as any other shopper here. Who knew how many different colours and shapes of pasta there was these days? And organic – a full thirty pee more! As if they charge you extra for leaving something out. I get the long and thin kind – not spaghetti, but the flat one. It's our Gary's favourite. O heavens! It comes upon me too quick, even though I promised myself I wouldn't let myself get distracted, would keep my eyes peeled for the Inconvenience, would come up with a plan, a strategy, an order of events. O! I look about in desperation. People shuffling about, too slow, with their trolleys. A pair of kiddies sliding up and down the polished floors on their knees. Beep beep at the checkouts. Someone else blocking the way with a sample tray. No I don't want to try the latest Cathedral City, thanks very much! Pray to God they have a disabled lavvy wide enough to take my chair, or the scooter. I daren't think about how I'm going to get myself from the scooter to the chair and from the chair to the toilet without making a mess, and I can already feel the inco-pad has taken about as much as it is going to, so no help there. I try and make myself breathe slowly, but the air isn't right – it's dry and sterile – tastes like cold plastic and frozen peas because I'm right at the freezer section and inhaling the warm draughts coming out of their ventilation units like outbreaths. I can feel my blood bubbling about in my chest and through the veins in my neck and cheeks like water coming to the boil. My hands tremble and I make a mistake with the scooter, turning the handlebars this way when I mean the other way. I ram the bottom of a wire display of KitKats, and before I can do anything about it, the packets slither downwards and under the wheels. I grab tight onto the handlebar and try and lean down to pick them up, but my pain comes back and I make a little groan and then straighten up quickly, trying not to draw attention to myself. Too late, a man no older than Gary, wearing a green apron and holding a pricing gun in one hand, turns around. 'Can I help you?' In a few moments, it's going to be too late. I can feel the pressure building like a bubble working up to pop. 'No! Everything's fine. Just go away!' And now it really is too late. I hunch over my tummy and wave at him with an outstretched arm as, before I can stop it, a bowel movement happens. I whimper a bit becuse the pain is back and I don't have my towel to bite on but the man talking to me can't see what's happening, and just stares at me and the KitKats, all confused. 'Are you looking for anything in particular?' he asks, glancing inside the basket attached to the front of the scooter. The little things inside it look ridiculous and small now. I should have bought a leg of lamb and had done with it. Soup. Tuna. Pasta. Martin could have got it all from the corner shop. I could have dipped into our food storage. I don't like to do it because the day is nigh and no one knows when we'll be needing these things. But all the same. I didn't have to make such a fuss over it. That Jeannie! Tears spill down my cheeks. I can feel the loose movement underneath me, moving across, behind and in front. I can smell it, and any minute he is going to notice the dark patches soaking through my clothes and smell it too. There's something hot on the back of my leg and I try not to move. 'Would you like me to —' 'I don't need any help! What's wrong with you? Go away!' The only thing for it is to get past him with the scooter, somehow, and get out of Richardson's. I buckle down and press down on the pedal, hard. I could ride the scooter all the way home if I needed to. If the battery held out. Just get out of here, and get home where Martin and Jeannie can give me a hand. It wouldn't be stealing – I'd get Jeannie to clean the scooter up properly and Julian could fix it up if the tyres needed replacing or the battery needed some jiggery-pokery. Then Martin would bring it back and explain and it would be all right. And I'd never, ever come in here again. I pass people, and they stop shopping and stare at me a bit but I don't care because I'm nearly at the doors. 'Excuse me, madam?' The man in the apron has jogged ahead and he's there again, standing between me and the doors, his arms out slightly either side of him as if he's afraid I'm going to ram him. 'Just – just shut up!' I say, and my voice cracks. 'Madam,' he says quietly, 'I can't let you leave the store with the scooter. As it says,' he points to the sign screwed to the side of the basket, 'it remains the property of the store at all times. You need to come over to the checkout and pay for your purchases.' I try and go round him. I'm nearly there, too – I can feel the breeze on my face from where it comes in between the automatic glass doors but then he sidesteps and catches hold of the basket on the front. 'Out of my way! You're going to need to move! I need to get past you!' 'I'm afraid I can't . . .' The wheels spin and I bat at his hands a bit, but he won't let go. 'Shoo! Shoo!' He frowns, braces himself against the front of the scooter, then his face changes shape completely because he's seen now, what a disgusting mess I've made of myself. 'Please. I need to go home right now!' Outside the main supermarket there's a wide lobby with a kiosk for cigarettes and magazines. There's an atrium and this part of the shop is lovely and bright. There's also racks of potted plants and flowers for sale, and maybe because I'm so aware of the filthy smell clinging to me, the aroma of lilies and primulas becomes overwhelming. 'Have you not got a mother of your own?' 'I don't see what that has to do with it.' There's another member of staff kneeling over the flowers, watering them or dead-heading them, and she looks up at me and I realise it's the nice girl, just as I see Maggie's grey head and camel-coloured coat over by the news kiosk. Maggie! Maggie Travers! An answered prayer is the sweetest thing! The man is still pulling at the scooter and shouting for someone to come and help him, to call the police or something, and I shout for her, relief flooding through me like a drug. 'Maggie! Maggie! Come and help me!' I realise I am sobbing. 'Maggie!' She turns and looks at me. She has her purse in one hand and a Galaxy Caramel and a copy of *The People's Friend* tucked into the other. She frowns and I see her eyes move from my face to my stained lap and then back up again. 'Maggie!' It's not ideal, but she's a Sister, and she'll help me. She should have come with me in the first place. That's what happens in Relief Society. We support each other, we bear each other's burdens. 'Maggie! It's me! It's Pauline! Come over here and help me with something, will you?' The shop assistant is tugging on the side of the scooter. His walkie-talkie is in his hand. I ignore the people who are staring at me and just smile at him. 'It's fine now. My friend is here. It's all just a very minor misunderstanding.' I look back up, expecting to see Maggie heading towards me, maybe even digging about for her mobile phone to call us in some back-up. But she's where she was, frozen by the counter. She can't *not* have seen me. Everyone in the whole shop has had a good stare by now. 'Maggie?' Maggie's recognised me all right, but she moves her eyes away and ducks her head as she tucks her purse into her handbag and then click-clacks over the hard shiny floor and out through the automatic doors towards Market Walk. I am speechless with shock, and the scooter stutters and stalls, and the man puts his hand on my arm and before I know what has happened I've picked up one of the tins from the front of the basket and lobbed it at him. I feel it leave my hand but I can't say the action was mine. It hits him on the forehead, on his eyebrow, and before it's hit the floor and stopped rolling blood unfurls itself down his face like a little red flag. There's a shocking silence, and he takes his apron off, screws it up in a ball and holds it against his head. 'I . . .' I start talking, but I can't think of anything to say. He leans over and does something with the walkie-talkie on his belt. 'Madam,' he says firmly, 'the police have been called.

142

We take all disturbances, assaults of staff and shoplifting or attempts at shoplifting,' he looks down at my lap and gags slightly, 'very seriously.' 'That was my friend, over there,' I say, 'she's just gone.' The woman who was dealing with the flowers has straightened up and I'm right, it is the nice one who set me up with the blasted scooter. 'Ant? Ant,' she says, 'are you all right?' She comes over and takes hold of the apron and pulls it away. He lets her look, and she's up on tiptoe staring at his head. Blood patters onto the floor. 'You'll live,' she says, 'it's just a little cut.' 'A cut! I've been assaulted!' I feel my mess getting cold against my legs. The longer it's on me, the more likely it is to give me inflammation, like a baby, and I can already feel my scar and my raw skin starting to sting. 'Calm down, Ant. You're all right. You don't need to get the police here really, do you? Look at her. She's ill. You send her to the police, and her picture will be on the front of tomorrow's *Chorley Guardian*. What's Tina going to say about that? *Great managerial potential, Ant. I'll leave you in charge more often.* I don't think so.' 'Get back to your flowers and leave this to me. I don't need you telling me what to do with my own store.' 'Have a bit of pity. She's sobbing her heart out here. Its two tins of dented soup and nothing a bottle of disinfectant and a bucket of hot water won't fix. I'll do it myself. If you call the police she'll be there all afternoon.' 'She should have thought about that before throwing hard produce at me, shouldn't she?' he says sniffily, and walks away out of the doors with his hand still to his head. She follows him and I see her gesturing towards me, their two figures dark in the light coming in through the glass. Because they are standing so near, the doors swish open and closed while they're talking. 'Look. I know the family. She's not well. She shouldn't even be out.' 'You know her? She's just *shat herself*.' 'She can't help it. She's dying. Come on, let me borrow the van and take her home.' Ant shakes his head. I'm dying? *Dying?* She sounds so certain that my head starts to pound, as if to reassure me that it's still working properly, the blood moving in and out, heating up my face and making my ears tingle. I hoick my chin up and grip very tightly to the handles of the scooter. People can stare all they want. Staring doesn't hurt you. But dying? Who said I was dying? Ant moves away from her, nearer to the automatic doors. Customers edge around him, tutting, but he doesn't notice. He's not leaving the shop, just standing in the entryway, looking backwards and forwards along the street and across the market as if he's hoping the police will arrive in a nice big riot van, with dogs and batons and electricity stun guns. I close my eyes for a second and murmur a prayer. You're not supposed to make bargains with Heavenly Father but I do it anyway. Gary home safe, first of all. And if this, today's humiliation, is what is takes – then fair enough. Fair deal. What mother wouldn't shake hands on that? But if I could, Father, if I could just get on home now, as quick as possible, without any more drama. Well, I'd be grateful. I'd like that to happen. When I open my eyes the nice girl from before has come back. She's young, and kind, and she has lovely clear skin – like someone from a magazine. Even close up there's not an open pore on her. 'He's not usually this much of a twat.' She doesn't sound like an answered prayer, but beggars can't be choosers. 'I don't feel very well.' I say, with as much dignity as I can. 'I know you don't. But don't worry,' she says, and rubs my arm. 'We're going to sort it out. He's only like this because it's the first time he's been left in charge.' She rubs my arm again, and it gets annoying, but I don't want to move myself out of her reach in case it hurts her feelings. 'The thing is, you're going to have to go to the police station. He won't let me talk him out of it.' I know people are still staring, but I'm so numb I can hardly work up the energy to mind about it now. 'I'm going to get arrested?' She smiles calmly. 'You did throw a tin at him.' I could explain, but what's the point? 'Listen, it doesn't matter. I'll come with you. And once you get to the station, it will all be sorted out really quickly. Last week there was a scally left here with three blocks of cheese and seven packets of bacon in his trousers and he'd done it before but he only got a little fine.' She keeps her eyes fixed tight to my eyes when she talks to me, like you do with someone who's got scars or a birthmark. 'I've got to go to the police station? Inside a cell? Like this?' 'Shall I ring Martin for you?' she asks. 'How do you know Martin?' I feel like I've started watching this three episodes in. What else have I missed? 'You're Gary's mum, aren't you?' She dips into her fleece and hands me a tissue. I dab at my eyes and nod. 'I'm Nina,' she says, 'we've met once before.' She must be a friend of Gary's. From his A levels, something like that. 'Martin won't be back yet. I haven't got any clean clothes with me.' I start to sob again. 'I only came out to pick up a few bits and pieces. I never come out on my own. And this is why!' Nina squeezes my shoulders. 'Sh, come on now. Get yourself together.' Ant is back with my chair and she helps me into it, ignoring the mess I've left on the scooter and floor. Ant gags again, and she scowls at him. 'Don't be such a baby,' she says, and swears at him. She'll get herself sacked if she's not careful. I want to warn her. A job is a job and they don't grow on trees. 'Sit tight. I just saw the car – they're here. The police will have a blanket or something. I'm sure they will.' She pushes me towards the door. I want to catch hold of the wheels and stop her, but I'm just too tired. I want to tell her about my hair, about how long it used to be, about the man who was going to pay me just to touch it. She probably wouldn't believe me, the state I'm in now. 'You can't leave,' Ant says, 'I'm understaffed as it is.' Two policemen arrive in the lobby and Ant trots off towards them, the strings on his apron bobbing jauntily.

MARTIN

The key fits into the lock snugly, as if it's magnetised, the house sucking me back towards itself.

'Back, Pauline. Has Jeannie been in with the food yet?'

Shoes off on the plastic mat covering the precious hall carpet. The shade of the paint on the walls (*Faded Birch*) was chosen to match it (*Smoky Latte* in a hard-wearing tufted-twist pile) as near to exactly as she could manage. *To increase the sense of space and light and cleanliness*, she says. I wrestle myself out of my jacket, knocking a picture of Gary askew with a flailing elbow.

'Pauline? Has the paper come? Shout if it hasn't and I'll bob back to the shop and sort it before I take my shoes off.'

There's no answer. It's with questions like these that I force myself back into this life, and her silence irritates me. She'll be perched on the couch, pouting because I'm twenty minutes later than I said I would be. Annoyed because I forgot the pack-up she made me, and wanting to know if I wasted a fiver on a bacon and sausage roll at Peggy's Place. And there will be other annoyances. Unknown to me. She likes me to spend my energy in guessing. Socks on the bathroom floor? Not brought her flowers for a month? Stared too long at the woman reading the news this morning? If I could remember half of what I'd forgotten, it still wouldn't be enough. Oh, Nina. Where are you?

Normally, there are two beige, brown and oatmeal quilted patchworks hanging on the wall over the living room door. They're a set. One says *As for Me and My House* and the other one says *We Will Serve the Lord.* The second one is down for washing, leaving the first one, on its own, to sound like a threat. Every day I have to walk in under that.

'Speak up, Pauline – I'm taking my shoes off.'

Gary's frame has scratched the paint on the wall slightly. It's only a bog-standard matt emulsion and there's half a tin of it left in the cupboard under the stairs but before Pauline can appear and start shrieking, I lick my finger and run it along the groove. An old trick, that – I learned it as a boy when I lived in Blackpool with not only a mother but an aunt, who both shared Pauline's interest in the moral dimensions of carpets, paint, net curtains and tablecloths. Push Gary straight, perpetually smiling despite his cock-eyed school tie and missing front tooth.

'Are you in the toilet?'

I climb the stairs and the house rings with silence.

'Pauline?'

Jeannie's room is neat and empty and smells faintly of deodorant and dusty radiators. The thin pink curtains are still half drawn and I lean over her bed and pull them back. Need to sort that mildew out around the window seal, can't be good for her, sleeping near that. Breathing it in. The spores. I'll mention it to Gary, once things have settled down.

Our room is empty. So is the bathroom. I bang on Julian's door once or twice, and get no answer. He fitted a lock to his door, a little Yale lock with his own key, and (he said) because Pauline makes him pay forty pounds a week board, he'd a right to the lock, and the privacy, and if she didn't like it he'd move out, and so she agreed to it. Right in front of me, who's supposed to take his board off him, but never does. I haven't the heart to do it, all things considered – even BrightHouse. But what stings is that he didn't even ask me to lie for him, he just assumed I would. Or he knew no one would hear a word I said anyway. No wonder Nina went cold on me.

'Julian?'

I bang again. Sometimes he comes home for his dinner, and a little sleep.

'Have you seen your mother?'

There's no answer, and my question spreads out in the quiet air at the top of the stairs, sounding lonely and desperate and foolish. Nina's phoned the house to speak to me, Pauline intercepted and got herself into a rage? Pauline's picked up and left? Don't be daft, you old sod.

On the landing bits of fluff and dog hair clog the gaps between the railings under the banister. It's one of Pauline's pet hates. She said she was going to attack that, this morning. Get out the attachments for the James Dyson and make a proper go of it. And she hasn't. If she'd left, left me, this house, she'd have left a letter, wouldn't she? Never one to let the opportunity for the last word pass her by, our Pauline. We used to leave each other notes. Little Post-its stuck to the television screen. *Baby Derek rang – wants to swap an early with you. Buy milk. Pay window cleaner, money in egg box.*

I go back down and duck my head round the living room door – nothing but an abandoned basket of half-folded bed sheets, shirts up on hangers dangling from the door frame. The telly's cold, and no messages on the phone. There are tell-tale marks on the living room carpet, little reminders of little accidents. The hall carpet was one thing, but she wants new carpet in here and doesn't understand why I don't think it's worth it. *It's not that I want new things for the sake of them*, she says, *it's a way of showing faith. I'm going to get better. Heavenly Father is going to heal me. And I won't spoil the new carpet. You've got to make the leap before he'll catch you.*

Marie Celeste, this is.

'Pauline?'

I stay by the phone a second, but really, who would I ring? The police? I can just see it. *Hello, sir, I've come home from work to find my wife absent.*

Not here.

Missing.

Last time I saw her? Just this morning, sir.

No, no, very high spirits. Happier than usual. Full of the joys, in fact.

Any health problems? Well, ho ho ho that's a can of worms we don't open round here, if it's all the same to you.

Bye-bye then!

The silence between the trills of the dialling tone sounds crackly and sinister.

What's she up to? I don't think I've come home to an empty house in, what, three years? Other than church on a Sunday, which is her sole exception, I don't think she's left it in two. Not since Gary's party, if I'm remembering correctly. When Bishop Jackson picked him up to drive him to Heathrow, a bit of her shut down. She keeps indoors now, floating between the rooms like a ghost. *Still keeping the home fires burning*, she says, when she emails him, sending herself out into the world through her computer. eBay. My LDSmail.org. Mumsnet and Amazon. She's a top one hundred reviewer for kitchen equipment. She has the sisters round here instead of doing her Visiting Teaching in person – shows them how to work the Ancestry website, prints out clip art from the LDS collection she's got on CD-ROM, makes newsletters, sends chirpy chain emails with links to pictures of kittens and videos of Primary kids singing hymns. She's in the world, but only virtually.

I put the phone down and go into the kitchen. Breakfast dishes drying on the rack, two tea towels folded neatly over the handle on the oven. Vanilla gel candles on the kitchen table in little glass dishes. No one's allowed to light them until tonight, but they ooze their sticky-sweet smell out into the room anyway, mingling with bleach and Stardrops and Flash and all the other things Pauline uses, frantic, whenever she's expecting Maggie round. She's ashamed of the mess she makes. Ashamed of our little house, only rented, and in arrears at that. I crack open a window, Bovril scrabbles out from under the kitchen table and I clap her round the ears a bit.

'All right, girl. All right. We've already been out once today. Where's your mummy gone? Where is she, eh?'

The garden? Quick peep out the kitchen window, but there's nothing there but the bins, the brambles, a slack washing line with a string-of-pearls raindrops along it. The greenhouse. I should sort that. Little sit-down first, though. I whipped through my rounds today; my feet feel like they're on fire. On one of the kitchen chairs I pull off my socks, sniff them, and leave them screwed up in front of the washing machine.

Nina won't have rung. I rushed things with her. Gave her the willies. I can see that now. And Julian stood there eyeballing us across the park, that wasn't going to help, was it? My hand goes over my eyes and the thought strikes me, because I've been holding it back all morning: I could be packing a bag anyway. The house is empty. What's stopping me?

Maybe Nina needs to see me get out on my own. She needs to see me manage a bit myself. She's not going to want a liability. A man who can't look after his own domestic arrangements. She's more modern than Pauline is – the sort of woman that expects a man to cook his own breakfast. To go halves on the rent. Failure to launch this morning doesn't mean the whole enterprise is scuppered, now, does it? If at first you don't succeed, what do you do? Change tack, that's what.

I go over to Pauline's computer. Command Central. I could book a train ticket. A hotel. No, think of the finances. A bed and breakfast then, maybe. And eat a good big breakfast and make it last until tea. I turn on the computer and sit down. Keep an eye out of the front window while it warms up. I thought it was going to be impossible. That I'd be shoving things into a holdall amid shrieks and recriminations, Julian blocking up the doorways, Jeannie wailing, Pauline raining down the contents of her dressing table on my head.

I type in 'bed and breakfast Chorley' and click on the first result. Pictures of bedrooms with shiny quilted coverlets on them, and pink valances, and little trays with miniature kettles and wicker baskets of paper-wrapped tea bags. There's no way of finding out the difference between a twin and a double room. Not what I can see, any road. I don't want to share. Can I not just get one to myself, with one bed in it? They want you to pay by card. There's a phone number. But then what would I ask? Cheapest option, please. I can't say that. There's a form to fill in. They want to know how many nights.

'How the hell would I know that?' I say it out loud, and surprise myself, so get up quickly and turn the computer off without shutting it down properly. I'll ring Nina first. Tell her sorry. That we can do it very slowly. Explain about Pauline. She's got the wrong end of the stick; Pauline is fitter than I am. Improving every day. Only today she decided to branch out and go for a spot of fresh air. That's a good sign. I'll tell her.

Nina, I'll say – or maybe I could write it. Get her a nice card. It would be better that way, wouldn't it? She'd take it more seriously, I think. *Nina, I like to think that my heart is a house with plenty of rooms in it. That love can be like a piece of crazy paving.* The scented air in here is drowning me. A man can have ten children and love them all, can't he? Why not women too? I'm not taking anything away. I'm adding. I'm growing my heart. Perhaps Pauline not being here really is a sign. The Red Sea parting. God making the path straight. The thought is embarrassing, so I shift myself in order to shift it.

We keep the suitcases in our bedroom. There's built-in wardrobes (*Sweetheart Wardrobes, they're called, love – one for him and one for her!*) either side of the bed, with another set of cabinets above. They frame the bed itself. The big marital mattress. The sagging, stained (*Milky Barleycup, Ovaltine Splash*) pad where me and Pauline have slept these past twenty-seven years. Twenty-seven. It's a life. I stand up on the bed, push open the cabinet and get down the case – a soft one, with a pull-out handle and little wheels. It's never been used, this one. She bought it (eBay again) for Gary for his nineteenth birthday – mission papers to fill in and send to the bishop tucked inside it. Some present. I slipped him a pair of twenties later that day, when she wasn't looking. He didn't end up taking the case and as it falls onto the bed it kicks up its own little halo of dust.

Undies, that's obvious. Dart into the bathroom for toothbrush, shaving essentials. The biscuit tin under the bed with Bovril's vaccination records, her Kennel Club documentation. I love looking at her family tree, all laid out like that. Her special, secret name. *Leeke's Endeavour*. Pauline thought it were stupid, and said we all had to call her Bovril. Nina doesn't think it's stupid, though. She understands what it's for. Her two are called *Madonna Rising* and *Lady Olivia*, the little madams.

Pauline's got a secret name too. The one that me and God are supposed to call her. Martha. Mine is Michael. She's not to know mine. It isn't necessary. I'm the one who's supposed to whisper to her and call her through the veil once this life is through. Her secret name is a magic word and when I speak it, it will pull her out of death and darkness and into light and the presence of God, to be reunited with me and the rest of her family. Provided we've all been faithful in keeping our covenants, there'll be chains of family waiting for her, all sealed together backwards and backwards and backwards to Adam.

Martha. Martha, Martha, Martha.

But what if I forget?

Since we'd had the endowment done I couldn't help but stare at Maggie, Lawson and Jackson in a new way. The strange film we had to watch, the handshakes and the secret passwords? I wanted to laugh, imagining them in the hats and aprons. *Have they done it?* It was like finding out about sex for the first time and looking at your headmaster and thinking, *Does he do it too?*

Sometimes, during a church social or fireside, someone would do something daft like trip over, or lose their keys, or tell a funny story about leaving their spectacles in the refrigerator, and someone else would make a quip about the Lord naming them his peculiar people. I'd had it explained to me. It meant special, not strange. But they'd look at each other with a secret look on their faces, like the ones who'd had it done were alluding to a secret the ones of us who hadn't been interviewed and found worthy and got the recommend weren't in on. And after I'd been through, I reckoned they meant strange as much as they meant special. Like they wanted to be strange, and a bit separate from everyone else. And that was me too, now.

I think Pauline were shocked about it all herself. You think you're going in to get a special service done so that you can qualify to get married, forever, their way. They don't tell you to expect the rest. She was so keen for it – pushed me through the baptism, confirmation. Waiting a year, then the endowment, then having the civil wedding in the chapel first so everything was right by the law of the land. A fair lot of hoops to jump through just so I could get married to her the way she wanted, and I can't say I was sold, personally, on any of it, but it was important to her. She'd had so little of her own. Achieved so few of her own dreams. I saw the way the other women looked down on her, even then. That Maggie's been the same since day one. So I thought, *Why not, what harm does it do? Play along, and it'll be over by teatime.*

It had taken us away from both of our families as well. Was bound to, really. Supposed to be the most important thing in your life, and you can't tell your mother about it? Pauline's people were C of E and put it all down to Pauline's fervour for the missionary that had converted her. Fifteen, she was. He'd met her in a train station. She'd heard of the Osmonds and even owned the *Paper Roses* LP so they were off to a flying start. Her mum and dad reckoned it was a phase, but going through the temple just cemented everything in, as far as Pauline were concerned. She'd been set apart. Bolted tight to her brothers and sisters in the gospel and set loose from her own family. My mum didn't ask, and then she died, and Pauline took her name to the temple and had all the ceremonies done for her – baptism, endowments, had her sealed to my dad, and us. Stood in as proxy herself. She insisted.

That was years later, though. That night, the first in this bed, the rest of it was yet to come and my brain was still whirling with the strangeness of it all: the aprons and the mirrors, the veils and hats and handshakes and chanting. What if I forgot my part of it and because of me Pauline were left in space, to wander through the darkness on her own? What if I messed it up, and because of me and my habitual incompetence the family chain was broken? I'd hoped she was thinking about it all as well, and it would be all right to bring it up. You're not even supposed to talk about it outside the temple. But we were in bed. No kids then, the door shut and the light off. What harm?

Pauline was shy, but she was keen too. She stuck her hand inside my pyjamas and held me softly, just like that, as easy as if she was shaking my hand.

'That's us, now,' she'd said, and snuggled into me. 'We'll stick together, won't we?'

'Course we will,' I said. There was a long silence while she did something under the covers. I can't imagine where she learned it, but I wasn't about to start complaining, either.

'It's Michael, love,' I whispered to her, 'in case you ever need it. In case I can't find you. It's Michael. We'll stick together. Thick and thin. Time and eternity.'

I put my hand over hers and she didn't say anything, but she squeezed and I could see her smiling in the dark by the light that came off the numbers on the radio alarm clock she had on her side of the bed.

I didn't know I was lying. That time would turn all those promises into lies and pull those convenants apart for us.

I slide the certificates back into their little plastic holder and put them in the special inside pocket of the case, where they won't get creased. Next, a spare work uniform and a couple of pairs of jeans. Building society book. Nothing but pence in the account and if there were more I probably wouldn't have got to this point, but pence is what there is and every little helps. What else? The case is only half full. Sentimental things? Photographs?

The chunky silver frames on the windowsill belong to Pauline. In each of the three photographs she's sitting up in a hospital bed holding a baby. In the one with Julian, she's wearing lipstick (*Creamy Fudge*), and has her hair up in a ponytail. She's not aged much between Julian's birth and Gary's, who in his picture is staring at the camera with his eyes wide open. She often brings this photograph out as evidence of the boy's 'remarkable spirituality', his 'valiance in the pre-existence'. *Just think, she says, a few seconds before this picture was taken Gary was the other side of the veil receiving counsel from Heavenly Father, saying goodbye to his grandma. Maybe promising to prepare the way for the others still to come.*

The third picture has caught her with her eyes shut, or perhaps she's just looking down, inspecting the drip on the back of her hand. Jeannie is in her arms, her body rigid, her mouth open wide, screaming with the colic that plagued her and made her wail night and day until she was three months old. In contrast to Gary's birth, when Pauline was so elated she laughed and cooed at him while the midwives were stitching her back together, Pauline let the midwives take care of Jeannie and kept silent about the new baby's passage through the veil. Maybe the girl had changed her mind at the last minute, took one look at us all and decided she didn't want to be here. I wouldn't have blamed her. But the angels pushed her through, their white hands pressed into her back. *Too late to change your mind now!* She nearly ripped her mother in half on the way out – angels pushing from one side, a doctor with a pair of forceps on the other. A tug of war between this world and that one, our Pauline the rope. She frayed, she snapped and broke and she's never been right since. It's not her fault. But it isn't mine, either.

Between the three pictures there are painted pottery doodads: shepherd boys blowing trumpets; milkmaids heaving pails; some man leaning on a stick with his hands over his eyes, staring into an imaginary distance. They're all hers too, and paid for in twelve monthly instalments of six pounds each plus p&p.

Or mine. Maybe they're all mine. I paid for them, didn't I? Brought the parcels back? Carried them up the stairs for her? I did do those things, didn't I?

If I did, I don't begrudge her it. She brought up the kids. Kept the house nice. All she asked for herself was me alongside her at church, and a few trinkets to put on the windowsills. Once Julian was big enough, he was in charge of dusting the lampshades and changing the bulbs, so I didn't even have to do that.

There's a pain in my hip. So sudden it's as if I've been struck. I lie down on the bed; claw my trousers open so I can inspect the skin. There's nothing there. My grey and white flesh, more flabby than I'm going to let myself notice, stares back at me. It throbs. My head rests back on the pillows and it isn't often I have this room, this bed to myself. What am I doing? I kick the bag off the bottom of the bed and curl up, nursing my sore hip, enjoying the feel of my palm against my skin. I overdid it this morning. Perhaps this is age. Not creeping up on me, but shooting me in the joints like a sniper, crippling me. Is it arthritis? Or cancer? Some rare kind: blackening my bones, eating away at the cartilage between my joints.

Cancer. That'll be it. I'll have to stay here, side by side with

Pauline in matching chairs (*A Sweetheart Set! One for her, and one for him!*), with Jeannie bringing up bowls of soup and mopping our chins until she's an old woman herself, and I'll dither and dribble and watch while she wastes her best years on us. Nina might walk past the window once every couple of years. Bracken and Heather will get fat and limpy and grey. One day Nina will come along with a fella. A year or two later, pushing a pram. And the house will have sucked me in. I can see that now. I leave, it will collapse.

Nina. There's nothing stopping me ringing her up apart from cowardice. Let's not put too fine a point on it. But I will do. I will. Get my bag sorted, and a place to stay for tonight. And she'll see I'm serious. And when I'm able to talk to her properly about Pauline, we'll laugh about it. That's what I'll do. Tomorrow morning, just turn up in the park as usual. There's something she's been overlooking about Bracken's deportment – when the girl's walking to heel, her tail should be up, curved above her back like a scimitar. The judges at Malvern will be looking out for details like that, and it's not an easy thing to address once you've let a bitch settle into her bad habits. I'll give her a few pointers. She'll be grateful and if we bring up the misunderstanding about Pauline at all, it will only be to laugh at it.

My trousers are still open and I look down at myself curiously. Well, well, well. It's been a while since *that's* happened. I try touching, just a little bit, and can feel the blood rushing in, flooding into the secret chambers under my skin and making my underclothes too tight. Poor thing. It's as if it's desperate to have someone notice, to have someone hold on tight and say: *Yes, yes, yes, you're alive, you're still here.*

Nina's got a firm, soft hand, hasn't she? Nicely clasped around that tennis ball. Some people buy plastic contraptions to fire them into the air, but she'd laugh if anyone offered her one.

'What's wrong with my own two hands?' she'd say.

It feels lovely, that does.

I carry on, and wonder if tomorrow would be the time to broach starting the water training for Bracken and Heather. We've been putting in the heel work that's the foundation for a controlled water retrieve. Heather's really good at it. Like I told Nina, if you walk past a dog, even which foot you lead with can be a command for her. Bovril knows when I lead with the foot closest to her, it's a signal. Nina's doubtful but after a week or so of practice she'll be able to walk past either of them while they're in the sit and either pick them up, or not, depending on which foot she places next to them as she passes. Once they can do that, they're ready for the water. Nina's been reluctant to do it, because we'd have to travel somewhere else to get the right conditions. But I could book a bit of leave off work, and
guide her
through it.

You can say anything you like about Bovril – primarily that she's still got a tendency to be skittish around traffic and dogs she doesn't know well and I'll probably never break her of that but that dog handles the water like she was born to it. All Labs do. Nina'll see; I'll guide her on what commands to give. She worries, perhaps, about
getting wet.

I can see her standing in the water, throwing the decoys in one after the other,
little drops of
splash clinging to the strands of her
hair that she can never get to sit still behind
her ears.
Her laughing when Bracken
bellyflops
in and
soaks us both,

standing together, close,
and watching Bovril
slip
into the water like someone
had greased her up and
shot her
out of a
cannon. O!

I try moving the leg, bending it and straightening it, and the pain is easing now. My heart is banging and my hand is wet. I rest for a little while with my cheek on the pillow, my knees up to my chest. The neighbours, if they peeped through the net curtains and saw me, might think I was just working a cramp out of a muscle, or coming round from a little nap. I wipe my hand on the duvet cover and realise the whole thing is going to need changing and that's one more thing to do and Pauline will want to know why and I'll need to explain myself, and there'll be more shouting and disgust and recriminations.

There are tears now, falling down the side of my face and annoying me by gathering in the corner of my mouth. The sweat on my hairline cools. What's this? Is this what getting old is like? Strange pains, nasty habits and crying fits over nothing?

If I leave, will it collapse?
If I leave, will I collapse?
If I collapse, will I leave?
Will I leave if I collapse?
If it collapses, will I leave?

I take the bag downstairs. Twitch the front curtains and look up and down the street for Pauline. Run a cloth over the cupboard fronts and coffee table, just so I can say I did something if she comes back. The holdall is on the kitchen table and I can't leave it alone. I know what this is going to look like. She'd put it in the ward newsletter if Sister Jackson would let her get away with it. *Brother Leeke Deserts Wheelchair-Bound Wife as Son Returns Triumphant. Weak Man Led by Lust into the Jaws of Temptation.* I won't get a word in. No one will want to hear my side of the story.

When I imagine what life will be like tomorrow, I can only see how pleased Pauline is going to be at this latest tribulation. God tests the righteous. Her health has been her main trial these past years, and she's cherished that. 'Opposition in all things' is her hobby. Pauline's illness has been a mystery for such a long time that we've all accepted it and her incontinence, her agoraphobia (where is she, though, where is she?), and her gradual insistence that walking was so difficult it was better for her not to have to do it, have become unremarkable.

None of us were that surprised, actually, when she bought the wheelchair on eBay. I think Jeannie truly believes that's how people usually get them. A frenzied bidding war, murderous mutterings about shill bidders and second offers, and then the throne itself – wreathed in brown tape and bubble wrap and delivered to her by a courier who asked if she was collecting props for a play. Pauline decants herself from bed to toilet, toilet to chair, chair to couch and back again. I try not to think that, somehow, she's cottoned on to what I've been planning and beat me to the punch.

Bovril nudges at my legs and I open the back door and we both go out. Outside the sky is heavy and the weather looks like rain. The grass waves backwards and forwards, the tops of the bin liners rattling where they're poking out of the overfull wheelie bin. I can feel bits of grit sticking to the soles of my bare feet as I quickly move onto the grass, which is damp and long and cool. It'd help, I think, if when she comes back she catches me in the act of sorting out the garden a bit. Not a full set-to, just a little spit and polish round the edges to show willing.

At the back, tucked in behind an overgrown privet hedge, is the tiny five-sided greenhouse. The glass is clouded with condensation and, in places, some kind of black algae. The plants inside have grown so much that the house itself looks like a giant transparent jelly mould. If you could lift it off and move it away, the plants would stay where they were – a thickly knotted, greenhouse-shaped block of leggy tomatoes, bindweed and ground elder. Bovril comes with me and we circle it, peering through the glass. She wags her tail and sniffs at the bare soil under the hedges.

'Leave that cat alone,' I say, and she looks at me with such an expression it makes me laugh. The fresh air is making me feel better. It always does. 'This is a right state, this is,' I carry on, muttering as I pull out clumps of chickweed from around the greenhouse door, throwing them behind me onto the path to be cleared away later.

The thing is, the garden was always Gary's job. Don't think he liked it much, but it was his domain, and he took charge of it. The weeding, cutting the grass, clipping the hedges. The greenhouse was my idea. I had a daydream and in my daydream I saw myself growing tomatoes, pinching out seedlings and sitting on a bench planting them into growbags. The moist heat plumping up the fruits. I could have plucked a handful of them and presented them to Pauline the next time she started on a spag bol for our tea. 'From our own vine, my love.'

It was also, and it's daft to admit, a plan for me to have a room of my own in our house. I should have asked for a shed, but Maggie Travers's husband has a garden shed that's fitted out as a home office – hooked up to the electric and everything and that's where he keeps his computer, and I'd never, ever have got her to agree to the idea of a shed because of that. It's the glass, see. She could look out of the kitchen window whenever she wanted and see what I was doing in there. There'd only be two windows between us. Pauline liked the idea, which did surprise me, but I didn't question it and she got on the phone and ordered a small greenhouse for me from Argos. She tried to pretend it was a big hassle, and too much expense, but she was smiling when the men delivered it in four flat cardboard parcels, and looked out of the kitchen window pointing and reading out the instruction sheet while me and Gary assembled it.

It was just a rickety little thing with five sides and a sloped roof with a pointy top. No room for a bench inside and, as we weren't willing to dig out the bottom, no room to stand unless you lined yourself up directly under the apex of the roof, and bent your knees a bit. No room for anything more than three growbags, laid out end to end in a little triangle, with a sprinkling of blue slug pellets in the centre. We kept the seedlings on the kitchen window-sill under tents made from cut in half lemonade bottles and Pauline watered them and told me when it was time to plant them out. Gary had more of a green thumb than I did, that was clear right from the start. So he sort of took it over and he'll be expecting, no doubt, to take it back up when he comes home.

I lean over and pull at the door. The ground isn't even here and you always did have to give it a few firm tugs, the whole structure wobbling, before it would open, but the grass is over-grown and even though I've ripped out most of the chickweed there's not a chance in cheese I'm getting it open without a fight. I stare at the door for a minute, knowing that really I don't have time for this and I should get into the house and address the matter of Pauline's absence, and maybe hoover round or peel a few potatoes or something, when the idea hits me that I could slide one of the glass panels out of the frame and climb in that way. That'd do, wouldn't it? There are some thick bin bags in the kitchen drawer and I could clear out the greenhouse, pushing the old leggy plants out of the gap in the door, and even give the grass a mow – that would only take twenty minutes, if that, and by the time Pauline gets back from wherever Ruth and Maggie have whisked her off to, she'll see the garden at least is in a decent state and perhaps remember how much Gary liked to spend time out there, and noticing that will give her some degree of comfort, if not now, then in the times ahead.

Or I could just go, couldn't I? I could put on my socks and shoes and pick up my bag and leave.

I press the flat of my hands against the glass and push upwards, feeling the pane move three-quarters of an inch in its, it has to be said, warped metal frame. I wiggle it backwards and forwards like this, and eventually manage to lever it out. My hip is still throbbing a little, and as I carry the glass across the grass and over to the side of the house where I'm planning to lean it against the wall before replacing it later, it slips from my hands, falls onto the edge of the patio and shatters over my feet. The tops of my feet feel instantly itchy – like someone's stroked them with a nettle – and a hundred tiny red scratches appear.

'Stay back, Bovril – stay,' I say, and show her the palm of my hand, and quick as that she drops and sits by the hedge with her head down and her paws arranged neatly in front of her. In spite of everything I feel proud of that, and wish Nina was here to see it. It's a dog's instinct to come to the assistance of its owner/ pack leader when it senses that owner is in Danger, Doubt or Distress. Trainers call it the three Ds, and most dogs can overcome, with their training, one of them and obey a command to stay put. Apparently a bitch can find her natural instincts harder to overcome in this department, which is why it has always pleased me that Bovril's a solidly reliable double-D dog.

But as I shake off my feet, tiptoe over the glass and start pushing the rest of the panes of glass into the greenhouse, watching them fall and smash and break the stems of the plants inside, I can see she's outdoing herself – she's a three-D dog now, watching me peacefully with her brown eyes and moving nothing, not even her tail.

'Good girl, good girl, good girl, sit nice for your daddy. Don't come near.'

I talk to her until I'm finished, and the greenhouse is just an empty metal frame, the glass cracked into jagged panels. I breathe in deep and smell the sharp smell of sap from the broken plants inside it, springing outwards now, reaching towards the sunlight. The light catches the shards of glass on the grass and sparkles, and it stings my eyes and makes them water. I wonder what I've done, and am suddenly very tired.

In the kitchen, I wrap a tea towel around my worst hand and sit at the table. I think again about calling Nina, but I don't move. The list of things I need to do feels overwhelming. Bovril stands by the open back door, her nose raised, and I kick it shut so she won't go out and hurt her feet on the glass. My holdall is still on the table and I rest my head on it and close my eyes for a little while. It's no joke, getting up at five every day for Jeannie and squeezing an eight-hour shift into five hours this morning. No one in this world is getting any younger, it isn't just me. The cuts on my hands and feet are stinging a bit and I should probably do something about it. People get tetanus from getting soil into cuts, don't they? Lockjaw, my father used to call it. Knew someone on the allotments who got it from standing on a rusty rake – went right through the bottom of his boot. I've not been hygienic today. Don't think about that. Ah, I'll sort it out later. And move the table into the living room, and hide the bag, and decide about Nina and deal with the glass in the garden. How often is it that I get a little rest in the middle of the day? I could go up to bed even, have a little doze, but I've done nothing about the duvet and just being able to sit for a minute on your own, it's not a lot to ask, is it? Bovril whines at the door and the phone rings, the sound throbbing through the empty house like a teething baby's cry. Come here, girl. Settle down. Jeannie is crying somewhere and in a minute I'll get up and take her a bottle and her gripe water. Take it easy now, girl. Jeannie's screaming – full throttle – what's wrong with her? I'll just rest my eyes for one minute longer I'll get her in a minute, Pauline, just give me one minute will you let me just close my—

GARY

The airplane lands. The singing woman wails as the wheels bump, lift again and then make their final connection with the runway. She falls silent as the plane comes to its gradual halt and then, as we're warned to keep still until we see the seat-belt light go off, she releases a torrent of noisy prayer that sounds like a sentence with all the spaces between the words taken out. James King grins at me.

'Home time!' he says, and is already up and unloading the overhead locker, jabbing his arms into his jacket before I can get out of my seat. I can't get up. For a moment – too long for James, who is cheerily impatient with the delay – I am paralysed, my eyes hot in their sockets. So. Here we are. Home to glory.

'What you waiting for? This is our stop!'

Elder Keller and I have had long conversations about this moment.

'What's the first thing you're going to do when you go home?' he said, perfect English tinged with the Provo accent of the MTC trainers who'd helped him memorise all the discussions.

'Go and see my mother, of course,' I said.

'Is that it?'

'Why? What are you going to do?'

'Burn this tie,' he said, and pulled at it. The collar of his shirt was limp with the heat. This was a subject we talked about often – too often, in fact; we were counselled to keep our minds away from our homecomings – but during the time of this particular transgression we were walking along the side of a road in rural

165

Tooele County, further out in the boons than we'd ever been before. We'd tracted in the city, tracted in the burbs. Nothing. So we decided to take the car and go further out, not so far away from the city we couldn't get home before our curfew, but outside the zone we were assigned to. It was disobedience. Wickedness can't ever lead to happiness – bad won't make good and the ends never justify the means – but we were desperate, looking for the white fields, ripe for the harvest that had been promised us. And then the car had broken down. There were miles between the houses.

'I'll burn every single one of the ties. Never wear one again. I used to want to be a teacher but I couldn't stand being buttoned into my clothes all day every day.'

We walked with our suit jackets over our shoulders and our top buttons undone. Keller strode off in front with his thumb out, hoping for someone to stop and give us a lift, but we were on a road to nowhere, and no cars passed us. I looked over my shoulder every few steps anyway, scared that the zone leader, prompted by the Spirit, would ride by and catch us. You got called into the Mission President's office if you were caught crossing the zone boundaries. Keller saw me looking and laughed at my anxiety.

'Relax, Leaky. We're adventurers.'

'We shouldn't be here.'

'We're God's army. A pair of stripling warriors,' he flexed a muscle, 'what does geography mean to us?'

'Keller . . . leave your tie alone, will you?'

'I'll stop torturing it now,' he flipped it over his shoulder and I watched as it lifted and fell in the hot breeze, 'so long as I can set fire to it as soon as I get to go home. Is that a deal, Elder Leeke?'

We laughed.

'I'll burn the shirts as well. Put on a pair of trainers. Eat at a Chinese all-you-can-eat buffet. Go swimming in a lake. Go and see a movie. Sleep in till lunchtime. Play my guitar, really,

really loud. "Smoke on the Water"!' As we trudged he clutched an imaginary guitar, cradling it over his crotch, and hummed the riff, 'Ba ba baaa! Ba ba ba baaa!'

'Is that it?' I said. 'I think I'd rather go and see my mother. She cooks better than some all-you-can-eat buffet.'

Our shoes were yellow with dust. Above us, behind us, to the side and in front – more mountains covered with spindly cottonwood trees and the same withered-looking sage-brush that grew everywhere. You could smell the crushed stems in the hot wind, but I didn't find it beautiful. I wanted to take my tie off and go home too, not to our apartment in the city, but real home – back to England.

'No. One more thing.' Keller smiled at me over his shoulder, looking sly and mischievous. 'I'll go and kiss my girl. Maybe. If I'm lucky.'

'You've got someone waiting for you?'

'Of course.'

'Ah.' I smiled. The rucksack on my back was heavy. We weren't noticing how far away from the car we'd got but now we stopped and turned and looked and saw it shimmering in the distance, parked where it had let us down. The road was long and straight and wide, yellow lines running down the centre of it, the verges either side sandy and dry. The sky, like a glass bowl over our heads, shimmering and benign. And a house, a big white house standing apart from the road in the distance, and trudging wasn't bringing it any nearer.

'*Ah?* What's that supposed to mean?'

I didn't say anything, but Keller dropped back to walk beside me and bumped me with his elbow. 'Come on. Out with it. What does Leaky think he knows?'

'Nothing.' I laughed, even though the talking was making me hotter.

'I'll sing if you don't tell me. "We Thank Thee O God for a Prophet" in nine languages. Do you want to hear that?'

'It doesn't mean anything.'

He started singing in the wavering, work-up-to-the-note tremble of the old women who sat nearest the piano in ward meeting houses everywhere.

'We feel it a pleasure to serve thee, and we love to obey thy command . . .'

'It won't work, you know.'

'Blödes Huhn, tell me.'

'No!'

'Arsch mit Obren.'

'I know what you're calling me.'

'What is it then?'

'Clara.'

'What about her?'

'That's your girlfriend's name, isn't it?'

As we got nearer to the house we lowered our voices, and Keller fixed his tie. It was a low, wide-fronted white house with a wooden porch. I still thought of these kinds of houses as huge – as mansions, with their own lands gathered around them, but in America this was a poor person's house. The front yard was littered with toys, a little girl's bicycle with a bent front wheel and a plastic inflatable paddling pool. There were plastic bowls for a dog and toy Tonka Trucks lying on their sides in the dust. The skeleton of last year's Christmas tree leaned against the sagging front fence. The blinds were down, but that wasn't unusual on a hot day. The gate and the front door stood open.

'How do you know that?'

'That's what you say when you're asleep. That and a load of German gobbledegook,' I said.

'I gave myself away!'

'You're not s-s-s-s-supposed to keep a girlfriend,' I said, and smiled, 'but I won't tell anyone. Come on. Let's try here. If they aren't members, we'll give them the first discussion. If they are members, we'll ask for a tow back to town.'

'Wait a minute, will you?'

Keller had this terrible habit of taking his shoes off when we were out of the apartment. Waiting for a bus, sitting in a diner – even during a church service. He said, even after all this time, he couldn't get used to men's dress shoes. He said they rubbed his feet, made his socks come down and bunch up around his toes. Two or three times a day we needed to stop while he made his adjustments.

'You can't do that here.'

He sat on the verge between the road and the fence, leaning against the post for the dented mailbox.

'*Meine verfluchten Füsse!*' He proceeded to unlace one shoe, shake tiny pieces of grit out of it and then fastidiously take off, shake out and replace his sock. I stood and waited, looking over the fence into the dim quiet in the house and praying that whoever lived there wouldn't come out until Keller had put his shoes back on.

'Haven't you got anyone to go home to? Everyone loves a missionary.' He grinned up at me.

'That's not what we're here for, Keller.'

'Are the girls so different where you come from?'

'Elder Keller, fasten your sh-sh-shoelaces and straighten your tie.'

He stumbled to his feet. We did what we always did before knocking on anyone's door. Stood together, hands clasped in front of each other, gelled heads bowed under the sun, and we prayed. Simple prayers, whispered over maps, in the back of our car, on street corners. We asked Heavenly Father to lead us to people who wanted to be found. After the prayer was over we waited in silence for the promptings of the Spirit.

'I'll take this one,' I said, and Keller nodded.

'You're speaking well today, Leaky. Keep it up. Let's see if you're as good in front of an audience.'

'Sh-shut up, Keller.'

We went through the gate and trod the path through the dirt and yellow grass to the silent house.

'Hello? Anyone home?' I called into the gloom. 'We're from the Church of Jesus Christ of Latter-Day Saints and we'd like to talk to you about—'

The little girl came out of nowhere. She must have been playing out back, or around the side of the house. She was wearing a long pastel-blue dress, the sleeves puffed at her shoulders and dangling low below her fingertips, the hem dusty where it dragged on the ground. Her feet were wet and she left behind dark footprints.

'Is your momma in?' Keller asked. 'Will you go and tell her there's someone at the door for her?'

The little girl smiled – her front teeth were missing but she was beautiful all the same.

'It's all right,' I said, 'we'll wait out here.'

We had instructions about that. Never enter a house until we were sure there was an adult man inside. Not because we weren't trusted, but to avoid even the appearance of evil. Some missionaries fornicated. Some women lay in wait, wanting to get alone with an Elder even for five minutes – so she could run to *The Tribune* and tell some Anti-journalist that she'd been taken advantage of by an Elder. That he'd come into her father's house while he was out at work and forced himself on her. We knew some girls lied about us Elders like that, even if we couldn't quite believe it.

'I'll get her.' She smiled again and went inside, her blonde plait hitting her between the shoulder blades as she ran. Elder Keller stared at the house and, when I caught his eye, grinned again and gave me a thumbs-up. *This is the place*, he seemed to be saying. These people would be worth breaking the rules for.

James and I stand by the baggage carousel. Music. Something soft and instrumental and forgettable. I take a Book of Mormon out of my rucksack and try to hand it to him.

'James, here's that book we were talking about earlier.'

He waves me away. The track around the carousel is empty. We wait. After a while, cases start to appear on it.

'Okay, son,' James says. 'Quit your pouting. I know what you want. I'll make you a deal. One man to another. Quid pro quo. Shake on it?'

'You don't need to make a deal with me. If you need help. with s-s-s-s-something, just ask. It's been a while, but if I remember right, you can get a taxi from right out front – and the train to the c-c-c-c-city isn't more than fifteen minutes—'

'My stuff!' James whoops and ducks and darts forward to pluck his case from the carousel. It's a brushed silver Samsonite, slightly weathered at the corners and festooned with a bunting of labels from airports in every corner of North America. 'It's like winning the lotto every time!'

He lays the case down and is oblivious to the obstruction he is causing as he hunches over it and undoes the red belt wrapped around its middle. I thought the sleep would sober him up. Looks like I was wrong.

'Got something in here for you.' He fiddles the combination locks with his huge thumbs and finally pops the lid open. White shirts and whiter underwear jack-in-the-box out of it and James leans back on his heels, surprisingly limber, and starts to dig behind the mesh panel on the inside of the lid.

I think about bombs, and step around him to retrieve my own case. I gave most of my shirts to Elder Keller the day before I left Salt Lake City and it is very light. There's just one sticker on it – the green shield of the Choose The Right emblem.

'James? I think we sh-sh-sh-should . . .'

People are staring, tutting and knocking James and his case as they flow around him, away from the carousel and towards Arrivals. Just over there. Down that corridor, past that counter and through a few sets of doors is Bishop Jackson and his car. And home.

For the first time in two years I am in the same time zone as Carole. I can remember what her hair smelled like. The colour of it. Toffee. But her features won't keep still in my head. Her hands – very small and very white. And her favourite dress – black with hundreds of tiny white flowers on it. That's all that's left. I tucked my picture of her between the mattress and the wall at home, tight in where the light won't fade it and where Julian can't get to it. I haven't said her name out loud in twenty-three months. Would have been twenty-four, but I prayed for her once. It made me cry so I decided not to do it again. Never mind the tie, or 'Smoke on the Water', or an all-you-can-eat buffet; finding that picture is the first thing I'm going to do.

James stands up. He's sweating slightly – the unnaturally black hair at his temples is damp. He has a small green plastic bottle in each hand.

'Just one minute, Elder. Hold your horses. You're going straight home to your momma, aren't you?'

'I will be, s-s-sir, that's right.'

'Here's the deal. You give me a few dollars and your contact details and I will give you the full sample set of the best and I mean Thee Best professional-level quality dishwashing and bathroom hygiene detergents that you *or* your momma will ever see. I don't care where you shop – you won't have come across better quality than this and you won't do in the future, either. You got fifty dollars on you? Twenty? Fifteen? I'll put you on my list, and once you've had a chance to settle in we'll get back in contact. You'll tell me that you've never used a finer home hygiene product, your momma's been raving about our merchandise to all her friends and personal networks and they are desperate for the good news – where can they buy more? And then, Elder, I'll tell you how *you* can change *your* life by joining the Amway family.'

'I'm not—'

'Quid pro quo, Elder. You look at what I've got to sell and

I'll do the same for you. Do you want to get shot of that book, or don't you? I'm doing you a favour. You'll be looking for a career. Planning to get married soon. Settle down. Maybe a few kids?'

'Yes, that would be nice, but—'

'Well, a man needs a job for a life like that. A position where a woman can look up to him and respect him. And you've already gone and got the training. You've got the skills. You've got the sense God gave you to keep your mouth shut when there's nothing to say. I like a man who knows how to do that.'

'Thank you, James.'

'I'm not blowing hot air, here. I admire your style, son. I could do a lot with you. Give it a few years, some hard work and a bit of luck and you could get to be Regional Coordinator. Doing what I do. Buy your momma a new house. How do you like the sound of that?'

My outstretched arm is starting to ache. The book is getting sticky in my hand. I've got a leather-bound edition in my suitcase but the copies we have handy to give out to contacts are more cheaply produced and bound in thin navy card that sheds its colour onto anything it touches.

'And you'll take a Book of Mormon? And promise to read it?'

'Come on, Gary. I offered to shake on it with you, didn't I? Are you calling me a liar?'

'Okay, James.' I dig around in my suit pockets, past the crumpled Round Tuit, and hand him the last of my money, twenty dollars or so in small bills and change. I write my address on the little card he gives me to fill in. James hands me the plastic bottles reverently.

'Best product you'll ever use,' he says. 'The very best.'

'Thank you.' I juggle the bottles into one hand and push the book at him.

'And here's the Book of Mormon. Take good care of it. Read

it as soo-soo-soon as you can. I wrote my testimony in the front of it for you. I promise you, James, if you take the time to read this and then get on your knees and pray about it, the Lord will send his Holy S-spirit to you and he will tell you that it's true. Don't take it from me, James, take it from the Lord.'

The cover has adhered slightly to my damp fingertips and I feel it peel away as it leaves my hand. James rifles through the tissue-paper pages.

'I love the smell of a new book,' he says and then tosses it into his open case.

Keller and I had waited in the clammy shade of the porch for the little girl to come back, but she didn't.

'You got any water, Elder?'

I shook my head. 'Maybe they'll offer us some.'

The house was still silent, as if it had taken her into itself and swallowed her up. Now and again a truck would speed past on the road, heading out to Tooele City or the big army depot, perhaps. As we waited, we began to see how big the building was. All American houses are big to my English eye – they're nothing like the rows of terraces that I was brought up in, but this house, lying a distance from the road and slanted away from it, like a shy girl at a party, was huge. And, we started to notice, shaped strangely, with most of the outbuildings, extensions and add-ons behind the main and original structure. Someone had been hammering in a fence along the back side of the house too. A real solid one, to replace the sagging panels across the front.

'There must be ten or twenty rooms in this place,' Keller said, and whistled gently between his teeth.

'Maybe that's why we're here,' I said. 'Big family. In-laws living in the annexe. Baptise them all. It's not pride to want a thing like that.'

We were leaning back to see how many floors the house had,

counting the blinded windows and gawping at the roof, when a man came to the door. He was wearing jeans and a dusty white tee-shirt, no shoes, clean shaven but with long hair. Face so weathered with outside working it was hard to tell how old he was. His hands were dirty. I guessed he'd been out the back building up that fence.

'You boys better come inside,' he said, in a flat, rural accent that I knew Keller would have difficulty in following. 'It's hot out here. I'll get my wife to get you something to drink.' He coughed, and it sounded like a laugh.

'We'd be very pleased to, sir,' Keller said, because even though I'd told him I'd lead the discussion this time, I'd forgotten to speak. It happened sometimes, even after all my training and practice, and when my jaw stuck Keller always stepped in as if that was what we'd planned anyway – and never made a big deal about it afterwards. I was grateful for it.

The girl who we'd seen earlier appeared behind her father. She held on to his leg and sucked the dirtied edge of her sleeve.

'Luanne,' he said quietly, 'go and get your mother. Tell her we've got company from the Church.'

I followed the man into the house. *The Church*, he said. Not *the Mormons*, or *some missionaries*. Not even *the Morg*. No. *The Church*. He was one of us. I sighed. We'd probably end up coming back on a P-Day to finish making that fence for him and not one discussion taught to show for it. Inside, it was too dark to notice anything except for the quiet and the oppressive smell of bread dough and dogs. Keller hung back a little, and didn't come after me until I glared at him.

'Members?' he whispered, incredulous and irritated. 'We come out all this way and the first door we knock on is *members*? What good is that?'

'Shh. It's good and bad. At least they'll let us wait a while, maybe even help us fix the car, or tell us where we can get it towed.'

As our eyes adjusted to the gloom we saw that we were in a huge kitchen. There were three fridges lined up along one wall, and an industrial-sized oil range against the other. There were seven large bowls draped in damp tea towels and lined up on the counter. Bread, left to rise by the smell of it.

'You going to sit down, or aren't you? My wife will be in to serve you in a minute,' the man said roughly. He motioned to the table – a Formica-topped, cafeteria-style trestle that would have seated twenty along each side, and comfortably. The three of us huddled at one end, as if we were cold. The house was cooler than outside, and the place, despite the doggy smell, was clean. I got out my scriptures, placed them open on the table.

'What ward are you from, Brother . . . ? Are you and your family active members, can we ask?'

'You can ask, you bet you can ask,' he said.

'Brother,' Keller said, moving his head from side to side. I'd warned him not to do that, but he just couldn't get used to wearing a shirt with a collar. 'Is there anything we can do for you while we're here? Do you have any yard work that needs doing? Perhaps some help fitting those new fence panels out the back there?'

'What you been looking at my fence for?' He spoke quietly, gruffly. I couldn't decide if it sounded gentle or sinister.

'Are you a priesthood holder? We'd be happy to give a priesthood blessing to anyone in the family you feel needs it. We could do that for you, if you like.'

'No,' the man said, and leaned back, 'there's nothing like that wanted here.'

There was a silence. We heard flies buzzing around the light fittings and the closed blinds. We were waiting, I think, for Luanne to come back with her mother. No priesthood in the house. So a member, but one in poor standing. I glanced at his body, but it was still too dark to see the line of his garments under his tee-shirt, to discern if he were wearing them.

We came across it sometimes. Angry members who'd been disfellowshipped, perhaps even brought to a Court of Love and excommunicated. It happens. People get offended, or study old books in the wrong context, without the guidance of the Spirit. They think they want to sin. They fall, and become apostate. Missionaries show them the way home. Rebaptise them, in some cases.

I smiled.

'Then perhaps we could sit with your family and just visit a while. We've got ourselves into a bit of a fix out there on that road—'

'Here she is. Marilyn. Serve these two boys, will you?'

The girl had entered the room so silently we hadn't heard her until she'd emerged from the gloom and come up behind her husband. She didn't touch him or say a word, so he must have sensed her presence there – something about her smell or the imperceptible rustle of her clothes. She was wearing a long denim skirt and a faded white tee-shirt with a picture of Donald Duck on the front of it. She moved to the side and we saw she was pregnant. Keller and I stood up.

'Let me help you, S-s-s-s-s-sister. You s-s-s-sit and tell me where everything is and I'll do it,' I said. Keller was looking at me, his eyes wide. 'Can we do something with that bread for you? Set us to work.'

She only shook her head, once, as if she barely heard us and then made her slow way over to the sink and opened the blinds. Light streamed into the room and we all squinted. The place looked even bigger and now I could see the decorations on the wall – familiar pictures of Joseph Smith and Brigham Young in simple wooden frames. Drawings in crayon done on butcher's paper of houses and cars and airplanes. Ten or fifteen pictures of children, all at various ages.

'Oh, for pity's sake . . .' Keller said, and yanked at my arm. Marilyn wasn't much older than Luanne herself. Fourteen, fifteen at the very oldest. She couldn't be anyone's mother. And yet, soon enough, she would be.

The man laughed at us and Marilyn stayed at the sink, rinsing out a jug and glasses.

'Amy? Amy! Get in here. Marilyn needs some help.'

Keller remained standing. I sat down again, and closed my scriptures.

'It's not the right way,' Keller said, 'it isn't what Heavenly Father wants for you.'

The long-haired man shook his head. 'Strikes me that it isn't the right way for an uninvited stranger to come into a man's house and tell him what he should be doing under his own roof, with his own family,' he said slowly. 'Strikes me that someone's mother should have taught him better manners. Strikes me that none of my children would be allowed to go on that way.'

An older woman came into the room. She stood behind the man and put her hand on his shoulder, looking at us and smiling faintly.

'Guests, Richard?' she said.

'Elders, this is my wife, Amy. Been married seventeen years, this spring. I took her into the Manti Temple and married her five weeks after I met her. She's the mother to the first four of my children. Marilyn.'

Marilyn tipped her head slightly, but otherwise carried on at the sink, her face turned to the bubbling faucet.

'Marilyn here is my wife too. She's what *you'd* call a stepmother to Luanne and her two sisters, whose mother Wanda is out back with the boys helping me with our new fence. Marilyn don't do yard work because she's due one of her own this September and Amy stays in the house with her.'

'Will you pray with us?' I said. I held onto my scriptures tightly, feeling the sweat run along my spine. 'Let's all of us kneel down here in your kitchen and pray for a blessing on your house.'

'We pray every day,' Amy said. 'Morning, evening. With the children. I teach them myself. We pray before we go to bed and while we're working. There's always a prayer in our hearts,' she tapped her chest lightly with her clenched fist, 'the Spirit lives here. In this tabernacle.'

Keller shook his head. 'The Spirit can't dwell in an unworthy house,' he said. His acne glowed indignantly. 'There's no Spirit here, Sister.'

He drew himself up to his full and unimpressive height. All those thundering Mission President's talks about how each and every one of us had been given the power to confound those who speak against the work had gotten to him. He forgot sometimes, in a way that I never did and sometimes became envious of, that we weren't Old Testament prophets, nor warriors, seers and visionaries, nor healers, nor representatives of Christ – but only boys, boys away from home. Richard stood up too, scraping his chair back so hard that Amy had to jump back to avoid him.

'Are you telling my wife she's a liar?' he said. 'Are you telling her, in front of me, that we're doing any different to what Prophet Joseph, Prophet Brigham did right here in this territory, and called holy? We live the Principle. We don't back out of it because a few suits up in Washington tell us it isn't allowed. We live the Lord's way, not the world's way.'

'Elder Keller,' I said, and touched his arm. Richard took a step towards him. Keller had tears in his eyes. The Spirit leaves when you argue points of doctrine. You can't convince someone into truth. You can't show evidence for right and wrong. You live right, and the Spirit shows you the way.

'We don't treat our women like this,' Keller said, and I pulled at his arm, 'the sisters are precious. They shouldn't be housed like this, like cattle, like dogs . . .'

Amy inhaled sharply and looked like she had something to say about Keller comparing her and her sister wives to a pack of dogs, but she held her peace and said nothing.

'Brother Joe didn't think so,' Richard remarked, smiling gently, 'but they probably never told you that, did they? How's that Kool-Aid tasting, Elders?'

'Elder,' I said again, 'it's time for us to leave.' I had become convinced that if Keller said one more word Richard would produce a gun, or tie us up in one of the outhouses and leave his sons to deal with us.

'I think you boys will be going now. Won't you?' Richard said. 'Amy, take that jug away from Marilyn, give them some water and then show them the phone in the hall. They can wait in the yard for the tow truck. If there's enough shade for the *dogs*, the Lord's chosen and anointed should be able to manage.'

In the yard Elder Keller rubbed his temples, and paced, and threw dark looks at the house, knowing that Richard was inside, staring back at him and perhaps laughing. He wouldn't drink their water, and called for Marilyn to come with us, but she just shook her head and laughed.

I went to the gate, leaned against one of the fence panels and looked up and down the road, trying not to think of those familiar pictures up on their kitchen walls. I'd heard of the apostates, the breakaway groups, the people who called themselves Mormons, but weren't. What if, I thought, struggling furiously to keep the words from materialising in my mind, what if they weren't the breakaway group, departing from the truth, but we were? Abraham was given two wives. Brigham Young had over forty. Good, righteous men. Prophets. Does righteousness change?

The rest of the day passed. We didn't talk about burning our ties again. Keller and I rode in the truck, accepted our dressing-down from the zone leaders, had our car privileges removed and were sent to be interviewed by the assistants to the President. We never spoke again about what we'd seen. *How's that Kool-Aid tasting?* I didn't even know what he meant.

* * *

The thread connecting James and me breaks, and I lose him. The back of his head appears once or twice between others, pacing quickly towards the main exit of the airport, but before I can shout his name, he's gone. Can't even smell his rotten cologne. I try to follow, but every face in the crowd looks the same. I swim through people, looking for him. My golden contact.

'James?' I touch someone on the arm – the wrong person. He turns, shrugs my hand away, frowns, and I stumble away, shuffling my suitcase and rucksack and the bottles of washing-up liquid.

There is a group of teenagers waiting outside a photobooth, laughing and twitching at the curtain as the flash pops inside. Teenagers have changed since I've been away. It's hard to tell the boys and girls apart. They wear the same slick, lopsided, brushed-forward hairstyles, with eyeliner under their eyes and giant trainers on their feet. Studded belts and hooded sweatshirts dangling from skinny shoulders. They're all skinny – knees and elbows and miserable-looking cheekbones. They're tapping and swiping their mobile phones or messing around with MP3 players. The sight of them waiting here, maybe on the way home from a school trip, makes me think about Jeannie and I stop dawdling and hurry towards the arrivals lounge, looking for Bishop Jackson and wondering if I will recognise him.

Someone behind me grabs my shoulders, turns me around, gives me a shake and laughs in my face. I don't see who it is in the gale of movement and sound but I know. Bishop Jackson.

'S-s-s-s-sorry . . . I was, have you been waiting for me?' I glance past him, still stupidly hoping for James. The bishop's face is red and there are tears in his eyes.

'I've been looking for you. Welcome home. Welcome home, Elder Leeke.'

I think we're going to shake hands but he pulls me into him by the wrist and squeezes me tight. The plastic bottles under my arm jab my chest. He kisses my cheek, releases me for a second and then grabs me again. He smells like pies. There's a row of pens sticking out of his suit pocket. One of them has lost its top and the ink makes a mark on my own shirt, but it doesn't matter. People are staring. Smiling. They probably think he's my dad. I hug him back. The shoulder pad in his suit presses against my eyebrow.

'We're so proud of you, Elder. We're just so pleased to have you home. This is the best bit of my calling, you know. Welcoming you boys back. You've done well. So well.'

I open my eyes very wide but the tears get out and spill down my face anyway. I need to tell him it's not like I was out in Afghanistan, that I didn't do that well really. But when Bishop Jackson releases me I see his face is wet too and, overcome again, he grabs my hand in both of his and shakes it.

'Well. Well. Look at you. Just look at you.'

He's still shaking.

'I tried to get in at the barber's before I left, Bishop. It wasn't so easy . . .'

'Forget about your hair, Elder. You're skin and bone. Don't they have food in Utah?'

I smile. Am suddenly very, very tired. He lets go of my hand.

'Can I get you something to eat now?' He waves his arms around. Millie's Cookies. WHSmith. 'Do you want a bag of Quavers? A sausage roll?'

'I'm fasting, Bishop. Up until you release me.'

This prompts a fresh torrent of shaking and squeezing.

'Fasting! Course you are. You're a good boy. One of our best. You've done us all proud.'

'Thank you, Bishop.'

'I'm going to drive you back right now. The roads are clear. You'll be back in your own bed tonight. How does that feel?'

'Pretty good.' I smile, and it turns into a yawn.

'Pretty good! Listen to you! You sound like one of them!

What's that under your arm? You been spending your dollars on Duty Free? Did you get something for your mother? Aren't you pleased to be back? You look like somebody died! I wasn't sure how much cash you'd have on you, so I've a bunch of flowers and a tin of Quality Street in the back of my car for you to give to your mum. No, no, you don't owe me a thing. It's a pleasure. A real pleasure. Is that washing-up liquid?'

'It's—'

'Never mind. Never mind. Just listen to me, mithering you. Let's get you in the car. We'll talk on the way home. You got your luggage, Elder?'

'Yes,' I whisper.

'Come on then. What are we doing standing here weeping like a pair of girls when your mother's at home cooking up a storm? Let's go!'

Bishop Jackson puts his arm around my shoulders and steers me like that through the concourse. I've seen men walking through Chorley like this, swaying and pleased at the football match they've just seen. We go, my shoulder tucked into his armpit, his suit jacket too tight across his shoulders, past Starbucks and KFC and Tie Rack and Wetherspoons. It's all glass and chrome, yellow lights and tannoy announcements.

He keeps squeezing my shoulder and every time I catch his eye he looks so happy I can hardly stand it.

JEANNIE

16.47. Hot inside the padding, and itchy behind the shin-guards. Mrs Leaming's down the other end of the pitch, puffing into her whistle and supervising a long corner, so I lean forward and spit through the mouth-guard onto the Astroturf.

'Get on with it, then. Which one of you is going to take it?' Leaming is shouting, but it's taking ages. Through the criss-cross netting around the pitch that's meant to keep stray balls from escaping onto the playing fields or shattering the windows of the art block, I can see the boys from the lower school practising their relay. There are four teams of five and Mr Barnes spreads them out along the lines chalked into the grass and hands out the batons.

I hate the relay. People think it's easy, but it's not. They think just because you don't have to run that far and there are four other people helping you win, it's lemon squeezy. I'm not a fast runner, and when we had to do it last year for sports day they put me last, as the anchor.

You're not supposed to turn and look at the one running towards you, but get into place with your hand palm out behind you, ready to receive. I did that, listening to my team-mate puffing and thudding her way along the track behind me, and then felt the baton in my hand, cool and light and the metal slippery and disgusting with her hand-sweat. No one told me you were supposed to hold it lightly, to dry your hands on your shorts. It slipped out of my hands like a bar of soap because I grabbed it too tight. We lost, and I had to walk back on my own between wooden benches full of everyone waving their hands and screaming because they'd already started the next race.

'Jeannie! Screw your head on, will you?'

My hands find their way to the catch under my chin that keeps the helmet on tight. Fingernail just flicking at the clasp. What would happen. What would. If I.

I undo the clasp.

Emily Higgins is leaning forward now, waiting for the whistle, the ball at her feet – a little cannon ball. It could hurt you. The whistle sounds, very far away, and Emily drives the ball through the air with such force that she nearly loses her balance and hits herself on the back of the head with the stick. She grunts. I don't know why she's even on the team, hoofing at the ball like that. She treats her stick like it's a spoon. Helmet is loose. The ball hisses through the air, followed by most of our side, charging their way down the centre, sticks glued to the pitch. It's curving, spinning like a little sun, much too high, and it'll be a foul but that won't help me if I'm. If it.

I put my head down, turn slightly and bite my lip. The ball catches me in the side and not in my head, bouncing off my padding and knocking my hip as it falls. The sweat on the back of my neck cools.

'Raised ball! Time! Time! What are you doing, Emily, trying to take her head off?'

Mrs Leaming jogs down the sidelines, blowing her whistle in a series of indignant little peeps.

'Jeannie's been hurt!'

The pain comes on slowly, a few seconds after the impact. Like it was called up by someone shouting, someone saying I was hurt, and then my body made it happen. 16.59.

Sister Fletcher once told me a story about a frog that managed to get itself boiled to death in a pot without a lid. I didn't ask her why the frog didn't just jump out, even though I knew she wanted me to. I'd heard it already. They must get together in their councils and decide all the youth need to hear this story at least once or twice a year until they're deaf to it. So I didn't ask. I didn't say anything.

'The thing is, a frog likes water. It likes being in a pan. And you can heat the water up degree by single degree until it's boiled. Till its skin drops off and it dies. No problem. If you do it slow enough, it'll sit there bathing until it's dead. Can you see the significance? No? *Jeannie*. Our elder brother Jesus Christ spoke and taught in parables, meaning he wants us to be a people that can interpret dark sayings, find the truth in unlikely places. You see nothing in this story? Read between the lines, eat the meat and spit out the bones. Frog soup!'

'It sounds sort of cruel,' I said, and she shook her head. 'Sorry.'

'Don't be sorry. Just listen.' She counted off the points I was too stupid to see on her fingers. 'We can become immersed in our sin, step by tiny step, until even fornication, murder, abortion, adultery, homosexuality or any other abomination you can think of seems almost normal. Unremarkable. Nothing much to protect yourself from.'

'Okay.'

'And something else we can learn. The lid was off. Off, Jeannie. The Lord doesn't shut people in with sin. He never allows you to be tempted more than you can bear. When the Lord closes a door, he opens a window. We've always got an escape hatch. Yes.'

Escape hatch. A way to jump out of that pan. I don't think she meant opening the catch on my helmet and standing in front of a ball that would work like a bullet if it hit me right where I wanted it to.

'All right, Jeannie,' Mrs Leaming is right here now, her mouth at my ear, her breath like coffee and Polos, 'deep breaths.'

The ball is rolling away between my boots and there's a hot, glassy throb that starts on the sticking-out bit of my hipbone and radiates outwards. I dig my stick into the pitch and lean over it, panting. Pain. Up and down, along my thigh and across my stomach. I lean forward, let the stick fall, kneel down, unclip the mouth-guard and retch, once, twice, three times, but nothing comes up. The helmet falls off and bounces on the pitch.

'Has she puked, miss?'

Leaming shouts for everyone to go back and get changed and mutters about helmets and padding and foul balls. My hands start to shake.

'It's all right, Jeannie. You're fine. Take a few minutes to settle down, then go in with the rest.'

She takes my stick, picks up the ball and walks away. It wouldn't have knocked me out. It would have killed me. Smashed my nose and teeth into my brain. Caved my head in. An eggshell, or a dropped melon. Drowned me in my own blood. That's me. I never think. That's half my. 17.04.

Emily, as part of her punishment, stands at the door of the changing room collecting the coloured bibs and rattling the hockey sticks back into the big plastic dustbin they are stored in. We throw them at her as we pass. The new team photos are up. Someone must have hung them during the Easter holidays. We gather around them, trying to find our own faces and bottle-necking in the entrance to the changing room.

From a distance, we all look the same. Navy pleated skirts, white polo tops with the school logo printed over the heart. Us in lines, hair scraped back, holding our sticks across our bodies like spears. On this picture, I am pale and straight faced, my hands grip the stick tightly, my hair knotted into a bun on the back of my head. I don't look anything like myself. We won all our county inter-school matches last term – the finals of the yearly tournament are coming up at the end of this term. We're going to wipe the floor. Beat them into the ground. Trounce them and send them home.

How big will I be by then? As big as a whale, a house. A big white blob, blocking up the nets, too fat for my padding. My hip still hurts and I run my hand across it, inside the padding and across my belly, which is little and flat, just like it always was. 17.12.

'Are you going to get your mum to buy you a picture?' Beth is taking a form from a pile on the table next to the office, filling out her details and posting it into the box fixed to the office door.

I shake my head and throw my helmet into the bucket under the table. 'They know what I look like in my PE kit.'

Beth laughs, and pulls her hair out of its knot, and shakes it out, damp and wavy, around her shoulders. There's a long graze on her forearm from where she skidded on the Astroturf and went down before she could get her balance. It gleams, red and wet, but she ignores it.

'You should leave that helmet out, if it's faulty. What if someone else gets it? She could have knocked you out. You could have *died*!'

Emily glances at us; mouths a silent 'sorry' with her frosted lips.

'Forget it. Just help me out of this, will you?'

Beth unclips the padding for me, pulls at the straps and Velcro, and it comes off in two sections. I pull it over my head, smelling the mouldy, damp smell. Don't be sick. Don't breathe in. Don't think about being sick. Think about water, and fresh air, and grass and.

'You look rough.' Beth props the padding up against the bin full of sticks. It falls over, but we both pretend we didn't see it and go on towards the showers. 'Is it still hurting?'

'I didn't get much sleep last night.'

I limp over to the wall and lean against it, pulling up my shirt to look at the red welt on my hip, hot and throbby.

'You'll feel that in the morning,' Beth says admiringly.

'I'm going to pack this in,' I say. Just testing to see what the words sound like out loud, but even before Beth has turned to face me, shocked, I know what I've just said is true, is what's going to happen.

'You're not. You can't!'

I'm the star goalie. I wait in the nets, bent over, head forward, testing the weight of my stick and moving from one foot to another. No one else gets to be goalie. When I'm not at practice, my side loses. I'm very good at this. 17.16.

Beth holds open the door with her boot and shakes her gumshield. Silvery ribbons of spit fly away from it, my stomach lurches, and I turn away quick.

'I'm going to tell Mrs Learning today.'

'Because you had a knock?' Beth laughs. 'You've had worse than that before. I remember the time you took one to the face, had the imprint of the guard on your cheek for a week, didn't you?'

I nod.

'Play to the end of the season, at least. The final's in May. We're going to win it. You can't miss that.'

'I don't want to any more.' I sound like a big baby, I know I do. I don't want Beth to see my face in case I am going red so I lean over my bag and start rooting about for my phone. He won't have sent a message, but I need to check anyway. 17.19.

'Jeannie? If I see that phone in your hand again, it'll go in my desk until the end of the week. Away, please. In your bag. *Properly.*'

Leaming is always appearing out of nowhere. When they hear her coming, some of the girls rush into the changing room and wrap themselves in a towel before she's had time to lock the sticks and balls away and get back. If they can get over to the sinks and splash their shoulders and hair before she comes out, it's all right for them to be sitting on the benches drying their feet when she comes in. She likes it when we get undressed and dressed quickly: she gives you ten sets of hockey rules to copy out if you don't.

I strip off my socks, pull my phone back out of my bag. Four missed calls from Mum. There was something I was supposed to do. Wasn't there?

'Come on, ladies. You know the drill.'

We get up and go, slowly. Leaming stands at the entrance to the showers with a clipboard, marking our names off on a second register. You've to go into the changing room, strip off and get your towel, then file past her into the nearest free shower cubicle along the row. She's wearing a Preston North End shirt, football shorts and white Nikes. Her legs are so brown you can tell she's always on the sunbed. But they're muscly, like a man's. She rubs Vaseline all down her shins before she takes us out because she says it keeps her warm while she's standing about on the sidelines.

'Jeannie!'

'It's away, miss. It's away.' I show her my empty hands.

'How's your hip? Are you all right?'

Beth, wrapped in her towel, is staring at me. If I'm going to say anything, now's the time. Let the side down. Be responsible for the squad losing our place. My fault, see, because no one's as good in the nets as I am.

'Do you need an ice pack?'

'I want to get home.'

Beth hides a smile, turns away from me. Bottled it. Taking one for the team.

'Don't go to bed. Walk around for a bit, have a hot bath. Bag of frozen peas. Don't let yourself seize up, we need you in full working order.'

'I won't, miss.'

'Good.' She makes a mark next to my name. 'Now hurry up.'

The tiles are ridged to stop you slipping, and there's dirt and hair caught in the patterned surface, and I try and walk on the sides of my feet because it's disgusting. Walking in other people's soapy run-off.

When I first started I was afraid of the communal showers. I'd seen them on telly in high-school films and things like that but actually when we came for the open day they were laid out like the ones in the swimming baths with two rows of cubicles facing each other and each one with a red curtain hanging down from a row of shiny metal rings. So on my first week when they said it was time for us to go in and do PE, I wasn't afraid and just wrapped myself up in my towel and took a bar of soap in one hand and went through. Mrs Leaming ticked off my name on her register and in I went.

But between the open day and then, someone had ripped all the curtains down – there was only one cubicle that still had that curtain and I wasn't ever getting into that one – and Mrs Leaming was at the end staring with her pencil in her hand and the edge of her tongue showing between her lips and they only replace the curtains when the open days come round again, so I had no choice but to hang my towel up on the hook and stand there under the lukewarm dribble of water rubbing myself with soap and slightly crying because you had to be naked in front of everyone and there was no choice about it. That's what the register is for. You can get out of it if you say you're on your period, but then she puts a dot near your name instead of a tick and if you get more than one dot every month she sends you to the school nurse to explain yourself. There's no way out of it.

We run through and keep our towels around us while we kick our legs under the spray. Beth starts chatting to me about some song we're supposed to be practising for the Youth Convention next month but I hold my face under the spray and pretend I can't hear her. 17.23.

* * *

191

Beth's shy like I am. We huddle in together right on the end of the bench and she stands between me and the others while I put my knickers back on under my towel. Then I do the same for her. Her towel is pink and thick and fluffy. She twists it around her hair and puts it on top of her head like a turban then sits to button her shirt.

'Are you on your phone *again*?'

I hang up and tuck it back into my bag.

'No.'

'I saw you!' Beth laughs. 'If he was stuck at the airport, your mum would have texted you and told you, wouldn't she?'

'He's not stuck. He'll be back tonight,' I sigh, 'definitely, this time.'

'Where are you going?' Paula says. She's hunched over a hand mirror, earwigging and running a pastry-coloured sponge loaded with foundation over her speckled forehead and cheeks.

'Nowhere.'

'I just heard you say you were.' She dabs at her chin. 'Is anything good happening?'

'Nothing.' I shake my head.

'She's not going anywhere,' Beth says. Paula smirks, and ignores her.

'You still grounded?'

'My brother's back.'

'So, what's that got to do with you?'

'He's been away for a long time,' Beth chips in, 'he's been serving a—'

'He's in the army,' I interrupt her, and elbow her away not accidentally as I stuff my hockey skirt back into my PE bag. The whole place stinks of mud and sweat and the rubber-studded soles of our boots. 'My mum wants us all there.'

'A soldier? Cool. I bet he's well fit. Are you having a party? Can I come?'

Beth frowns again. 'He's not been in the army,' she says, 'I don't know why you'd say that, Jeannie. He's been serving a mission for our Church. We're Mo—'

'It's just a dinner,' I say quickly, 'he's been away for a while, and now he's coming home, and we're having a special dinner together. No party.'

Paula screws up her nose. 'Boring. You should come out with us,' she says, 'bring Lewis with you if you want. Get him to bring his friends. It'll be a laugh.'

Beth's face is reddening, her eyes getting bigger. I'd never be allowed to hang around with Paula. Mum doesn't want me getting in with a bad crowd and making best friends out of non-members. Beth scowls at me and Paula snaps her make-up case shut, drops it into her bag and heads over to the queue in front of the cloudy, crazed mirrors over the sinks. 17.32.

'Lewis?'

'It's nothing, Beth. Just leave it, will you?'

'Who is he?'

Mrs Leaming appears, striding through the steam with her clipboard tucked under her arm.

'If you girls have got time to gossip, you've got time to knock the mud off those hockey sticks for me.' Silence. 'No? Didn't think so. Get on with it then.' She stalks away, her whistle rattling against her chest.

'Jeannie? Have you got a boyfriend?'

'Mind your own.'

I roll up my towel, drop it into the carrier bag and shove it into my bag. Slip my feet into my shoes without undoing the laces.

'I'm not being nosy. I'm concerned about you.'

Concerned. I want to laugh. Concerned is one of those words that mean something different when someone at our church says it. It goes along, most of the time, with *inappropriate. I'm concerned, Jeannie*, Maggie might say, one of these days, *you're acting out in inappropriate ways. Is this something we can talk about?*

Concerned is a sticky, beady-eyed sort of kindness. These harmless words are loaded. They are gentle ways of telling you that you're doing something wrong, and even if you didn't know, everyone else can tell and has had a good old chat about it behind your back.

'You *are* going out tonight, aren't you? With this Lewis? Gary's back and all you can think about is getting out with a boyfriend? Your own brother. Don't you think he'd rather you stayed at home and spent time with him?'

Beth opens her eyes wide and shows me the palms of her hands. Maggie in training. This is what we will all turn into if we behave ourselves and don't do anything too concerning.

'I'm going to be there for the dinner,' I say. Because I want to explain it to her. Because I want someone to tell me that this is not a stupid idea. She ducks into her bag and pulls out a packet of Haribo.

'Here,' she says, 'eat something.'

We sit on the benches together and chew. Julian says these sweets are made out of pig bones but I love them.

'I just need to go and do something first. Something important.'

Beth is staring at me.

'I need to do a . . .' I can't tell her. 'It's important,' I try again, 'to sort this out before Gary comes home. Before I speak to him.'

'Sort *what* out?' she says, and frowns at me. 'You're not making any sense. You've been weird all day. Do you not think he'll be dying to see you?' She chews noisily. I can see the red and yellow gummy bears sticking to her molars.

The day of Gary's going-away party I went up to the bedroom he shared with Julian to see if he was ready to go. He was ironing shirts and ties and putting them on hangers. The room was steamy and smelled like flowers because Gary liked to put Shake n' Vac on the carpet and hoover up when Julian wasn't around. They had bunk beds. Julian had the bottom one and it was a kind of dark pit with hundreds of pictures of cars ripped out of magazines and stuck to the wall. Gary had the top one. He always made his bed and had little pictures of the temple, the one of Jesus in the red cape that everyone's got, the Articles of Faith, other things he was trying to learn off by heart so he could get a head start before he went. A little shelf with his scriptures on it and a glass of water and a reading light and a packet of mints so he wouldn't offend us with his breath first thing.

Julian's still on the bottom, he just uses Gary's bed to put stuff on now. His spare overalls and that.

'All right, Jeannie?'

'Dad's sent me up to get you. He's just putting Mum in the car.'

He turned the iron off and sat on the edge of Julian's bed. The mattress sagged under him.

'Right then. I better get my shirt on. Should I wear the white one with the blue tie, or the ivory one with the navy tie?'

I didn't get the joke, but he laughed at it for himself and then took my hand and pulled me over and made me sit on his knee. I was too big for it even two years ago. He knew I was but did it anyway and I let him.

'What's wrong with your face, Shortcake, Little-Leeke, Jeannie-in-the-Lamp?'

'I don't want to go,' I said. 'There's going to be loads of people there. They'll all be staring at us the whole time.'

He laughed. 'Angela will be there. Ask if you can take her outside. Show her the flowers or something.'

'Mum's already told me if I sneak off she'll send Maggie after me.'

Gary laughed again.

'Looks like you're stuck then.'

'That's no help.'

'If I could help you, I'd help myself.' He squeezed me round the waist and whispered in my ear, 'I don't want to go either.'

'It's your party!'

'It's like a funeral,' he said, 'more for Mum and Dad and all the others than it is for me.'

'They'll give you presents, though,' I said.

He laughed. 'Ties and stamps and envelopes. Shoe polish and black shoelaces. A raincoat. I've seen the list she's sending round.'

I put my head on his shoulder. It was uncomfortable, sitting like that. We had to duck a bit to keep from hitting our heads on the top bunk.

'Can I have your Xbox?'

'You can borrow it. Keep it in your room. Don't let Julian sell it.'

'Can I have the games as well?'

'Let me sort them out. I need to send some to Cash Converters.'

'Gary!'

'They're not meant for girls. If you moan, I'll save Julian the trouble and send the whole lot to Cash Converters.'

'You're miserable, you are.'

'Shut up.'

'You shut up.'

He laughed and let go of me then and I jumped off his knee. Even though he was just in his jeans and tee-shirt, his ironed shirt hanging up off the door frame for the party that afternoon, he still felt like a missionary. Someone you weren't allowed to cuddle or touch even if he was your brother.

'You'll be sh-sh-shaking hands with me next, Sister Leeke,' Gary said. I laughed. I am his sister. His real sister.

'Are you going to write me letters while I'm away? Tell me your worries? Maybe I should be the one buying you stamps.'

'I might,' I said, 'if I can be bothered.'

'You'll be grown up when I come back. Old enough to go on the Youth Conventions. Meet boys.'

I shook my head and pulled a face. 'I'll be fourteen.'

'Nearly a grown-up.' Gary looked sad then, and I went and stood next to him. Didn't want to sit on his knee again, but I let him hug me. He'd had his hair cut extra-short and it tickled the side of my neck. 'Poor Jeannie. Poor Gary, but poor Jeannie too.'

I wondered if he was thinking about Carole. He wouldn't let anyone say she was his girlfriend because he knew as soon as he turned nineteen he'd be putting his papers in and it wouldn't be fair on her to ask her to wait. We weren't ever allowed to mention her in front of Mum. She'd have gone mental. *No girls before your mission.* But in the front of his scriptures, tucked in along with his bookmarks, there was a picture of her standing outside the temple. Julian told Gary he'd put a tenner on her being married by the time he got back, and Gary turned white and went and pulled out brambles in the garden for two hours while Julian laughed at him out of the kitchen window.

'It's you who's leaving, not me,' I said. 'You're leaving me with *them*. And Julian.'

'I know,' he said, and stood up, 'but doing the right thing isn't always easy, is it?'

He didn't leave for another two weeks, but that was the last proper conversation we had. From the night of the party onwards he wouldn't watch television or listen to the radio. He put all his DVDs and computer games in my room, gave all his magazines to the hospital, wouldn't wear anything but a shirt and tie, even when he was taking the bins out or picking up the dog poo from the back garden.

Beth is staring at me and I don't want to talk to her any more.

'Jeannie. Why are you crying?'

Smells are working on me today. These damp towels wafting

about and sickening me, making me think about that blanket. 17.41.

When Gary comes back tonight I will tell him that, after a bit inside that garage when I was already past bored and wanted to go home, Lewis shut the car door and leaned over me.

'Stop messing about and come here, you little tease.'

He kissed me and I felt a little current, like I was licking a battery and turning my whole body into a tongue. *That's enough*, I thought, but he leaned forward, grabbed my knees and tipped me over so I was lying along the back seat and he was on top of me. The blanket fell down from the parcel shelf and across my face and he didn't move it for me right away. I didn't say anything because I was that embarrassed.

I'd had information about this, at Young Women's. Heavy petting counts as sex even if you've got your clothes on so by that point I was a lost cause anyway. Jeannie the little froggy. Because lying down, even if you've got one foot on your bedroom floor or whatever, turns kissing into heavy petting. One of our prophets didn't even kiss his wife until after he'd taken her to the temple. It's just not necessary if you're looking at someone with your spiritual eyes.

I stayed lying down, my skirt had come up around my knees and once Lewis pulled the blanket off my face I saw he was looking right up it as if he didn't know what was up there. Your first time is supposed to be a special time to seal the marriage between a husband and wife and make you one flesh but it had gone past that now anyway. Far too late.

I let myself lie there limp. My arms and legs were so heavy. The front of his overalls had poppers up them and he was undoing them from the top down. Then when it was open he pulled the overall off past his shoulders. He was wearing a tee-shirt underneath and ordinary blue boxers. I shut my eyes tight like I was having my hair washed and was scared of getting suds in my eyes.

'Don't go all shy on me now,' he said.

I tried to move away but he caught my hands and pressed them to my chest. My neck crumpled against the plastic moulded bit on the inside of the passenger door, you know, the bit that's meant for keeping your hankies and a glasses case in or something?

'You're hurting my neck.'

'Don't wriggle about then,' Lewis said and my brain flew like a bird out of the window and I couldn't talk.

He. Then he. After a while he. Then I. When he.

'Please, Jeannie.'

We're the last in the changing room now. 17.45. Leaming will come in soon and usher us out so she can lock up, but there isn't the same rush after school as there is during the day. It's silent; the only sound the rushing inside the pipes.

'It's . . .' My tongue has been stuck tight to the roof of my mouth for weeks. Mum thinks I am giving her the silent treatment. Beth's doing up the laces on her shoes, and isn't looking at me when I say the words.

'I'm going to have a baby,' I say.

She leans back on the bench and lets her hands rest on her knees. Palm up, little shocked cups. Fingers curled limply. Tears come quite easily for her, and she blinks them back a bit, then lets them go.

'You have to speak to your mum,' she says, 'Jeannie, you've *got* to.'

There are girls in the fifth year who it has happened to. They go off for a bit and get the operation, or they go off for longer and come back on their own for their exams while their mothers take care of the . . . It's not like it's something we've never heard of. It just doesn't happen to us.

'I know.'

'Tell Bishop Jackson. He'll tell her for you.'

I nod and stuff my trainers into the top of my school bag.

'Is Lewis your boyfriend?'

I shake my head. 'No. I don't . . . I didn't want to.'

'He *made* you?'

Because if he did, that's all right.

'I didn't like it.'

But he didn't tie me up or hit me or anything.

'Did he know you didn't want to do it? Did you shout at him and scream and stuff?'

Beth is trying to figure out if I am bad or not. I know this. We've all done it. We know what the rules are. That's what Gary's going to ask me.

'No,' I whisper. I rub my eyes with the heel of my hand.

'That poor baby,' she whispers, and just sits there, and lets me walk off.

All the blood has left my arms and legs. I want to go home and sleep. I need to go back though. I need to have a do-over. Fix it so when I speak to Gary I can say, *Yes he did definitely know I did not want to do that.*

I look at the clock. 17.49.

Lewis will be expecting me.

PAULINE

This Nina can lie like she's been born to it. She takes charge at the police station, standing at the counter and telling them all she's a good friend of the family, a junior but long-standing employee of the store and a witness to all the events. There's been, she says, a horrible mistake that she knows I'll be good enough to overlook if I can be processed quickly and get out before teatime. She tells them all about Gary and his mission, about Jeannie's recent problems and, as I'm wondering how she knows so much about me and mine, she lays a twenty-pound note out and says she knows for a fact that will more than cover any damage or cleaning costs incurred. There are two police officers this side of the counter, the ones that came to Richardson's to get me, and they just stand back and raise their eyebrows and shake their heads a bit. 'I hope that isn't a bribe?' There are another two behind the counter (and that's what my tax is going on – your comfy chairs and swish computers! That brew you've been sucking at the past ten minutes!). One's blonde with clumpy blue mascara on, and the other one who looks young enough to be at school just sits there taking phone calls and hammering away at his computer like I'm not even there. 'It's not for you,' Nina says, and takes the note back off the counter and puts it into her back pocket. 'It's for that prick at Richardson's. Jobsworth.' 'You're going to need to settle down and moderate your language a bit, or you'll end up in a cell with her,' the one with the blue mascara says. She's typing things into a computer too, her short nails clattering away on the keyboard. 'Are you her carer?' Nina looks at me and one eyelid lowers, just a flicker.

'I'm staying here with her,' Nina says. 'Can you confirm your name and address with us, and empty your pockets?' 'Don't say anything to them,' Nina whispers, then looks across the counter, points at me with her thumb. 'She's not a criminal, is she?' 'We've a process to go through.' Blue mascara woman waves Nina away, and looks down at me over the counter. 'We've fully accessible cells here, love. Have you any other medical needs we should know about?' 'This is bloody ridiculous,' Nina says, breaking in before I can say anything. 'This woman is terminally ill. She's dying. Can you not understand that?' There are posters all over the place here. Maybe they think if they give the derelicts and delinquents something to read they'll be a bit calmer. HIV and drunk driving and needle exchanges – whatever they are when they're at home. Crying, pouchy-eyed women advertising domestic violence helplines, and lots of pictures of pretty girls with scars on their faces to show you what happens when you go joyriding in stolen cars. The posters are tattered around the edges and faded, the boards loaded to bursting, and there are notices about Neighbourhood Watch meetings with dates on them going back to when Adam was a lad. Dying. She's so certain about it. And something about her voice; the mixture of outrage and pity. It's hardly a thing a stranger would lie about. But she's not a stranger, is she? A friend of Martin? Did she say she used to work at the sorting office? 'At least get her a warm drink, will you? And a blanket – a change of clothes?' Dying. She's telling the truth. But how would she know? How would she know, and me, not? Could you be dying, and not know it? Could you have something seriously wrong with you, and still use the telephone, and look things up on the internet? If that's the case, then anyone could be dying, any time. Could happen to all of us. Gary could be dying. Getting ready to get off the plane and then *poof*! Is there something wrong with me? Something specific? I go all floaty and faraway, that behind-glass sort of sensation I used to get when I was Jeannie's age, it was my time of the month and

I was getting ready for a faint. 'I want to see a doctor,' I say, but very quietly. No one listens. 'Get me the forms to make a complaint,' Nina demands, and lays her hands flat on the black shiny surface of the counter. Their voices fade in and out, like they're on the telly and someone's messing about with the volume buttons. Blue mascara comes out from behind the counter and wheels me into a side room. She says something, and then gently pushes my hand onto a computer screen. The screen takes a picture of my fingers and she tells me my fingerprints are on the system now as if that's something to be proud of. They push me in my chair and line me up between two black marks on the wall and the floor. I'm not looking in any particular direction when a light flashes and I realise they've got the computer to take another picture. Blue mascara woman smiles and she's got brown marks on her teeth. She tells me I'm in the hall of fame now, and did I want her to turn the screen round so I can check they got my best side? 'I want to see a doctor. I'm dying.' I must be whispering because she gives no sign of having heard. Then she takes my fingerprints again, this time the old-fashioned way with ink and sheets of card. 'All right, lovey, can you stand at all? We're just going to have to ask you to get up a minute so we can search the chair. You've nothing in there that you shouldn't have, have you? Fags? Any weapons or drugs? Nothing like that?' She takes my arm and pulls me upwards and my knees start to tremble, as if the bones in my legs and especially my pelvis are made of paper and I am going to hurt myself by putting so much weight on them. The tiny bones in my feet start to crackle and bend and I'm about to cry out in pain when she eases me down into a plastic chair, the one she's been sitting in. 'I'm sorry . . .' I say, when she uses the handles on the chair to tip it forward and look underneath the seat. She screws up her nose, turns her face away. 'We'll get someone to sort that out for you,' she says, spinning the wheels with one hand, pressing at the tyres with her fingers as if I've put a gun inside the inner tube. 'Don't worry, we've all seen worse.' I keep on asking for the doctor but blue mascara woman doesn't seem to mind that I am dying. I don't understand this at all. She is polite and gentle with me and she wipes down my chair before putting me back in it. But once she's done that, she still puts me in a cell. 'There's an emergency button there,' she says, letting go of the handles and pointing to a little red button on the wall near the door. She backs out, drawing it closed behind her. 'You can reach it all right?' I nod. 'Now don't go pressing on that every five minutes. Only if there's a real emergency. Do you hear?' I was expecting that the sound of the door being closed and locked would be sheer terrible – that the thud and clank of her closing the metal gates along the corridor behind her would drive me mad. I counted them, the second closing before the echoes of the first had died away, and again with the third. The squeak of her sensible flat-soled shoes on the polished floors, the jangle of her keychain, both getting fainter as she walked away back to reception. But it wasn't that bad. At least here in this room on my own my humiliation is over and no one can see me. I cry a bit, but not much. Eventually a nurse comes. 'You decent, my love?' she calls, but she comes in anyway, locks the door behind her and brings me some water and a big roll of blue paper to dry myself on, and some clean clothes. They're only tracksuit bottoms and a bit small at that, but she grabs my elbow and helps me onto the little ledge. 'That better?' I nod, 'Thank you,' and she sits next to me and watches while I struggle with the laces on my plimsolls. She's big and fat and has thick round glasses, and her hair is thin but permed, so the gelled-up curls lie against her pale scalp and stick up around her cheeks. 'Now what's all this about? I've tried to get in touch with your GP and he hasn't got any record of an ongoing medical condition. Are you on any medication? Did you change your doctor, maybe?' 'I don't see doctors.' My throat starts to feel narrow. 'I can't. I won't be interfered with.' She shakes her head, takes her glasses off, cleans them and puts them back on again. Her eyes look round and swollen behind the glass – like she's on the verge of bursting into tears herself, though she's smiling and seems happy enough. 'Well now, that doesn't make any sense, does it? There's a young girl out there telling us you're at death's door and if we keep you locked up we're as good as murderers. I'm not even supposed to be on shift, but they got me sent over from the other police station 'cos she was making such a fuss.' She stares at me until I feel like I've got to say something. 'Sorry,' I say, 'I didn't know.' I have to lean back in my chair because that fuzzy feeling is coming back again. Could be the condition, whatever it is. Something brought on by stress, and I can't think of a person who's got more stress in their life than I have. 'Well, never mind about that now.' She leans back, crosses her thick legs at the ankle. We both look at her shoes, black lace-ups with little pink beads in the shape of teddy bears threaded into the laces. A woman her age. I wonder if she's borrowed them from someone. 'I'm not here to interfere with you. I can't even touch you unless you say it's all right. But your friend out there is convinced you're not long for this world and seeing as they've called me in, I might as well take a look at you. What is it?' she says. 'Cancer?' Cancer! She's so matter of fact! 'It's . . .' I can't talk, but just nod towards my lap. I know well enough what the problem is. But I never knew you could die from it. It's almost a feeling of relief. Yes, it really has been that bad. For the doubters out there, and I know who they are, thanks very much, this is a serious condition. I am properly ill! 'Down below?' Nod again. 'Do you always have problems like this? With your water and bowel movements?' I can't help it, and start crying again. It's not my fault, I want to tell her. Does she think I want to go outside and make a state of myself in public? I think about Maggie and the tears really get going. It's a minute or two before I can get a grip on myself. It's all that Jeannie's fault, I want to explain, she was supposed to bring the shopping. 'All right, love. It's only me here. What started it off? Do you know?' I swallow hard. 'I had a baby. It was a hard birth.' She waits, but I can't bring myself to say more. 'Lie back then, let me have a peek.' Does she mean what I think she means? 'A what?' She hands me a tissue and I blow my nose. 'On your back, feet flat together and let your knees drop open. As far as you can without causing strain.' I can feel my eyes going big, the heat building up in my cheeks. But the way she talks about it, like every day she has someone laid down with their knees spread like a Christmas turkey. And do you know what? I do what she tells me. The foam mattress has a waterproof, plastic-y cover and it squeaks and sticks and nips the skin on my backside. I'm scared, and just look at the writing scraped into the wall, my head turned away from her. She doesn't touch, or shout, or turn away to be sick, which is something. 'Dear oh dear,' she says, and my blood runs cold. 'What is it? How long have I got?' Maybe it is some kind of cancer. 'I can see there's been a lot of damage to your perineum,' she says, 'but it's the scarring that's the problem, isn't it?' She peers again, then pats my knees and gives me a hand so I can get back up again. 'You don't see work like that any more. If you don't mind me saying so, you look like you were stitched up by a vet.' Honestly? I don't know what to say to that. 'There's no need for you to suffer like this,' she says. 'How old is the baby now?' 'Fourteen,' I say, 'and more like a cat than a girl, she's so sneaky.' 'Fourteen?' I nod. 'It's a hard age.' 'You've been like this for fourteen years? And no one's offered you surgery? Jesus Christ,' she shakes her head, 'the last time I saw someone in a state like this, she'd delivered in a refugee camp and her uncle – a shoemaker – had sewn her back up with a length of home-made catgut. And that was eight years ago.' 'My GP's a man,' I said, 'it were bad enough getting the babies out. I'm not putting my legs in the air and letting some stranger loose down there. I won't have it.' 'Well, that's up to you, but that pain you're feeling, that loss of control over your movements – it's all down to scar tissue, my love. Unless you get that sorted out, it isn't going to get any better. You'll be in and out in a day. A decent plastic surgeon would have that dealt with in under an hour. It'll change your life.' She makes everything sound so – so *possible*. 'Scar tissue. Is that all?' She nods. 'Not rocket science, is it? Have you never had a look yourself? What has your husband got to say about this? Have you been having intercourse?' My eyes feel like they're about to drop out of my head. She laughs. 'Didn't think so. The poor sod.' 'It's too . . .' 'The muscles, love. It's all to do with the muscles. That's what's causing your other problems too.' 'The walking?' 'It's *all* muscular. Can be fixed, very easily. A little operation, and some practice. You need to build your core strength back up.' She takes off her glasses, folds them up and slips them into her top pocket. It's as if she's disappointed I don't really have some rare and interesting disease. 'I bet you could stand up right now, if you wanted to.' She's got blue eyes and very fine, very long blonde eyelashes. No looker, but a kind face. 'Could I?' 'No medical reason why not,' she said, 'just take it easy. Don't strain yourself. Do your pelvic floors. It'll be like trying to move your ears at first, but persevere.' My heart starts beating ever so fast. My hands flutter over my tummy, feeling the way the muscles there have thinned and separated, like there's nothing between my skin and my precious internal organs. I fold my arms over myself like a shield. 'Are you sure you know what you're talking about? If you're a proper nurse, how come you're working here and not in a hospital?' She laughs. 'It's livelier here,' she says, and puts her hands on me, touches my tummy gently. 'These muscles here are connected,' she reaches behind me and tugs at the waistband of the jogging pants, 'to your back, to your pelvic floor. The muscles around your vagina, your back passage, they're all linked.' She prods gently. 'Do you ever get backache?' 'Terrible,' I say, 'like there's a metal band round me. It's torture. I can't sit, can't stand, can't lie. That's why I got the chair. I couldn't stand it any more.' 'You need to get yourself out of that chair, love,' she says, 'and get those muscles moving. A little bit every day. Have you got a dog? Start walking it. It's not going to get better if you don't. I'm surprised you've not had a prolapse. That's what you've got to look forward to, if you carry on the way you are. How old are you?' 'Forty-seven.' 'Well then. That's hardly anything at all, is it? Your best years are ahead of you. You don't want to spend them in this chair, do you, not if you don't have to?' I shake my head. 'I'll leave you to think about it,' she says, 'and I'm going to write a letter to your GP. All right?' She takes the dirty clothes away and puts a little squirt of Febreze through the hatch in the door to make me more comfortable. I call after her, wanting to tell her thank you, but my voice has gone all scratchy and whispery so she must not have heard me. When I come out, Nina is still waiting and she says she's not been able to get through to Martin – she's rung the phone off the hook but no one's answering at the house – so she'll pay for a taxi and come right home with me. She's got it all planned out. She's got a carrier bag in her hand and when I realise it's my stained and unrinsed clothes and underwear I can't look at her. She swings it against her leg like she doesn't know what's in it, and takes my arm as she helps me into the taxi. The officers at the counter make me sign something. 'You look like you've lost a pound and found a fiver,' the one with the blue mascara says, 'have you enjoyed yourself that much?' I shake my head and then, before I know it, start to laugh my head off. *Lost a pound and found a fiver!* Yes, that's about right. I want to stay and chat to them a bit, find out how that poor lad with the cut on his head is getting on, but Nina takes hold of the chair and pushes me past the desk and out of the automatic doors. 'I think we should get out while we can, don't you?' she says. Outside it's late afternoon all of a sudden and there is a group of kids – little girls, really – bouncing a tennis ball off a wall and singing 'Queenio Cokio'. They remind me of Jeannie when she were that age, and I just want to get home and snatch her up and give her a cuddle. How long has it been since I've done that? Nina gets into the taxi next to me and even holds my hand a bit while the tears run down my face. She thinks I'm sad. 'I'll get the food for you, give me your list,' she says. 'Oh, it doesn't matter about that. I'll send Martin out. There's a few boxes of tins in the airing cupboard for hard times and rainy days. It's all been something and nothing. Am I going to have to come back here?' 'No, no. They talked to the manager; she said they weren't to charge you. I explained everything. I bet she'll send you a bunch of flowers as well.' 'No, really?' She nods. 'She won't be leaving Anthony in charge of the store again either.' 'Maybe you'll get a shot at it next time, love. Do you think? I bet you've impressed them today.' She shakes her head and smiles. 'Let's just concentrate on getting you home, eh?' My insides are churning with excitement and I keep catching sight of the two of us in the rear-view mirror. Nina, looking all pale and bothered, and me, having to press my lips together, tight shut, to stop myself from smiling. What a picture we must look. Even the taxi driver catches my eye in the mirror once or twice, and I see him wondering about me, thinking I'm a criminal mastermind, a burglar or a member of the mob, and Nina's my assistant, or my solicitor, and we've just been let out on a technicality. A loophole that has saved our bacon. We stop at lights and I look through the windows and into a bus that's stopped right next to us, full of people in grey and brown coats facing the same direction and looking right into the back of each other's heads as if the rest of the world doesn't exist. I want to bang on the glass and stick my tongue out at them. *Look at me!* I could say, and get up and dance on the roof of the taxi. I feel glamorous, and I want to giggle. Poor Nina, she looks rotten. 'How come you're being so nice to me, Nina? What have I ever done for you?' Nina pats my hand, but she won't look at me. She bites her lip before she speaks. 'I'm only doing what anyone would have done.' 'That's not true, though, is it?' I say, thinking about Maggie. I wait because I know after a bit the silence is going to get too much for her and she's going to have to answer. I'm not daft, am I? She starts blushing. I can't think what it would be, except somehow she's mixed up with Julian. I sneak a look at her tummy, but she's solid – not glowing. Still, even *that* would be a relief where he's concerned. 'I know your husband,' she says, eventually, and pats at my hand again, as if there's something on it she wants to rub away, 'we've been friends for a while,' she ducks her head. 'I didn't know you were' – poor thing looks completely stricken – 'so poorly.' 'I'm not,' I say, very slowly. I can feel pins and needles running along my shins and into my feet, and I know it's because the blood is moving fast in me. My favourite story was always the one about Jared, who prayed and asked Heavenly Father to touch some stones and make them glow so that he'd have light in his raft when he set off across the sea to America. What faith. With God, nothing is impossible. And I'm the one who's glowing now, every bit of me buzzing and shining and coming back to life. A stone touched by the finger of God. 'I'm all right now. I'm better!' All that praying. And now, on the day Gary comes home, it happens for me. I've been waiting so long, but the Lord works in his own time, doesn't he? He provides answers to prayers through his servants, our brothers and sisters. Miracles happen every single day. Heavenly Father isn't far away, he's in the world, and he loves us. 'I've not been as good as this in years. I could sing!' Nina looks at me, and starts talking again, too fast for me to get the thread of what she's saying. 'I didn't know, and I wouldn't have carried on meeting him if I'd have known he thought—' I grab her hand and pull it into my chest and smile. 'Shh shh. Whatever it is, we can sort it out, can't we? Everything's going to be fine, my love. Come home and have tea with us. Come and meet our Gary. It's the least we can do. Tonight's going to be a real celebration!'

JULIAN

The sky is white: obliterated by clouds. Behind them, the sun starts to sink, then the air gets greyer. The registration plates on cars become less distinct.

Suffer the little children Gary your brother on time tonight time to set an example straighten up clean white shirt your brother give me children else I die sometimes the younger must lead Jeannie to think of your brother and the dog the dog on the hall carpet a bit of effort and the list for tonight your brother my little children let us not love in word, neither in tongue, your brother your brother.

I keep on walking. I never have a set route. I go quickly and enjoy the feel of my legs slicing the air and my trainers eating up the pavement as I go.

Fast, faster, fastest.

Fast faster fastest.

Fastfasterfastest.

Fsfsfsfsfsfsfsfsfsfsfsfsfsfsfsfsfsfsfsfsfsfsfsfsfs

I do not realise I have been speaking out loud until I feel the air buzz through my lips and the sibliants fizz around my teeth. And my lips are chapped, and people stare at me as I hurry past, walking so quickly my knees hurt and it is almost a jog.

Fast, faster, fastest.

Say any word often enough and its meaning goes. Repeating words like this tumbles their rough edges against the inside of my skull, smoothing them into ball-bearings. My head is rattling.

I speed up, and then I am jogging – my trainers battering the pavement. I watch them, and decide not to worry about lamp-posts or who else I might be sharing the pavement with. You can get out of town quickly – onto the A6 and walk down it towards the hospital and the new roundabouts until you hit the House of Handshakes. Then further on, following the road past Travelodges and old people's homes, industrial estates and on to Preston. I have gone all the way a few times. It takes four hours and the last time one of my feet had a blister the size of an egg on the sole. But it is possible. With planning, anything is possible. The street lights start to hum as they warm up. My teeth can feel it in their little spidery nerves. It hurts. I walk.

The sky darkens.

I walk again.

*Fsfsfsfsfsfsfsfsfsfsfsfsfsfsfsfsfsfsfsfsfsfsfsfsfsfsfsfsfsfsfsf
sfsfsfsfsfsfsfsfsfsfsfsfsfsfsfs*

Time vanishes.

There is a new cash-machine on the corner. Is it the right time to get my money out yet? Nine thousand, three hundred and eighty-six forty on instant access. Interest rate is shit, but I can get it whenever I want. As soon as I decide the time is right, it is there, in my hand. I like the idea of the machine spewing the paper out into my hands. Of other people looking.

I spit in the gutter, jam my hands into my pockets and speed up. Stupid Bastard. Me. That is what I am. That is what I should have done. Instead of letting Drake and then Mum get me worked up, I should have visited Nationwide and got the whole lot out in little bundles. Asked them to put it in a jiffy bag and kept it tucked into my waistband until tonight. I spit again, blowing it out so the lump of curdled white foam flies onto the windscreen of a double-parked BMW. Sometimes a long walk is not enough. Sometimes getting into bed during the day and lying there with my face pressed into the pillow is not enough. Nor a little feel. Holding tight to the Iron Rod. Sometimes it is not enough to wrap my dressing gown cord around my neck and pant until the light in front of my eyes breaks into spots and dances, and all those fuckers dissolve and get away from me. When it is not enough, I do something else.

Ruth and Andy have got a good big house. It is on a nice street too. Someone would call the police quick if they saw a stranger hanging around the cars for too long. The people who live here hose down their drives and scrape the moss out of the cracks between the crazy paving. They cover their wheelie bins in that plastic stuff that is supposed to look like leaves and plants and hedges. The whole street smells like lilac and honeysuckle and valeting.

I spit on a few more cars.

Ruth and Andy have got their house the wrong way round and for some reason they use the front room as a dining room. During the day you can see the table and the tops of the chairs in the gap between the windowsill and the bottom of the drawn blind. Six inches. Sometimes less. They have placed picture frames and wooden bowls with shells and pebbles in them on the sill. A cat sometimes sits there, getting black hairs on the back of the blind and looking out of the empty house.

But at night when they are all in they draw it right up. There is a bit of arrogance about that. As if they think their house is a shop and they are selling something. The lights are blaring and they sit in their window eating their food and laughing and talking to each other like they are actors in an advert selling the perfect family togetherness dining experience. You can see them from across the road. Easily.

When I was little, I used to think that people lived inside the television set. Mum encouraged it. She would turn off the telly and then we would hold hands and rush around to the back of the set as quickly as we could, to see if we were quick enough to catch them climbing out and sliding down the wire into the plug socket. The people in the television went down the wire and into the walls when we turned off the set. I believed it for almost as long as I believed all the other shit she told me about the world.

Children trust their mothers: we can't help it. When you stop believing, it hurts. It is important to take Angela out of all this. If someone had come to me and taken me away from people inside television sets, Santa Claus, worlds without number, the Tooth Fairy and the building of Zion, never mind the cupboards full of soup tins, powdered milk, cracked wheat and water purification tablets, then I think I would have been glad.

It is impossible to project your mind into an earlier self and know for sure. More impossible to put your mind into someone else's and speak for them. But as far as I can be sure, I am sure that I would have wanted to be taken away and that as she grows Angela will become glad of the opportunity I will give her. When it gets dark.

Ruth is standing at the head of the table spooning out a brownish sauce from a pan. Mum says Ruth has John Lewis duvet covers and Primark sheets and this means something other than what it means but I do not know what. The juice is crusty around the sides. Andy is sitting next to her holding up a plate – white shirt with his collar open, his jacket and tie over the back of his chair. Between the two of them they have got a conveyer belt going.

Ruth spoons onto the plate – one, two, three – and then Andy takes it and wipes the rim with a tea towel, and takes it along the table and puts it in her place at the opposite end of the table. She serves again, into a little plastic dish, and Andy takes it and sets it down and uses a spoon to mush up whatever is inside it before he hands it down again, to Angela. Without looking, Ruth reaches out her hand and pushes the bowl so Angela can see it, but not touch it. She is probably worried about it being too hot, or does not want Angela to try feeding herself until she sits down and helps her.

Ruth and Andy are laughing and talking to each other the whole time. I see their mouths moving and it is just like an advert with the sound turned off. They are in good moods. Ruth's got a nice dress on. Before Andy comes back she always puts on lipstick. There is a little fruit bowl on the dining room table and I have seen her chuck her lipstick and comb in it before she opens the door for him. The Profits of the Church have spoken about women and their adornments. After all, *even an old barn looks better when it's painted*. Andy sits down, and because Ruth is standing up and leaning over Angela, he can see down the front of her dress. I catch him looking, and then Ruth catches him, and she swipes him with a tea towel and Andy is putting his hands up, shaking his head, playing the innocent.

What? What did I do?

Angela is sitting facing the window, between them. She is hitting her plastic table mat with the palms of her hands, and does not understand the joke passing between her parents. She has a special plastic chair attached to the ordinary chair, a sort of booster seat that she is strapped into. The straps are red and they have yellow animals printed all the way along them. Ruth shuffles Angela in her chair closer to the table, serves Andy an extra helping of whatever it is that is in the pan, fills their two glasses with water from a jug and then sits down.

There is one empty seat. The chair nearest the window, opposite Angela, is always pushed in and no one sits in it. Sometimes I catch myself thinking about that seat as mine, and even though I have never said it out loud, to anyone, I get embarrassed about the pictures in my head – me sitting there in my overalls with my own plate, probably knocking glasses of water over and ruining the conversation. But I think about it anyway. I can't always get rid of the idea and it makes me angry. I catch hold of a bit of the hedge I am standing in front of, pull it away from the plant roughly, strip the leaves from the stem. They flutter to the pavement.

I am startled by a knock and my stomach clenches, my arms fly up as if I have just been hit. Instantly, I am panting, my system flooded with adrenaline. *Fight or flight?* It is a decision your body makes, not your mind. I look around. It was a knock. Someone knocking on the inside of their window. He is standing there now – the reflections on the glass obscuring everything but a flash of grey hair, a navy shirt and stooped shoulders turning away.

See? I am not supposed to be here, touching this privet, breathing this air, loitering on this pavement. The trembling in my muscles subsides, I breathe, turn back and take two steps to the left so I am out of sight of the knocker's window. I carry on watching.

Ruth is laughing and pushing a basket of bread over the table to Andy. I like it that they put out the bread nicely in a basket with a little white linen lining, even when there is nobody but them at the table. When they have the mishies over for a meal they set it out exactly the same way. Andy raises his eyebrows and says something while he takes a roll and balances it on the side of his plate, and Ruth laughs again. Even Angela's mouth is going, open and closed, grinning and waving her pink plastic spoon and fork about. Ruth stands up again and I duck, quickly, feeling the coldness of the paving stones through the knees of my overalls.

I carry the sight of the inside of Angela's mouth down with me to the cracks in the pavement. Angela's mouth is red and wet and soft. She dribbles a lot. Sometimes her tongue is whit-ened with scales because Ruth still lets her have milk out of a bottle when she screams. There is a faded crisp packet caught in the lower stems of the hedge. I pluck it like it is a fruit growing and fold it up. Tuck it into my pocket. That is a good deed, to show the old codger inside I forgive him for knocking his window at me. No hard feelings because we are even stevens now.

When I dare to put my head up again I see Ruth has not come to the window but only moved to put a bib on Angela. It is a stiff pink plastic bib that looks like it came in a set with her cutlery. The bottom edge of it is curved upwards, making a little trough to catch the dropped food. I would never have imagined such a thing existed. It is amazing what people can invent. Angela bangs her spoon on the table and her mouth starts moving again. She is not speaking. She never speaks. They finally bow their heads and fold their arms in front of them. Andy says the prayer against Angela's wailing but it's just a short one. Fast, because good smells are going up his nose along with the steam from his plate. They start to eat. My mouth waters just watching them.

The only thing that made Gary's party tolerable was Angela. I had been sitting on one of the padded benches in the lobby looking out of the big windows at the road that runs past the Stake Centre and towards the House Handshakes. Just counting the cars going in and out of the car park, thinking about what Jackson and Lawson had said to me – had tried to imply – and turning the numbers of cars over and over. Adding up the registration plates, multiplying the numbers in the front bays by the numbers in the back bays, dividing them by the registrations on the cars in the middle, and watching for a space so I could get Dad's car out and go.

And then she was there, right next to me, the sunshine catching in the folds of her skirt. I remember the thing she had on – a navy tartan dress with a big, white, wide, flappy collar over her shoulders. She was sitting on the floor, leaning against the window and making sticky handprints on it, half crawling, half shuffling with her hand patting the cool glass.

She must do that, sometimes – just crawl away. But I reckon

Ruth only lets it happen at church. Everyone there is family; they all know about Angela. Know to watch her if she is eating, be ready to slap her on the back. Know not to let her try crawling up any stairs, not to hang around near the swinging doors. She belongs to everyone. Our own perfect, not testable soul. Sent to Chorley Fourth Ward, a mascot, a marker of how righteous the rest of us are. I do not think that policy of theirs — letting her roam around free at church — is good parenting at all.

'What's all this?' I said.

She had an empty plastic cup in one hand and a doughnut she was busy sucking the jam out of in the other. Her face was sticky; the front of her dress and her collar soaked with whatever it was that had been in the cup.

'You are a real mess,' I said.

She made an owly sound, a bit like laughing. Her little girl's teeth were wet and perfect.

I stood up and looked around, up and down the lobby, through the doors into the empty chapel, last week's hymn numbers still slotted into the rack. Along to the right and through the glass panels in the doors to the cultural hall, where Gorgeous Gary was waving a Book of Mormon about and machine-gunning his way through his victory speech. The self-righteous little prick.

Where was Ruth? Parents carry bags full of extra clothes and food and cleaning things for their children, don't they? I was going to take her to Andy and tell him he needed to take better care of her. Angela was their responsibility, not anyone else's.

I turned around and nearly tripped over her. She had followed me on her hands and knees and her bare skin was red raw from the bristly carpet. She had come after me, right up to the doors. When I looked down at her she made a noise that was so like Gary trying to say something that it made me laugh. She put her arms up to me.

And something happened.

I was blown apart. Blown. Like a dandelion clock. Fragments

of me went all over the place and I discovered I had no centre. The roof of my mouth started to hurt. My eyelids stung.

She must have been three or four years old at that time and she was wearing sticky little bangles made of chalky sweets with holes in the middle threaded onto elastic. I remembered that Jeannie had some like that. I used to pull them tight and ping them onto her wrists.

She was only little.

I don't know why I did it.

'Come on then, you big dirty mess,' I said, and lifted her up. The muscles in my arms were trembling. 'Let's get you clean.'

I get a bit closer to the window. They are still eating like they have nothing else to do with their night than stuff their faces, talk about how lucky they are, laugh and stare adoringly at each other. Ruth keeps getting up and down, bringing water, extra bread, a cake and some small plates for afterwards. Andy is poking food into his mouth like it is his last meal. He leans back in his chair, rubs at his gut, smiles, and then puts his plate out for cake, like a child. I want them to open the window because I cannot hear a thing, but while I have been here it has started to drizzle. Light and warm, putting spray on the cars and dark spots on the pavement. I wonder if the ash is caught up in the rain. If I am getting showered with filth from the centre of the world. I doubt it.

I always knew it would not be easy to take Angela. Most of the time Ruth is tirelessly minding her defective little chick. It would have to be all or nothing because no one was going to let me just *borrow* her for a while, to get that feeling again. I need it. Need it today, and tomorrow – increasingly. I need it. But for a while I could not see how I would make that happen. Not babysitting, not breaking into the house at night when they are all asleep. I even thought about pretending I had had a change of heart and had decided to go back to sacrament meeting once a week. Starting the process of my repentance. Then swipe her from the nursery – put my head round the door and tell them I was taking her to Andy, that he had asked me to step out and get her for him. I even bought a shirt. Thought about cutting my hair. But I could not do it. It would finish me.

Last summer I came over to their house, thinking again about the conversation I had had with Lawson and Jackson at Gary's party and what it meant, and wanting to spend some time with Angela to ease away the feelings I was having about it. They were in the front garden. The sun was streaming down from a cloudless sky, reflecting off the windows in the houses, the windscreens and wing mirrors of cars. I peered at them through the darkening lenses of my glasses. Ruth was walking along the drive, holding Angela's arms above her head and trying to encourage her to walk in front of her. There were two glasses on the front step – an ordinary glass one and the special plastic thing with the spout and the handle that Angela's got to have.

'Come on then, just lift your foot! Lift your foot and come with me and look at the flowers!'

Ruth's voice was shrill and desperate, stretched through a smile even I could see she did not feel. Angela was bowlegged, wobbling, struggling to pull her wrists away from her mother's hands, her feet too far apart and stuck, almost in terror, to the drive.

'Will you try it on your own then? Shall Mummy let go of your hands? Maybe you'll take me to go and see the pretty flowers. Maybe, Angela, maybe there's even a frog down there?'

I moved forward a bit, standing at the open gate at the end of the drive. I thought about coughing, or saying hello. Ruth did not see me, even though she was only a few feet away – too busy looking down at Angela, clamping her hands tight around her spindly wrists.

'Try for Mummy, Angela,' Ruth said, '*please*,' and bit her lip, and let go.

Angela fell. There's nothing to her, no strength in her legs. I remembered the time I held her, the feeling that she wasn't made of bones and muscle, just a bag of skin half filled with warm water and elastic. Her knees hit the drive, and she started howling, spit running out of her open mouth. Ruth did not pick her up straight away, but straightened up, put a hand over her eyes and sighed.

'Come on up then,' I said. I was onto the drive and close to Angela before Ruth had time to notice me. I scooped her up and blew, hard, on her face. It was a trick I remembered from when Jeannie was little and would get into a paddy because she was never allowed to touch the video player, or pull the pages out of magazines. It worked. Angela stopped crying, like a switch had been flicked, and stared at me, her wet mouth open. I felt it again, throbbing through me like her breath was a hand brushing the strings of the harp that I was made of.

'Julian,' Ruth said, and stepped towards me. 'What a surprise.'

'Is this little one all right?' I said. 'Did she scrape her knees?'

'She'll be all right,' Ruth said, and stepped towards me with her arms outstretched. I let her take Angela, who slumped heavily onto her mother, resting her head against her neck. She looked at me from between half-closed eyes, then found a lock of Ruth's hair and started sucking it. The vibrations died away slowly: I felt them longest in my ears and cock.

'Poor little thing,' I said, 'she nearly had it then, didn't she?'

Ruth didn't answer.

'Good job I was here,' I said.

Ruth turned and walked away, stooping to pick up the glasses on the front step. I followed. She held them like a collector at a bar does – two in one hand, her fingers inside her glass, her thumb looped through the plastic handle of Angela's.

'You should come in,' she said, at last, not moving from the front door. 'Andy's at work but . . .' She shook her head and smiled. 'It doesn't matter. Of course it doesn't. What am I saying?

Come in and have a glass of water, it's warm out, isn't it? You look like you're about to pass out.'

The inside of their house looked like a catalogue – all white walls with huge black and white blown-up pictures of Angela in brightly coloured frames.

'What a nice house you have got,' I said to her, because you're supposed to, and as soon as I had said it I hated myself.

We went through the living room and out into a kitchen with wide windows looking out onto a patch of grass and another hedge.

'Is she all right?' I said.

Ruth licked her finger and rubbed it against the red wet spot on Angela's knee. Angela struggled to get away, and started to rock, pushing her head against Ruth's chest until she gave up and put her down on the floor. She shrugged.

'Children fall. It happens all the time. She'll never learn to walk if she doesn't fall down a few times.'

Straight from Relief Society, that one was. *Our Heavenly Father is a loving parent, and that means he sometimes lets us make our own mistakes so that, from the consequences, we can learn.* I pasted a smile on my face, and did not roll my eyes.

See how good I can be when Angela's in the room? The fists in my pockets unknotting without me telling them to, my eyes, the buzzing in my brain. It goes when she is there. It just . . . *goes.*

'Will she learn to walk?' I asked. 'I mean, eventually? Will she be able to do it?'

Ruth smiled. 'I hope so. There's so much the doctors can't tell us. They told us she'd never know who we were, and look at her now.'

Angela was still sitting on the floor, rubbing her hands along the ridge where two floor tiles met. Ruth leaned against the kitchen counter and watched me while I drank the glass of water she had given me. The cupboard under the stairs was open, and I glanced inside – saw a jumble of cardboard boxes, brooms, an ironing board and a vacuum cleaner. On the inside of the cupboard door someone, I like to think Ruth herself, had taped up an OU poster of Darwin's *Tree of Life*. She caught me looking at it, but when I smiled she didn't shrug or move to close the door.

That is just the sort of thing that would get mouths flapping in the ward – and scandalise the likes of Maggie if she ever saw it. I could not decide if Ruth did not care what they thought of her, or if she was relying on the sad fact that none of them would know what it was they were looking at even if they did see it.

'Was it the way she was born?' I asked. I had heard the story from Mum; her hushed, tragic tones, lowered eyes and clasped hands – typical indicators of her glee. 'Was it what happened with the cord, or would she have been different anyway?'

'We're all different, Julian.'

I laughed. It is true that I do not laugh very often. It sounds forced and it makes my face look odd and for a second I forgot and laughed and then I panicked because I did not know how I was supposed to stop it. In that second I thought about all the laughs I had ever heard. Do you let them fade out, like tracks on a CD, or are you supposed to just stop them and say something else? I bit it off.

'You're right about that,' I said, and Ruth smiled. She did not have any make-up on. Must not be expecting Andy back for a while. Plenty of time to chat. The laugh faded into the corner of the room and I breathed again, pretending that I was inhaling Angela's exhaled oxygen, mouthing molecules of her shampoo. The skin cells that are lifting from her body and floating into the air every time she moves landed on me like snow, melting into my skin, becoming part of me.

'We've had that many opinions on her, that many

examinations, scans, tests, all sorts. She's only four. I think it's more important to accept her how she is than spend all her childhood working out how to fix her. She's not ill.'

'She's not in pain?'

'No, of course not. She's happy. Learning things will just take her a long time. And the limit on what she can learn is probably a bit . . .' – she doesn't say lower, lesser, a word like that, but the word is there anyway, spinning in the air between us, we can both hear it echoing – '*different* than it is for you and me. But that's all right.'

'Because we're all different,' I said. I decided that if Ruth told me Angela was here for a reason, that she was so valiant in the pre-existence she only needed to be here to get a body, and not to be tested, I would throw the glass I was holding against the window, grab Angela from the floor, and run for it.

I waited, the muscles in my throat tightening. She did not say anything, and I sipped the water slowly. It clicked past the uncomfortable lump in my throat.

'Sometimes I wonder, just now and again, when things get difficult. You know, when I see all the things that other children her age can do, and Angela still can't. Well, I wonder what Heavenly Father's plan was for her. Why he wanted her to come to earth like this.'

'So why do you do it then?'

'Do what? Church?'

'Yes. All that time. Having to make yourself fit in. You do not like my mum. You do not like Maggie. Sisters in the gospel. It is all a big pretend with you, isn't it?'

I do not know what made me say all that. Seeing that poster, I think, felt like a secret signal. Like I might have an ally. Someone who understood what it was like to be born in the covenant, and hate it, and feel it clanking like a chain around your ankles even when you did not believe in it any more. They might, I thought, even start inviting me around for meals.

'I do it because it works,' she said, and not in a tone of voice that made me feel like she was annoyed with me.

'Works? But she is still ill. Still — like she is. She is not all right.'

'No. She isn't. But I am.'

'Just all right?'

'Isn't that enough?' Her voice wavered. She was getting emotional. It was me. Making her cry. 'It's enough to know he has a plan for us all, and that Angela's an important part of it. Even if I don't know what the plan is. What's the plan?' She threw her hands in the air, wiped her eyes and laughed. 'Who knows? I don't know. I don't suppose any of us will know the answer to that one until we're back home with Him. We'll find out everything then. It'll all be revealed, and make sense to us, and we'll understand.'

Her lip was still trembling, so I decided to make a joke.

'When you find out about dinosaurs, and fossils, and Aids, and natural disasters — all those kinds of things, will you send me a postcard and let me know? I will not be with you, but I would certainly appreciate the information all the same.'

She frowned at me. 'What do you . . . ?' and I pointed my thumb at the floor to finish off the joke.

'I'll be down there, I reckon.'

She looked like I had just told her I had incurable cancer. Brain rot, bone rot, blackening of the blood. She did not laugh, did not even look angry. That much sincere and unhidden pity was almost impossible to take.

'Oh, Julian,' she said, 'there's no such thing as hell, and even if there was, you wouldn't be going there. That's why I love the gospel so much. Don't you think it's a beautiful thing that Heavenly Father's only task for us in this life is to make our families into a heaven on earth, so that the only hell that exists afterwards would be our separation from them?'

There was not a great deal I could say in response to that. I just moved towards her to put my glass on the draining board and she stepped aside quickly. I saw her looking at the dirty marks my fingers had made on the outside of the glass.

'I expect you'll want to get on,' she said, once a moment or two had passed. 'Have you got a job on round here?'

'No, just walking.'

'It's a bit out of the way for you, though, isn't it?'

'Not really.'

'I'll let you go then,' she said, 'I won't keep you here indoors when there's a bit of sunshine outside.'

I said goodbye to her and let myself out. She did not come to close the door behind me.

The Loonie Tuners say Angela has a particularly pure soul but they are quite wrong about that. She has no soul. She is like me: all faulty machine and no ghost, the cogs and circuits not quite doing their thing. She smiles and she holds her arms up to you just like a normal child but I think these are things she has learned to do to please her mother. Inside her skin she is just a perfectly silent and empty space. Maybe we will get a sleeper train to Scotland, or even, if I can manage it, swipe one of the cars from the garage and go up in that. A huge throb starts in my chest and works through me, making my cock twitch and my eyelids flicker. Eyes half closed and swaying in the street like a dirty glue sniffer. I watch my flicker book of images, spirited into life by speed and the persistence of vision:

1. Me holding her hand as we look out of the train window at green fields and cows. She presses the tip of her nose to the glass.
2. Me and her sitting on a wooden bench on a pier somewhere. One of the remote islands. Sanday, Staffa. Baleshare. Coll. Grey rocks, grey sand, seals and silence.

3. Lighthouses, maybe. Can you live at the very top of a lighthouse? Could it be our job to crank the lens and ventilate the lantern room? I suppose not. It is all computerised now.
4. Watching the whirlpools form and suck between Scarba and Jura.
5. Arriving on a boat at Auskerry: population 5 (then 6.5).

The images stutter and quiver into life, and the real world, the impossibility of it all, recedes. She is there, through that glass and behind the curtain. And I am here on the other side. It would be all right in the end. She would get used to me. There are lots of things wrong with me but I am not cruel. Sometimes when you want something all you need to do is reach out your hand and take it.

6. Us both on that bench, side by side like a still from an arty film. Say we are in Flodaigh.
7. Black and white. A sea-defence wall, at night. Her with her feet dangling, white socks, black shoes. Me in my usuals. Our mouths and eyes clamped shut against the wind.
8. Rewind. Tonight I will buy nappies. Hair dye. She can be a redhead, and I will cut off my hair and get contacts. I will pay cash and say she is my sister.
9. Our parents have died, like they do in all the best kinds of fairy tales. It is my job to take care of her now. We want to be alone in our grief.

I know Ruth does not like me. Something she has not put into words yet, some pheromone moving from my groin to her nose whenever she is in the room with me. She has never seen or heard me say anything wrong, but she perceives it all the same. The spirit of her discernment makes her suspicious. Or simpler: Ruth does not like me because I asked her once what size shoes Angela wore. She asked me why I wanted to know and I just said something about her getting taller all of a sudden, then held my breath until there were tears in my eyes.

That day in the Stake Centre was the first time I touched her. It was like putting my hands on a magnet. All the hairs on my body twitched in her direction. And she was light in my arms, her floppy limbs feeling warm but not quite human. I held her against my chest and went down the corridor, in the opposite direction to the door where I knew Jackson and Lawson were, on their knees and totting up what Gary owed them for his mission. I started looking round the classroom doors, kicking them open and calling, looking for someone from the Relief Society to hand her over to. The place was empty – everyone was congregated in the cultural hall listening to Gary's speech. I could not go in there.

Most kids are chubby at her age, aren't they? But she was not. The truth is she felt like a hot nothing: as frail and bubble-headed as an alien. Maybe she would have been fine if they had managed to get her born a bit quicker. No. Ruth just wants to think it was nothing but an accident. That she is stuck inside a damaged body; somehow camping out inside her skin and soaking up all that love and Makaton and educational television as it slowly filters through to her.

'We are all right now, Angela,' I said, and could not stop myself staring at her. She looked a bit different to the way Jeannie looked at a similar age – less substantial, with too-pale skin and a long fuzz of transparent, babyish hair. I do not know why I had not noticed it before. Finally, I found the room they call 'the cry room'.

When they first built the Stake Centre and we started coming here the women talked about the fact they were getting this room like it was the same thing as Christmas. Along with the temple itself, the new Stake Centre was fully equipped – enough classrooms for everyone, a new and better font for baptisms, a whole corridor for Primary, *and we're even getting a cry room!*

I remembered how many of them would cry – the whole gamut from spitty sobbings and nose blowings to silent, dignified overflowing – when they got up and bore their testimonies. *I know the Church is true-oo-oo without a shadow of a doubt with every fibre of my bee bee beeing!* I thought that was what this room was for – somewhere for them to go and leak and wet their fronts in private while they thanked God and Jesus for making them so special.

There were three comfy armchairs in there, a side table and a box of plastic toys and dolls. A painting of Jesus suffering the little children to come unto him on the wall and, in every corner, plastic speakers. As soon as I was in, I could hear Gary – jack-hammering his way through a list of people he wanted to thank, 'but obviously most of all, my mother'. I could *smell* Mum smirking, did not need to see her. I let the door whoosh shut gently behind me, and squeezed Angela tight against my chest and felt the fragile bird bones of her ribs under my big hands.

The zip on her dress ran under the collar, and I could not figure out how to get it off her at first. I had to flick the entire collar up – it was so big it nearly went over her head. She sagged against my arm as I unzipped her dress and let it fall around her feet. She had on a pink vest, and I took that off too, then screwed it up into a ball and used it to wipe her bare, flat chest, her neck and face. She closed her eyes and moved her head from side to side.

I am not sure if that meant she liked what I was doing, or was trying to get me to stop.

'The final and most important thing I'd like to share with the youth is to listen to what your leaders, teachers and parents tell you. Avoid evil, run from temptation and make sure your dress, words and thoughts are church standard. Then there'll be nothing stopping you from putting in your mission papers too. I'm

talking to the young women now as well as the young men. Sisters, if you're reaching twenty-one and you haven't yet found the one Heavenly Father wants you to marry, pray earnestly and see if it is his will that you serve a mission. Talk to your father, and then to your bishop.'

I imagined Gary swelling to fill his Matalan suit, his voice growing, copying the slow deep drone of the General Authorities on the General Conference broadcasts that he'd been boning up on for months. He had no idea how much of a dick he sounded. I bet myself twenty quid he would come back with an American accent and do nothing to shift it. The absolute and utter knobhead.

I looked for a switch on the wall to shut his fucking noise out of the room, but there was nothing. The ladies holding their crying babies in this room would be out of their minds to want to block the service out, wouldn't they? Angela was not much better off than she was to start with, but without water and a clean set of clothes, there was nothing else I could do for her. I turned her, and she smiled. Maybe she thought we were playing a game. I started turning her round and round.

'Twirling? Do you like that? I used to know a little girl who liked twirling.'

I held onto her shoulders and carried on. Her hair brushed my arm and, after a while, she stopped making any sound at all and so did I and she let her head hang loose and her arms fly about limply until I almost thought I had put her to sleep on her feet. I stopped, and just stared at the skin between her shoulder blades, the fine hair that disappeared down the small of her back and into her nappy, a brown birthmark on the back of her elbow.

I stared at her until it was time to get her dressed and give her back to Ruth and Andy, who did not even ask where she had been, and never chased me up about the vest.

Which I kept.

*   *   *

They have finished eating now. Ruth is pointing at Andy, and then at the ceiling. She could be talking about God or loft insulation. He argues back. Ruth usually leans forward, picks Angela up out of her chair and carries her over to the window. I know what she would see if I do not get out of the way now. Some guy she half recognises, standing leaning against her opposite neighbour's hedge, twirling an empty crisp packet around in his hands. Dirty fingernails. Ripped overall and a denim jacket with greasy cuffs. Light-reactive spectacles, the oblong lenses shaded brown and speckled with the light drizzle. I keep still. Maybe the light inside the house blinds her to what goes on outside in the darkening street.

Let's see. It is a game of chicken.

Ruth goes through an elaborate ritual about waving goodnight to the garden, to the sky, to the plastic-covered fucking wheelie bin. She hoists the girl up on her hip and they wave at everything in the garden before pulling down the blind. Angela stares right at me. I doubt she can see me but our eyes meet anyway.

This is urgent. It is getting darker – the sky turning navy and the street signs too hard to read. I want to shout out in the street as I run away from the house, but I bite my lip and smile at the same time, until I can taste blood. I slow down to a fast walk and wipe my lips with my jacket cuff. Between home and work there is a paper shop and I head towards it. Going to need a bit of something to get me through tonight. Small bottle of vodka, another of 7Up. Pour half of the Seven down the drain, empty the vodka into it, and get most of the wretched-tasting stuff down my neck before I turn up home. Dad knows, but he never says anything.

Later, I will come back. Then we will go.

GARY

On the M6 passing Stoke. The car windows are smeared with the greasy handprints of Bishop Jackson's children and James was right: the jet lag is worse this way round. Maybe that's why I feel so bad. Jet lag isn't just about being tired, or wanting your breakfast in the middle of the night. Though the tiredness is part of it. The bone-deep, soul exhaustion that leaves you weeping at the array of options on the boards in Denny's window.

When I arrived in Salt Lake, feeling like it was three in the morning when most Utahns were just settling down after their dinners, I felt I'd come to a washed-out, watered-down version of all the films I'd ever seen. Maybe it is the fatigue that reduces the world to something else – something faded and remote and too familiar at the same time. People had been telling me for months how huge the country would seem to me – how vast and inspiring I would find the experience of being Stateside after existing in one tiny corner of one tiny island all my life. How strange I would find it, that these people would drive four hours to go to an outlet store, and four hours back – all on the one day. How brash and huge and rude I'd find Americans.

But all I noticed was how small the place felt – the city itself nothing more than a series of strip malls on the sides of the freeway with a glossy postcard of the snowy Wasatch Front propped up against the horizon. Downtown filled with actors dressed up as tourists, office workers, missionaries. Films about America are larger than life – America is just itself.

But it wasn't just America I was going to. It was *Utah*. For this Chorley boy, the Beehive State was the motherland. Beautiful

Deseret. I'd been told I'd feel, being among members the whole time, like I'd gone home. Bishop Jackson told me I wasn't *leaving* home, I was *going* home, to be with my greater family: the rest of the Saints in Zion. We knew members who'd saved up and moved there. The Harris family were in Bountiful and had promised to introduce me to some non-member friends of theirs. Allan Redbury had won a scholarship to BYU and had married there, lived for a year in Provo, had a son and then moved to Idaho. Even Sister Travers had a niece in from one of the Shropshire wards who'd fallen in love with a missionary from Brigham City. Two weeks after her missionary had arrived home, she'd received an airmail package containing a photograph of his mother and father standing on the steps of the family home, a diamond ring and a one-way plane ticket.

So why was going to church there almost a disappointment? The profusion of chapels: identical red-brick buildings with white spires and satellite dishes; the comforting lettering of the sign, the same all over the world: the franchise, the logo; the green hymn books; the cry rooms; the little plastic cups full of water slotted into their holes in the sacrament trays; women crying as they bore their testimony, or took their children up to the stand and whispered the words into their ears so even the little ones could tell us what they knew to be true.

Mum had made the place out to be some sort of Mecca and I was disappointed. She'd said that the Saints in Utah were more faithful because they were closer to the source. These people didn't have to waste their time defending their faith, justifying their practices to outsiders. They could just get on with living it. But in the end it was no different to the way it had been at home and I never thought to ask her, if that was the case, why was it that the Prophet had been led to send me there. What's one more missionary, in a ward where half the membership are wearing tags?

And now I really am coming home. I've never seen Chorley

on the television – no one's ever made a blockbuster film set in Astley Village or Clayton Brook. In the world's greater mind these places are so shrunken that they are invisible.

And in my mind too. I put home away, along with Carole, my Xbox, my little garden, and secret thoughts about university. I have locked home up along with my other childish things in the secret pocket of my suitcase that contained the calendar I used to mark off the days with. All seven hundred and thirty-one of them. My days: gifts, given freely to the Church – the tithe of my life.

'What's the matter, Elder. Something troubling you?'

It seems easier to talk in the car. Perhaps because he doesn't look at me, but keeps his eyes on the grey road ahead, the car in front, the wipers slapping the light rain off the windscreen.

'I'm not looking forward to getting back as much as I probably sh-sh-sh-should be.'

'Is that right? Have any idea why?'

There's a sticker with the instructions for turning the passenger airbag off on the dashboard in front of me, and I read it again and again while turning the miniature-sized bottle of washing-up liquid over in my hands.

Guiltily, I tell him about my failure.

'Is that all? I thought you were going to tell me something awful. I've been worried.' He laughs with relief and I wonder if he's resisting the urge to ruffle my hair. 'You're looking at it all upside down. Being too hard on yourself. You're bone tired, that's all. The Lord is pleased with you, very pleased.'

He doesn't understand. I have not been able to communicate the depth of this well enough to him.

'I don't think I should speak on S-s-s-s-sunday, Bishop. I don't think my experience is going to inspire anyone.'

'All you need to do is stand up there and tell the truth,' he starts to call me Gary, and checks himself, 'bear your testimony. Speak to the youth in particular; they'll be looking up to you.'

'I'm not s-s-s-sure the truth of how I did out there in the mission field is going to go down too well. Not one person? Really? That's going to inspire some-some-some-someone?'

'That's not as uncommon as you think it is. It's not how we measure the success of a mission. You must have been told that.'

'I've never heard of a missionary that didn't baptise even one person. I looked for those s-s-s-stories, Bishop, I promise you.'

'I bet you did a lot that was good out there, didn't you?'

I think about the service projects – the afternoons spent painting fences, moving trash out of a widow's yard, coaching basketball teams, helping out at the Scout Troop meetings.

'We s-s-s-s-s-served as best we could,' I say, 'but that wasn't what I went out there to do.'

'You made people laugh? Walked alongside them and lightened their burdens for a while? That's what Christ asked of you.'

I want to tell him about Keller, the way he had with a piece of gum – blowing a bubble bigger than his head. All the Primary kids loved him. But Bishop Jackson doesn't know Keller. Why would he care? They're not going to want to hear that.

'I guess I'm just a little afraid of the talk you're all expecting me to give. I can imagine what my mother's been saying about me. Those kinds of s-s-s-stories are hard to live up to.'

Bishop Jackson chuckles. 'I've never met a mother who didn't believe the sun rose and set for her own children. It's the way it's supposed to be. Don't you think your Heavenly Father and Mother look on you the same way? Won't rejoice in the same way when you come home to them? There are many ways to talk about your experiences out there.'

'I can't do anything except tell the truth.'

'Yes, but you can emphasise the most important aspects. The times when you felt the hand of the Lord guiding you. The times when the Spirit witnessed to you that you were engaged in the right work, the most important work. The friendships you made with your companions, the membership. You saw Temple Square, you got to listen to the Tabernacle Choir! Do you know how many of the members wish they'd been able to spend even a few minutes in your shoes?'

'I could s-s-s-say all that, but it wouldn't be everything, would it? Wouldn't that be wrong? Dishonest, almost? It feels that way.'

There's a long silence that neither of us hurries to interrupt. Speaking is becoming more exhausting. I can see Bishop Jackson bite his lip and force himself not to speak the stuck words for me. But sometimes I wish he would. I read that sticker again, the road signs, a leaflet about discounted garden furniture crumpled and muddy in the footwell. The plastic bottle gets damp in my hands and the paper label starts to pucker and peel.

'I've been sitting here praying, thinking about what to tell you. The Lord is prompting me to remind you that the Church is the bride of Christ. Think of that word *bride*. What do you think of?'

Carole. Carole, her toffee-coloured hair. Black and white dress. Tiny flowers. Cello music. Her silence. Letters. Shh.

'A girl?'

'Not just any old girl. Heavenly Father could have said wife, could have just said woman. But he didn't. He said bride. No man loves a woman more than on the day that he marries her. No woman is as dainty, as beautiful as she is when she's arranged in white and waiting for you at that altar. The Church is the bride of Christ. The *bride*. We are that *delectable* to him.'

'Yes.'

'Well, there's no sense sending that bride out into the world with her skirt pulled up and her knickers showing, is there? There are enough people in the world wanting to throw mud at her, treat her like a common woman, talk down to her . . .'

'I understand your point.'

'You've got a teachable heart, Elder. You're humble. These

are testaments to the quality of your character. What the ward is after is inspiration, not a list of facts and figures. You don't need to lie. There were obstacles in your way, but you overcame them. Satan made some of your seed fall on stony ground, but you persevered. You're being too hard on yourself. You did well.'

'I understand what you're saying, Bishop. But I can't do that. I can't s-s-s-stand up there and tell a lie. Not to make myself look better than I am. I failed. I let everyone down. I couldn't count the hours I spent taking this to the Lord in prayer. I don't s-s-s-speak well, I know, But I prayed with my heart. And nothing.'

'You're just tired. And you've been travelling for days. This ash cloud. When's the last time you saw a bed, a proper meal? It's just jet lag.'

'No, it's not that. You were the one who s-s-s-spoke about character. My character and my word are all I have. Look at me. I'm never going to have a fancy house, a nice job. And that's all right. I'm healthy. I've got my family. And my word. If I s-s-stand up there tomorrow and tell a pack of lies then that's gone. I'm gone. I won't be able to look at myself in the mirror again.'

'You're talking about it as if truth is just one thing, or another. It's how you look at things. We can all look at things differently, can't we? I'm just asking you to look at things in the best possible way. And to help other people to do that too. That's still your job, Elder. Isn't that all you were doing when you wrote all those letters and emails to your mother? Presenting the facts in the best possible light?'

My cheeks burn and I turn away from him and look out of the window. I never once, not in any of my letters, said outright that I'd baptised anyone. Never. I talked about the strength of the convert's testimony, the wonder of conversion, the challenges that face converts as they start their new lives in the gospel. In general terms. Hypothetically. The heat spreads over my face and downwards — even the hairs on the back of my neck are prickling with shame. I could say that I didn't know how my letters would be interpreted. That I am not responsible for the misunderstandings of others. That my mother's mistakes do not reflect on my honesty. I could say that. And people would believe me.

'What are you thinking about, Elder?' He pats my knee and looks at me sympathetically. 'Come on. Speak.'

'It isn't my job to s-s-s-stand at a pul-pul-pit and lie.'

'You know it isn't as simple as that. You've been serving for two years. You could teach me about the best ways to introduce someone to our Church. I shouldn't have to tell you this.'

I think about it. *Never give meat when milk would do. Don't answer the question they asked, answer the one they should have asked. Don't mention polygamy, gays, blacks or freemasons. When in doubt, bear your testimony. Behaving is more important than believing. Not secret, but sacred. Some things that are true are not very useful.* I've done that. I've been doing it. Lying for the Lord? I shake my head.

'I'm so-so-so-sorry, Bishop. I can't. Do it any more. The truth is a number. A big fat zero. There's no way to polish that one up.'

'Don't you remember the talk you gave us all at your farewell party? The deacons were quoting that in Fast and Testimony meeting for months. *Months.* You're a kind of inspiration, not just for the youth in our ward, but across the stake. Didn't you know that? Course you didn't. But you *are.* For a young man your age to overcome such challenges, both with your speaking, and with your family life, your mother's difficulty – for you to get over all that and serve an honourable full-time mission – is nigh-on unheard of. That's why you're the inspiration, Elder. It doesn't matter how many people you baptised.'

The stammer was very bad that day and I don't remember what I said, just the rows of smiling, kind and eternally patient faces staring up at me from the folding metal chairs laid out around the sides of the cultural hall. The way my hand shook and grasped my plastic cup of Shloer too hard and made it slosh over the sides. Carole was sitting a way away, near the door. I glanced at her once and saw she wasn't looking at me, but out of the window at the trees growing around the side of the Stake Centre.

After my talk was over, people milled around with paper plates, eating and listening to music. Jeannie's gobby friend Beth had brought some tapes, and was in charge of staying by the music player and turning the sound down whenever the lyrics became unwholesome. Jeannie was sitting with her, both of them cross-legged and nodding their heads in time to the music. I tried to give her a thumbs-up but she wouldn't look up from the floor, and other people, even people I didn't know, kept wanting to stop and shake my hand and give me things. Girls from other wards in the stake were there – familiar faces from conventions and youth dances, who pressed scraps of paper and envelopes into my hands and promised, straightened hair swinging, strawberry lip gloss shining, that they'd write – that they wanted to support the Chorley Fourth Ward missionary.

Before I was halfway across the room my arms were filled with envelopes, stamps, shoelaces, packets of biros and boxes of monogrammed handkerchiefs. The lapels of my suit smelled like perfume and were damp with other people's tears.

'What a hero you are,' someone said, and I turned to see an old man, his suit too big for him, his face like a piece of paper someone had screwed up in their fist. Spit gathered in the corners of his mouth. He wouldn't let go of my hand, pulled me down into a stoop so we were face to face. 'Take care of yourself,' he said, and winked, 'stay away from the girls. Read your scriptures every day.'

'I will,' I said, and smiled, and started to say something else but the stammer took hold again then, gripping my throat, turning me into a fish drowning on dry land. He squeezed my hand, I could feel the thick veins protruding on the back of his. 'Don't worry about that,' he said, 'if you pray enough, Heavenly Father will take it away from you. And you've heard by now, I'm sure, that Moses had an affliction just like yours? And look what a leader he turned out to be . . .'

I nodded and let go of his hand, looked over people's heads for Mum, who could take all these bits of stuff off my hands. But I couldn't find her either. She was, I found out later, angry with Dad because he'd missed my big moment, too busy talking to the girl who'd dropped the food off, and now she was in the kitchen complaining to little Angela's mum about how useless he was.

Just as it became overwhelming, I found Carole.

'Shall we go outside?' she said, and I just nodded because by that point my words were gone and it was all I was capable of.

The Stake Centre is separate to but in the same grounds as the temple. They are both beautiful buildings, but with their own purpose and function. Except for the times she did baptisms for the dead, Carole hadn't been inside the temple before. We walked around it in the gardens, smelling the roses and listening to bees move in and out of the flowers. We looked up at the smooth pale walls and the beauty of the spire, pointing the way to heaven. It had been only a few days since I'd been in to take my endowments – with Bishop Jackson at my side because Dad, who should have been there, didn't have a recommend any more. Carole must have guessed what I was thinking about because she didn't speak for a long time. I watched our shoes as we walked. She knew she couldn't ask me what the endowment was like.

'I've been dreading that talk all week. Did I make a mess of it?'

Carole didn't say anything, but tilted her head. She's so small. She comes up to the second button down on my shirt. She smiled.

'I used to get teased about him, when I was at school,' she said.

'About who?'

'Moroni.'

There are myths about him. Apparently the brethren in Salt Lake pay Manchester airport a million pounds a year to divert the airplanes that fly over the temple in preference to painting over the shining gilt of his robes, which distracted the pilots. Or the top of his head opens up and the Urim and Thummim are inside of it, stored there because we're the oldest stake in the world, Lancashire the home of the first European Mormons, landing place of the very first missionaries and Heavenly Father has got a soft spot in his heart for us. Or when the Second Coming is near, Moroni will come to life and blow his horn and on that signal we'll all pack up our stuff and travel to Missouri to assemble ourselves in the Garden of Eden and wait for Jesus to come and start the Millennium. Or because the temple itself cost so much they ran out of tithing money, so Moroni is actually made of spray-painted polystyrene, replaced annually in the dead of night between Christmas and New Year.

And that's just what we say about ourselves.

'We *all* got teased about him,' I said. 'One of Julian's friends asked him if the trumpet really worked. If when we heard it, we all came to the temple no matter what time of day it was, went up into the sp-sp-sp-sp-sp-spire and fastened our s-s-seat belts as the whole thing took off and took us to the moon.'

Carole laughed but very gently, with her hand against her top lip. I was talking again and, for the minute, the stammer seemed to have vanished. I know some people think that I put it on sometimes, that I work it up to get out of things that I don't want to do. But it isn't like that. It's got a mind of its own. The more important the speaking is, the tighter the string wraps around my throat.

'And what did your Julian do?' she asked softly. 'Or do I not want to know?'

'Oh, I don't know. Punched him, I suppose. Followed him home and s-s-stamped on his hamster. You're better off not asking, where Julian's concerned.'

'Poor Gary.'

'No,' I shook my head, 'I'm the lucky one. Poor Julian.'

Carole said nothing, which meant she probably disagreed with me, but had decided not to push it.

'Where is he, anyway?'

'I don't know. I didn't expect him to be here, not really.'

'He was here for the food,' she snorted, 'first in the queue for the buffet.'

'Carole.'

'What? I'm just saying, that's all.'

'Today can't be easy for him either, can it?'

'How do you mean? He had to drive Jeannie here. That's it. It's not him leaving his whole family. All his friends. For two years.'

Her voice wobbled. I put out my hand but didn't touch her. 'Well, that's the point, isn't it? He's five years older than me. People are bound to start asking him why he hasn't turned his papers in. Why it's the younger brother that has to lead the way. It can't be nice for him to hear that day in, day out. For months.'

'*Wickedness never was happiness*,' she said.

'Carole.'

'I'm just saying. You can't do wrong and feel right. It isn't possible. It would be nice if he could put his pride aside and turn up and support you for one lousy afternoon.'

I didn't tell her, but right then I was thinking about the first time that I caught sight of her, and knew without a shadow of a doubt that Heavenly Father had sent her here for me, to be my wife. I'd have been sixteen, maybe seventeen.

It was Pioneer Day. Jeannie was in the Primary Parade and had spent most of the day in a prairie dress and bonnet, being pushed around in a wagon made out of a cardboard and fabric-covered Morrisons trolley. Mum had been learning to make quilted scripture cases with the rest of the sisters in Relief Society, and me and Julian had been on a Pioneer-themed treasure hunt on Beacon Fell. Now it was night-time and we'd all eaten, and the whole stake had got together in the cultural hall for the talent shows.

They'd set it up like a theatre; dark with the stage at one end lit up by spotlights because we were doing the roadshows – each ward's skit or song or performance over, and us being certain we'd won it until Carole and the rest of the youth from her ward got up, all dressed in black and every one of them wearing cool dark glasses. They all had instruments of one kind or another – and between them they played 'Livin' on a Prayer', Carole in the middle with her knees around the big wooden boat of her cello and her head down, her hair falling all around her face because she was so shy about being on stage. Everyone else was roaring and stamping and clapping, but I just leaned against the wall, forgot to keep an eye on Julian and stared. If I felt anything at all, it was awe, and a sense of gratitude, and comfort in the knowledge that when the path is the right one, the way is always clear.

'All right now. Let's not talk about it any more.'

Once we'd made one circuit of the temple, we did another, walking more and more slowly to delay the time when we'd have to go back in. The paths were lined with flowering shrubs and every now and then there was a plastic trellis arch over our heads, wound up in clematis and honeysuckle. I watched Carole stepping carefully, making sure she never put her foot down on the join between the paving stones.

The thing is, she was right about Julian. And even at the time I knew that me being kind about him impressed her, which made me take his side even more, whether I really felt it or not. When I stopped to reflect on it, I got into a tangle. I could agree with her about Julian, which would be honest – but that would be wrong too. Once, in a Gospel Doctrine class I came close to saying that the only real way to tell the truth was to shut up and keep quiet, so imperfect is our human understanding of the world. But the words didn't sound right in my head and I'd never have been able to stand up and say the sentence in one go without practising, so I kept my mouth shut and just underlined the verses in the scriptures we were looking at with my coloured pencil.

'Let's wait here for a bit, before we go back in.'

There's a spot right in front of the temple that is just made for taking pictures. The bride and groom always stand in this exact place, just so, with the bride laying her hand very gently on her new husband's sleeve. We paused there, just for a second, and looked at the greenish water bubbling in the marble troughs.

'Two years is a long time, Carole,' I said. 'You'll be nineteen when I get back. I'll be twenty-one. That's old enough.'

'Yes, it is,' she said, and ducked her head so her hair fell over her face. I saw her cheek, the mottled blush creeping up along the sides of her neck and ears. I wanted to laugh. Not at her, but because I was so happy.

'I'll write to you. And when I come back, I'll take you to the temple.'

She didn't say anything.

'Shall I?'

It isn't right to get engaged to a missionary before he leaves. She wouldn't do it. But she wasn't going to say no, either.

'Look,' she said, and wouldn't look at me, but pointed over to the Stake Centre, where Mum was being wheeled out by Maggie. I saw her arms waving, her shawl dangling off one shoulder and the paper plate on her knee bumping along as the chair negotiated the kerbs in and out of the car park. Her face was a picture. She hates people wheeling her places, *especially* Maggie.

'Woman, behold thy mother-in-law,' I said, and made my voice all deep and boomy.

Carole started to giggle. I joined in, and we moved apart – fully laughing now as Maggie started trying to ram the wheelchair up the kerb of the pavement alongside the road that leads from the Stake Centre to the temple.

'Gary! Gary! *Gary!* Brother Lawson's mother's come down from *Ulverston* just to meet you. Ulverston! That's near Barrow! Gary! Get back in here!'

'Carole?'

'Come on. We'd better get back before Pauline drops her vol-au-vents.'

'Bishop. I want to ask you something. Between us.'

'You know you can ask me anything, Elder. Do you need me to pull over?'

'It's about Carole. Did Carole get married? I asked my mum how she was doing, every single time I emailed her. But she didn't ever say anything about her. I wondered if . . .'

'Let me see. I wonder which Carole you could be speaking about. Carole Jenkins? Chorley First Ward?'

I nod. Stare at my hands.

'She didn't write to you?'

'A card at Christmas, signed by her whole family. It had her name on it too, but it wasn't the same. The Young Single Adults knitted some socks for Christmas last year. She helped with that, I suppose. But she never sent a proper letter.'

'You wrote to her?'

'A few times. And when she didn't reply, I stopped. I hoped she was holding back because she wanted me to concentrate on my mission. But then I wondered if. Well. I'd just rather know, if that's the way it is. And I'd like to know before I have to see her.'

Bishop Jackson squirts wiper fluid up the windscreen and turns on the wipers. They make a semi-circular window in the dusty marks caused by the rain.

'I don't think this is an appropriate topic of conversation for this point in time, do you, Elder? You've still got your badge on. Keep a lock on your heart. Your love belongs to the Lord and him alone for a little while longer.'

'I only—'

The bishop turns to me, his round face damp and pale. The sky is dull above us, and now the cars coming down the other side of the motorway beside us have their lights on. He opens his mouth, looks like he's about to chastise me again, when his phone rings. He shakes his head, as if to tell me we'll talk about it later, and then reaches into the inside of his suit jacket to retrieve it.

'Hello?'

I look out of the window. I don't like to eavesdrop but he's not talking, just nodding his head and saying 'uhum' or 'aha' every now and again. Listening. He wouldn't be answering it if it wasn't an important call, not while he's driving. He must be under such a heavy burden: he's the first point of contact for members who are struggling in their temporal and physical lives.

I used to want to be a bishop, used to want to overcome my difficulty and have the Lord use my talents in taking care of a small ward of Saints. During my mission I'd sometimes hear the members complaining about something or other their bishop had said, or done, or not said, or not done. People expect, somehow, that just because the Lord has chosen a man to serve the Church in this way, he becomes perfect – that the mantle sanctifies him somehow. I always wanted to tell them – look, this man, he's not getting paid for this, he's not been trained, he's still got his own job to do, his family to feed. Heavenly Father wants you to help yourself, wants you to pray for your bishop, give him love, offer to help support his wife because her mantle is heavy too.

'I don't think now's the time to talk about that, Beth. No, no, I know it's important and I know that you're very upset. Of course.'

The knuckles of his free hand tighten around the steering wheel.

'Listen. I'm going to hang up now, and I'll deal with this. There's nothing you need to do now. Talk to your mother, and tell her I'll handle it. She isn't to phone anyone. That everything will be fine. No, no. Beth – that's not what I want you to do.'

I can just about hear the voice on the other end of the phone line. No words, just a voice – a desperate, high-pitched twittering.

'Okay. Okay, sweetheart. Say your prayers and go to bed early. That's right. That's all. Bye-bye now.'

He tucks the phone into his pocket and doesn't say anything. It doesn't matter, though, because we're nearly there now – turning off the motorway. I can see the temple, the spire rising up behind the houses and trees, and it feels like only seconds pass before we're turning onto my street.

'You're going to have to be strong now,' he says, and there are tears in his eyes again. 'I'm getting an impression from the Lord that the next season is not going to be easy for you, for your family. There's going to be challenges ahead. But the Lord has sent you home, and your ministry now is with your mother. Uplift her. Can you do that?'

He fumbles as he reaches for the gearstick, taps at my knee and then grabs my hand.

'Is there bad news?'

'Just be there for them, Elder. That's all you need to do.'

Bishop Jackson doesn't say anything else as the car slows and makes its final turn onto my street. It looks smaller, somehow. The houses jammed in tight next to each other, the windows little joke panes of glass – like doll's houses. I think of the cramped garden, the tiny, rickety greenhouse. My lawn. Bovril.

Jeannie-in-the-Lamp, Shortcake, Little-Leeke. My heart starts hammering against my ribs.

'You all right?' he asks. I nod my head quickly, swallow a few times.

When we park, I wait a while, like a girl who wants her date to open the car door for her. Bishop Jackson pats me on my knee and then goes around to the back of the car where he pops the trunk and takes out my suitcase.

'Come on then, Elder,' he says. I pick up my rucksack from between my knees, grab the Legacy of Clean sample bottles, and stumble out of the car. The little bit of grass in front of the house is just the same. The front windows have been cleaned. You've still got to lift the gate up with the top of your foot. The same old curved scrape on the cracked cement of the front path where the drooping gate has scored itself for years.

'You're not the first, you know,' he says. 'I heard of a boy in Liverpool Stake who got into John Lennon airport and jumped in a taxi rather than go home. It can be a facing.'

'It's not that,' I say, but the words won't come out of my mouth and I start coughing.

'I'm going to leave you here,' he says, and I look back at him, standing at the gate. His suit jacket is crumpled. His face is shiny and tired, the skin under his eyes pouchy and grey. He puts his hands in his pockets, and takes them out again. Bishop Jackson has five children and he's a primary-school head teacher and his wife is probably pregnant or trying to be and he didn't ask for this calling. I want to say something but I can't.

'I'll come in the morning. Take you to High Council. Put a clean shirt on, shine your shoes. They'll want to know how it went. You're still a missionary. They'll ask you about your mission, your conduct on the way home. Today, tonight – you're still wearing your tag, Elder. Act like it. Then they'll release you. You can ask them to give you a blessing, if you want one. But tonight, just eat and rest, all right? Let your mother hug you, let her cry a bit. Show her your pictures. Then sleep. Pray. Do your best. Be strong.'

'Okay,' I say – but it sounds like I'm speaking in a foreign language. I'm starting to hear that my accent is all wrong. Half Utahn, half Elder Keller. 'I'll see you tomorrow, Bishop.'

I knock on the door.

JEANNIE

18.23. I walk along the side of the road, carrying my kitbag over my shoulder, my rucksack weighed down with my seminary stuff as well as my school stuff on my back. Cars pass by and it carries on raining, spitting fat drops onto the pavement and speckling the flags. Inside my school jumper I start to sweat and I can smell myself – damp from the outside in and the inside out. I get my head down and carry on and the shower is over before I've had time to get properly wet and I'm this close to just slinging everything I'm carrying and letting the wind dry the wet patches under my arms, the rain spots on my shirt, and go on lighter without the rest of it.

The sky is a whitish grey, and the street lamps stick up hard and straight against it like wires holding it up. A den made with an old sheet draped over the kitchen chairs. The pavement is grey, the road a darker grey with dirty white lines running along it. Lewis and Julian's garage is at the end of the street. I can see the light is on in the office. I walk on, like a dog going back to lick up its own sick.

Last Sunday, Sister Lawson, the Young Women's first counsellor and the Mia Maid teacher, brought a big stack of paper plates, sticky tape, string, old cornflakes boxes and newspaper, and read scriptures to us, asking us questions and trying to get us to memorise things as we made ourselves suits of cardboard armour of God.

We have our lessons in one half of a big room in the back of the Stake Centre, while Mum was at Relief Society meeting and

Gary at Priesthood meeting. The deacons and Teachers – boys the same age as us – met in the other half of the room. We were only separated by a corrugated divider that you could push backwards and forwards depending on what you wanted to use the room for. Sometimes Sister Lawson would get annoyed and tap on the divider if she thought the boys were being too raucous, or the one time they were learning about proper care and control of their 'little factories' and she felt it was inappropriate learning for the Sabbath, and for us to overhear.

'Beth, will you read from Ephesians, chapter six verse eleven for me?'

Beth found it quickly. She used to get embarrassed about how slow she was to find her way around her scriptures. One day, Sister Lawson noticed and went to the distribution centre at the temple and bought her a set of little tabs to stick to the edges of the pages in her scriptures to help her keep up with the rest of us. Since then she's seemed much happier reading in lessons.

'*Put on the full armour of God that ye be able to stand against the wiles of the devil*,' she read, in the special, slightly quieter voice we all use when we're doing the scriptures for a class.

'Now, girls, we're talking about armour today. Who wears armour?'

Beth, still standing with her scriptures in her hand, shrugged. 'Soldiers?'

'Yes, that's right. And in these Latter Days, and through all times, faithful members of the Lord's Church have always thought of themselves as soldiers – in constant and active battle against Satan and his schemes to harm us and draw us away from Heavenly Father and the kind of lifestyle we should be living. And all soldiers need armour. Rebecca, will you stand to read, please?' She handed Rebecca a slip of paper, and we waited while she flipped expertly to the right page. It took her less than three seconds.

'*Stand, therefore having your loins girt about with truth and having on the breastplate of righteousness*. That's verse fourteen.'

'Thank you, sweetheart. Hold that thought, all of you. Girt loins and a breastplate of righteousness.' She produced a piece of paper and attached it to the chalkboard with a bit of Blu-Tack, even though you're not really supposed to. It was a picture of Aragorn from the film version of *Lord of the Rings*, sitting on his horse and holding a big round shield to the side of him.

'Nice big shield,' Sister Lawson said, 'and not unpleasant to look at either.' We giggled, but we knew when to stop our light-mindedness and look serious again. 'Nothing's getting through that, is it? A shield of righteousness. Good works to protect you from the devil. If you look over on that table,' we stood up, taking our scriptures with us, and looked, 'there are some materials for you there. I want you to work together and make Beth here a shield. You can leave her loins alone, but make her a nice big shield.'

On the table there was an array of paper, cardboard, paper plates and Sellotape and string. Rebecca and I started to sellotape bits of cardboard together. Beth, our soldier, stood there waiting awkwardly.

'Now what else does a soldier have?'

'Shoes?' Esther suggested, doubtfully. We were still sticking things together on the table.

'That's exactly right! Did you do this lesson for family home evening, Esther? Tell the truth now.' Esther shook her head slowly, smiled and then nodded. 'Then Heavenly Father must think you need to hear it again,' Sister Lawson said. 'Shoes! And not just any old shoes. Verse fifteen, please, Jeannie.'

'*And your feet shod with the preparation of the gospel of peace.*'

The picture that came out this time was of Russell Crowe, in his full gladiatorial outfit. Tanned bulky arms and a frowny, sort of puzzled look, as if he wasn't quite sure why he was wearing what he's wearing. Sister Lawson leaned close to the picture and tapped his legs with a pencil. They were brown too, and nicely hairy, and encased in a sort of metal shin-guard that curved round to cover his sandals and protect his feet.

'He's not going to get his toes trampled now, is he? Do you see how important even the smallest detail is when you go out into the world? Girls, evil is everywhere and it's your responsibility to make sure you're properly defended. And the best way to do that is with knowledge, in-depth and detailed, of the restored gospel of Jesus Christ. The only place to get this knowledge – the full, true and reliable facts of the gospel, is through the living prophet. No other church has a living prophet. No other church can give you the information you need – the truths that are essential for your safety and salvation. These are the Last Days. Do you think Heavenly Father wants you to spend time painting your nails, or learning an aspect of Gospel Doctrine you'll be teaching your children one day?'

'He wants us to be learning,' Beth said, and looked shame-faced. Perhaps she was thinking about the lack of homework, the bookmarks and handouts lying crumpled in the footwell of her dad's car.

'But, Sister Lawson?' Esther had her hand up.

'What is it?'

'If it is the gospel of peace,' she said, and hesitantly gestured towards Beth, bent over to slip the paper-plate shoes over her shiny Sunday shoes, and not paying attention, 'what's all this about soldiers, and fighting, and battles and stuff?'

Sister Lawson sighed slowly. 'What wouldn't I give for a priesthood holder in there right now,' she said, almost under her breath, and then looked square on at us all. 'When Jesus comes back, not on a donkey but carrying a sword, he will vanquish evil, bind Satan and then reign from Zion – which we know will be in America, just as Eden was. His reign will last one thousand years, and during this time there will be peace in the world. We wait for Jesus, fight on, endure to the end and *anticipate* his glorious peace. Does that make sense?'

'I think so.'

'Good. Let's get on with the lesson, or sacrament meeting will be upon us and I'll have to send you home to learn the last references on your own. Rebecca. Chapter seventeen, please.'

Rebecca had the next scripture queued up ready, and was quick off the mark.

'*And take the helmet of salvation, and the sword of the Spirit which is the word of God.*'

'Good. Well done. Now, girls, what kind of thing do you need a helmet for in real life?'

'Horse riding,' Beth suggested. Sister Lawson smiled and nodded.

'Cycling, rock climbing,' Rachael added.

'Oh yes, all these things. Very good, girls.' She stuck a picture cut out of a magazine of Tom Hanks in *Saving Private Ryan* onto the chalkboard. He was in full soldier kit, including his little green helmet. 'Soldiers all over the world have worn helmets since the very dawn of time,' she said.

We carried on sticking, unrolling the tape around Beth's head to get the paper hat to fit.

'Even before modern medicine discovered the brain, people knew that it was vital to protect your head from injury. Now, girls, looking at this with your spiritual eyes, what kind of things would you need to protect your *mind* from?'

'Bad influences?'

'That's exactly right,' she said, pleased that we were catching on so quickly. Beth shuffled and puffed her hair out of her eyes, where it immediately stuck to a raw edge of Sellotape on her paper hat. We looked at each other, bit our lips and said nothing.

'Bad influences, unwholesome thoughts. Inappropriate music, books and magazines. Off-colour jokes, or films that are R-rated. (That means they aren't church standard.) As Latter-Day Saints, we seek after things that are "virtuous, lovely or of good report or praiseworthy" and we avoid all those things that are apt to drive away the Spirit. Do any of you girls have any examples of things that you've avoided in your own life?'

'Pornography,' Beth said quickly, because it's always the right answer, and Sister Lawson reddened and looked away.

'That's very good, Beth. More of a challenge our young men face, though, I would think. Anyone else?'

'Novels that glorify immorality,' Esther said. 'I ask my dad to check all my books before I get started on them.'

I looked at Esther and wondered if that was really true. She's got pierced ears, and I can't imagine her reading anything except for *Twilight*, which the Young Women's Presidency are keen on anyway.

'And music? What about the music you listen to?'

'We don't have the radio on in the car. My mum bought us a lot of Tabernacle Choir CDs and we listen to those instead.'

'That's right, girls. Protecting your mind with the helmet of salvation is not only about avoiding what is unwholesome, but seeking out that which is good. The mind is like a sponge and once an image, a line from a song or even a character from a book gets in there, you can never, ever fully erase it.

'There's one thing that we're missing though. One item this soldier needs that *isn't* armour. That isn't about defending himself from the blows of the world,' Sister Lawson said, and we were all giggling now because she had stuck up a picture printed off the internet of Mel Gibson as William Wallace in *Braveheart*, next to Tom Hanks, Russell Crowe and Aragorn. Mel was looking long-haired and untidy, with a leather cuff around his arm, but he was holding, as if he was aware of the camera, a shiny silver and gold sword.

'A sword is a weapon to fight off evil. To both defend himself and his loved ones, and to attack his enemies. Something to have in his hand when he *stands against the wiles of the devil*.'

Beth looked fit to topple over at any second, and her face was really red inside the helmet. It must have been stifling under her long-sleeved blouse and her long skirt, with all the newspaper and cardboard piled on top. From next door came the stop-start of singing – the Young Men practising their part for the mixed-choir piece we're all going to do at Youth Convention next month.

'So, girls, who's going to make our soldier here a sword, and who's going to read the scripture?'

Rebecca and Esther were on it before she'd finished speaking, rolling up newspaper and wrapping the loose ends with tape to make a pointed tube. Amy cut a curved crossbar out of a piece of cardboard and they started to attach it with a piece of string. They were getting into it now, wrapping the string between the paper tube and the crossbar in a fancy, criss-cross pattern.

'Jeannie, will you read one more scripture out for us?' She wrote it on the blackboard next to Mel Gibson: Hebrews, chapter four, verse twelve, although none of us copied it down into our journals because we were busy sticking the sword down between Beth's droopy belt of truth without dislodging her breastplate of righteousness, which was starting to come unstuck. It didn't matter; if we don't remember the references this time we'll be getting bookmarks and clip art later so we can learn it at home.

'*For the word of God is living and active. Sharper than any double-edged sword, it penetrates even to dividing soul and spirit, joints and marrow; it judges the thoughts and attitudes of the heart.*'

18.37. I stand in the courtyard and read the sign.

Mike Drake and Son, MOTs, bodywork, servicing and repair. Call-out service avail. Where not the cheapest but where the best.

Something about it makes me shake violently. Julian gets angry because his name isn't on it. He started out as an apprentice and now he's the main assistant and does more with the cars than Lewis does, but it's a family business, it always will be and he's just staff: he doesn't belong. I don't knock on the office door, but go right into the garage. The sliding door is up as far as it will go and I can see Lewis in at the back, bending over the counter.

It would be good if I could go right up and surprise him, make him drop that metal thing he's holding and frighten him, but he hears my shoes on the concrete floor, turns around slowly and smiles at me.

'Hiya,' he says, 'I thought you weren't coming. What's all these bags? You moving in?' He's going to keep asking questions until I say something, isn't he? 'What's to do?'

I put my head on one side and try and smile but my mouth won't do it. It's freezing again. My muscles feel like they're going to seize up and leave me standing here like the Tin Man caught in the rain. He moves around the workshop putting tools away.

'You've only rung me ten times today,' he says, 'and now you won't talk? You're keen one minute, giving me the cold shoulder the next,' he says, 'I can't answer the phone every time you fancy a chat. What if your brother found out? I'm taking a risk letting you come here at all. What if he turned up now? Just out of the blue?'

I watch his hands move across the strange metal objects, wiping them down, fitting them into plastic cases or hanging them up on hooks along the wall. He does it slowly, without looking or rushing. Big hands moving gently over the tools, pushing plastic bottles into a row, brushing down the counters with his palms.

'It would be a bit of a thrill, though, wouldn't it? Getting caught in the act?' He laughs.

How long have him and Julian worked here? Since Julian left

school – that's ten years, and Lewis started it with his dad only four years before that. So Lewis has been here doing this same job, half in the dark, sitting in that hole under cars for as long as I've been in the world. I was a baby, and he was already getting started on his grown-up life, learning to handle the tools as smoothly and unworriedly as this. 18.41.

'Julian won't come,' I say at last, 'don't worry. We're all busy tonight.'

I can't look at him for very long. I can't look at the car even though it's a different one. There's nothing in here that's safe to look at. Even the smell makes me want to gag a bit. I hold it back but maybe I shouldn't. Maybe I should open my mouth and chuck up all over the floor and see what he does then.

'He better not, the sneaky bastard. Do you know what he did?'

18.42. I shake my head.

'Left me here. Fucked off at lunchtime and didn't come back. Is he at yours?'

'I don't know.'

'You sure? I'm going to dock his pay this time. I've threatened often enough, but this time I'm really going to do it. I've got a business to run. Walked off with his own tools and half of mine. If he's got a job somewhere else that's fair enough, but he could at least work his notice.' He points at me. 'And I'll expect those tools back. I lend them out to no one. No one.'

18.44. He moves out of the workshop, into the light and the little courtyard between the road and the garage. The ground here is stained with oil, and there's a tyre leaning against the metal fence. Lewis half kicks, half lifts it and then rolls it in front of him, back into the garage.

'Keep things tidy,' he says, 'or the neighbours complain. And anyway, stuff gets lifted if you don't put it away properly. As I've found out today.'

'Lewis? There's a—'

'Sorry, sorry. That's not what you came for, is it?'

Lewis plucks the rag from his shoulder – maybe it used to be red – and wipes his hands on it as he's walking towards me. He drops it onto the bonnert of the car and then dusts his hands off, leans against it and smiles.

'Come on then,' he says, and pats the curved metal surface next to him, 'come and sit down here. He won't come, you've nothing to be worried about. And if he does . . .' he coughs, 'you can tell him you came looking for him. Wanting to know why he wasn't home for his milk and biccies.'

I don't move, and he frowns at me.

'What's the matter?'

I still don't say anything.

'Ah, I get it. You're shy, are you? Well, that's easily fixed.'

18.45. He crosses the workshop quickly, towards the large square door where the cars drive in and out, and reaches up to the metal shutter. The noise as he pulls it down sounds like the whole building is made of metal and is creaking under the burden of some giant weight about to crush it. It seems to go on for ever, while the watery sunlight shrinks to a slit at the bottom. For a moment, it's dim – not completely dark, because the electric light from the office and the open door, letting the sunshine into the waiting room and through the windows between there and where we are, give off a bit of light, but dark enough to wash the colour out of everything, and make me move away from Lewis quickly as he retraces his steps towards me.

'Nice and private now,' he says.

'Maybe . . .' I struggle to speak, the light going makes me feel like there are a pair of thumbs pressing into my throat. I swallow and wonder if he can hear it. 18.46.

'What is it?'

'Maybe you should turn the ringer off on the phone. You're still open, officially, aren't you? Someone might ring up.'

Lewis winks. 'I never thought of that,' he says, and heads off to the office. I watch him disappear through the door, flinching even though I know to expect the sound of the wooden frame hitting the bare wall and banging back again. I'm frozen for a second more as I stare through the window at him hunching over the counter and fumbling with the little black switch on the bottom edge of the receiver, getting impatient and finally pulling the cord out of the wall, grinning at me, like it's some big romantic gesture or something. Only seconds pass before I lean down, dip into my school bag and pull out the perfectly weighted, tiny, shining little screwdriver I took from Technology this afternoon. 18.47.

Leaming says the most important thing is to keep breathing, and keep your feet moving. It's easy to let your body cool down when you're in goal and all the action is happening on the other side of the pitch. And if your body cools down, your muscles shorten and start to go back to sleep, and when the ball does come hurtling towards you, you're less likely to be ready with hands, feet, stick – whatever it takes – to stop it getting past you. Which is why you'll see goalies dancing on their own between the posts of the net, moving from foot to foot. They're keeping warm. Making sure the blood is moving. They are staying ready. Beth says when I do it, it makes me look like I need a wee but she and the others don't complain when I save anything that comes near me.

Lewis comes back, wiping his face and smiling. He sits next to me on the front of the car. I put my hand behind me and pull my bobble out. I can smell him. I bet he can smell me. It wouldn't be right to do anything if it weren't self-defence. If you're fighting for your life you can do what you like. So I let my hair fall over my shoulders and watch him look at it and I wait.

'I had a dream the other night,' I say, and Lewis edges a little closer to me and puts his hand next to mine on the bonnet of the car. 'I was little in the dream, and riding a horse, and holding onto something heavy. I don't remember what. Just the sound of the hooves, and a big clanging sound of metal hitting metal. And then when I woke up I remembered what the dream was about. A sort of memory, really. From when I was little. And as soon as I pieced it together it all made sense. Which is why I decided . . .'

Lewis isn't really listening to me. He's got that look about him people have when they're pretending to be listening, but just waiting for you to get through your story so they can say what they want to say, or move away and talk to someone else, or go back to the television programme they were watching. So I carry on talking, talking and talking, and watching his eyes wander from my hair to my face, the space over my head, down to my knees, to the wall behind me, and then to his own hands, which are clenching and unclenching on his knees. Sitting here is a bit more comfortable for him than it is for me because he's bigger and his legs are longer, and I keep on talking but slither back a little bit, and put my feet up on the bumper to stop myself sliding off, 18.49, and Lewis watches me moving, then jumps down from the car and stands in front of me, really quite close so he's pressing against my knees, nudging them with his thighs and smiling, and I keep on talking, and he's nudging my knees open and I can tell by the look on his face he wants to stand between them so I stop talking, right in the middle of a sentence about Camelot, leaving the log-shaped carriage we are sitting in teetering at the top of the drop, and he smiles again and leans down and puts his head on one side and I think he thinks now is just the right time to kiss me to get things started. I let the screwdriver fall down my sleeve into my palm, and lean into him so that for one minute only my face is against his chest and my eyeballs are burning.

'You hurt me,' I say, and the words are muffled by his overall so I pull my hand back and jab him, once, really hard with the screwdriver. I thought about getting him down low in the softest bit of his belly, but I've misjudged and get him in the inside of his leg. It doesn't go in very far, but right away my hand is wet and when Lewis pulls back he looks at me, half smiling still, as if someone's given him bad news halfway through him telling a joke. He leaves his mouth open and steps back and I let go of the screwdriver, and it stays in his leg, but blood is patter-pattering to the floor. It sounds like leaves. 18.51.

You know, Gary, I was scared to do this but it felt just like the time Mum asked me to get the barbecue skewer and stab some holes in the Christmas lamb so she could poke cloves of garlic in right deep down inside to make it taste good. I didn't think I was going to be able to manage but now I have it feels like nothing else in the world.

Lewis panics a bit, and keeps touching the plastic end of the screwdriver, and moving around the garage, and the blood is coming out of him so quickly the mark he leaves on the floor follows him around like a ribbon. He's got his back to me, and I jump down from the car and he turns, gesturing at the screwdriver.

'What did you do that for?'

The blood is running down his leg, soaking into his overalls and trickling down the front of his shoe. It pools around my foot. The screwdriver is acting like a plug, I think, stopping up its own hole, and this leakage is nothing. If I whipped it out right now – and I tap on it a little, just to watch his face, and he bats at my wrist and shouts something, but doesn't move away – the spray would be halfway up the walls, I reckon.

'Don't,' he says, 'please don't,' and I laugh again and let go of the screwdriver, and Lewis falls away from me, backwards, and against the wall.

18.52. I take a deep breath and scream as loudly as I can. My throat feels like it's breaking, the skin inside stretching under the pressure and splitting, making a thousand tiny cracks. I don't

care. I've never heard a sound like it and it's brilliant and I want
to do it again so I do and

18.53.

18.54.

18.55.

18.56.

18.57.

18.58. There's nothing stopping me, just this dark room and
me inside it screaming as loud as I can over and over.

18.59. Until Lewis is crumpling down the wall, scrabbling
with his feet to get away from me. Gary, he looks terrified.

19.00.

JULIAN

The lights of the shop appear at the end of the street. There is a neon sign in the window saying MILK SOLD HERE and a folding street easel with a poster attached to it – the headline of today's paper, which is again about the volcano and the ash cloud. The light comes soft through the window – on which is stencilled GROCERY TOILETRIES BOOZE N NEWS. I can see Ahmed through the letters, leaning over the counter. I pick up the pace, feeling the sweat gather against my back, under my rucksack.

Inside, he is rolling himself a little tab while half watching the telly that is sitting on top of the wine and beer fridge. The wire loops down the side of the fridge, taped to the door with bits of gaffer tape here and there as a nod to Health and Safety. Bits of baccy fall all over the counter, and when he sees me come in through the door he swipes them away and back into his pouch with the side of his hand.

'All right, J?' he says, in this fake gangsta accent that always makes me want to laugh, because he is brown and tiny and has the most perfect, shiny little black bob I've ever seen on a human being. He's dapper, with a permanent facial expression last seen on Brian Molko.

'Getting there, getting there.'

'You going somewhere?' he says, nodding at my back. The shop is so cramped I slip the rucksack off my shoulders and put it between my feet.

'Somewhere new every day. Exploring worlds within and beyond, through time and space and into a glorious and uncertain future,' I say. It is sort of an impression of Carl Sagan but

I do not expect him to pick up on that and, indeed, he does not reply, his eyes are fixed over my head. On the telly, a gang of people come rushing down a set of stairs. They're all wearing glittery dresses, their hair done up and their eyes painted. They're singing a song – the one that people who die of cancer always ask to have played at their funerals.

'Turn this shit off, will you?'

'You're cold, man.'

'It is doing my head in.'

'I'm watching it! What do you want?'

'I want you to turn this shit off and do your job. "*How can I help you, sir,*" that would be nice.'

This is the way me and Ahmed always talk to each other. We do not socialise outside of the shop but when I came in here he once asked for advice about a chip in the windscreen of his van and I told him about the five-pee rule and from that point forward we have shared bits of conversation here and there. He once let me take a loaf of bread for nothing because it was a day past its sell-by date but still perfectly fine. I would say, as a matter of fact, that Ahmed is the nearest thing I have got to a friend. But he does not turn the television off and I am about to pretend to get really angry with him when the bell attached to the top of the door goes and a person comes in.

She is probably thirty-five with three kids at home but for some reason is dressed as if she is much younger than she actually is. This person wears tight black leggings and fluffy boots worn down on the instep. A black vest. Arse hanging out at the back, tits at the front. Arms all wobbling white and blue. She reminds me quite a lot of the plucked chickens and ducks dangling on their hooks in the butcher's brightly lit window.

'Stacey! You are looking beautiful tonight. Are you on a night out? A few wines with the ladies?' Ahmed says, and leans back, as if he is expecting her to leap at him.

'All right,' I say in greeting, seeing as she is a friend of his. I am only trying to be decent, to get through this next and last bit of time, but this person ignores me, walks right past and leans over the counter, her face in her hands, fluttering black eyelashes at Ahmed. She stinks of fags and gravy.

'Nah, I've got the kids, haven't I?' She shrugs, and the tattoos on her shoulders wink. Winnie the Pooh holding a balloon on one shoulder, and '*Lindsey Joe 12.10.09*' in black gothic letters on the other. 'I'm bored out of my fucking skull,' she says, and jerks her head at the telly, 'I hate this programme. Has he picked one yet?'

'Opening credits, lovely lady. You going to stay and watch it with us?'

She shrugs again. 'Might do.'

'You should write away. Send them your photo. They'd put you on there, no bother. You'd be the star.'

She ducks her head, tries not to smile in an affected gesture that would look fake on someone Jeannie's age.

'Do you think so?'

'I wouldn't say it if I didn't, sweetheart. You want to think about it. Get yourself out there. How long has your Nathan been gone now?'

'He's not gone, he's just in the army.'

'Out of sight is out of mind, in my book.'

'You cheeky bastard. And while he's away serving his country an' all – just so the likes of you can move in and take all our jobs,' she laughs. 'I'll tell him when he comes back, you know, and he'll be round here with a stick.'

Ahmed laughs, and pretends to duck and hide behind the counter. The pair of them find this hilarious, and stand there for a while, braying like fucking donkeys. Every time one of them stops, the other lets out a giggle, which starts the other one off. I stand there and wait. I find that I am not sure what to do with my arms, and put my hands in and out of my pockets too many times. Eventually I clasp my hands behind my back. There is no point rushing Ahmed when girls like Stacey are in the shop. His priorities are clear and they are not me.

'Did you want to buy something, pretty girl?' he says, eventually.

'Can I have some fags? And a lighter?'

He turns around and throws them onto the counter without asking her brand. She does not reach for her purse, but looks over her shoulder at me. Her hair is lighter at the roots and it makes her look a bit bald along the parting.

'Who's your friend, Ahmed?'

'Him? Just some derelict. Why? Do you like him?'

She tilts her head, purses her lips, stares. I can feel my face getting hot and it makes me want to smash things up. I turn my face towards the ceiling light for a second. It is an excellent trick I learned in my early teenage years. The transition lenses of my glasses darken immediately and when I turn back to her I can stare past her, out of the door, and ignore her without her knowing it. I keep my hands behind my back and straighten up a bit.

'He's all right. What's your name, derelict?'

I am not certain she is talking to me. And, anyway, conversation would just keep her in the shop longer and I am in too much of a rush to bother with small talk. I try not to look at the television in case it brings on one of my headaches so I just keep my eyes focussed on a row of tinned dog food and wait.

'Tell her your name, you pillock!' Ahmed says, and they laugh at me. I stand there, the joints in my knees and neck and back rusting up. Even if I wanted to tilt myself over the counter, stare down her vest and wink at her, I would not be able to.

'He's called Julian. He's cool.'

'A quiet type, yeh?'

'Five-eighty, sexy girl. He's quiet, all right. But deep. A real tricky customer.'

'Shut up early and come out tonight, Ahmed. I'm bored.'

'I can't,' he says, and smiles, shaking his head so his little bob swishes about his ears. 'No workee, no money.'

'Come on. Bring Carole. I've not seen her for ages.'

Ahmed shakes his head.

'I'm not seeing her any more.' He puts his hands in front of him, sketches out a big bump. For a minute I think Ahmed is telling Stacey that he left his girlfriend because she put on too much weight and became too fat to be attractive.

'You sod,' Stacey says, and laughs. Ahmed purses his lips and shrugs.

'But you're free now then?' She licks her lips. 'You and your friend. Silent but deadly over there, yeh? Both single young men around town.' Stacey looks back at me, and puts her hand into the front of her leggings. A mobile phone emerges. 'Give me your number, and I'll text you tonight. Are you on Facebook?'

'No.'

'Don't blame you, there's loads of weirdos on there. Just give me your number then, and I'll text you.'

She stands there, staring at me with her square-edged and lacquered thumb on the pink phone, her hip cocked towards me.

'I do not remember it,' I say.

I should tell her some of the things Ahmed has said to me. Him and his mates. They are disgusting. They have got a little tally going. I should introduce him to Drake – they would get on like a house on fire. The scores go like this: one for a munter, two for a slag, three for a goer. One extra on top if she's white, one less if she's ginger, but if she's a ginger munter you don't get a zero, you get a minus two for being so desperate. All bets off for a virgin (unless she's ginger).

I think about Jeannie and before I can picture anyone touching her I want to push his telly off the fridge and right into his shiny, pouty little face. Stacey is staring at me, frowning so much her eyebrows are nearly touching.

'You can't remember it? All right, I get the message. What a bastard! I wasn't offering you a shag, or anything, all right?'

She points at me, the painted and filed nail gleaming. There is a gap between the fake bit of the nail and her real nail. I wonder about the pressure it would take to snap them off, if her real nail would come out along with it.

'There's something wrong with you.'

Behind her, Ahmed is shaking his head at me and giggling. He puts one hand over his face.

'I don't know who you think you are!' she says, turns, and scoops up the fags. 'I'll have to owe you for these, Ahmed my love,' she says, 'I've just had to put money on the gas and I'm short till tomorrow.'

'All right, my sweetness,' he says, but he's still laughing behind his hand. She slams the door behind her, the bells rattling fit to break the glass.

'Julian. Julian. Julian.' Ahmed makes a show of straightening the papers on the counter, shaking his head at me slowly and sucking in the air between his teeth, 'That was poor, man, that was really poor. What's she going to think of you now? Don't remember your number? What's wrong with Stacey? A night out with a keen girl like her. It'd be what you need. It'd loosen you up,' he wiggles his hips, 'relax you. It's medical, isn't it? A man needs a woman now and again. Then he can concentrate, do his job well, not get into arguments with his mother. Don't remember your number!'

'I need a drink,' I say.

'I could have told you that. Look at you!'

'Give it a rest,' I say, and hate myself a bit more. 'I have only come in for a bottle.'

'Little bit of the usual?' he says, and reaches behind him.

'You know me too well, mate.'

I hate people who say 'mate'. The words feel filthy in my mouth, greasy and foreign. I get the Seven out of the fridge and fling it at him. I am still a bit out of breath from the run. I am not unfit and out of condition. Far from it. It is the rucksack. I have been carting it around all afternoon. During my rage, when I walked for miles and ended up in Bamber Bridge without knowing how. I should eat if I am going to drink. I could ask Ahmed to make a Pot Noodle for me. We usually stand and chat a while, him watching the telly over my head.

'You want one of these, bro? Do you mates' rates on it, shall I?'

There is a new display on the counter between the papers and the till. Candyfloss in blue and pink, jammed into little plastic pots with foil peelback lids.

'I am all right for candyfloss,' I say, and he raises an eyebrow. I worry he thinks I am flirting with him sometimes.

'Seven-eighty-five,' he says. 'You in a rush? What's all the running about? Special occasion? You got a date? What's in the bag? Is the J-Man expecting a bit of pussy after all?'

He does this ridiculous thing with his hand, swiping his fingers through the air over his head until something clicks.

'No.' I unscrew the top on the Seven and hold it out to him. 'Just sling a bit of that out for me, will you? And here.' I dip into my pocket for my wallet.

Nothing.

The other. Gone. Ah, fuck.

In a second, I see it – like a picture in a glossy magazine. It is back at the garage on the counter next to the phone and the broken milk bottle. My wallet and cards. My nine thousand. All my tomorrows on that grey beach with the stones and the seals and the lighthouse. The telly screams out its pink twinkles and its applause and Ahmed is looking at it and not me as I run my hands through the inside of my jacket one more time.

I start counting up in sevens. It does not have to be a big deal. I have my keys. I can dash over to the garage, come back and give Ahmed a ten-pound note. I will let him keep the change to keep him sweet. I will be later than I had planned. I wanted to take up a position by eight o'clock and wait there until Ruth and Andy's house was dark. This happens between ten and eleven on a usual evening. I wanted to make sure I was in position early. That I could look over Angela's evening routine and measure the mood in the household before entering. I clench my fist around the strap of my rucksack and sling it onto my shoulder.

'Ahmed, mate.' I pick up the vodka. 'I am going to have to owe you for this. My wallet,' I do a big stupid mime, patting my pockets, 'left it at Drake's. I will bob and get it now. Be fifteen minutes, twenty tops. Mate.' I am already heading out of the door. The carpet is worn right through in places – the holes stuck together with gaffer tape.

'No can do, I'm afraid, my man,' he says, in his real voice – no gangsta now.

'I will owe you,' I say, 'I will be fifteen minutes,' and he is shaking his head.

Why don't I leg it out of the door anyway? I could. The bottle is in my hand. What would it matter? But he is not even watching me, still has his big dark eyes on the telly, his girly eyelashes fluttering. No one takes me seriously.

'No try before you buy!'

'I will tell you what,' I say, and before I know it the vodka leaves my hand and I feel my arm fly through the air, the sleeve of my jacket clapping against my wrist, 'you can take your bottle and you can stick it up your arse!'

The bottle hits the tobacco display and shatters. Disappointing. I wanted to break the window. The reek of alcohol nips at my eyes.

'J-Man! What the hell are you doing?'

I pick up the sheaf of newspapers from the counter and toss them at him. Words shuffle through the air.

'You can fuck off!' I scream. 'Suck on that!'

I am crying. My lip has started to bleed again and I can feel it dribble onto my chin, making me look like some sort of retard. The pots of candyfloss roll off the counter and all over the place and Ahmed is standing there, his mouth going, his hands flat out and towards me.

'Mate,' he says, 'take a bottle of Kirov. You come in tomorrow. The next day. Whenever you like.'

I kick at the chest freezer. I want to dislodge the telly and smash it but pain darts up my leg like an electrical current. The Birds Eye waffles and Viennettas wobble slightly. That is all.

'J. My friend. What's the matter? Come on now, stop kicking and fighting. You are spoiling my shop.'

He is still holding a fresh bottle out. I take it off him and he nods. Smiles.

'I will come back,' I say, 'I will go to Drake's and I will come right back.'

'Julian,' he says, 'look at what you've done to my fags.'

I nod. 'I know. I will go and get my wallet. I have got cash. Credit cards.'

'What's wrong with you?'

'Forget it, mate. Just leave it. I will get you your money.' I know what I am going to say next, and it makes me smile, even though I do not want to, even though I know the blood on my teeth will make me look weird, even though I have not much of a face for smiling anyway, it bursts out of me and I can't help it. 'I am going away, Ahmed. For good. I will give you my credit card and the pin number and you can use it. I will not be the one paying it back.'

He sighs. The slags start squealing and clapping over my head. The man presenting the show laughs. I am missing the punchline, losing the thread. The noise feels like wasps in my ears.

'What's going on with you, brother? Did you argue with your mother again? Stay here and mop up with me and we'll have a smoke together. Do you like a smoke? If you have a problem, we'll chat about it. Man to man. But none of this wrecking the shop. Running off, chucking your credit cards about. It's not on, is it?'

I shake my head. Loosen the cap on the bottle and back away. Stand on one of the pots of candyfloss and feel it squeak between my trainer and the floor, like fibreglass.

'I am going. Right now. Do not call the police. Right? I will come back and I will pay you. Whatever you want.'

'Come on, Julian . . .'

I shoulder the door and leg it. No hesitation – right off towards Drake's, swigging the vodka neat like a marathon runner sucking on his Evian. The air is cold on my face.

MARTIN

—the walls are made of glass and they are coming in, whooshing in like the wind, and pressing against my arms and face and as they move they make a noise, a banging noise, one that echoes as if it's coming from far away, but grows nearer and there's a pain in my neck and something pushing against my foot, something wet, and warm, and Bovril is wanting to be let out and I lift my head up from the kitchen table and feel dribble on my chin and wipe it, looking out the back window. That Viv Potter will be on to Pauline, all concerned eyebrows and arch nods, asking her if I'm ill, slumped on the kitchen table in the middle of the day. Banging. And I stand up, and feel the pain in my hip again, and wipe my hands over my face and the top of my head. Banging. The door. Pauline?

I've been sleeping on my arms but my hands are coming to life now. Pins and needles like nobody's business, and I fumble with the lock, seeing the dark shape behind the rippled glass panel in the door, and realising who it is, working faster with the snib and chain against the jolts fizzing through my skin. I drop the chain and swear at my fingers that are like dead rubber, belonging to someone else and not me. It's important, what I say next. First words the boy has heard from his father in two years. And what with everything that's to come. I should have prepared something.

'I'm sorry, I'm sorry, Gary. I'll be with you. In a minute.'

I fumble again, and finally get the thing open. He'll think I'm an old man. Arthritic. Feeble and senile. Need to stand up tall, give him my best Bill Henrickson smile. Welcome Home.

Glad to see you, son. Shake his hand, something like that. The door opens and outside, cold and petrol-smelling, comes in.

'Dad,' Gary says quietly. His suit is hanging on him, and he's staring at his shoes. Bishop Jackson waves a fat hand out of his car window.

'See you in the morning, Elder Leeke!' he says. 'Get some rest!' He guns his engine like a boy racer and we both watch him, both smile like idiots, wave like he's the Queen. The car trails its noise behind it, then the silence closes in.

'Sh-sh-sh-shall I come in now, Dad?'

'Sorry. Sorry, son,' I say, and pull the door open wide and stand back and let him come home.

He stands in the hallway for a second, staring at the pictures on the wall. He looks at me so intently I rub my hair even though I've banned myself from doing that because of how sparse it's getting on top. After a few moments, he puts down his case and shrugs off his rucksack. He's juggling all this as well as a tin of toffees and a bunch of bent yellow tulips. There are more bottles under his arm, some sort of hand soap. I take the lot off him and put them on the bottom step. I don't ask.

'Do you want a drink? A slice of toast?'

He shakes his head.

'You'll want to sit down for a bit, though. You look half dead.'

We go through. When he turns to sit down I lean forward and grab him, hug him awkwardly. It unbalances us both, and we totter for a while, like drunks.

'I'm glad you got back safely. The flight, all that ash. Your mother was worried.'

'Where is sh-sh-sh-she?'

'She's out. Jeannie's out. Julian, well, you know Julian. He said he'd come back from work early.'

'Mum's out? On her own?'

I shrug. I know without looking that I'm the spit of my own father when I do this. And his father too, probably. We Leekes are a long line of shruggers. Abdicators of responsibility. King Martin the Reluctant, that's me. Gary is looking around the room as if he doesn't recognise it.

'That's a brand-new suite you're sitting on. The hall's been painted. And the carpet is new. Your mother will want you to mention it.'

He is sitting forward, his hands on his knees. I sit down next to him, pat his hand. Stand up again.

'She's thinking about new curtains for in here too. We're still in debate about that, though. No doubt the conversation tonight will touch on the issue. She may well consider your vote to be the decider. Think on.'

'Where is sh-sh-sh-she, Dad? Sh-sh-sh-she never goes out on h-h-h-her own.'

I sit down again.

'I think they're fine, just need a stint at the dry cleaners. They weren't cheap when we got them. But perhaps she's right. I'll tell her she can have them, when she comes back. You can help her put them up, she'll need someone to go up the ladder.'

'Are you all right?'

He's staring at me, and I realise I've slumped back into the settee. I sit up properly and do another smile.

'I've been dozing. Still coming round.'

'I mean your hands, Dad. And your feet. What's happened to you?'

I look down at myself, the red and brown criss-cross of tiny cuts and scratches. My skin feels hot, tight, tender. I rub the palm of one hand over the back of the other, massage the ball of muscle under my thumb.

'I haven't really kept up with the garden while you've been away . . .'

'It's all right, Dad,' he's smiling now, and squeezing me round the shoulders, 'it's all right.'

'I thought I'd try and get on top of it. Once and for all.'

'I'll get onto it, at the weekend. I'll s-s-s-s-s-sort it out.'

He stands then, and because I'm worried he's going to go into the kitchen and look out of the window and see what I've done, I start speaking again, too quickly.

'It'll be a case of starting from scratch, I reckon. Maybe even abandoning the idea of a greenhouse altogether.'

Gary is looking around the room, as if for help. He moves along the settee until his leg is touching mine, and puts his arms around my shoulders again.

'Has Mum got a mobile?'

'I wouldn't think so. No.'

'We'll manage then, won't we? What did sh-sh-she have planned for tea? Sh-sh-sh-shall we get s-started on it?'

'She'll be pleased to have you back, you know. More than anything.' Gary stands up again now and I can see he's easing back into the house, feeling more comfortable. He leans against the wall with one hand in his trouser pocket. 'If you've got any photographs, any pictures or souvenirs or anything. Best get them out. Unpack them first, she'll want to see.'

He glances into the kitchen, then bends down to look under the table for Bovril. He stands up, turns around.

'She's printed out all your emails too. Look at this.'

I get up and go over to the stand the telly is on. There's a drawer in it, meant for DVDs or computer games, probably, but inside it is a big three-ring binder, with a picture of Gary standing outside the temple taped to the front of it. It's bulging with emails and airmail letters, carefully unfolded, smoothed flat, with holes punched in them. I pull it out and show it to Gary. It's heavy.

'She reads these out when she's got people round,' I say, wanting to make him smile a bit at her antics. 'You might want to bone up on them a bit yourself before she gets here. Jog your memory. She'll want chapter and verse.'

Gary still doesn't say anything. I am holding out the folder to him, and it's getting heavier by the second. My arms are drooping so I put it down on the coffee table. He stares at it. I can't quite get the expression on his face. What's wrong with him? The greenhouse? I cough, and realise I've been remiss.

'Not just your mother, of course, son. Me as well. All of us. We're all anxious to hear about how it all was. Did you do all right? Did you get done what you wanted?'

He crumples a bit. Takes his hand out of his pocket. I start to ask him if he's sure he won't take a bit of toast, when he waves his hand to stop me, and turns away.

'I don't think I did, Dad. Those letters. They may contain one or two. Exaggerations.'

He goes into the kitchen, braces himself against the kitchen sink and sobs. He doesn't make a sound, though. His shoulders move. I can hear the tears coming off his face and hitting the stainless steel. I watch through the open door and, after a few minutes, close it gently. He's overtired, and will want his privacy.

The carriage clock on the mantelpiece ticks and twirls behind its glass. Gary remains next door for fifteen minutes. He runs the taps then, and I can hear the fridge door opening and closing. In a minute or two he'll have gathered himself and everything will be all right. He'll be as good as new by the time Pauline turns up.

The phone rings.

'Pauline? Where on God's earth have you been?'

'Dad, it's Julian. Is Gary there?'

'He's here. Where are you?'

'Put him on, will you.'

'When are you coming home? Have you heard from your mother?'

'Put Gary on, Dad.'

'He's not feeling too good. You can talk to him when you get back.'

'Put him on.'

'You know he's not good on the phone. You get home and I'll give him a message for you.'

'For fuck's sake, will you go and get Gary from wherever he's sitting snivelling and put him on the fucking phone? Or shall I come back myself, and let Mum know about that blonde I saw you pawing at in the park this morning?'

That's a kick in the chest. I can actually feel my lungs retreat, the air come hissing out of them. It takes me a second before I'm able to breathe in again. Can he hear me gasping down the receiver?

'Is Nina with you? I need to speak to her. There's something I need to explain.' I still can't catch my breath. The sentence comes out as a whisper, and he speaks over me. I doubt he even heard me.

'Just put him on.' For just a moment he sounds like he's frightened. But that's daft. Julian's never been scared of anything in his life. That's why, in the end, he always gets what he wants. He's more like his mother than he realises.

I put the phone down on the side, Julian ranting into the air, and tiptoe over the carpet to the kitchen. I can hear Gary in there, talking softly. I can't hear what he's saying. Can't tell if he's praying, or catching up with Bovril. I chap a few times and then open it. He's sitting at the kitchen table, running his finger around the top of a glass of water.

'You had a breather?' I say, and before he can answer, 'Julian's on the phone for you. Mad keen to talk to you. I reckon he must have missed you.' I can't stop smiling, and Gary raises an eyebrow and it feels good, that does, that we've managed to share a joke.

Gary goes into the hall. He puts the receiver to his ear, then I see him frown before he reaches over and pushes the living room door shut.

'Suit yourself,' I say, to the closed door, but there's nothing but silence on the other side of it. So I go back through and start pushing the settee and chairs back towards the edges of the room. Wheel the telly table back so it's flat against the wall, and then go into the kitchen and start bringing the chairs in. The doorway is too narrow to just push the table through it. How do we do it at Christmas? Julian and Gary and me, we tilt it, and jiggle it in at a crazy angle.

'Gary? Are you done yet? I really need you to help me with this table.'

'Dad,' Gary shouts from the doorway, 'I'm going out. I need a bit of fresh air. Need to get myself together before Mum comes back.'

'You must be joking.'

'Dad. Please.'

He comes in and I have a good look at him. He's pale, his face pinched and tear-stained, his eyelids swollen. His mother comes home and sees him like that, and there'll be hell to pay.

'Fresh air? Open a window, then.'

'I need to go out.'

He's lying. He's not going to come back, is he? The panic rises and threatens to engulf me totally, like hot water closing in over my head. He's feeling about in his pockets for keys that he hasn't had on him in two years.

'Dad,' he says, and nothing else. He's struggling, the words getting tangled in his throat. I can hardly lock him in, can I? He's an adult now. I chuck him the spare set from the mantelpiece. Fair's fair. He's entitled to the keys to his own house, no matter what else happens.

'Where are you going, Gary?'

He won't look at me, just shakes his head and presses his lips together. He can't lie, this one. It's not in his nature. He owned up to things he hadn't done, when he was a lad, just to stop Pauline going on about it.

'I won't be long,' he says, and I hear the front door slam

again. And that's that. I might as well finish dragging the kitchen chairs through from the kitchen to the living room.

We bought a rabbit for them when Jeannie were about six or seven. We had the hutch in the back of the garden, against the side of the house to give it a bit of shelter. The talks we gave them – lists of rules, about feeding, and changing the straw, and not letting Jeannie hold it on her own, teaching them to keep their fingers out of the way when they poked dandelion leaves through the chicken wire on the door of the hutch. Geoffrey, it was called. Julian's idea. He thought he was being funny. Pauline didn't get it but he did have a point; it was funny.

It would have been two or three months after we got the thing – no more than that – the novelty had not worn off and Jeannie liked to visit it in the garden as soon as she woke up. So not long after we got it, Gary went down with her this particular morning – early, before school. Still in their pyjamas. Jeannie had some pink ones with purple horses on them. Gary in tartan, the trouser legs three inches over his ankle. It was Jeannie shrieking that brought me out into the garden to see what was what.

The door was open. There was a mess of straw and fur on the grass, nothing more. It could have been a cat. Maybe even a fox – we get them even this far into the town. Chicken carcasses and ripped up pizza boxes in the street, sometimes. I looked closer and saw a little bit of blood on the grass, but Gary had his arm round Jeannie's shoulders, pulling her away from it, trying to convince her it had just run away. Telling her a story about a family of wild rabbits living in Astley Park, who visited gardens at night, found pet rabbits, and set them free.

'He'll be in a burrow right now,' he was saying, 'being introduced to all his new brothers and sisters. Drinking lemonade out of acorn cups, eating a grass sa-sa-salad with dandelion flowers for his pudding.' Where he got all that from, I don't know.

She was crying and laughing at the same time, and I held back, standing in the kitchen doorway and listening to them. And then I noticed Julian was out there too. Lurking to the side – though you couldn't accuse him of hiding: he was just standing there, but somehow less visible than the other two. That's his way. He was just starting with his acne, wearing jeans and a tee-shirt he'd probably slept in and scuffing at the grass around the edge of the patio with his bare feet. His face was shiny with sweat and oil, flushed dark and angry.

'Who fed him last night?' I said. Julian looked up from his feet and threw off the Leeke shrug. 'Who was it? Who fed Geoffrey and left the hutch open?'

Jeannie started crying again, pressing her face against Gary's stomach. He rubbed the back of her head and looked from me to Julian, observing the tension in the air like it was weather.

'It was me,' he said quietly, and crouched down, holding Jeannie by the shoulders. 'I'll come and get you from sc-sc-sc-school. We'll go into town and I'll get you another rabbit. A white one this time. And we'll call it Sno-sno-snowy, and it'll be just yours to love and look after, all right?'

Jeannie was sniffing back her tears and already starting to chatter about new straw, and getting her mother to knit a blanket for Snowy so it wouldn't get cold at night, and Gary led her into the house to get ready for school, and Julian went back to kicking at the grass. His toenails were filthy and he was smiling and me and his mother had to punish Gary anyway, seeing as he'd admitted it.

There's dog hairs sticking to the legs of the chairs. Short of anything better to do, I get the cloth from the kitchen sink and turn the chairs upside down and start wiping off the bottoms of them. At least Pauline won't be able to accuse me of ruining her carpet or making a mess in the living room.

As soon as I think it, a car pulls up outside. Speak of the devil.

I twitch the curtains like an old biddy. A taxi. And how much is that going to cost? I should go out, should help her into her chair, pay the taxi driver, though with what I don't know, push her along the path and hold the door open for her, bump her up the front step. Should dart through to the kitchen and put the kettle on, give the table top a quick wipe and maybe a couple of squirts of air freshener. She'll be behind schedule. She'll be stressed, lashing out at anyone who comes near her, desperate to see Gary. And it's my fault that he isn't here. Of course. Oh God.

I wait in the kitchen, the damp cloth in my hand. Bovril is lying on her side under the table, spread out in the space where the chair legs usually are. I kneel down, put my hands on her belly, where her fur is finest and the pink of her skin shows through. There's a smell that comes off her – warm and oily – that brings tears to my eyes. I should nip up the stairs right now and hide my bag. Put it in the airing cupboard, or poke it on top of the wardrobe, right at the back where she can't reach it. Whip my toothbrush out and put it back into the mug on the bathroom windowsill. My electric razor back in its holder. I leave my hands on the dog. The front door opens. There's always tomorrow.

'Martin! Martin! Come and give me a hand out here. Is Gary in there? Send Jeannie out. It's tipping it down. Here, Nina, just pull the handle back and bump me up the front step, will you? Don't want to strain myself at this early stage, do I?'

Nina?

I hear the hall door open and close, the creak of the sofa. Because I can't think of what to do, I do nothing – just hold onto the dog and watch her swipe her tail backwards and forwards across the lino. There's scuttling and shuffling next door, like they're bringing in a present or trying to hide a surprise. I look inside myself for more rooms, for plenty, for enough. But all I can hear is the front door slamming shut. Oh, Bovril. What are we going to do, girl?

When Pauline comes in, she's standing.

Standing, right up. On her legs!

'Pauline.'

She nods at me, smiling. Doesn't ask what I'm doing down on the deck.

'Go and get Gary,' she says. 'Is he upstairs? In the shower? Wake him up, will you? I want him to see this. Go and call him.'

I don't move because I can't get my eyes off her. The weight she's carried around her middle since she decided to go into the chair full time droops, and makes her look like she's wearing a rubber ring. Her ankles, poking out of the jogging pants that, for some reason, she's decided to wear today, look pale and bare and almost delicate. I look up at her, along her body, past her breasts and her shoulders to her face – which is shining. Just shining. Whatever she's done today has put roses in her cheeks, and knocked years off her.

'Look at me, Martin,' she says, '– I've had a day of it, I really have. But look at me now.'

Slowly, with one hand on the kitchen door handle to steady her, she turns around. Her wide backside, the crumpled back of her blouse, her soft, brushed hair. She looks over her shoulder. 'Almost as good as new,' she says, and then she turns back to me. She's filling up. It's been years since I've seen her move about like this. Years. Now it's me who feels weak for no particular reason, who can't muster up the energy or the inclination to get to my feet.

Behind her, Nina's face appears.

'You two have already met, so I've heard,' Pauline says, and giggles into her hand like a girl, 'you daft sod.'

Bovril sits up then, sees Nina, wags her tail and lets her ears point up. Nina smiles at the dog but not at me.

'Go on, make Nina a hot chocolate and then let's get this table shifted. She's staying for tea.' She shouts up the stairs, 'Gary! Come down here!' and when there's no reply, frowns at me.

'Where are the lads? Have I lost track of the time? How long have I got? Fire up the oven and then get out of the way – we need space in this kitchen.'

I turn and obey.

JULIAN

Jeannie is still sitting on the floor, leaning against the Peugeot that Drake was working on this morning. He must have finished the job after I left because he's taken it down from the ramp and the back doors are open. I know it sounds stupid, but when I see cars with both their doors open like that, the sight of it always reminds me of big-eared little boys. The Citroën has been shifted out, which is, despite everything, a bit of a relief.

I walk around, touching the car and the counters. Laying my hands over Drake's tools, unpacking my own tool bag and slotting everything back into its proper place. Far away, through the corrugated metal door of the garage and out on the road, I can hear the beep beep of the recycling van reversing as it turns in the courtyard and makes its nightly trip back to the depot.

I thought it was spilled coffee when I got in here. It is all over the floor, her legs, her hands.

'Jeannie?'

She looks up at me and I see how pale she is and check, again, that there is no blood coming out of her. She has been veering between whimpering and screaming and nothing at all, which I expect is a psychological response to the shock of the situation rather than any actual physical pain, because as I have said, I have checked several times and she does not seem to be injured. Her silence now is a kind of dopey, quiet withdrawal that makes me think that whatever reason she had for doing what she did, it was a good one. I will not press her on it in case she starts screaming again.

'Julian? What are you doing?'

I screw up the canvas tool bag and throw it into the bottom of the cupboard where it always is when Drake and me are not on a call-out. My wallet is on the counter, next to my sandwich tin and the broken milk bottle.

'Cleaning up. It's all right,' I say, for the fourth or fifth time. 'I got through. Gary's back. He is coming to get you.' I look at the clock on the wall, the cheap cardboard face furred with dust. I try to speak in a comforting tone of voice. 'He won't be much longer. And then he will be here. You will be pleased to see him, won't you?'

'What did you say to Gary? You didn't tell him, did you?' she says, then turns her face away as if she does not want to hear my answer.

I take another swig of the vodka and notice there is only a quarter of the bottle left. I consider offering the last bit to Jeannie to relax her, to help her with her shock, which I think you can actually die of (I am sure I read that somewhere), but in the end I think better of it and finish it up myself. I pick up my wallet, flip it open and look inside. There are no pictures, just a scrap of pink and white fabric tucked into the compartment where the paper money is supposed to go. Three inches of Angela's vest was all I dared to keep. I take it out, hold it against my mouth and nose for a second and smell nothing but the inside of my wallet and my own unwashed hands. It is quiet in here. For the first time in what seems like months I am able to think without interruption.

The phone at home had rung three times, four, five before Dad picked it up. *I only came back for my wallet*, I thought. I paced up and down beside the car, stepping over Jeannie and turning my eyes away from Drake every time I passed him. I thought Dad was going to refuse to put Gary on but eventually and with some persistence I managed to convince him.

'Gary? Bit of a problem.' I laughed again. 'Big fuck-up, actually. Pains me to say it, but I need your help. It is Jeannie.' I could hear my voice wasn't right. I was speaking too quickly, as if I was about to give him the punchline to a joke I had been waiting two years to tell him. I took a breath, tried to settle myself down. Seven, fourteen, twenty-one, twenty-eight, thirty-five . . .

I could hear Gary on the other end of the line. Breathing and swallowing. Chewing at his lips and struggling to talk – struggling as if the air was drowning him. I knew he would be bad, but mute? He had never been this bad before. They have broken him, I think.

'It is all right, Gary. Do not say anything. Just listen to me. Tap on the phone once for yes and twice for no, all right?'

One tap.

'Do you remember where I work?'

Tap.

'Do you remember the way to get here?'

Tap tap.

'I am going to give you directions now. Do not bring the car. You are going to have to run, though, you need to get here quick.'

He started grunting and sighing again, tiny sounds of protest, and I lost it for a second and swore at him, then told him, pointlessly, to shut up.

'Jeannie is here with me. I need you to come and get her. Take her back home for me. This is an emergency. I am not asking, I am telling. All right?'

A long pause. Tap.

'Okay. Good. There is one other thing you need to do before you go. It is important. Go up into Jeannie's bedroom and fetch some clothes for her. Does not matter what. Jeans, jumper – whatever. Just go in her cupboard and grab the first things you see, put them in a bag and then get here.'

Gary started to tap away urgently then, but I cut him off.

'She is not hurt. She is all right. But you need to come, right now, and you need to tell Dad that you are a bit overwhelmed with all the travelling and you want to have a quick walk before tea, but you will be home in an hour.'

I hung up.

'We will just have to trust him,' I said to Jeannie, who didn't answer. 'I hope he gets his act together.'

It occurred to me then it was better for us to turn the lights out, to sit quietly like that in the dark to wait. So I checked the lock on the office door and turned off everything apart from the little light in the bathroom. I left the door open so we were not sat in the pitch black, but we still could not see much of Drake or the mess he had made in the garage, which was the idea.

It was not quiet for long. She started making that horrible noise, a growling little cry, a ragged series of drawn-out, half-formed and throaty sobs. And she would not stop.

Jeannie stands and starts to pick her away across the floor, wailing and chopping her hands through the air like all she can see is a picture and she wants to rub it out.

'Shut up, will you? He will be here any minute, then you can go home.'

I cannot tell how loud she is. It sounds loud, but with just us and no other sounds in here, who is to judge?

The thing is, I am not frightened at all. Ten, twenty years in a little room? Not scared at all. I can take Angela with me, in my mind. Take her into my solitude in that dirty place. They can stuff me in a box but I already know what they do not – the inside of me is a great hall and I have already filled it with her. Her frizzy hair and bird bones. Her bubble skull, blue veins and silence. I look at my wallet again. I was kidding myself. When I close my eyes and feel the throb of my imaginings ripple through me, from eyelashes to groin and back again, I know that I am not frightened at all and I never will be. Scotland would not have worked out, not really. So long as Gary plays along I am going to get the next best thing. This is what Ruth meant. Each of us, in our own way, must find the thing that works and hold tight to it even if it threatens to shatter in our hands and cut us to shreds.

Jeannie starts wailing again. She sounds like a creaking door.

'You really, really need to shut up now,' I say, and turn around fast, hoping to scare her into silence. She is still making noise when I put my hand over her mouth, gesturing towards Drake, towards the dark pool under his legs.

His eyes are closed, but every now and again he opens them and looks around. For some reason this in particular seems to upset Jeannie, though she does not stop looking at him all the same. He does not try to talk and I am not sure how much of what he hears he can understand.

My palm over her mouth is wet. I am suddenly concerned that she is going to be sick. Be better, I think, to take her into the office, to get her out of his sight. But the less trace she leaves in here, the better. I know what they do for a murder; the way they check the drains and collect fibres from the carpet. The things scientists do to get even low-copy DNA are actually very interesting. It is all right that there is a little trace of her here. What sister would not want to come and see her brother at work now and again? I am on her way home from school. I could even have carried her in here myself – tiny particles of her essence tangled up with my overalls and caught under my nails. But not too much. No blood, no vomit. No hair in the office or tears in the workroom. I turn her around and push her away from Drake, sit her on the other side of the car. When I take my hand away from her mouth she starts crying again and I hit her.

It was too hard, that. My hand stings. Immediately I can see red fingerprints across her mouth and cheek. Her head lies limply against her shoulder and for a minute I think I have knocked her out. My hands make themselves into fists and batter against my knees. But her eyes are open. Tears are sliding down her cheeks.

'Just shut up, Jeannie. The only thing you have to do now is,' what is it? 'exactly what I tell you. Just shut your mouth and let me think.'

I sit back down next to her. Blood is running under the car and it soaks into the back of my jeans. The smell of it is bright, coppery – catches in your throat. I push Jeannie out of the way; sit her in the corner where it will not dirty her. *Forty-two, thirty-five, twenty-eight, twenty-one, fourteen, seven, suffer the little children suffer suffer seven, fourteen, twenty-one . . .*

'Tell me about the volcano again,' she says, after a while. 'How do you say it?'

'It is pronounced *Eye-ab fee-yapla yurkal*.'

'That one. Tell me about it again.'

She wants a story, just like a baby.

'Everything that happens, happens the way it does because of the magma,' I say, and she settles her head against my shoulder as if she wants to go to sleep. I do not blame her, to be honest. 'Magma is the term for the molten or liquid rock under the mantle of the earth. It moves around. This is called a convection current. If it were just liquid rock moving around, it would be all right. But it is not. There is gas in there too. Additional substances. So when the magma rises, up through the layers of the earth, the pressure drops, and the gas starts to emerge from the liquid and make bubbles.'

'Like pop,' she says. She knows this story.

'Yeah. Like pop. And you know what happens when you shake up a bottle of lemonade? The bubbles under there start moving, bouncing about and making the magma frothy. And eventually. Well, it can't take it any more. There is too much energy. So it explodes. Pop . . .'

'The biggest sneeze in the world,' we say it together and we should be laughing together too, but we are not. It strikes me that I am not good at telling stories. I am not good at being an older brother. If I was, things like today would not have happened.

'What else?' She has got to prompt me to start again. I do not even do this little thing right. Stupid Bastard. It is true.

'As it comes out, it rips open the mantle: that is, all the earth and rock and all sorts on the surface of the world. It makes a volcano, and the ash goes right up into the air and this time, it has made a massive cloud.'

'But it's over now,' she says, 'and Gary's back home and he's going to be here any minute and he'll sort all this out, won't he?'

Her little fingers claw at me.

'It's not quite over. Sometimes these volcanoes can carry on erupting for months. Years, even. Gary was just lucky to get on one of the first flights.'

'Poor Gary, being the guinea pig. He must have been scared.'

'It was safe. They would not have let the plane go otherwise.'

'How would they know?'

'There were tests, and satellite pictures, and all sorts.'

She is silent. I can feel her shivering. I should probably put my arm around her.

'When the first test flights went through the cloud the pilots said the air – even inside the plane – smelled like sulphur. Rotten eggs. Because that is what is in the ash – it has come out from the middle of the earth and into the sky. Everything is upside down. It must have stunk like hell.'

She shakes her head and I can feel her nose bumping against the top of my arm.

'There's no such thing as hell,' she says, sleepily.

'Yes, there is,' I say.

I hold her hand and we wait. She doesn't make a peep. Not a peep.

PAULINE

Touched! Touched by the finger of God! That doesn't happen to everyone, does it? Some people pray for years and nothing happens. You only need to look at Ruth and her little scrap of a girl to see that. Fair enough, sometimes it's not that the faith is insufficient, sometimes it's that the answer is no. But you can't tell, you just can't tell. How do you know that there's no one answering until your hands are bloody with the knocking on that door between you and the Lord? A door of your own making, constructed out of sin and stiff-neckedness! Knock knock! That's a laugh. 'Pauline,' Nina says, hovering at my elbow. 'Sit down. Don't overdo it.' Overdo it! Things are looking up for the Leekes now. Look at Martin's face! 'You're right, love,' I say, and ease myself back into my chair, 'one little step at a time.' The pain is still there but it's hardly significant now. How could it be? 'Shall I get tea started?' Martin says, hovering, pulling at his sleeves like an old woman. 'You get out of the road,' I say to him, 'leave it to us women.' I get Nina to come in with me to the kitchen. 'Okay, go into that top cupboard and pull down three tins of Campbell's soup. The one with the red label. There should be both chicken and mushroom in there. Can you see them?' She pulls them down, shows me them. 'These ones?' They're from storage, they are. We shouldn't be using them until they're really needed. The Lord wants us to be self-sufficient. But time is getting on and if I send Martin to the corner shop he'll decide to combine it with a trip out for Bovril and it'll be a good hour before he's back. Storage it is, and we'll sort the rest out tomorrow. 'That's right. Make sure you get the mushroom, though. Gary's favourite is the mushroom.' 'Okay. What else?' 'Is that pasta done? Tip it all into that big casserole there – the one with the chickens on the side. There's a chip in the lid but it's the biggest one we've got so it will have to do. If I'd have thought, I'd have picked one up today. Hang on. Let me taste a bit first. Hand it over here on the spoon. It's got to be cooked properly. None of this aley denty nonsense.' She leans over me with the spoon like I'm a baby and I don't like it, I want to stand up at my own cooker, but she's right, might as well save my strength for when Gary turns up. 'Is that all right, Pauline?' 'It'll do. Put it all in the dish. And put the soup in too. And you'll need to keep that tin opener handy. You need to get two or three tins of tuna – best do three, and drain them in the metal sieve – that's probably still in the sink from last night, you'd think Maggie would have been able to shift herself to do a tiny bit of washing-up, but no – in fact get Martin to sort it all out. He can get his hands dirty for once, the silly man. Where is he?' Nina looks towards the living room door. She's got guilt written all over her, the poor little thing. The idea of Martin tipping his hat at her. Well, it's just hilarious, isn't it? As if he'd never took a long hard look at himself, and her, and noticed what's plain to everyone else. Dreamer. 'I think he's watching the telly, Pauline.' Best place for him, actually. 'Never mind. Leave him. Put the tuna in the dish. Stir it all around. Tilt it, let me have a look at it.' Nina does as she's told, which makes me think there's nothing much at her house to get back for. It's probably the Lord, this is, bringing her into our lives so we can gather her up and save her for Gary. That's what he needs. A nice, clean, moral young woman to get stuck into. Some go off the rails after their Missions but I won't let that happen to our Gary. He needs a life plan. 'Should it look like that?' She screws up her nose in an attractive way, and I smile. Yes. She'll do nicely. 'Oh yes. That looks lovely. You wait till we get the crust on and stick it in the oven. It makes a smell that fills the whole house.

It's the smell of home cooking that turns a house into a home, you know. Do you cook much yourself, Nina?' Nina smiles. 'I don't do many casseroles like this,' she says, 'but I can do a belting roast dinner. And I make cakes too.' Perfect! 'Cakes, eh? That's a blind spot of mine, Nina. I think we'll have to spend some time with each other. Casseroles are my speciality. They call me one-pot-wonder at Relief Society. We need to get the crust on and get this into the oven. Gary can't be much longer. Then you'll meet my boys properly, and Jeannie too, if they've managed to round her up from wherever she's crept off to this time. Go into that cupboard over the microwave. Careful when you open it, though – Julian never puts everything back properly and you're just as likely to get brained by a bag of sugar as you are to find the Ritz Crackers. There you are. Cheesy ones, not plain. Bring them out, lovely.' Nina shows me the box. I like the way she can take direction, that she leaves me in charge, understands that it's my kitchen and she's the helper, not the chef. 'You'll want four or five handfuls. Your hands are clean enough, aren't they? I can see that. Just reach in, grab them and smash them up a bit in your hands before sprinkling them on top. Not to a powder! Not to a powder! We want a bit of bite to it.' I look at my own hands. My fingers are black with the ink from the police station. It's smeared all over my arms. I glance around the kitchen, see my fingerprints on the door handle, on the walls where I tried to take a little walk around the kitchen. Heavens! As if we've not got enough to do. 'Pauline, are you sure you want me to put this on top of your pasta thing?' I lean half out of my chair and call for Martin. He pokes his head round the door, looking sheepish and shamefaced. As well he might. 'Look at the state!' I say, and show him my hands. 'Will you get me something? Don't ask. Just bring me something to sort it out with, will you?' Martin frowns, and then his face lights up like something has just occurred to him. 'I've got just the thing,' he says, pops away and comes back with a little green bottle of soap. 'Gentle on delicate skin,' he reads, 'just perfect for you, my love. This is top-quality stuff, this is.' I take the bottle and get out of my chair, stand at the sink. It's not that I've not stood up before these past months, just that it never felt as easy as it does today. A load has been lifted right off. Nina's still standing there with the crackers. 'Just do as you're told,' I tell her, up to the armpits in soap suds. 'And then you and me can sit down here and get to know each other a bit better. It's nice to have a bit of company while I wait. My nerves are in tatters after today. Tatters! And I'll eat that casserole dish and the lid as well if Julian's not behind it one way or another. Trouble follows that boy.' Ah, who cares, though? Things are looking up for us Leekes. This is the good news: we're making a fresh start together. All five of us. And just you wait, Maggie Travers, I think to myself, hardly able to stop myself from cackling at the idea of it, just wait while we all go into that church together on Sunday – me up on my feet again, Gary on my arm. I might even get my hair done. Good news!

GARY (FINALLY GETS HIS TEA)

It's almost completely dark and I feel faint from jet lag and lack of food, but I run, inhaling car exhaust fumes, kicking pizza boxes, marvelling again at how close together the houses are, how narrow and crooked the streets, how the sky appears only in grey strips between buildings, how grass is allowed only in parks. I run, missing Jeannie-Little-Leeke-Shortcake-Jeannie-in-the-Lamp-Jeannie, missing her, and feeling my tie hit my shoulder, my suit jacket flapping around me. If Keller was out he'd be in jeans by now, holding Clara's hand, maybe sliding his palm along her bare arm. Keller. He knew what being a brother to someone meant. I run anyway, not knowing what I am running towards. And pray, half under my breath.

But they that wait upon the LORD shall renew their strength; they shall mount up with wings as eagles; they shall run, and not be weary; and they shall walk, and not faint.

The metal shutter is down over the door of the workshop and I tap on it, looking up and down the road in case someone stops me and asks me what I'm doing. There is a drift of faded crisp packets and brown leaves against the bottom of it. I pant and shiver and can't get used to how cold it is, how thick and damp and heavy the air. You're breathing in water, all the time, and it must do bad things to your lungs after years of it. It must do.

'Julian? Come on, let me in.'

Maybe it's just my pride but there's something undignified about being locked outside of a place, and having to knock on the door and wait for someone like Julian to let me in. It is certainly my pride and I try and observe this about myself, forgive it and let it go, to move on from it and on to better thoughts and attitudes, but I have difficulty. Keller was more of a brother to me than Julian has ever been and I miss him too.

'Julian?'

I can hear something going on. There's a gap in the shutter that corresponds to the letter box in the door behind it. A little oblong mouth. I bend over and put my ear to it.

'J-julian?'

I don't stutter. Not really. It is more of a hitch in the sentence, like a bubble popping on the back of my tongue. Nothing as humiliating as not being able to speak in front of Julian. And knowing that is the thing that causes it. He makes it happen. He does.

'Is that you, Gary?'

How does he not recognise my voice? He doesn't sound any different. Furtive, defensive – always ready to complain about an imagined slight or injustice. Thinks the world owes him a living. Whatever he's done, he better not have dragged Jeannie into it.

'Yes, of course it's me. Who else w-would it be?'

He's stolen a car. Crashed a car. A hit and run. He owes money to someone. Drug dealers, criminals. He's got a girl pregnant and her dad is waiting out here somewhere, ready to kill him. If it's money he wants, he can whistle. I'm not even going to bother asking if Jeannie managed to stop him selling my Xbox – he wouldn't tell me the truth anyway. But I'm not going to be the one to shield him from the consequences of his own decisions.

'Julian? What's this about? Where's Jeannie?'

He opens the inner door and the shutter scrapes and rumbles as he draws it up. His face is pale in the yellow street lights. He's lost weight. So it's drugs? Maybe.

Dad caught him with a packet of cigarettes once and made him stand out in the garden and smoke the lot, one after the other. Dad thought it would make him sick, put him off for life. But Julian just lay back on the grass with his legs crossed, eyes half closed in the sunshine, his free hand curling and uncurling on his chest. He'd have been thirteen, maybe twelve. Is that when it started?

'You'd better get in. Hurry up.'

He's so skinny his overalls are hanging off him. How is it we were brought up exactly the same way, and he's the one who makes all the bad decisions? Is there something wrong with him? Heavenly Father doesn't make rejects. They sell posters with that on. Because it's true. Everything that happens is because you choose it. Julian has his free agency, exactly the same as me.

He stands back, in the shadows, one hand up on the shutter and I bend my head to duck under his arm and go inside. He's sweating, I can smell it. And he's been drinking. Even inside the lights are dim – has he been sitting here in the dark? There's a thick, almost meaty smell in the air along with the powdery pub smell of stale cigarette smoke.

'Don't talk,' he says, and pushes me out of the way so he can pull the shutter back down. Unopened envelopes and shiny takeaway flyers crumple under my shoes. There's a big rucksack leaning against the wall and I stumble my way past it, hitting it with my shins because it's dim in here. I can't see anything.

'Did anyone see you come?'

I shake my head. He gets behind me and nudges me forward, along the narrow hallway and through the door that connects the office and waiting area to the main workshop. Have I been in here before? I must have, but the when and why of it are gone from my memory. The drop in temperature is startling – it's even colder in here than it is outside. And it's so dark. Can't make out much. The hunched shape of a car with the back doors open, and tools hanging up on the walls. A stack of – what are they? – maybe wheels, tyres in one corner.

'Where's Jeannie? What's the matter with her? You haven't been drinking with her, have you? Has she been sick?'

Someone down there, over there. Someone moving.

'Jeannie? Are you ill?'

'Gary. Shut up. I am going to turn the lights on. If you think you are going to be sick, you need to keep your mouth shut and swallow it. Do you hear me?'

I don't have time to ask him what he means before he snaps on the lights. They hum and flicker into life. Julian once broke the kitchen strip light into pieces with his cricket bat because he couldn't stand it. Just like him. The rest of us have to put up with life's disappointments and discomforts. But he's too good for—

There is a man half lying, half leaning against the wall between the office and the workshop. There's something sticking out of his leg – Blood – Hundreds? No – Pints. How much is there in a man? As I move towards him, my legs and feet doing their own thing, he opens his eyes. I feel a flood of pity rush through my chest – my throat and the roof of my mouth ache with it.

'Are you all right? Can you hear me?'

He blinks once or twice, slowly, as if his eyes are sticky. His hands are shiny where he's tried to stem the flow of blood.

'Oh you . . . are you in pain? Julian, have you called an ambulance for him? Where's the phone – let me do it.' Julian is leaning crookedly against the wall.

'Don't get blood on your clothes,' he says, 'you must leave no trace of your presence here.'

How drunk is he? 'What have you done?' I say, and turn to go into the office. I stumble on the rim where the floor turns from concrete to carpet tiles, the metal – what's it called? Catching on my shoe. It takes a long time for me to get my balance back. Like the floor has tilted, gone all spongy. I never knew blood had such a hot smell.

'He's going to lie there and bleed to death if we don't do something to help him.'

'You will not be phoning anyone, Gary,' Julian says, 'that is not what you are here for.'

He comes up behind me and grabs my arm so tight I know I'll have a bruise there in the morning. His breath reeks of alcohol and his face is sweaty and flushed.

'We can't just leave him to die!'

'That is exactly what we are going to do.'

I shake my head.

'I won't do it, Julian. If I've got to hit you, I w-w-w-will do. Let go of me right now. You know full well I won't let you do it, or you wouldn't have called me and made me come here. Where's Jeannie?'

'Gary. Gary.' Julian squeezes my arm tighter. His strength is astonishing. You couldn't tell from his face that he was even really trying. The phone is on the floor behind the counter, the wire looped around it. Julian's too strong for me, too quick. How can that be? I'm taller, I'm healthier, I'm sober – right is on my side. But he sets his jaw and prevails and when I won't stop struggling he shouts – a wordless cry. I feel his spit land on my face and flinch away in spite of myself. Some stripling warrior.

'Jeannie was the one who did it. She phoned him up, got him to meet her here after school, brought a screwdriver from God knows where and stabbed him with it.'

He looks at the man through the office window. I can see the top of his head, the spiky red hair against the wall.

'She was probably aiming for his balls,' Julian says, smiling ruefully, 'the poor bastard.'

'Don't you *dare* try and b-b-b-blame this on Jeannie. That's the most disgusting thing I've ever heard you s-s-s-say.'

Julian stares at me. He isn't offended. He doesn't try to defend himself. I think he expected every single thing I've thought and

301

said since he called me an hour ago. I feel a tiny stab of shame but it goes quickly. I'm not the one who's half killed a man and tried to blame it on my baby sister.

'I should be s-s-s-surprised, but I'm not. How low can you get? Where's Jeannie? I'm calling an ambulance and I'm taking her h-h-home.'

'Gary? Gary? Shut up for one fucking minute and look at her. Look at her.'

Julian lets go of the phone and pushes open the office door. He expects me to stop struggling for the receiver and follow him, and I do. We walk across the workshop. I sweep my eyes around, wincing when the injured man shifts against the wall and groans, but I still can't see Jeannie.

'She's there.' Julian points at the car and I think she might be inside it, then I hear a tiny noise – something halfway between a squeak and a sob. I look down and there she is, leaning against the closed driver's side door with her legs stretched out in front of her.

Her hair has come out of its ponytail and is dangling in front of her face.

'Jeannie?'

She doesn't even look at me.

Her hands are red, the front of her school jumper – her hair. She's soaked in the stuff.

'Jeannie?'

'She won't answer you. She has been like that for an hour. I have tried everything. I slapped her face for her, threatened to call the police myself if she did not snap out of it. She is in shock.'

I look again at her hands. The smell is coming off her in waves. That offally, heavy smell I noticed as soon as I came in. It's floating off the warm bodies of Jeannie and this man. Blood, slowly pooling and clotting on the floor and soaking into their clothes.

'Is she hurt?'

'Not a scratch on her. It is only his blood,' Julian jerks his head, 'Drake.'

'Drake? Your friend Drake?'

Julian looks like he's about to spit, or vomit.

'You are wasting time. Making this more dangerous for us and Jeannie.'

'Are you sure she did this?'

Julian shows me his hands. 'Sorry to disappoint you, Gary – but this one was not my fault if that is what you are asking.'

'Why won't you let me call an ambulance? I'll give them blessings.'

Julian laughs.

'Gary. Lewis Drake is covered in blood. From eyebrows to arsehole. There is probably more of his juice on the floor than there is inside him. Do you really think you are going to fix him up with a bit of your abracadabra?'

'If it's the Lord's will, then yes.'

Julian crosses the workshop and kneels down beside Jeannie. He tucks her hair behind her ears and shakes her shoulders gently.

'Come on, it is time for you to get up and change your clothes. You need to go now,' he says, in that weird, tick-tocky way he has of talking to us. Like he's written down everything he wanted to say in advance and learned it off by heart first. I look at him, kneeling in front of her and putting his hands on her like a good brother should, and can see that he's playing a part. There's not a person inside him, not really. Jeannie can see it too. She looks at him, and shakes her head.

'Fuck this then,' he says calmly and without moving. He looks up at me. 'I am telling you. Explaining that we do not want Drake to get better, do we?' He doesn't wait for me to answer. 'Drake needs to lie there nice and still until he falls asleep. Or he will talk to the paramedics and then the police about what happened to him. About what Jeannie did to him. And that is no good at all.'

I look over towards Drake. I've never seen anyone so pale before. And now he is shivering. His eyes are open, but misty. The dark puddle around him is widening, but he's awake, and it's impossible to tell how much he can hear.

'What are you planning, Julian?'

I eye the office door. I could rush at it, shoulder Julian out of the way. Maybe even lock myself in to call the ambulance. But then what? I remember Julian pulling the shutters back down and turning off the hall light so, from the street, the workshop looks empty and closed up for the night. How long would it take the police and ambulance to get here? And what would Julian do to me in the meantime? I have no idea what he is capable of. Julian looks at me, and at the door. He stands, shakes his head – as if he can read my mind.

'Here is the plan. We are going to get Jeannie cleaned up, stick her in some fresh clothes and send her home with you.'

'Sh-sh-she can't—'

'Shut up.' He holds up a finger, prissy, like an old woman. 'And the rest of the plan. I am going to wait here with Drake. I don't think it will take too long. I will have a drink and,' he glances towards Drake, 'make sure I am sufficiently contaminated. Fluids. We had a fight. A drunken brawl. The sort of thing that two men who work together might get into one night. Could easily get out of hand. And the final part of the plan. When he is gone, I will call the police myself. And they will come. And I will be the only one here. They will see a drunken brawl gone wrong.'

While Julian has been talking he's stood up and plucked a pair of greasy overalls from a hook on the wall. He shakes them out and then throws them at me. Automatically, I catch them. They stink. Sweat and oil and who knows what else.

'When he's gone? When he's *gone*?'

'Have you got a better idea?'

'They'll send you to jail.'

Julian nods.

'You're going to lie about it all?'

Julian smiles, shakes his head and draws an imaginary zip across his mouth. 'I won't need to say a thing,' he says.

'You can't.'

'If I don't, then they will send Jeannie to jail. Except she is probably still too young for a real jail so it will be a children's home. Or more likely a kind of secure unit where she will spend ten years hanging out with slags and skagheads. People who really have done things like this,' he gestures towards Drake. 'Is that what you want?'

I shake my head.

'She is pretty, isn't she? Our baby sister. Growing up nicely. Blooming early, Mum says. Do you know what that means? I think she is talking about breasts. Do you think that is what that means? Blooming early. So we can notice how pretty she is even though she belongs to us. The prison officers will probably think so too. They will notice. Ten years getting fingered by middle-aged men who take turns with her and then compare notes in the staff room. I know what that sort of man is like. Do you like the sound of that?'

'I s-s-said no, didn't I?' I am still holding the overalls, clutching them in my fists.

'So you are going to help me.' It wasn't a question. 'You are going to put those on over your fancy suit and help me get Jeannie cleaned up and then you are going to take her home and you are going to do whatever it takes to get her to keep her mouth shut. For her own good.'

I shake out the overalls and step into them, my shoe catching in the leg. I need to force my foot through, but it goes.

'Even if I could do that, it's a stupid idea. It won't work. Sh-sh-sh-she's covered in blood. Sh-sh-sh-she's in no fit st-st-state to go home and pretend everything's all right. The police are going to see through this in about five se-se-seconds.'

The other leg goes in fine, and I pull them up around my waist, searching for buttons, armholes, anything. How can he work in these all day? They're filthy.

'You took one look at him and you were convinced I had done it,' Julian said calmly, 'and you are my own brother. I trashed a shop tonight. My friend's shop. For no reason at all. That proves I am unstable, the odd one out and likely to be a participant in a brawl gone wrong.'

I can't look at him, but carry on groping. The overalls do up at the front with a series of press-studs. There's a long, dark hair caught in one of them. I pull it out and throw it to the floor.

'Let's say I am half pissed, which is true and verifiable. Sleeping it off in one of the cars. He has warned me about that before. He comes back to lock up. Finds me. Then we had a fight.'

He shrugs, smiles – a wide smile that shows the gap in the side of his mouth where he lost a tooth playing football. No? Not playing football. Watching the football game from the side of the pitch. That would be right, I think. Standing there watching – would it have been me, in the team? Taking a stray ball full to the face. We laughed our heads off at that. He is still smiling. I can't remember the last time I saw him smile. It doesn't suit him.

'It is simple,' he says, through that terrible smile, 'of course they are going to believe me. You would, wouldn't you?'

'You're asking me to si-si-sit here and watch a man die, and then lie about it. I can't do that.'

Julian laughs and I think he's going to punch me. I flinch a bit – my body getting ready to duck, to run for cover.

'You are not going to sit here and watch. You are going to help me get Jeannie cleaned up.'

'I can't.'

Why would Julian have been watching us play football? Was

I even on the team? It's Jeannie who likes competing, not me. Not Julian. The memory uncurls itself very slowly now. Julian walking alone in the park. Walking slowly and staring at things. Like he didn't know the reason why he was always on his own was because he insisted on doing weird things like that. And me, with a ball under my arm, out with friends. No shortage of them. *Look, look at this, I bet he won't even know to duck.* Who was holding the ball? Was it my football? Who said that?

Julian laughs, 'Course you can, Gary,' he says, 'it is very easy. Unless . . . ?' He pulls Jeannie onto her feet, holds her by the shoulders so she's standing between us. 'Unless you want to stay here and let me take her home? That would be a nice thing to do for her, wouldn't it? For me. The ultimate sacrifice. Lay down your life for your brother, eh? How about it, Gary?'

He pushes her towards me and she stinks and yes she has bloomed early and very suddenly. I step back, appalled. Julian lets her fall back against the car and I can hear him laughing. I put my hands over my ears. I can't bear the sound of the laughing, of Drake's heels scraping the concrete floor of the workshop or the sight of them making tracks through the blood. It runs away from him in all directions, as if Drake is on the top of a little concrete hill inside the garage, blood running over the oil-spotted floor towards the three of us as if it wants to point out who did this to him.

I walk away and sit on one of the chairs in the office. My legs are shaking so much I spill a pile of magazines from the little table onto the floor. I stand up again, then kneel, and press my forehead against the rough material covering the seat of the chair. It smells like cigarettes. I try to pray. The Liahona inside me is whirling crazily.

There are some prayers that don't use words. It goes like this: you are on a small raft in the middle of a dark sea. The tide is sucking you away from land and the spray spits at you and fills your eyes so you can't see, and the waves toss the craft up and down until you're convinced you're going to be thrown over and die. And prayer is nothing more than a distress flare shot up towards the windows of heaven. *If it be thy will.* I imagine my little light appearing in the vastness of the firmament, a milli-second's worth of glow in the blackness. Heavenly Father and Mother looking down on me while I'm crouching here, in this place, wearing Julian's clothes and too frightened to do this thing that he is asking of me. I wait. I listen.

Sometimes the answers to prayers come as an immediate conviction – a sense of motivation and energy where previously there was only confusion and torpor. Heavenly Father touches the compass, steadies it, makes it glow. You know what to do. At other times the answer comes as a confirmation of something I already knew. Like being bathed in soft light and peace. It was like that when I prayed over turning in my mission papers and asking Carole to wait for another two years. I already knew what the right thing to do was, but I was weak, and I needed the Holy Spirit to confirm my path with that sweet feeling of peace and rightness. And that is what happened.

But not all prayers are answered immediately. Sometimes Heavenly Father wants me to wait, to study things out in my own mind further, to use my talents and my free agency to make my own decision on the matter. But even when the answer is 'not yet', I am comforted. The still, small voice of the Spirit whispers to my soul and even during the darkest times of perse-cution and failure I have felt it and I have been comforted.

I send up my little light again. The emptiness echoes around me. I breathe deeply and it feels like I'm taking the cold coming up from the concrete floors of the workshop and tucking it deep down inside my lungs. The coldness spreads through me, into my bones and even my soul, and I feel nothing. Nothing at all. This is what it feels like to be without the Spirit. To lose the presence of God. Julian must feel like this all the time. The needle whirls and whirls and there is no rod for me to cling on to.

It isn't any wonder. I've come to this evil and blood-soaked place – a place where the Holy Spirit can't follow me. If I'd been a better missionary, if I'd done even a portion of the work God allotted to me. I must have a fault, some sin that I am not aware of and have left too long to address. I'm already enmeshed in this wickedness and God has stopped speaking to me.

I raise my face from the chair and Julian is standing at the door staring at me. His clothes and face are streaked with blood. That's what he meant by 'sufficiently contaminated', I realise, with a dim horror that makes me want to scream into his face. But I don't. But it doesn't matter now what I do. The world is dark.

'All right,' I say. 'I'll help you.'

Julian looks unsurprised. I get up and walk with him into the workshop, the overalls chafing against my thighs. Jeannie is kneeling on the floor where we left her, opening her mouth and trying to scream. She's hoarse. Her voice cracks and all she can come up with is a whisper. Probably best.

'Grab her right side.'

Julian grabs Jeannie under the armpit and pulls her off the floor.

'Come on!'

I grab her on the other side. Julian grunts with the effort of hauling her dead weight. We half carry, half drag her through to the office. We prop her against the sink and Julian unbuttons her shirt and pulls down her skirt and tights, which he stuffs into a carrier bag. She's wearing a white bra and white knickers and socks, but these are unstained and, thank goodness, Julian leaves them where they are.

I try not to look at her. She's fatter than she was. Her hair is longer and greasy at the roots. The smell of sweat rises from her damp, white skin. Julian screws her school jumper up into a ball and hands it to me.

'You are going to need to dispose of all that lot too. Take it home and burn it. Sling it in the canal, stuff it in the attic, just get rid of it.'

'Why did sh-sh-she do it?'

Julian shakes his head. 'I can make a good guess. She's been as sick as a dog. Crying in her bed at night. I did not suspect Drake but I should have. You will figure it out in a few months, if not before. Take her uniform and put it in the bag.'

'We can't throw out her uniform. Mum'll notice.'

Julian laughs. 'She has been planning your welcome home dinner for two years. When the police come to the door in the middle of it and tell her they have carted me off to Strangeways in a van, do you think she is going to remember to wonder about what happened to Jeannie's uniform?'

Julian runs the water and we lean her over the sink, splashing her hands and face and neck. Blood has collected and dried along the edges of her fingernails and Julian holds her up, supports her with his body and puts her hands under the taps while I clean her fingers with the nail brush and the grey cake of slimy soap. It's a long time before the water runs clear. Every time I think we're finished, Julian turns her around and notices some other smudge or smear on her skin and we have to start again.

'Will this work?'

Julian grunts. 'Probably not,' he says, eventually. 'Worth a try, though.'

He leaves both taps running and we haul Jeannie back into the waiting room, put her on one of the plastic chairs and get her dressed. My hands are numb with the cold water and it takes me lots of tries before I can get her shoelaces fastened. She stares at us and puts her arms up like a baby when we put the tee-shirt over her head.

'Gary,' she says, and even her voice sounds different. 'Gary. I need to tell you something. I need to . . .' Julian catches my eye and shakes his head.

'Not just now,' I say. 'Plenty of time when we get home. Or tomorrow.'

Julian kneels in front of her and grabs her chin. His hands up to the middle of his forearms are white – the skin on the palms pruned. I've never seen his fingernails so clean. You'd never tell he was a mechanic. Not now. Jeannie flinches and tries to turn her head away but he won't let her.

'Jeannie. This is what is going to happen. Your part of the plan. You need to keep your end up. Or it will not work. Gary is going to walk you home. You are going to take some deep breaths in the fresh air and get yourself together. When you get home, you are going to get a bollocking from Mum. Best one of your life. She is going to ask you where you have been. Say you have ruined Gary's special dinner. You might get a clip. Ignore her. Do not upset yourself. Tell her you were out with your boyfriend, but you have packed it in with him now. Tell her you were at Beth's. Whatever you like. Gary has a part in the plan. We're going to work together. He is going to take you home and look after you and you are going to get your bollocking and have your tea and then you are going to go to bed and go to sleep. And Gary will carry on looking after you. When . . .' He stops talking, looks at me, and then nods at her. Whatever he is trying to say to her, she understands. She looks at him for a while, tears forming in her eyes, then slowly nods.

'Gary.' Julian flips his wallet out of his pocket, hands me a card. 'Don't let Mum and Dad see you with this. Don't tell anyone about it. I do not know if you will be able to get the money out. It could be that I will need to write a letter. But all the same I want you to get it out and keep it safe. The passbook is under my mattress. Give it all to Jeannie. Give all the money to Jeannie. She will need it.'

'How much money have you got, Julian?'

'Enough to be going on with,' he says, and smiles. 'There are some benefits to living at home. Well, one, anyway. It gave me a chance to save enough money to disappear on.'

I slip off my overalls and hand them to him. The card goes into the inside pocket of my suit. Should I thank him? Ask him for his pin number? Tell him to keep his running-away money? There isn't anything to say. Jeannie doesn't ask Julian what his part of the plan is. What role he's going to play. But she knows because she is crying and moving towards him. He's going to kiss her, or hug her. Show her some kind of affection, at least. But at the last minute they both break off and he just nods at her. His clothes are bloody and he is set apart for something else now. He can't get near her.

'All right then, Gary. Take her home.'

He unlocks the shutter and holds it up for us as we go out into the night. Jeannie walks slowly, as if through a dream, but I don't need to drag her along. She waits at the gate between the main road and the enclosed courtyard in front of the garage where the cars are parked, a little way from us. Julian stares at me for a moment, as if trying to judge if I will let him, let them both down, or not, and then, perhaps realising he doesn't have any choice at all, turns quickly and draws down the shutter behind him. I wonder if Drake is still alive but then Jeannie is leaning, almost falling into me, and I grab her arm gently and we start walking.

'Gary,' she says, very quietly – so quietly that her voice is almost inaudible beneath the traffic sounds and our feet hitting the pavement. My legs are shaking and I wonder how we look, hobbling, leaning into each other, pinched and giggly with horror.

'What is it?'

'Are you glad to be back? Are you still pleased to see me?'

She's biting her bottom lip, pulling her coat around her even though it isn't cold, not really. That voice. Like a child – someone much younger than she really is. Time has been busily dragging her on towards being an adult while I've been away and she hasn't had a say in it. But inside, deep down where it counts, she's no different. I can't tell if that's a good or a bad thing and while I'm trying to think of myself at fourteen, or more usefully, trying to remember what the girls who I knew at fourteen were like, I suddenly realise what has happened. Why she did it. Why Julian wants to give her his money, wants me to look after her. She tugs at my arm and I realise I haven't answered her.

'Yes,' I say, 'very. Very, very.'

'Lewis isn't my boyfriend. I didn't—'

'Shh now,' I say, and find her hand, hold it, put it along with mine into my pocket. We used to walk like this, how many years ago? Ten? A trick to keep her tiny hand warm on the way to school.

The front door is ajar, the light on. We go in quietly and wait on the hall carpet. There are school pictures on the walls, one of Julian's denim jackets hanging off the newel post at the bottom of the stairs. Dad's Post Office Dr. Martens lying side by side on a piece of newspaper. The door from the hallway into the living room is open and I can see Mum has got Dad to move the kitchen table in. Mum is sitting there, with Martin on one side of her and some blonde woman – probably someone from Relief Society – on the other. They're waiting for us. There's a casserole dish on the table, with a grey and lumpy sauce bubbling down the sides.

'You're back!' Mum puts her hands against her chest and tears run down her cheeks. She steadies herself on the table and stands up. 'Both of you! Come in and sit down. Martin, you move down so Gary can sit next to me.' She weeps, and dabs at her eyes with a paper hanky she finds in the sleeve of her cardigan. 'We've been sat here waiting. Waiting!'

'We'll just take our shoes off, Mum.'

Jeannie hesitates behind me. There's a dark blur and Bovril leaps through the doorway and jumps up at us both.

'It doesn't matter, Jeannie,' I whisper. 'You don't have to say anything. I will speak to Mum, Dad – anyone else who asks. You can hide behind me. All right?'

She's distracted, Bovril leaping at us so much we're at risk of falling over. At first I think the stupid thing is pleased to see me and am half moved that she remembers me with such obvious delight. But then, with a chilly column of vomit rising up and filling my throat, I realise it's not me the dog is after, it's Jeannie. Or rather, her hands.

Bovril jumps and dribbles and pushes her nose into Jeannie's palms, licking at her fingers, and when Jeannie tries to push her away Bovril takes it as an invitation and gets even more excited.

'What's wrong with the dog, Martin? She's gone doolally,' Mum calls.

'Get out of it, get out of it, Bovril,' I say, and use my knee to nudge her away. She won't be dissuaded, though, and when I look at Jeannie's face her eyes are wet. I put my arm through hers and try and pull her into the living room. 'She'll leave you alone once you're sat down,' I mutter, but Jeannie leans back and resists me. 'We've got to go in. They're waiting for us.'

'I can't,' she says, 'that smell . . . what is it? Tuna?'

The blonde stranger looks up from the casserole dish, a loaded spoon halfway between it and Jeannie's plate. The pasta twirls from the spoon in long, greasy strands and the sauce oozes slowly down them and onto the tablecloth. Bovril starts to nose at Jeannie's hands again and Jeannie turns away and is noisily sick onto the hall carpet. She's been eating gummy bears. Mum shrieks like someone's shot at her.

'My carpet! That's brand new! It's not been down a fortnight! Gary, get into the kitchen and get a bowl of hot water, will you? Nina – you'll have to help him, we've had a switch-round and he won't know where anything is. Oh, you'd have to go and get the new carpet, wouldn't you? Couldn't you be sick in the garden or on the lino? Typical! Martin – you sit there, you've made

314

enough of a mess in that kitchen as it is. You can serve up. Jeannie – how could you? What's the matter with you?'

The blonde stranger – Nina – stands, but Mum gets up anyway, and so does Martin, and the three of them are heading towards us, bumping into each other as they edge round the table, too big for the front room, and try to join us in the tiny hallway. Jeannie is nudging at me, and wiping her mouth, and I find myself sighing. I try and catch Dad's eye but it's no good.

'Hang on,' I say, and Mum is there, hanging on my arm. Moving quickly, and on her own too. She must really love that carpet. I put my arm around her shoulders, squeeze her tight and kiss her on the top of her head. 'You're up, Mum,' I say, 'on your feet. What a blessing. I prayed for it.' She beams – her whole face is alight, and while she's smiling I take Jeannie's clammy hand and pull her towards the stairs.

I start moving, faster than I think Mum can manage.

'I think this one needs a talking-to.' I carry on tugging Jeannie along after me. 'And do you know what? I'm starving. Is that your one-pot special, Mum? Is that what I can smell?'

Mum, taken aback, nods.

'Brilliant. Just what I was hoping for. Can someone serve up for me, and I'll be back in two ticks?'

Mum's still hanging onto my arm.

'Gary, what's happened to your voice?' I dislodge her and take the steps, two at a time. Is she talking about my accent or my stammer?

'I'll just be a minute,' I shout from the top of the stairs, shove Jeannie into Julian's – my bedroom, and close the door.

'You're going to have to get yourself together,' I say to her. I want to sound stern, like I'm not messing about, but my heart is pounding fast, breaking itself for her, and I can't. We sit on the bed and the mattress creaks under us. The room smells like Julian – dirty clothes, oil and cheap deodorant. The wardrobe door is ajar and my clothes are gone. What has he done with them? The top bunk is loaded with his stuff. It's as if I never existed here.

'What am I going to say to her?' she asks. 'What will we do? About a baby?'

'Whatever you want to do,' I say.

'But . . .'

Tears are sliding down her face and spattering onto her hand. It's easy, in this house, to forget about the garage, about the blood and the darkness and about Drake. I wonder if it's the same for her too. I hope that it is.

'None of this is your fault, Jeannie. None of it. You're fine. Here, look.' I put my hand under the mattress, feel around and pull out Julian's bank book, just where he said it was. I open it and show it to her; point out the columns of printed figures, climbing and climbing every month. His running-away money. He'd been planning to get away from us for years.

'It's not money I need,' she says, and shakes her head. 'Tell me this. Tell me the truth now, Gary, and I'll know if you're lying. What would you say if you knew that your sweet Carole was pregnant too? Right now,' she sketches her hands in front of her, draws a shape that doesn't fit her, '– like this. You haven't heard the way people have been talking about her. She can hardly show her face. Sister Williams is trying to organise people to do a shower for her, but she won't come, she's that upset. Embarrassed.'

Carole?

'None of us were allowed to say. No way. Not in an email, not in a letter. In case it interfered with the work. Caused a distraction or made you want to come home early, or get depressed or something. But it's true. She's massive.' She scowls at me intently. 'They want her to get it adopted. But she's not signed anything, not yet. She won't do. What do you think about it?'

Carole.

'Well?'

'Right. Well. That would be a . . .'

My insides are tumbling about, railing at the unfairness of it all. I can hear myself whining, like a little boy: *why me?* And tears building up, that hot feeling across my nose just before I lose it completely. Carole.

'You don't know, do you?' Jeannie is almost triumphant, or she would be if she could bring herself to speak above a whisper. It is a very long time before I can answer.

'No,' I say, 'I don't know.'

'And what am I going to do?'

This is easier. 'I don't know that, either.'

'You don't know much, do you?'

I shake my head slowly. 'Not a thing.'

Guiltily, I realise that I'm feeling more peace now, more calm, than I ever have before. The cramp in my jaw, the words turning to rocks in the back of my throat, my worry over choosing my words – making sure I have the right ones, or at least, not the wrong ones, is gone. Gone – just like that. I can talk. That must have been what Mum meant. What's the matter with my voice? What's the matter? Nothing. I've heard people say that Heavenly Father does not call the equipped, he equips the called. And they were right. Along with the words, comes the way.

We can do this, I nearly say to her, *we'll stick together and we'll do it, whatever it takes, whatever it is. We'll visit Julian, or write letters. We'll bring up a baby, or we won't. I'll marry Carole, or I won't. She'll decide to keep her baby, or she won't. One or the other. I don't know, but whatever it is, we'll manage.*

I want to laugh because after two years of teaching people what it's all supposed to be about, I feel like I've figured out the tiniest bit of it. And it isn't too little, and, I hope, it isn't too late.

'Jeannie,' I say, 'we're family. I can't pretend to understand what has happened. What it must feel like. But—'

I've got it all planned out, and she interrupts me.

'Just leave it, Gary.'

She's holding the blue book between her hands, opening and closing it, when Dad opens the door and comes in. He looks bashful; perhaps ashamed of his wobble earlier, the anticlimactic way he welcomed me home. He's still pale and tear-stained, moving quietly, as if he wants to disturb the air as little as possible.

'Your mum's sent me up here,' he says apologetically. 'She's worried about the food getting cold. She wants me to explain. About Nina. A friend of the family. Someone we'll be taking under our wings from now on. She's worried you're upset that there's an outsider here. She says you've not to feel uncomfortable, Gary. Your mum's got her to agree to taking the first discussion. She wants to know if you could pop down and do it now, while she's keen. While she's here.'

'I don't think . . .' I could just about laugh, remembering my golden contact James and wondering what he's up to now – whether our paths will cross again. Dad looks stricken so I smile. 'Maybe later,' I say, 'there's no rush, is there?'

'Right enough,' Dad says, and starts to go. But then he turns back, jolting his head around. 'What's that?' He nods at the book in Jeannie's hands.

'It's Julian's bank book,' I say, and Dad pulls it off her, opens it, looks down the figures, his eyebrows raised. 'Does he know you've been poking about in his things?'

'He told us to,' I begin, but Dad's still examining the paying-in book.

'There's thousands here,' he breathes, and runs his fingers down the page. 'Thousands. Where did he get all that from?'

'Dad. Julian's in trouble. He wanted to give this money to . . .' Jeannie shakes her head urgently, '. . . to the family. He thought we could use it.'

Dad leans against the wall, opening and closing the book as

if he's expecting the numbers to disappear each time he looks at it.

'There's *thousands* of pounds here and he's giving it all to us?'

I nod.

'Where did he get it?' He closes the book firmly, holds it away from him for me to take. 'This isn't dodgy, is it? Is this why he's in trouble? This money? Has he nicked it?'

'He saved it up,' I say, and push the book back towards him. 'From his wages. All above board. He wants us to have it. He thought we could do with it.'

Dad opens the book again. He looks at the ceiling, as if he's doing sums in his head. His fingers twitch, like he wants to count on them, but won't do, not in front of us.

'Thank God,' he whispers, and runs a hand over his eyes, 'I've not been able to sleep, Gary. Thank God. It's a bloody miracle.'

Jeannie looks at me, shrugs. She doesn't know what he's talking about either. The money? Some sort of miracle? We've always been hard up, no money for extras, no luxuries. Like leather-look sofas. And flat-screen televisions. And new hall carpets.

'Has it been that bad?'

Dad wipes his face again and nods behind his hand. 'You're not kidding, son. The arrears. BrightHouse . . .' He lets his words fall away in a sigh. The cuts on his hands are stained yellow with TCP and he's wafting the smell of it around the room. He takes a breath and lowers his hand. 'But why? Why is he doing it? What sort of trouble is he in, Gary?'

Before I can answer there's a heavy tread on the stairs, the sound of huffing and panting.

'I like this! Have we relocated the dinner to upstairs and no one's told me? Does someone feel like telling me exactly why I'm sat downstairs like a lemon?'

Mum. I get up, go out onto the landing and try and grab her arm. She waves me away.

'Let me do it,' she says breathlessly, 'I need to build myself back up. God helps those who help themselves.'

Jeannie looks at us helplessly, and then pushes past Dad and dashes along the landing. The bathroom door slams, the lock snaps shut. Mum leans against the banisters and fans her face with her hand.

'What's up with her? What is this?' She points at Dad. 'Did you tell him? She's sitting down there, Gary,' she shakes her head at me, 'white and ready for the harvest. You might be all grown up now, and jet-legged, and you might have just got back, but I'm still your mother and . . .' She takes a breath and, perhaps for the first time since I've got back, takes a good look at my face. It stops her dead.

'What is it?' she asks, quietly. 'What is it, son? Is someone ill? I'm not stupid, you know. I might be,' she looks at Dad, 'self-absorbed, and a bit, well, nervy. I might miss some things,' Dad ducks his head and reaches for her hand. She clutches at him, and pulls his hand to her chest, 'but I'm not stupid. I'm not. Will someone please, please tell me what is happening? You're not sick, are you?'

'No. I'm all right. No one's ill, Mum.'

'What then? Don't lie to me; you've never been any good at it. What's wrong with Jeannie?'

'It's not Jeannie,' Dad says, 'it's our Julian. He's in trouble. Julian's in trouble and Gary won't say what it is.'

Slowly, and without stammering, I start to talk. The words come, if not easily, then without too much struggle.

'He's had a falling-out,' I begin, 'with Drake. The police are involved.'

'He's been in a fight?'

'Yes.'

'Is he hurt?'

'No, he's all right. It's Drake. Drake's been hurt.'

'Bad?'

I nod.

'Martin, get your coat on. You'll have to get down to that station. Sort it out. Bring him home to us.'

'Quiet.' Dad waves his hand, but he's looking at me, his eyes fixed to my face as if he's trying to read my mind. Mum is still chunnering. 'Shut up, Pauline, will you? Let the boy say his piece.'

She shuts up, then, probably for the first time ever, and if we were in a different time and place I'd probably be laughing. But her hands, clutching at Dad's, kneading it between her fingers, are trembling.

'He's hurt bad. Julian's with the police now, I suppose. He won't be,' how much to tell them? 'He won't be back soon. Not for a long time.'

My voice is calm and strong and my hands do not shake.

'How do you know about all this? He's not got you covering for him, has he? What were they fighting over?'

I decide to ignore that, for the time being. 'There's something else you need to know, Mum,' I say. 'It's about Jeannie. Be calm, all right? She's having a baby.'

Mum stares at me. She doesn't say anything for a while. Maybe she's doing her own mental calculations. Some secret, feminine thing about months and weeks and cycles of the moon. Or maybe she's making a list of the boys in Jeannie's class at school, the guys in Young Men's who have shown an interest in dancing with her at Youth Convention this year. Whatever she's doing, the calculation takes some time. I can feel Dad's eyes boring into my head and I know he's put it together already – or, at least, some version of it. Is he going to remember the phone call from Julian? Me leaving the house? Creeping out, unexpected, and coming back with Jeannie? Maybe not. Maybe it will come later, perhaps. Some stray fingerprints and a missing school uniform. There's no way to tell.

Mum takes a breath. I expected shrieking, or frantic phone calls, or tearing about the house closing the curtains. But not this silence. It seems to go on for hours.

'Who did it?' she says at last. 'Was it someone at school?' She doesn't wait for us to reply, but takes a deep breath, wipes her eyes on the sleeve of her tee-shirt and hobbles down the landing towards the bathroom. She trails her hand along the banister but bears her own weight.

'Jeannie, my love,' she chaps at the door gently, 'there's no need for this. Come on now, love. Whatever's happened, it's not the end of the world, babies get born every day.'

After a few seconds, which me and Dad fill by looking at each other in worried silence, the lock slides back, the door falls open and the three of us go in. Jeannie is sitting on the edge of the bath.

'It was Lewis that did it,' Jeannie says. She grits her teeth. I can see she's steeling herself for their reaction. She's prepared, even now, to take the flak she thinks is coming. 'Lewis Drake did it.'

Mum looks at me, back at Dad, then nods. Lewis. Grown up, older than Julian, Lewis. Too old to be a boyfriend, even a secret one, Lewis. Lewis Drake, who Julian's just had a bit of a falling-out with, and hurt. Bad? Oh yes. Bad. As bad as it gets.

'Say something then?' Jeannie says. 'Don't just stand there staring at me. Say something.'

'You poor love,' Mum says, and Dad clenches his fists and puts them inside his pockets, and we all cram ourselves into the bathroom. Mum sits on the side of the bath next to Jeannie, and Jeannie leans into her and starts to cry. Dad closes the door gently, avoiding my eye.

'Sorry,' Nina says, 'I did knock.'

When Nina's face appears at the bathroom door I notice she's blushing red, and sweating slightly. What must she think of us? And what's she been doing down there all this time? Waiting for her first discussion? Where on earth did Mum find her?

She's holding the cordless phone in her hand. 'It was ringing,' she said, 'so I answered it. I hope you don't mind. He says it's Bishop Jackson. He wants to make a visit. Tonight. Says it's important.'

We look at Mum, who, perched on the closed lid of the toilet, tucks her hair behind her ears, sighs, glances at Jeannie and then shakes her head.

'Tell him we're occupied, will you, love? Family business. I'll get back to him in the morning. Or when I feel like it.'

'Shall I tell him that?' Nina asks. 'When you feel like it?'

'Yes,' Mum says, decisively. Jeannie sneaks a shocked look at her, and half smiles. 'Tell him I'll ring him when I'm good and ready, and until then he's to look after his own family and leave me to look after mine.'

'You sure?' Nina asks. She won't look at my dad, and since she's opened the bathroom door Dad's kept his eyes so firmly fixed on my mum it's like he's never seen her before. I wonder, just for a second, what's going on there – what Nina's part of this jigsaw puzzle is and if she really is my last chance, my one golden contact – but put the thought away along with all the other questions I'll never know the answer to before it can distract me from what's important – which is here, and now, inside this bathroom.

'I'm sure,' Mum says. Nina nods, looks round at us all again, and disappears, reverently closing the door behind her like she's interrupted a board meeting. There's a minute or two of silence then Dad starts wheezing. I remember the greenhouse; maybe he's losing it again. He's got Julian's blue book in his hand and he fans himself in the face with it, his shoulders shaking.

'Are you all right, Dad?'

'Occupied!' he says, nodding at Mum, who is unrolling a

piece of toilet paper and dabbing at her eyes. 'That's a good one, Pauline. Occupied!'

'Martin!' she says, and shakes the piece of toilet roll at him. 'Honestly. At a time like this!' But she's laughing too, and suddenly, so am I – our brays and squawks echoing off the white and water-spotted tiles and falling around Jeannie, like prayers.

ACKNOWLEDGEMENTS

The first draft of this novel was written in the time and space provided to me by a Writing Fellowship at the Centre for New Writing at the University of Manchester. It was finished while in post at the Department of English and Creative Writing at the University of Lancaster and my thanks go to my colleagues and friends there, in particular to my advisor Andy Tate.

While researching, I was reminded of the warmth, humour and diversity of the LDS community both in Lancashire and in Utah. Many of the people who were willing to help needed to remain anonymous. To them: thank you. Thanks are also owed to the Mormon Stories community, FAIR, FARMS, FLAK, Faces East, PostMo and ExMo communities for information and fellowship. Thanks especially to John Dehlin who welcomed the 'writer from far away' to Utah.

The writers Carys Bray, Russ Litten, Kim McGowan, Jacob P. Young, Zoë Sharp and Andy Butler all provided support and information and in some cases, checked final drafts for inconsistencies. Best thanks go to all at the Northern Lines Fiction Workshop, my editor Carole Welch and my agent Anthony Goff.

JENN ASHWORTH

Cold Light

Sometimes friends are the last people you should trust.

This is the tale of three fourteen-year-old girls and a volatile combination of lies, jealousy and perversion that ends in tragedy. Except the tragedy is not quite what it seems, or how their tight-knit community is persuaded to view it. Ten years on, as a body is unearthed, it looks as though the truth might finally emerge.

With a surreal edge to its portrait of a Northern town, this blackly funny novel captures the intensity of teenage girls' friendships and the dangers they face in a predatory adult world – especially one all too willing to let sentiment get in the way of the facts.

'That most uncommon delight – a literary page-turner'
Gary Cansell, *Sunday Times*

'Jenn Ashworth leavens a bleak but pacey story with dry, wry humour, resulting in an extraordinarily perceptive and beautifully written novel' *****
Sunday Express

'In the best possible way this novel is an uncomfortable read.'
Lucy Scholes, *Sunday Times*

'Haunting . . . told by the hand of a true storyteller'
Anita Sethi, *Independent*

SCEPTRE

JENN ASHWORTH

A Kind of Intimacy

Annie is morbidly obese, lonely and hopeful. She narrates her increasingly bizarre attempts to ingratiate herself with her new neighbours, learn from past mistakes and achieve a 'certain kind of intimacy' with the man next door. But hard as Annie tries to repress a murky history of violence, secrets and sexual mishaps, her past is never too far behind her.

'An intense and intriguing novel that never quite lets the reader get comfortable. It understands about the fuzzy boundary between the normal and the strange, and weaves them together in a gripping, ever-darkening narrative'
Jenny Diski

'Who wouldn't kill for a comic gift like Jenn Ashworth's?'
Guardian

'A hugely readable debut novel . . . about the inability to know others and ourselves'
Independent

'Evokes a damaged mind with the empathy and confidence of Ruth Rendell'
The Times

SCEPTRE